Mills & Boon is synonymous with romance and in this sparkling anthology, you can enjoy timeless stories from three favourite authors, each filled with new romantic promise.

The Tycoon's Virgin by Penny Jordan

A Mills & Boon Modern romance™
...International affairs and seduction guaranteed

The English Bride by Margaret Way

A Mills & Boon Tender romance™
...Sparkling, emotional, feel-good romance

Rescuing Dr Ryan by Caroline Anderson

Mills & Boon Medical romance™
...Pulse-raising romance, heart-racing medical drama

You'll find brand-new Mills & Boon Modern, Tender and Medical romances available every month from all good booksellers.

Penny Jordan has been writing for more than twenty years and has an outstanding record, with over 130 novels published and hitting the *Sunday Times* and *New York Times* bestseller lists. Penny Jordan was born in Preston, Lancashire, and now lives in rural Cheshire.

Margaret Way takes great pleasure in her work and works hard at her pleasure. She enjoys tearing off to the beach with her family at weekends, loves haunting galleries and auctions and is completely given over to champagne 'for every possible joyous occasion'. She was born and educated in the river city of Brisbane, Australia, and now lives within sight and sound of beautiful Moreton Bay.

Caroline Anderson has the mind of a butterfly. She's been a nurse, a secretary, a teacher, run her own soft-furnishing business and now she's settled on writing. She says, 'I was looking for that elusive something. I finally realised it was variety, and now I have it in abundance. Every book brings new horizons and new friends. My teacher husband John and I have two beautiful and talented daughters, Sarah and Hannah, umpteen pets and several acres of Suffolk that nature tries to reclaim every time we turn our backs!'

THE TYCOON'S VIRGIN

by

Penny Jordan

CHAPTER ONE

'MMM.' Jodi could not resist sneaking a second appreciative look at the man crossing the hotel lobby.

Tall, well over six feet, somewhere in his mid-thirties, dark-suited and even darker-haired, he had an unmistakable air about him of male sexuality. Jodi had been aware of it the minute she saw him walking towards the hotel exit. His effect on her was strong enough to make her pulse race and her body react to him in a most unusual and un-Jodi-like manner, and just for a second she allowed her thoughts to wander dreamily in a dangerous and sensual direction.

He turned his head and for a shocking breath of time it was almost as though he was looking straight at her; as though some kind of highly intense, personal communication was taking place!

What was happening to her?

Jodi's heart, and with it her whole world, rocked precariously on its oh-so-sturdy axis; an axis constructed of things such as common sense and practicality and doing things by the book, which had suddenly flung her into an alien world. A world where traitorous words such as 'love at first sight' had taken on a meaning.

Love at first sight? Her? Never. Stalwartly, Jodi dragged her world and her emotions back to where they belonged.

It must be the stress she was under that was causing her to somehow emotionally hallucinate!

'Haven't you got enough to worry about?' Jodi scolded herself, far more firmly than she would ever have scolded one of her small pupils. Not that she was given to scolding them very much. No, Jodi loved her job as the headmistress and senior teacher of the area's small junior school with a passion that some of her friends felt ought more properly to be given to her own love life—or rather the lack of it.

And it was because of the school and her small pupils that she was here this evening, waiting anxiously in the foyer of the area's most luxurious hotel for the arrival of her cousin and co-conspirator.

'Jodi.'

She gave a small sigh of relief as she finally saw her cousin Nigel hurrying towards her. Nigel worked several miles away in the local county-council offices and it had been through him that she had first learned of the threat to her precious school.

When he had told her that the largest employer in the area, a factory producing electronic components, had been taken over by one of its competitors and could be closed down her initial reaction had been one of disbelief.

The village where Jodi taught had worked desperately hard to attract new business, and to prevent itself from becoming yet another small, dying community. When the factory had opened some years earlier it had brought not just new wealth to the area, but also an influx of younger people. It was the children of these people who now filled Jodi's classrooms. Without them, the small village school would have to close. Jodi felt passionately about the benefits her kind of school could give young children. But the local authority had to take a wider view; if the school's pupils fell below a certain number then the school would be closed.

Having already had to work hard to persuade parents to support the school, Jodi was simply not prepared to sit back whilst some arrogant, uncaring asset-stripper of a manufacturing megalomaniac closed the factory in the name of profit and ripped the heart out of their community!

Which was why she was here with Nigel.

'What have you found out?' she asked her cousin anxiously, shaking her head as he asked her if she wanted anything to drink. Jodi was not a drinker; in fact she was, as her friends were very fond of telling her, a little bit old-fashioned for someone who had gone through several years at university and teacher-training college. She had even worked abroad, before deciding that the place she really wanted to be was the quiet rural heart of her own country.

'Well, I know that he's booked into the hotel. The best suite, no less, although apparently he isn't in it at the moment.'

When Jodi exhaled in relief Nigel gave her a wry look. 'You were the one who wanted to see him,' he reminded her. 'If you've changed your mind...?'

'No,' Jodi denied. 'I have to do something. It's all over the village that he intends to close down the factory. I've already had parents coming to see me to say that they're probably going to have to move away, and asking me to recommend good local schools for them when they do. I'm already only just over the acceptable pupil number as it is, Nigel. If I were to lose even five per cent of my pupils...' She gave a small groan. 'And the worst of it is that if we can only hang on for a couple more years I've got a new influx due that will take us well into a good safety margin, providing, that is, the factory is still operational. That's why I've got to see this...this...'

'Leo Jefferson,' Nigel supplied for her. 'I've managed to talk the receptionist into letting me have a key to his suite.' He grinned when he saw Jodi's expression. 'It's OK, I know her, and I've explained that you've got an appointment with him but that you've arrived early. So I reckon the best thing is for you to get up there and lie in wait to pounce on him when he gets back.'

'I shall be doing no such thing,' Jodi told him indignantly. 'What I want to do is make sure he understands just how much damage he will be doing to this village if he goes ahead and closes the factory. And try to persuade him to change his mind.'

Nigel watched her ruefully as she spoke. Her high-minded ideals were all very well, but totally out of step with the mindset of a man with Leo Jefferson's reputation. Nigel was tempted to suggest to Jodi that a warm smile and a generous helping of feminine flirtation might do more good than the kind of discussion she was obviously bent on having, but he knew just how that kind of suggestion would be received by her. It would be totally against her principles.

Which was rather a shame in Nigel's opinion, because Jodi certainly had the assets to bemuse and beguile any red-blooded man. She was stunningly attractive, with the kind of lushly curved body that made men ache just to look at her, even if she did tend to cover its sexy female shape with dull, practical clothes.

Her hair was thick and glossily curly, her eyes a deep, deliciously dark-fringed, vibrant blue above her delicately high cheekbones. If she hadn't been his cousin and if they hadn't known one another since they had been in their prams he would have found her very fanciable himself. Except that Nigel liked his girlfriends to treat flirtation and sex as an enjoyable game. And Jodi was far too serious for that.

At twenty-seven, she hadn't, so far as Nigel knew, ever had a serious relationship, preferring to dedicate herself to her work. Nigel knew that there were more than a handful of men who considered that dedication to be a total waste.

As she took the key card her cousin was handing her Jodi hoped that she was doing the right thing.

Her throat suddenly felt nervously dry, and when she admitted as much to Nigel he told her that he'd arrange to have something sent up to the suite for her to drink.

'Can't have you driven so mad by thirst that you raid the mini-bar, can we?' he teased her, chuckling at his own joke.

'That's not funny,' Jodi immediately reproved him.

She still felt guilty about the underhanded means by which she was gaining access to Leo Jefferson's presence, but according to Nigel this was the only way to get the opportunity to speak personally with him.

She had originally hoped to be able to make an appointment, but Nigel had quickly disabused her of this idea, telling her wryly that a corporate mogul such as

Leo Jefferson would never deign to meet a humble village schoolteacher.

And that was why this unpleasant subterfuge was necessary.

Ten minutes later, as she let herself into his hotel suite, Jodi hoped that it wouldn't be too long before Leo Jefferson returned. She had been up at six that morning, working on a project for her older pupils, who would be moving on to 'big' school at the end of their current year.

It was almost seven o'clock, past Jodi's normal evening-meal time, and she felt both tired and hungry. She stiffened nervously as she heard the suite door opening, but it was only a waiter bringing her the drink Nigel had promised her. She eyed the large jug of brightly coloured fruit juice he had put down on the coffee-table in front of her a little ruefully as the door closed behind the departing waiter. Good old plain water would have been fine. Her mouth felt dry with nervous tension and she poured herself a glass, drinking it quickly. It had an unfamiliar but not unpleasant taste, which for some odd reason seemed to make her feel that she wanted some more. Her hand wobbled slightly as she poured herself a second glass.

She read the newspaper she had found on the coffee-table, and rehearsed her speech several times. Where was Leo Jefferson? Tiredly she started to yawn, gasping with shock as she stood up and swayed dizzily.

Heavens, but she felt so light-headed! Suspiciously she focused on the jug of fruit juice. That unfamiliar taste couldn't possibly have been alcohol, could it? Nigel knew that she wasn't a drinker.

Muzzily she looked round the suite for the bathroom. Leo Jefferson was bound to arrive soon, and she wanted to be looking neat and tidy and strictly businesslike when he did. First impressions, especially in a situation like this, were very important!

The bathroom was obviously off the bedroom. Which she could see through the half-open door that connected it to the suite's sitting room.

A little unsteadily she made her way towards it. What on earth had been in that drink?

In the suite's huge all-white bathroom, Jodi washed her hands, dabbing cold water on her pulse points as she gazed uncertainly at her flushed face in the mirror above the basin before turning to leave.

In the bedroom she stopped to stare longingly at the huge, comfortable-looking bed. She just felt so tired. How much longer was this wretched man going to be?

Another yawn started to overwhelm her. Her eyelids felt heavy. She just had to lie down. Just for a little while. Just until she felt less light-headed.

But first…

With the careful concentration of the inebriated, Jodi removed her clothes with meticulous movements and folded them neatly before sliding into the heavenly bliss of the waiting bed.

As Leo Jefferson unlocked the door to his hotel suite he looked grimly at his watch. It was half-past ten in the evening and he had just returned to the hotel, having been to inspect one of the two factories he had just acquired. Prior to that, earlier in the day, he had spent most of the afternoon locked in a furious argument with the now ex-owner of his latest acquisition, or rather the ex-owner's unbelievably idiotic son-in-law, who had done everything he could at first to bully and then bribe Leo into releasing them from their contract.

'Look, my father-in-law made a mistake. We all make them,' he had told Leo with fake affability. 'We've changed our minds and we no longer want to sell the business.'

'It's a bit late for that,' Leo had replied crisply. 'The deal has already gone through; the contract's been signed.'

But Jeremy Driscoll continued to try to browbeat Leo into changing his mind.

'I'm sure we can find some way to persuade you,' he told Leo, giving him a knowing leer as he added, 'One of those new lap-dancing clubs has opened up in town, and I've heard they cater really well for the needs of lonely businessmen. How about we pay it a visit? My treat, we can talk later, when we're both feeling more relaxed.'

'No way,' was Leo's grim rejection.

The gossip he had heard on the business grapevine about Jeremy Driscoll had suggested that he was a seedy character—apparently it wasn't unknown for him to try to get his own way by underhanded means. At first Leo had been prepared to give him the benefit of the doubt—until he met him and recognised that Jeremy Driscoll's detractors had erred on the side of generosity.

A more thoroughly unpleasant person Leo had yet to meet, and his obvious air of false bonhomie offended

Leo almost as much as his totally unwarranted and unwanted offer of bought sex.

The kind of place, any kind of place, where human beings had to sell themselves for other people's pleasure had no appeal for Leo, and he made little attempt to conceal his contempt for the other man's suggestion.

Jeremy Driscoll, though, it seemed, had a skin of impenetrable thickness. Refusing to take a hint, he continued jovially, 'No? You prefer to have your fun in private on a one-to-one basis, perhaps? Well, I'm sure that something can be arranged—'

Leo's cold, 'Forget it,' brought an ugly look of dislike to Jeremy's too pale blue eyes.

'There's a lot of antagonism around here about the fact that you're planning to close down one or other of the factories. A man with your reputation…'

'Oh, I think my reputation can stand the heat,' Leo replied grittily.

He could see that his confidence had increased Jeremy's dislike of him, just as he had seen the envy in the other man's eyes when he had driven up in his top-of-the-range Mercedes.

Out of the corner of his eye he caught sight of the newspaper that Jeremy had rudely continued to read after Leo's arrival. There was an article on the page that was open detailing the downfall of a politician who had tried unsuccessfully to sue those who had exposed certain tawdry aspects of his private life, including his visits to a massage parlour. The fact that the politician had claimed that he had been set up had not convinced the jury who had found against him.

'I wouldn't be so sure about your reputation if I were

you,' Jeremy warned Leo nastily, glancing towards the paper as he spoke.

Giving him a dismissive look, Leo left.

Leo frowned as he walked into his suite. There was no way in a thousand years he was going to change his plans. He had worked too hard and for too long, building up his business from nothing…less than nothing, slowly, painstakingly clawing his way up from his own one-man band, first overtaking and then taking over his competition as he grew more and more successful.

The Driscoll family company was in direct competition to Leo's. Since their business duplicated his own, it was only natural that he should have to close down some of their four factories. As yet Leo had not decided which out of the four. But as for Jeremy Driscoll's attempt to get him to back out of the deal…!

Tired, Leo strode into the suite without bothering to switch on the lights. At this time on a June evening there was still enough light in the sky for him not to need to do so, even without the additional glow of the almost full moon.

The bedroom wasn't quite as well-lit; someone—the maid, he imagined—had closed the curtains, but the bathroom light was on and the door open. Frowning over such sloppiness, he headed towards the bathroom, closing the door behind him once he was inside.

Giving his own reflection a brief glance in the mirror, he paused to rub a lean hand over his stubble-darkened jaw before reaching for his razor.

Jeremy Driscoll's bombastic arrogance had irritated him to an extent that warned him that those amongst his family and friends who cautioned that he was driving himself too hard might have something of a point.

Narrowing the silver-grey eyes that were an inheritance from his father's side, and for whose piercingly analytical and defence-stripping qualities they were rightly feared by anyone who sought to deceive him, he grimaced slightly. He badly needed a haircut; his dark hair curled over the collar of his shirt. Taking time out for anything in his life that wasn't work right now simply wasn't an option.

His parents professed not to understand just where he got his single-minded determination to succeed from. They had been happy with their small newsagent's business.

His parents were retired now, and living in his mother's family's native Italy. He had bought them a villa outside Florence as a ruby-wedding present.

Leo had visited them, very briefly, early in May for his mother's birthday.

He put down his razor, remembering the look he had seen them exchange when his mother had asked wistfully if there was yet 'anyone special' in his life.

He had told her with dry humour that not only did his negative response to her maternal question relate to his present, but that it could also be applied indefinitely to his future.

With unusual asperity she had returned that if that was the case then it was perhaps time she paid a visit to the village's local wise woman and herbalist, who, according to rumour, had an absolutely foolproof recipe for a love potion!

Leo had laughed outright at that. After all, it was not

that he couldn't have a partner, a lover, if he so wished. Any number of stunningly attractive young women had made it plain to him both discreetly and rather more obviously that they would like to share his life and his bed, and, of course, his bank account… But Leo could still remember how at the upmarket public school he had won a scholarship to the female pupils had been scornfully dismissive of the boy whose school uniform was so obviously bought secondhand and whose only source of money came from helping out in his parents' small business.

That experience had taught Leo a lesson he was determined never to forget. Yes, there had been women in his life, but no doubt rather idiotically by some people's standards, he had discovered that he possessed an unexpected aversion to the idea of casual sex. Which meant…

Unwantedly Leo remembered his body's sharply explicit reaction to the woman he had seen in the hotel foyer as he had crossed it on his way to his meeting earlier.

Small and curvy, or so he had suspected, beneath the abominable clothes she had been wearing.

Leo's mother did not have Italian blood for nothing, and, like all her countrywomen, she possessed a strong sense of personal style, which made it impossible for Leo not to recognise when a woman was dressing to maximum effect. This woman had most certainly not been doing that at all. She had not even really been his type. If he was prepared to admit to a preference it was for cool, elegant blondes. Most definitely not for delectably sexy, tousled and touchable types of women, who turned his loins to hotly savage lust and even distracted his mind to the extent that he had almost found himself deviating from his set course and thinking about walking towards her.

Leo never deviated from any course he set himself—ever—especially not on account of a woman.

With an indrawn breath of self-disgust, Leo stripped off his clothes and stepped into the shower.

As a teenager he had played sports for his school, which, ironically, had done wonders to increase his 'pulling power' with his female schoolmates, and he still had the powerful muscle structure of a natural athlete. Impatiently he lathered his body and then rinsed off the foam before reaching for a towel.

Once dry, he opened the bathroom door and headed for the bed. It was darker now, but still light enough, thanks to the moonlight glinting through the curtains, for him not to need to switch on the light.

Flipping back the bedclothes, Leo got into the bed, reaching automatically for the duvet, and then froze as he realised that the bed—*his* bed—was already occupied.

Switching on the bedside lamp, he stared in angry disbelief at the tousled head of curly hair on the pillow next to his own—a decidedly female head, he recognised, just like the slender naked arm and softly rounded shoulder he could now see in the lamplight.

The nostrils of the proudly aquiline nose he had inherited from his mother's Italian forebears flared fastidiously as they picked up the smell of alcohol on the softly exhaled breath of the oblivious sleeping form.

Another scent—a mixture of warm fresh air, lavender

and a certain shockingly earthy sensuality that was Jodi's alone—his senses reacted to in a very different way.

It was the girl from the foyer. Leo would have recognised her anywhere, or, rather, his body would.

Automatically his brain passed him another piece of information. Jeremy Driscoll's oily-voiced suggestiveness as he had tried to persuade Leo to go back on their contract. Was this…this girl the inducement he'd had in mind? She had to be. Leo could not think of any other reason for her presence here in his bed!

Well, if Jeremy Driscoll dared to think that he, Leo, was the kind of man who…

Angrily he reached out to grasp Jodi's bare arm in strong fingers as he leaned across her to shake her into wakefulness.

Jodi was fathoms-deep asleep, sleeping the sleep of the pure of heart—and the alcohol-assisted—and she was having the most delicious dream in which she was, by some means her sleeping state wasn't inclined to question, wrapped in the embrace of the most gorgeous, sexy man. He was tall, dark-haired and silver-eyed, with features reassuringly familiar to Jodi, but his body, his touch, were wonderfully and excitingly new.

They were lying together, body to body, on a huge bed in a room with a panoramic view of a private tropical beach, and as he leaned towards her and stroked strong fingers along her forearm he whispered to her, 'What the hell are you doing in my bed?'

Her brain still under the influence of her 'fruit cocktail' Jodi opened bemused, adoring eyes.

Why was her wonderful lover looking so angry? Smiling sleepily up at him, she was about to ask him, but somehow her attention became focused on how downright desirable he actually was.

That wonderful naked golden-brown body. Naked. Yummy! More than yummy! Jodi closed her eyes on a sigh of female appreciation and then quickly opened them again, anxious not to miss anything. She watched the way the muscles in his neck corded as he leaned over her, and the sinewy strength of his solid forearms, so very male that she just had to reach out and run an explorative fingertip down the one nearest to her, marvelling at the difference between it and her own so much softer female flesh.

Leo couldn't believe his eyes—or his body. She, the uninvited interloper in his bed, was brazenly ignoring his angry question and was actually daring to touch him. No, not just touch, he acknowledged as his body reacted to her with a teeth-clenching jerk that gave an immediate lie to his previous mental use of the word 'unwanted'. What she was doing—dammit—was outright stroking him, caressing him!

Torn between a cerebral desire to reject what was happening and a visceral surge of agonisingly intense desire to embrace it, and with it the woman who was tormenting him with such devastating effectiveness, Leo made a valiant struggle to cling to the tenets of discipline and self-control that were the twin bastions of his life. To his shock, he lost. And not just the campaign but the whole war!

Jodi, though, fuelled now by something far more subtle than alcohol, and far stronger, was totally oblivious to everything but the delicious dream she had found her way into.

Imagine. When she touched him, like so, the most extraordinary tremors ran right through his whole body—and not just his, she acknowledged as she considered the awesome fact that her own body was so highly responsive, so reactive to every movement of his.

She was so lucky to be here with him on this wonderful private island of love and pleasure. Tenderly she leaned forward and flicked her tongue-tip delicately against the hollow at the base of his throat, revelling in the sensation of his damp skin against her tongue, its texture, its taste, the way that fierce male pulse thudded to life at her touch.

Leo couldn't believe what was happening. What she was doing; what he was letting her do. He found himself lying back against the pillow as she was the one to arch provocatively over him, whilst her tongue busily and far too erotically laved his skin.

Even in the less than half-light of the shadowy bedroom he could see the naked outline of her body with its narrow waist and softly flaring hips; her legs were delectably shaped, her ankles tiny and delicate, the shadowy triangle of hair between her thighs so soft and tempting that…

His throat dry with angry tension and gut-wrenching longing, Leo felt his whole body shudder.

He could see her breasts, soft, rounded, creamy-skinned, with darkly tender crests and tormentingly erect nipples.

Unable to stop himself, he lifted his hands carefully, cupping them. He could feel their warm weight, and he could feel, too, the tight hardness of those wanton peaks, tauntingly challenging him to…

Jodi gasped and then shivered in delight as she felt the rough pressure of her lover's tongue against her nipple.

'Oh, it feels so good,' she whispered to him, closing her eyes as she gave herself up to the sensations he was arousing. Her hand slipped distractedly from his arm to her own body, flattening betrayingly against her belly as she drew in a juddering breath of delirious pleasure.

Leo could scarcely believe the sheer wantonness of her reaction to his touch. He tried to remind himself that she was there for a purpose, doing the job she had been hired for, but his senses were too drugged to allow him to think rationally.

He had known then, in that fleeting second he had seen her in the hotel foyer, that she could affect him like this; that he would want her like this, no matter what the stern voice of his conscience was trying to tell him.

His hand slid to the curve of her waist and flared possessively over her hip, which fitted as perfectly into his grip as though they had been made for each other.

Her hands were on his body, their touch somehow innocently explorative, as though he was the first man she had ever been so intimate with—which was a ludicrous thought!

The soft whispers of female praise she was giving him had to be deliberately calculated to have the maximum effect on a man's ego—any man's ego—he tried to remind himself. But somehow he couldn't stop touching her—couldn't stop *wanting* her!

Jodi sighed blissfully in a sensual heaven. He seemed to know instinctively just how and where to caress her, how to arouse and please her. Her body soared and melted with each wonderful wave of erotic pleasure. Voluptuously she snuggled closer to him shivering in heady excitement as she let her hands wander at will over his body—so excitingly different from her own.

The bedclothes, which she had pushed away an aeon ago so that she could look at the powerful nakedness of the male body she was now so hungry for, lay in a tangled heap at the bottom of the bed. Moonlight silvered her own body, whilst it turned the larger and more muscular shape of her lover's into a dark-hued steel.

She ached so much for him. Her hands moved downwards over him, her gaze drawn to his taut, powerful magnificence.

Deliberately she drew her fingertips along the hard length of his erection, closing her eyes and shuddering as a deep thrill twisted through her.

Leo couldn't understand how he was letting this happen! It went totally against everything he believed in! Never before in his life had he experienced such intense and overwhelmingly mindless desire, nor been so driven by the fierce pulse of it to take what he was being so openly offered.

Every single one of his senses was responding to her with an uncheckable urgency that left his brain floundering.

The scent, the sight, the feel of her, her touch against his body, even the soft, increasingly incoherent sound of her husky, pleading moans, seemed to strike at a vulnerability inside him that he had never dreamed existed.

He reached out for her, giving in to the need burning through him to kiss every delicious woman-scented inch of her, and then to do so all over again, slowly and thoroughly, until the unsteadiness of her breathing was a torment to his senses. He finally allowed himself the pleasure of sliding his fingers through the soft, warm tangle of curls concealing her sex, stroking the flesh that lay beneath and slowly parting the outer covering of her to caress her with full intimacy.

She felt soft, hot, moist and so unbelievably delicate that, ignoring the agonised urging of her voice against his ear, he forced himself to love her slowly and carefully.

He could feel her body rising up to reach his touch as she writhed frantically against him, telling him in broken words of open pleasure that jolted like electricity through his senses just what she wanted from him and how. She somehow managed to manoeuvre both of them so that he was pushing urgently against her and then inside her, as though the intimacy was beyond his own physical control.

She felt. She felt…

Jodi heard the low, visceral male sound he made as he entered her, filled her, and sharp spirals of intense pleasure flooded her body.

Just hearing that sound, knowing his need, was almost as erotically exciting as feeling him move inside her. Long, slow, powerful thrusts lifted and carried her and caused her to reach out for him, drawing him deep inside her. The pleasure of feeling her body expand to accommodate him was so indescribably precious that she cried out aloud her joy in it and in him. She loved this feeling of being wrapped around him, embracing him, holding him, somehow nurturing and protecting his essential male essence.

Somewhere on the periphery of his awareness, Leo recognised that there was something that his mind should be aware of, something important his body was trying to tell him, something about both the intensity of what he was experiencing and the special, close-fitting intimacy of the tender female body wrapped around his own. But the age-old urgency of the need now driving him was short-circuiting his ability to question anything.

All he knew was how good she felt, how right, how essential it was that he reciprocate the wonderful gift she was giving him by taking them both to that special place that lay so tantalisingly almost within reach…another second, another stroke, another heartbeat.

He felt her orgasm gripping her; spasm after spasm of such vibrant intensity that its sheer strength brought him to his own completion.

As she lay in his arms, her body trembling in the aftershock of her pleasure, her damp curls a wild tangle of soft silk against his chest, he heard her gasping shakily, 'That was wonderful, my wonderful, wonderful lover.'

And then as he looked down into her eyes she closed them and fell asleep, with all the speed and innocence of a child.

Broodingly Leo studied her. There was no doubt in his mind that she was a plant, bought and paid for with Jeremy Driscoll's money.

And he, idiotic fool that he was, had fallen straight into the trap that had been set for him. And he suspected, now that he had time to think things through properly, that this was something more than Jeremy Driscoll supplying him with a bedmate for the night.

Jeremy was simply not that altruistic. Not altruistic in any way, shape or form, and Leo knew that he had not mistaken the dislike and envy in the other man's eyes earlier in the day. Jeremy knew that he, Leo, was not about to change his mind. Not unless Jeremy Driscoll believed he had some means of forcing him to do so.

Now, when it was too late, Leo remembered the newspaper article Jeremy Driscoll had been reading,

For a man in his position, an unmarried man, the effect of a public exposé, a woman selling her kiss-and-tell story to one of the national newspapers, would not be devastating. But Leo would be pilloried as a laughing stock for being so gullible and, as a result, would lose respect in the business world. If that happened he would not be able to count on the support and belief he was used to. No businessman, not even one as successful as Leo, wanted that.

He got out of bed, giving Jodi a bitter look as he did so. How could she lie there sleeping so peacefully? As though…as though… Unable to stop himself, Leo felt his glance slide to her mouth, still curved in a warmly satisfied smile. Even in her sleep she was somehow managing to maintain the fiction that what had happened between them was something special. But then no doubt she was a skilled actress. She would have to be.

The reality of what he had done pushed relentlessly through his thoughts. His behaviour had been so totally alien that even now he couldn't imagine what had possessed him. Or, at least, he could, but he couldn't understand how he had allowed it to get so out of control.

Or why he was standing beside the bed and continuing to look at her, when surely his strongest urge ought to be to go and have a shower as hot and strong as he could stand until he had washed the feel, the scent, the taste of her off his body and out of his senses. But for some incomprehensible reason that was the last thing he wanted to do…

Just in time he managed to stop himself from reaching out to touch her, to stroke a gentle fingertip along that tender cheekbone and touch those unbelievably long, dark lashes, that small, straight nose, those soft, full lips.

As though somehow she sensed what he was thinking, her lips parted on a sweetly sensual sigh, her mouth curling back into another smile of remembered pleasure.

What the hell was he doing, letting her sleep there like that? By rights he ought to wake her up and throw her out. He glanced at the alarm clock supplied by the hotel. It was two o'clock in the morning, and he told himself that it was because of his inbred sense of responsibility that he could not bring himself to do so.

It just wasn't safe for a woman—any woman, even a woman like her—to wander about on her own so late at night; anything could happen to her!

But he wasn't going to get back in that bed with her. No way!

Going into the bathroom, he pulled on the complimentary robe provided by the hotel and then made his way into the sitting room, closing the bedroom door behind him as he did so and snapping on the light.

The first thing he saw was the almost empty cocktail jug and the glass Jodi had drunk from.

Grimacing, he pushed it to one side. She had even had the audacity to order a drink on Room Service. Because she had needed the courage it would give her to go to bed with him?

He warned himself against falling into the trap of feeling sorry for her, making excuses for her. She had known exactly what she was doing… Exactly… He frowned as he moved a little uncomfortably in his chair.

He was wide awake now and he had some work he could be doing. When his would-be seducer woke up they were going to need to have a short, sharp talk.

There was no way he was going to allow Jeremy Driscoll to blackmail him into backing out of the contract he had made with his father-in-law.

Still frowning, he reached for his briefcase.

CHAPTER TWO

RUBBING her eyes, Jodi grimaced in disgust at the sour taste in her mouth. Her head ached, and her body did too, but they were different sorts of aches; the ache in her body had a subtle but quite distinctly pleasurable undertone to it, whilst the one in her head…

Cautiously she moved it and then wished she had not as a fierce, throbbing pain banged through her temples.

Instinctively she reached across, expecting to find her own familiar bedside table, and then realised that she was not in her own bed.

So where exactly was she? Like wisps of mist, certain vague memories, sounds, images, drifted dangerously across her mind. But no, surely she couldn't have? Hadn't! Frantically she looked to the other side of the large bed, the sledgehammer thuds of her heart easing as she saw to her relief that it was empty.

It had been a dream, that was all, a shocking and unacceptable dream. And she couldn't imagine how or why… But… She froze as she saw the quite unmistakable imprint of another head on the pillow next to her own.

Shivering, she leaned closer to it, stiffening as she caught the alien but somehow all-too-familiar scent of soap and man rising from the pillow.

What had been vague memories were becoming sharper and clearer with every anxious beat of her heart.

It was true! Here in this room. In this bed! She had. Where was he? She looked nervously towards the bathroom door, her attention momentarily distracted by the sight of her own clothes neatly folded on a chair.

Without pausing for logical thought she scrambled out of the bed and hurried towards them, dressing with urgency whilst she kept her gaze fixed on the closed bathroom door.

She longed to be able to shower and clean her teeth, brush her hair, but she simply did not dare to do so. Appallingly explicit memories were now forcing themselves past the splitting pain of her alcohol-induced headache. She couldn't comprehend how on earth she could have behaved in such a way.

She had been drinking, she reminded herself with disgusted self-contempt. She had been drinking, and whatever had been in that potent cocktail Room Service had sent up to the suite had somehow turned her from the prim and proper virginal woman she was into a…an amorous, sexually aggressive female, who…

Virginal! Jodi's body froze. Well, she certainly wasn't that any more! Not that it mattered except for the fact that, driven by her desire, she hadn't taken any steps to protect her health or to prevent…

Jodi begged fate not to punish her foolishness, praying that there would be no consequences to what she had done other than her own shocked humiliation.

Picking up her handbag, she tiptoed quietly towards the bedroom door.

Leo was just wondering how long his unwanted guest intended to continue to sleep in *his* bed, and whether or not five a.m. was too early to ring for a room-service breakfast, when Jodi reached for the bedroom door.

Even though his body ached for sleep, he had been furiously determined not to get back into his bed whilst she was in it. One experience of just how vulnerable he was to her particularly effective method of seduction was more than enough.

Even now, having had the best part of three hours of solitude to analyse what had happened, he was still no closer to understanding why he had been unable to stop himself from responding to her, unable to control his desire.

Yes, he had felt that bittersweet pang of attraction when he had first seen her in the hotel foyer, but knowing what she was ought surely to have destroyed that completely.

He tensed as he saw the bedroom door opening.

At first, intent on making her escape, Jodi didn't see him standing motionlessly in front of the window.

It was light now, the clear, fresh light of an early summer morning, and when she did realise that he was there her face flushed as sweetly pink as the sun-warmed feathers of clouds in the sky beyond the window.

Leo heard her involuntary gasp and saw the quick, despairing glance she gave the main door, her only exit from the suite. Anticipating her actions, he moved towards the door, reaching it before her and standing in front of it, blocking her escape.

As she saw him properly Jodi felt the embarrassed heat possessing her body deepen to a burning, soul-scorching intensity. It was him, the man she had seen in the foyer, the man she had thought so very attractive, the man who had made her have the most extraordinarily uncharacteristic thoughts!

Out of the corner of her eye Jodi could see the coffee-table and the telltale cocktail jug.

'Yes,' Leo agreed urbanely. 'Not only have you illegally entered my suite, but you also had the gall to run up a room-service bill. Do you intend to pay personally for the use of my bed and the bar, or would you prefer me to send the bills to Jeremy Driscoll?'

Jodi, who had been staring in mute distress at the cocktail jug, turned her head automatically to look at him as she heard the familiar name of her least favourite fellow villager.

'Jeremy?' she questioned uncertainly.

Jeremy Driscoll's father-in-law might own the local factory, and Jeremy himself might run it, but that did not make him well-liked in the locale. He had a reputation for underhand behaviour, and for attempting to bring in certain cost-cutting and potentially dangerous practices, which thankfully had been blocked by the workers' union and the health and safety authority.

But what he had to do with her present humiliating situation Jodi had no idea at all.

'Yes. Jeremy,' Leo confirmed, unkindly imitating the anxious tremor in her voice. 'I know exactly what's going on,' he continued acidly. 'And why you're here. But if you think for one minute that I'm going to allow myself to be blackmailed into giving in…'

Jodi swallowed uncomfortably against the tight ball of self-recrimination and shame that was lodged in her throat.

Did Leo Jefferson—it had to be him—really think that

she was the kind of person who would behave in such a way? His use of the word 'blackmail' had particularly shocked her. But was the truth any easier for her to bear, never mind admit to someone else? Was it really any more palatable to have to say that she had been so drunk—albeit by accident—that she simply had not known what she was doing?

To have gone to bed with a complete stranger, to have done the things she had done with him, and, even worse, wanted the things she had wanted with him… A woman in her position, responsible for the shaping and guiding of young minds…

Jodi shuddered to think of how some of the parents of her pupils, not to mention the school's board of governors, might view her behaviour.

'Well, you can go back to your paymaster,' Leo Jefferson was telling her with cold venom, 'and you can tell him, whilst you might have given me good value for his money, it makes not one jot of difference to my plans. I still have no intention of cancelling the contract and allowing him to buy back the business.

'I have no idea what he hoped to achieve by paying you to have sex with me,' Leo continued grimly and untruthfully. 'But all he gave me was a night of passably good if somewhat over-professionalised sex. If he thinks he can use that against me in some way…' Leo shrugged to underline his indifference whilst discreetly watching Jodi to see how she was reacting to his fabricated insouciance.

She had gone very pale, and there was a look in her eyes that under other circumstances Leo might almost have described as haunted.

Jodi fought to control her spiralling confusion and to make sense out of what Leo Jefferson was saying. She was going to avoid thinking about his cruelly insulting personal comments right now. They were the kind of thing she could only allow herself to examine in private. But his references to Jeremy Driscoll and her own supposed connection with him were totally baffling.

She opened her mouth to say as much, but before she could do so Leo was exclaiming tersely, 'I don't know who you are or why you can't find a less self-destructive way of earning a living.'

Ignoring the latter part of his comment, Jodi pounced with shaky relief on his 'I don't know who you are'.

If he didn't know who she was, she certainly wasn't going to enlighten him. With any luck she might, please fate, be able to salvage her pride and her public reputation with a damage-limitation exercise that meant no one other than the two of them need ever know what had happened.

She had abandoned any thought of pursuing her real purpose in seeking him out. How on earth could she plead with him for her school's future now? Another burden of sickening guilt joined the one already oppressing her. She had not just let herself down, and her standards, she had let the school and her pupils down as well. And she still couldn't fully understand how it had all happened. Yes, she had had too much to drink, but surely that alone…

Cringing, she reflected on her reaction to Leo Jefferson when she had seen him walking across the hotel foyer the previous evening. Then, of course, she had not known who he was. Only that…only that she found him attractive…

She felt numbed by the sheer unacceptability of what she had done, shamed and filled with the bleakest sense of disbelief and despair.

Her lack of any response and her continued silence were just a ploy she was using as a form of gamesmanship, Leo decided as he watched her, and as for that anguished shock he had seen earlier in her eyes, well, as he had good cause to know, she was an extremely accomplished performer!

'I have to go. Please let me past.'

The soft huskiness of her voice reminded Leo of the way she had moaned her desire to him during the night. What the hell was the matter with him? He couldn't possibly still want her!

Even though he had made no move to stand away from the door, Jodi walked towards it as determinedly as she could. She had, she reminded herself, faced a whole roomful of disruptive teenage pupils of both sexes during her teacher training without betraying her inner fear. Surely she could outface one mere man? Only somehow the use of the word 'mere' in connection with this particular man brought a mirthless bubble of painful laughter to her throat.

This man could never be a 'mere' anything. This man…

She had guts, Leo acknowledged as she stared calmly past him, but then no doubt her chosen profession would mean that she was no stranger to the art of making a judicial exit.

It went against everything he believed in to forcibly constrain her, even though he was loath to let her go without reinforcing just what he thought of her and the man who was paying her.

Another second and she would have been so close to him that they would almost have been body to body, Jodi recognised on a mute shudder of distress as Leo finally allowed her access to the door. Expelling a shaky, pent-up breath of relief, she reached for the handle.

Leo waited until she had turned it before reminding her grimly, 'Driscoll might think this was a clever move, but you can tell him from me that it wasn't. Oh, and just a word of warning for you personally: any attempt to publicise what happened between us last night and I can promise you that any ridicule I suffer you will suffer ten times more.'

Jodi didn't speak. She couldn't. This was the most painful, the most shameful experience she had ever had or ever wanted to have.

But it seemed that Leo Jefferson still hadn't finished with her, because as she stepped out into the hotel corridor he took hold of the door, placing his hand over hers in a grip that was like a volt of savage male electricity burning through her body.

'Of course, if you'd been really clever you could have sold your story where it would have gained you the highest price already.'

Jodi couldn't help herself; even though it was the last thing she wanted to do, she heard herself demanding gruffly, 'What...what do you mean?'

The cynically satisfied smile he gave her made her shudder.

'What I mean is that I'm surprised you haven't tried to bargain a higher price for your silence from me than the price Driscoll paid you for your services.'

Jodi couldn't believe what she was hearing.

'I don't...I didn't...' She began to defend herself instinctively, before shaking her head and telling him fiercely, 'There isn't any amount of money that could compensate me for what...what I experienced last night.' And then, before he could say or do anything more to hurt her, she managed to wrench her hand from his and run down the corridor towards the waiting lift.

A girl wearing the uniform of a member of the hotel staff paused to look at her as Jodi left Leo's suite, but Jodi was too engrossed in her thoughts to notice her.

Leo watched her go in furious disbelief. Just how much of a fool did she take him for, throwing out a bad Victorian line like that? And as for what she had implied, well, his body had certain very telltale marks on it that told a very different story indeed!

To Jodi's relief, no one gave her a second glance as she hurried through the hotel foyer, heading for the exit. No doubt they were used to guests coming and going all the time.

'Stop thinking about it,' she advised herself as she stepped out into the bright morning sunlight, blinking a little in its brilliance.

The first thing she was going to do when she got home, Jodi decided as she drove out onto the main road, was have a shower, and the second was to compose the letter she would send to Leo Jefferson, putting to him the case for allowing the factory to remain open—there was no way she was going to try to make any kind of personal contact with him now!

And the third: the third was to go to bed and catch up on her sleep, and very firmly put what had happened between them out of her mind, consign it to a locked and deeply buried part of her memory that could never be accessed again by anyone!

Jodi opened the front door to her small cottage, one of a row of eight, built in the eighteenth century, with tiny, picturesque front gardens overlooking the village street and much longer lawns at the rear. After carefully locking up behind her she made her way upstairs.

It was the sound of her telephone ringing that finally woke her; groggily she reached for the receiver, appalled to see from her watch that it was gone ten o'clock. Normally at this time on a Saturday morning she would be in their local town, doing her weekly supermarket shop before meeting up with friends for lunch.

As luck would have it, she had made no such arrangement for today, as most of her friends were away on holiday with their families.

As her fingers curled round the telephone receiver her stomach muscles tensed, despite the fact that she knew it was impossible that her caller could be Leo Jefferson; after all, he didn't even know who she was, thank goodness! A small *frisson* of nervous excitement tingled through her body, quickly followed by a strong surge of something she would not allow herself to acknowledge as disappointment when she recognised her cousin Nigel's voice.

It was no wonder, after all she had been through, that

her emotions should be so traumatised that they had difficulty in relaying appropriate reactions to her.

'At last,' she could hear Nigel saying cheerfully to her. 'This is the third time I've rung. How did it go with Leo Jefferson? I'm dying to know.'

Jodi took a deep breath; she could feel her heart starting to pound as shame and guilt filled her. The hand holding the receiver felt sticky. She had never been a good liar; never been even a vaguely adequate one.

'It didn't,' she admitted huskily.

'You chickened out?' Nigel guessed.

Jodi let out a sigh of relief; Nigel had just given her the perfect answer to her dilemma.

'I…I was tired and I started to have second thoughts. And—'

Before she could tell Nigel that she had decided to write to Leo Jefferson rather than speak with him her cousin had cut across her to say tolerantly, 'I thought you wouldn't go through with it. Never mind. Uncle Nigel has ridden to the rescue for you. My boss has invited me over to dinner tonight, and I've asked him if I can take you along with me. He'll be speaking to Leo Jefferson himself next week, and if you put your case to him I'm sure he'll incorporate the plight of the school into his own discussion.'

'Oh, Nigel, that's very kind of you, but I don't think…' Jodi began to demur. She just wasn't in the mood for a dinner party, and as for the idea of putting the school's case to Nigel's boss, who was the chief planning officer for the area, Jodi's opinion of her own credibility had been so undermined that she just didn't feel good enough about herself to do so.

Nigel, though, made it clear that he was not prepared to take no for an answer.

'You've got to come,' he insisted. 'Graham really does want to meet you. His grandson is one of your pupils, apparently, and he's a big fan of yours. The grandson, not Graham. Although…'

'Nigel, I can't go,' Jodi protested.

'Of course you can. You must. Think of your school,' he teased her before adding, 'I'm picking you up at half-past seven, and you'd better be ready.'

He had rung off before Jodi could protest any further.

Wearily Jodi studied the screen of her computer. She had spent most of the afternoon trying to compose a letter to send to Leo Jefferson. The headache she had woken up with had, thankfully, finally abated, but every time she tried to concentrate on what she was supposed to be doing a totally unwanted mental picture of Leo Jefferson kept forming inside her head. And it wasn't just his face that her memory was portraying to her in intimate detail, she acknowledged as she felt herself turning as pink as the cascading petunias in her next-door neighbour's window boxes. Mrs Fields, at eighty, was still a keen gardener, and as she had ruefully explained to Jodi she liked the strong, bright colours because she could see them.

Jodi's own lovingly planted boxes were a more subtle combination of soft greens, white and silver, the same silver as Leo Jefferson's sexy eyes.

Jodi's face flamed even hotter as she stared at her screen and realised that she had begun her letter, 'Dear Sexy Eyes'.

Quickly she deleted the words and began again, reminding herself of how important it was that she impress on Leo Jefferson the effect the closure of the factory would have not just on her school but also on the whole community.

All over the country small villages were dying or becoming weekend dormitories for city workers, although everyone here in their local community had worked hard to make theirs a living, working village.

If she could get Nigel's boss on her side it was bound to help their case. Frowning slightly, she pushed her chair away from her computer. She ought to be used to fighting to keep the school going now. When she had first been appointed as its head teacher she had been told by the education authority that it would only be for an interim period, as, with the school's numbers falling, it would ultimately have to be closed.

Even though she had known she would get better promotion and higher pay by transferring to a bigger school, as soon as Jodi had realised the effect that losing their school would have she had begun to canvass determinedly for new pupils, even to the extent of persuading parents who had previously been considering private education to give their local primary a chance.

Her efforts had paid off in more ways than one, and Jodi knew she would never forget the pride she had felt when their school had received an excellent report following an inspection visit.

Her pride wasn't so much for herself, though, as for the efforts of the pupils and everyone else who had supported the school; to have to stand back and see all the ground they had gained lost, the sense of teamwork and community she had so determinedly fostered amongst the pupils destroyed, was more than she wanted to have to bear.

She had proved just how well the children thrived and learned in an atmosphere of security and love, in a school where they were known and valued as individuals, and Jodi was convinced that the self-confidence such a start gave them was something that would benefit them through their academic lives. But somehow, trying to explain all of this to Leo Jefferson was far harder than she had expected.

Perhaps it was because she suspected that he had already made up his mind, that, so far as he was concerned, the small community he would be destroying simply didn't matter when compared with his profits. Or perhaps it was because all she could think about, all she could see, was last night and the way they had been together…

With every hour that distanced her from the intimacy they had shared it became harder for her to acknowledge what she had done. It just wasn't like her to behave in such a way, and the proof of that, had she needed any, was the fact that he, Leo Jefferson, had been her first and only lover!

Too overwrought to concentrate, Jodi stood up and started to pace the floor of her small sitting room in emotional agitation.

Shocking though her behaviour had been, she knew and could not deny that she had enjoyed Leo Jefferson's touch, his lovemaking, his possession.

But that was because she had been half-drunk and half-asleep, she tried to defend herself, before her strong sense of honesty ruthlessly reminded her of the way she had reacted to him when she had first seen him, when she had quite definitely been both sober and awake!

It was nearly six o'clock. Her letter wasn't finished, but she would have to leave it now and go and get ready for the evening.

Nigel was going to a lot of trouble on her behalf and she ought to feel grateful to him. Instead, all she wanted was to stay at home and hide from the world until she had come to terms with what she had done.

CHAPTER THREE

LEO grimaced as he ran a hand over his newly shaven jaw. There was no way he felt like going out to dinner, but when Graham Johnson, the chief planning officer for the area, had rung to invite him to his home Leo had not felt he could refuse.

It made good business sense to establish an amicable arrangement with the local authority. Leo had already met Graham and liked him, and when Graham had explained that there was someone he would find it interesting to meet on an informal basis Leo had sensed that Graham would not be very impressed were he to turn him down. And besides, at least if he went out it would stop him from thinking about last night, and that wretched, unforgettably sexy woman who had got so dangerously under his skin.

As yet, Jeremy Driscoll had made no attempt to contact him, and Leo was hoping that he had the sense to recognise that Leo was not to be coerced—in any way—but somehow he doubted that Jeremy had actually given up. He wasn't that type, and, since he had gone as far as paying his accomplice to play her part, Leo suspected that he was going to want value for his money.

Did Driscoll avail himself of Leo's tousle-haired tormentor's sexual skills? It shocked Leo to discover just how unpalatable he found that thought! Was he crazy, feeling possessive about a woman like that, a woman any man could have? Unwantedly Leo found himself remembering the way her body had claimed him, tightening around him almost as though it had known no other man. Now he *was* going crazy, he told himself angrily as he peered at the approaching signpost to check that he was driving in the right direction.

'Jodi, you aren't listening to me.'

Jodi gave her cousin an apologetic look as he brought his car to a halt outside his boss's house.

'Come to think of it, you're not exactly looking your normal, chirpy self.' He gave her a concerned look. 'Worrying about that school of yours, I expect?'

Ignoring his question, Jodi drew a deep breath, determined to tackle him about an issue that had been weighing very heavily on her mind.

'Nigel, what on earth possessed you to order that cocktail for me last night? You know I don't drink, and because it never occurred to me that it was alcoholic...well, there was so much fruit in it...'

'Hey, hang on a minute,' Nigel protested in bewilderment. 'I never ordered you anything alcoholic.'

'Well, whatever the waiter brought to Leo Jefferson's suite definitely was,' Jodi informed him grittily.

'They must have misunderstood me,' Nigel told her. 'I asked them to send you up a fruit cocktail. I thought it seemed expensive—what a waste; I bet you didn't touch it after the first swallow, did you?'

Fortunately, before she was obliged to lie to him, he took hold of Jodi's arm and walked her firmly towards the front door, which opened as they reached it to reveal their host, Graham Johnson, a tall grey-haired man with a warm smile.

'You must be Jodi.' He shook Jodi's hand, and introduced himself. 'I've heard an awful lot about you!'

When Jodi gave Nigel a wry look their host shook his head and laughed.

'No, not from Nigel, although he has mentioned you. I was referring to our grandson, Henry. He's one of your pupils and an ardent admirer. With just reason, too, according to his parents. Our daughter, Charlotte, is most impressed with the dramatic improvement the school has achieved in Henry's reading skills.'

Jodi smiled her appreciation of his compliments and a little of the tension started to leave her body as they followed Graham into the house.

Mary Johnson was as welcoming as her husband, informing Jodi that she had trained as a teacher herself, although it had been many years since she had last taught.

'My daughter was a little concerned at first when she heard that you were an advocate of a mixture of traditional teaching methods and educational play, but she's a total convert now. She can't stop telling us how much Henry's spatial skills have improved along with his reading ability.'

'We like to encourage the children to become good all-rounders,' Jodi acknowledged, explaining, 'We feel that it helps overall morale if we can encourage every child to discover a field in which they can do well.'

'I understand from our daughter that you've actually got parents putting their children's names down for the school almost as soon as they are born.'

'Well, perhaps not quite that,' Jodi laughed, 'but certainly we are finding that our reputation has been spread by word of mouth. We're above the safety limit we need to satisfy the education authority as regards pupil numbers and likely to stay that way, unless, of course, the factory is closed down.'

Jodi gave Graham Johnson an uncertain look as she saw his expression.

'The final decision with regard to that rests with Leo Jefferson,' he told her gently, 'which is why I've invited him to join us for dinner tonight. It was Nigel's idea, and a good one. It might help matters if the two of you were to meet in an informal setting. I suspect that from a businessman's point of view Leo Jefferson hasn't really considered the effect a closure of the factory would have on the village school. And, of course, it isn't inevitable that he will close down our factory. As I understand it, of the four he has taken over he only intends to close two.'

Jodi wasn't really listening to him. She had stopped listening properly the moment he had said those dreadful words, 'I've invited him to join us for dinner tonight'.

Leo Jefferson was coming here. For dinner. She was going to be forced to sit in the same room with him, perhaps even across the table from him.

She felt sick, faint, paralysed with fear, she recognised as the doorbell rang and Graham went to answer it.

Frantically she looked at the French windows, aching to make her escape through them, but it was already too late, Graham was walking back into the room accompanied by Leo Jefferson. The man she had spent the night with... Her lover!

* * *

Leo had been listening politely to his host as Graham showed him the way to the sitting room, opened the door and ushered Leo inside. He proceeded to introduce Leo to the other occupants of the room, but the moment he had stepped through the door Leo stopped hearing a single word that Graham was saying as he stared in furious disbelief at Jodi.

She was standing by the French windows, looking for all the world like some martyr about to be taken away for beheading, her eyes huge with anguish and fear as she stared mutely at him.

What was going on? What was she doing here? And then Leo realised that Graham was introducing her to him as the local school's head teacher.

He felt as though he had somehow strayed into some kind of farce. He accepted that things were different in the country, but surely not so damned different that a village headmistress moonlighted as a professional harlot!

The surge of furious jealousy that burst over the banks of his normal self-control bewildered him, as did the immediate antipathy he felt towards the man standing at her side.

'And this is Nigel Marsh, my assistant and Jodi's cousin,' Graham Johnson was explaining.

Her cousin. To his own relief Leo felt himself easing back on his ridiculous emotions.

'A little surprise for you!' Nigel whispered to Jodi whilst Mary was talking to Leo.

Jodi gave him a wan smile.

'Jodi, can I get you a drink?' Graham was asking jovially.

'I don't usually drink, thank you,' Jodi responded automatically, and then flushed a deep, rich pink as she saw the look that Leo Jefferson was giving her.

'She's always been strait-laced, even before she qualified as a teacher,' Nigel informed Graham humorously. 'Can't think how we came to share the same gene pool. I'm always telling her that she ought to loosen up a little, enjoy life, let herself go.'

Jodi didn't want to look at Leo Jefferson again, but somehow she couldn't stop herself from doing so. To her shock he had moved closer to her, and whilst Nigel responded to something Mary was saying he leaned forward and whispered cynically to Jodi, 'That's quite a personality change you've managed to accomplish in less than twenty-four hours.'

'Please,' Jodi implored him, desperately afraid that he might be overheard, but to her relief the others had moved out of earshot.

'Please… I seem to remember you said something like that to me last night,' Leo reminded her silkily.

'Stop it,' Jodi begged in torment. 'You don't understand.'

'You're damned right I don't!' Leo agreed acerbically, adding, 'Tell me something; do your school governors know that you're moonlighting as a hooker? I accept that schoolteachers may not be overly well-paid, but somehow I've never imagined them supplementing their income with those sort of private lessons.'

'No, you…'

Jodi meant to continue and tell Leo he had it all wrong, but her vehement tone caused Nigel to break off his conversation with Mary Johnson and give her a concerned look. He knew how passionate she was about her school, but he hadn't expected to hear her arguing with Leo Jefferson so early in the evening. It did not augur well. However, before Nigel could step in with some diplomatic calming measures Mary was announcing that she was ready for them to sit down for dinner.

'That was absolutely delicious.' Nigel sighed appreciatively as he ate the last morsel of his pudding. 'Living on your own is all very well, but microwave meals can't take the place of home cooking. I keep saying as much to Jodi,' he continued plaintively to Mary, giving Jodi a teasing glance. 'But she doesn't seem to take the hint.'

'If you want home cooking you should learn to cook yourself,' Jodi returned firmly. 'I insist that all the children at school, boys and girls, learn the basics.'

'And I think it's wonderful that they do,' Mary supported her, turning to Leo to tell him, 'Jodi has done wonders for her school. When she first took over they had so few pupils that it was about to be closed down, but now parents are putting down their children's names at birth to ensure that they get a place.'

Jodi could feel herself starting to colour up as Leo turned to look at her.

The whole evening had been a nightmare, and so far as she was concerned it couldn't come to an end fast enough.

'Oh, yes, Jodi is passionate about her school,' Nigel chimed in supportively.

'Passionate?'

Jodi could feel the anxiety tensing her already over-stretched nervous system as Leo drawled the word with an undertone of cynical dislike that she hoped only she could hear. Was he going to give her away?

To her relief, Leo went on, 'Oh, yes, I'm sure she is.'

'I think,' Graham began to say calmly, with a kind smile in Jodi's direction, 'that she is also concerned about the potential effect if would have on the school if you were to close down the Frampton factory.'

When Leo gave him a sharp look Graham gave a small shrug and told him, 'It's no secret that you intend to close one and possibly two of the factories—the financial Press have quoted you on it.'

'It's a decision I haven't made as yet,' Leo responded tersely.

'So are you considering closing down our factory?' Jodi couldn't resist demanding.

Leo frowned as he listened to her. She had hardly spoken directly to him all night. In fact, she had barely even looked at him, but he could feel both her tension and her hostility as keenly as he could feel his own reaction to her.

It infuriated him, in a way that was a whole new experience for him, that she should be able to play so well and so deceitfully the role of a dedicated schoolteacher when he knew what she really was.

She must be completely without conscience! And she was in charge of the growth and development of burgeoning young minds and emotions. How clever she must be to be able to dupe everyone around her so successfully; to be able to win their trust and merit their admiration and respect.

Leo told himself that the intensity of his own emotions was a completely natural reaction to the discovery of her duplicity. If he was to reveal the truth about her—but, of course, he couldn't, after all he wasn't exactly proud of his own behaviour.

But why had she done it? For money, as he had originally assumed? Because she enjoyed flirting with danger? Because she wanted to help Driscoll? For some reason, it was this last option that he found the least palatable.

Jodi could feel Leo's bitterly contemptuous gaze burning the distance between them. If he should mention last night…! If Nigel had given her the slightest indication that Leo was going to be a fellow guest no power on earth would have been able to get her within a mile of Mary and Graham's.

She had cringed inwardly, listening to the others singing her praises, hardly daring to breathe in case Leo said anything. But of course last night's events did not reflect much more credibly on him than they did on her. Although he, as a man, at least had the age-old excuse of claiming, as so many of his sex had done throughout history, that the woman had tempted him.

Soon their current school term would be over. Normally she experienced a certain sadness when this happened, especially at the end of the summer term, since their eldest pupils would be moving on to 'big' school. Right now she felt she couldn't wait for the freedom to quietly disappear out of public view.

A couple of friends from university had invited her to join them on a walking holiday in the Andes and she wished that she had agreed to go with them. Instead, she had said she wanted to spend some time decorating her small house and working on her garden, as well as planning ways to make the school even better than it already was—something which in Jodi's eyes was more of a pleasure than a chore.

Now, thanks to Leo Jefferson, all the small pleasures she had been looking forward to had been obscured by the dark cloud of her own guilt.

'Well, we shall certainly be very disappointed if you choose to close down our factory,' she could hear Graham saying to Leo. 'We're a small country area and replacing so many lost jobs isn't going to be easy. Although logically I can understand that the Newham factory does have the advantage of being much closer to the motorway network.'

'Unfortunately, it is all a question of economics,' Leo was replying. 'The market simply isn't big enough to support so many different factories all producing the same thing…'

Suddenly Jodi had heard enough. Her passionate desire to protect her school overwhelmed the fear and shame that had kept her silent throughout the evening and, turning towards Leo, she told him angrily, 'It managed to support them well enough before your takeover, and it seems to me that it would be more truthful to say that the economics in question are those that affect your profits—not to mention the tax advantages you will no doubt stand to gain. Have you no idea of the hardship it's going to cause? The people it will put out of work, the lives and families it will destroy? I've got children at school whose whole family are dependent on that factory—fathers, mothers, grandparents, aunts, uncles. Don't you care about anything except making money?'

Jodi could feel the small, shocked silence her outburst had caused. Across the table, Nigel was giving her a warning look, whilst Graham Johnson was frowning slightly.

'We all understand how you feel, Jodi.' he told her calmly. 'But I'm afraid that economics, profits, can't just be ignored. Leo is competing in a worldwide marketplace, and for his business to remain successful—'

'There are far more important things in life than profits,' Jodi interrupted him, unable to stop herself from stemming the intensity of her feelings now that she had started to speak.

'Such as what?' Leo checked her sharply. 'Such as you keeping enough pupils in your school to impress the school inspectorate? Aren't you just as keen to show a profit on your pupil numbers in return for Education Authority funding as I am on my financial investment in my business?'

'How dare you say that?' Jodi breathed furiously. 'It is the children themselves, their education, their futures, their lives, that concern me. What you are doing—'

'What I am doing is trying to run a profitable business.' Leo silenced her acidly. 'You, I'm afraid, are blinkered by your own parochial outlook. I have to see the bigger picture. If I was to keep all the factories operating inevitably none of them would be profitable and I would then be out of business, with the loss of far more jobs than there will be if I simply close down two of them.'

'You just don't care, do you?' Jodi challenged him.

'You don't care about what you're doing; about the misery you will be causing.'

She knew that she was going too far, and that both Nigel and the Johnsons were watching her with concern and dismay, but something was driving her on. The tension she had been feeling all evening had somehow overwhelmed the rational parts of her brain and she was in the hands of a self-destructive, unstoppable urge she couldn't control.

'What I care about is keeping my business at the top of its field,' Leo told her grimly.

'Precisely,' Jodi threw at him, curling her lip in contempt as she tossed her head. 'Profit… Don't you care that what you are doing is totally immoral?'

Jodi tensed as she heard the sharp hiss of collective indrawn breath as she and Leo confronted one another in bitter hostility.

'*You* dare to accuse me of immorality!'

Had the others heard, as she had, the way he had emphasised the word 'you'? Jodi wondered in sick shock as she tried to withstand the icy contempt of the look he was giving her.

'Jodi, my dear.' Graham finally intervened a little uncomfortably. 'I'm sure we all appreciate how strongly you feel about everything, but Leo does have a point. Naturally his business has to be competitive.'

'Oh, naturally,' Jodi agreed bitingly, throwing Leo a caustic look.

Nigel was standing up, saying that it was time that they left, but as Graham pulled out Jodi's chair for her she still couldn't resist turning to Leo to challenge, 'In the end everything comes down to money, doesn't it?'

As he, too, stood up he looked straight at her and told her softly, 'As you should know.'

Jodi could feel her face burning.

'Oh, and by the way,' Leo added under cover of Mary going to fetch them all their coats, 'you can tell your friend Driscoll—'

Jodi didn't let him get any further.

'Jeremy Driscoll is no friend of mine,' she told him immediately. 'In fact, if you want the truth, I loathe and detest him almost as much as I do you.'

She was shaking as she thanked Mary and slipped on her coat, hurrying out into the warmth of the summer night ahead of Nigel, who had turned back to say something to their host.

As she waited for him beside the car, her back towards the house, she was seething with anger. At the same time she began to feel the effects of the shock of seeing Leo Jefferson and the way she had argued with him so publicly.

As she heard Nigel come crunching over the gravel towards her, without turning to look at him, she begged fiercely, 'Just take me out of here…'

'Where exactly is it you want me to take you? Or can I guess?'

Whirling round, Jodi expelled her breath on a hissing gasp as she realised that it wasn't Nigel who was standing next to her in the shadow of the trees but Leo Jefferson.

'Keep away from me,' she warned him furiously, inadvertently backing into the shadows as she strove to put more distance between them.

Her reaction, so totally overplayed and unwarranted, was the last straw so far as Leo was concerned.

'Oh, come on,' he snarled. 'You haven't got an audience now!'

'You don't know anything,' Jodi spat back shakily.

'That wasn't what you were telling me last night,' Leo couldn't stop himself from reminding her savagely. 'Last night—'

'Last night I didn't know what I was doing,' Jodi retaliated bitterly. 'If I had done I would never…' She was so overwrought now that her voice and her body both trembled. 'You are the last man I would have wanted to share what should have been one of the most special experiences of my life.'

Jodi was beyond thinking logically about what she was revealing; instead she was carried along, flung headlong into the powerful vortex of her own overwhelming emotions.

Leo could hear what she was saying, but, like her, his emotions were too savagely aroused for him to take on board the meaning of her words. Instead he held out to her the handbag she had unknowingly left behind in the house, telling her coldly, 'You forgot this. Your cousin is still talking with Graham and Mary and he asked me to bring it to you. I think he probably wanted to give you the opportunity to apologise to me in private for your appalling rudeness over dinner…'

'*My* rudeness.' Jodi reached angrily for her handbag and then froze as her fingertips brushed against Leo's outstretched hand.

Just the feel of his skin against her own sent a shower

of sharp electric shocks, of unwanted sensation, slicing through her body.

'Don't touch me,' she protested, and then moaned a soft, tormented sound of helpless need, dropping her handbag and swaying towards him in exactly the same breath as he reached for her. He dragged her against his body and the feel of him was so savagely, shockingly familiar that her body reacted instantly. She looked up into his face, her lips parting. His mouth burned against hers like a brand, punishing, taking, possessing. She felt him shudder as his fingers bit into the tender flesh of her upper arms. But then as his tongue-tip probed her lips he seemed to change his mind. He released her abruptly and, turning on his heel, walked away.

It was several seconds before she could stop shaking enough to bend down and pick up her bag. Whilst she was doing so she heard Nigel saying her name.

'Sorry about the delay,' he apologised as she stood up and he unlocked the car. 'Feeling better now that you've got all that off your chest?' he asked her wryly.

'Better?' Jodi demanded sharply as they both got into his car. 'How could I possibly be feeling better after having to spend an evening with that…that…?'

'OK, OK, I get the picture,' Nigel told her, adding, 'In fact, I think we all did. I do understand how you feel, Jodi, but ripping up at Leo Jefferson isn't going to help. He's a businessman and you've got to try to see things from his point of view.'

'Why should I see things from his point of view? He doesn't seem to be prepared to see them from mine,' Jodi challenged her cousin.

Nigel gave her a wry look.

'There is a very apt saying about catching more flies with honey than vinegar,' he reminded her, 'although something tells me you aren't in the mood to hear that.'

Jodi could feel her face starting to burn.

'No, I'm not,' she said tersely.

'Why couldn't things have just stayed the way they were?' she moaned to Nigel as he drove her home. 'Everything was all right when the Driscolls owned the factory.'

'Not totally,' Nigel told her quietly, but shook his head when Jodi looked at him. He had already said too much, and he wasn't yet free to tell her about the fraudulent practices that Jeremy Driscoll was suspected of having operated within the business.

Jodi didn't push him further on that point; instead she burst out, 'Leo Jefferson is the most hateful, horrid, arrogant, impossible man I have ever met and I wish...I wish...'

Unable to specify just exactly what she wished, and why, Jodi bit her lip and looked out of the car window, glad to see that they were already in the village and that she would soon be home.

Leo grimaced as he paced the sitting-room floor of his suite. He had a good mind to ring down to Reception and ask them to transfer him to a different set of rooms; these reminded him too much of last night and her—Jodi Marsh!

That infuriating woman who had by some alchemic means turned herself from the wanton, sensual creature who had shared his bed last night into the furious, spiky opponent who had had the gall tonight to sit there and accuse *him* of immoral behaviour! How he had stopped himself from challenging her there and then to justify herself Leo really didn't know. And she was a schoolteacher! Perhaps he was being unduly naïve, but he just couldn't get his head around it at all.

And as for her comments about his plans for the factory and the effect it would have on other people's lives if he was to close it down…!

Leo frowned. Did she think he enjoyed having to put people out of work? Of course he didn't, but economic factors were economic factors and could not simply be ignored.

Well, he just hoped that she didn't get it into her head to come back tonight and pay him a second visit, because if she did she would find there was no way he was going to be as idiotically vulnerable to her as he had been last night. No way at all!

CHAPTER FOUR

'You pushed me.'

'No, I didn't.'

With gentle firmness Jodi sorted out the dispute caused by one of her most problematic pupils on her way across the school yard.

Left to his own devices, she suspected, seven-year-old Ben Fanshawe might have been a happy, sociable child, but, thanks to the efforts of his social-climbing mother, Ben was a little boy with an attitude that was driving the other children away.

Jodi had tried tactfully to discuss the situation with his mother, but Ben's problems were compounded by the fact that Myra Fanshawe was not just a parent, but also on the school's board of governors. It was a position she had single-mindedly set her sights on from the minute she and her husband had moved into the village.

A close friend of Jeremy Driscoll and his wife, Myra had made it plain to Jodi that she would have preferred to send her son to an exclusive prep school. It was only because her in-laws were refusing to pay their grandson's school fees until he was old enough to attend the same school as the previous six generations of male Fanshawes that Ben was having to attend the village primary school.

Having bullied and badgered her way into the position of Chair of the Board of Governors, Myra had continually bombarded both the board and Jodi herself with her opinions on how the school might be improved.

Having lost her most recent battle to impose a system of teaching maths that she had decided would be enormously beneficial for Ben, Myra had made it abundantly clear to Jodi that she had made a bad enemy.

For Ben's sake, Jodi had tried tactfully to suggest that he might benefit from being encouraged to make more friends amongst his schoolmates. But her gentle hints had been met with fury and hostility by Myra, who had told Jodi that there was no way she wanted her son mixing with 'common village children'.

'Once Benjamin leaves here he will be meeting a very different class of child. He already knows that, and knows too that I would have preferred him to be attending a proper prep school. I do wish I could make his grandparents understand how much better it would be if he was already in private education. Jeremy and Alison were totally appalled that we could even think of allowing him to come here. At least now that I'm Chair of the Board of Governors I shall be able to make sure that he is receiving the rudiments of a decent education.

'The vicar's wife commented to me only the other day how much better the school has been doing since I became involved.' She had preened herself, leaving Jodi torn between pity for her little boy and amazement at Myra's total lack of awareness of other people's feelings.

As it happened, Anna Leslie, the vicar's wife, had actually told Jodi herself how unbearable she found Myra and how much she loathed her patronising attitude.

With only such a short time to go before the end of term, it was perhaps only natural that the children should be in such a high-spirited mood, Jodi acknowledged as she made her way to her office.

By the time the school bell rang to summon the children to their classes she was so engrossed in her work that she had almost managed to put Leo Jefferson right out of her mind.

Almost…

Leo tensed as his mobile phone rang. He was in his car, on his way to meet with his accountant at the Frampton factory that had been the subject of his heated exchange of views with Jodi on Saturday night.

He frowned as he registered the unavailable number of his caller. If Jodi was ringing him in an attempt to… Reaching out, he answered the call using the car's hands-free unit, but the voice speaking his name was not Jodi's and was not, in fact, even female, but belonged instead to Jeremy Driscoll.

'Look, old boy, I just thought I'd give you a ring to see if the two of us couldn't get together. The word is that you're going to have to close down at least a couple of the factories and I'm prepared to make you a good offer to buy Frampton back from you.'

Leo frowned as he listened.

'Buy it?' he challenged him curtly, waiting for Jeremy to threaten to blackmail him into agreeing, but, to his surprise, Jeremy made no reference whatsoever to either Jodi or her visit to his bed.

'Look, we're both businessmen—and we both know there are ways and means of you selling the business back to me that would benefit us both financially…'

Leo didn't respond.

Jeremy Driscoll had been away on holiday in the Caribbean with his wife when his father-in-law had accepted Leo's offer to buy out the business, and it was becoming increasingly obvious to Leo that for some reason he did not wish to see the sale go through.

'I haven't made my mind up which factories I intend to close as yet,' Leo informed him. It was, after all, the truth.

'Frampton is the obvious choice. Anyone can see that,' Jeremy Driscoll was insisting. Beneath the hectoring tone of his voice Leo could hear a sharper note of anxiety.

Leo had almost reached the factory. Reaching out to end the call, he told Jeremy Driscoll crisply, 'I'll call you once I've made up my mind.'

As he cancelled the call Leo's frown deepened. It disturbed him that Jeremy Driscoll hadn't said a single word about Jodi. Somehow that seemed out of character. Driscoll wasn't the sort of man to miss an opportunity to maximise on his advantage and, even though Leo knew he wouldn't allow himself to be blackmailed, he was still in a potentially vulnerable position.

But nowhere near as delicate and vulnerable as the one Jodi herself was in, he acknowledged grimly. What on earth had possessed her?

'So what you're saying is that I should close this factory down?' Leo asked his accountant as they finished their tour of the Frampton site.

'Well, it does seem to be the obvious choice. Newham has the benefit of being much closer to the motorway system.'

'Which means that it would be relatively easy to sell off as a base for a haulage contractor,' Leo interrupted him wryly. 'That would then allow me to consolidate production at Frampton, and use the Newham site solely for distribution, or if that proved to be uneconomical to sell it off.'

'Well, yes, that could be an option,' the accountant acknowledged.

'Frampton also has the benefit of having recently had a new production line,' Leo continued.

'Yes, I know. It seems there was a fire, that destroyed the old one, which brings me to something else,' the accountant told him carefully. 'There are one or two things here that just don't tie up.'

'Such as?' Leo challenged him curiously.

'Such as two fires in a very short space of time, and certain anomalies in the accounting system. It seems that this factory has been run by the owners' son-in-law, who prior to working in the business gained a reputation for favouring practices which, shall we say, are not entirely in line with those approved of by the revenue.'

'So what we are actually talking about here is fraud,' Leo stated sharply.

'I don't know, and certainly I haven't found anything fraudulent in the accounts that were submitted to us on takeover. However, it may be that those accounts are not the only ones the business produced. Just call it a gut feeling, but something tells me that things are not totally as they should be.'

Had his accountant unwittingly hit on the reason why Jeremy Driscoll was so anxious to retain ownership of this particular factory? Leo wondered.

'If you're serious about finding a haulier buyer for the Newham land,' his accountant continued, 'I might know of someone.'

Leo stopped him. 'I might well opt to set up my own distribution network. With distribution costs rising the way they are, it makes good economic sense to be able to control that aspect of the business.'

'Mmm…'

What the hell was he doing? Leo asked himself in inner exasperation. He was finding arguments to keep Frampton open! Surely he wasn't allowing himself to be influenced by the emotional opinions of a woman who knew nothing about business? Although she did know everything about how to please a man. This man! How to infuriate and drive him insane was more like it, Leo decided in furious, angry rejection of his own weak thoughts.

He and the accountant parted company at the factory gate. It was almost lunchtime, and Leo recalled that there was a pub in the village where he could no doubt get something to eat.

If he was to change his plans and retain the Frampton factory it would mean spending a good deal of time in the area; several months at least. He would have to rent somewhere to live.

Perhaps predictably the pub was almost opposite the church, and separated from the church by the graveyard and a small paddock was the school.

Her school!

Since it was lunchtime, the school yard was filled with children.

Turning into the pub car park, Leo parked and then

got out to walk round to the main entrance to the dining room.

As he did so his attention was caught by a small group of children clustering around a familiar figure.

Jodi's curls were burnished a deep, rich colour by the sunlight. She was wearing a cotton skirt and a toning blouse, her legs bare beneath the hem of her skirt.

She hadn't seen him, Leo acknowledged, and she was laughing at something one of her pupils had said, her head thrown back to reveal the taut line of her throat, with its creamy smooth skin, the same skin he had caressed and kissed.

Leo could feel the sensual reaction filling his body. He still wanted her!

She looked completely at home in her chosen role and Leo could see that the children were equally relaxed with her. And then, as though somehow she had sensed his presence, she looked towards him, her whole body freezing and the joy dying abruptly from her face as their gazes battled silently across the distance that separated them.

As though they sensed her hostility the children too had become still and silent, and as he watched Leo saw her ushering them away from the school boundary out of sight.

The pub dining room was surprisingly busy, but Leo barely paid any attention to his fellow diners. His thoughts were taken up with Jodi, a fact which caused him to wonder grimly yet again just what the hell was happening to him.

He ate his meal quickly without really being aware of

it. In his mind's eye he could still see Jodi surrounded by her pupils. She had looked…

He shook his head, trying to dismiss her image from his thoughts, and caused the waitress who had served him to give a tiny little shiver and reflect on how dangerous and exciting he looked—and how very different from her boyfriend!

Having finished his meal and refused a second cup of coffee, much to the waitress's secret disappointment, Leo got up, oblivious to her interest in him.

On his way back to the car he noticed that the school playground was now empty, the children no doubt back at their desks.

For God's sake, he derided himself as he drove back towards the town, didn't he have enough to think about at the moment without being obsessed by a schoolteacher?

'Well, we don't normally have many rental properties,' the agent in the local town was informing Leo. 'But it just so happens that we've been asked to find a tenant for a thoroughly charming Georgian house, just outside Frampton. I don't know if you know the village.'

'Yes, I know it,' Leo confirmed a little grimly.

'I live there myself.' The agent smiled. 'I don't know if you have children, but if you do I can thoroughly recommend the village school. Jodi Marsh, the head teacher, is wonderful—'

'I know Jodi,' Leo interrupted him brusquely.

'You do?' The agent gave him a discreetly speculative look. 'Well, if you're a friend of Jodi's you'll find you get a very warm welcome in the village. She's as popular with the parents as she is with the children, and deservedly so.

'My wife dreads the thought of her leaving; she says the school just wouldn't be the same without her. We all admire the way she campaigned so tirelessly to keep the school open and to raise enough money to buy the playing field adjacent to it to stop Jeremy Driscoll from acquiring it as building land. That didn't make her popular with Jeremy at all, but Jodi has never been a fan of his, as you'll probably know…'

Again he gave Leo a speculative look, but Leo discovered that he was strangely reluctant to correct the other man's misconceptions. For one thing he was too busy analysing the agent's surprising comments about Jodi's antipathy towards Jeremy Driscoll to notice.

'If you'd like to view Ashton House?' the agent continued questioningly.

Leo told himself that he should refuse, that deliberately choosing to live anywhere within a hundred-mile radius of Jodi Marsh was complete madness, but for some reason he heard himself agreeing to see the house, and accepting the agent's suggestion that they should drive over to view it immediately.

'I rather get the impression that Jeremy Driscoll isn't the most popular of people around here?' Leo commented to the agent half an hour later as they stood together in front of the pretty Georgian property.

'Well, no, he isn't,' the agent agreed. 'And, despite the fact that he's married, Jeremy fancies himself as something of a ladies' man. Of course Jodi, in particular, is well known for her strict moral code, so I suppose it was almost inevitable that she should make it very plain to him that his advances were unwelcome.'

Leo struggled to absorb this new information as the agent changed tack to tell him about the house. 'It was built originally for the younger son of a local landowner; it's listed, of course, and with all its original internal decorative features—a real gem. If I had the money I would be very tempted to put in an offer for it. The elderly lady who owned it died a few weeks ago, and the beneficiaries under her will ultimately want to sell it, but until the estate is sorted out they need to find a tenant for it so that it doesn't fall into disrepair. Shall we go inside?'

The house was undoubtedly, as the agent had said, a 'gem', and had he been looking for a permanent home Leo knew that he too would have been tempted to acquire it. As it was, he was more than happy to meet the relatively modest rent the owners were requesting.

However, as Leo followed the agent back to his office, so that they could complete the paperwork for the rental, it wasn't so much the new temporary home he had acquired that was occupying his thoughts as the agent's revelations about Jodi.

Just why was it that everyone seemed to think that Jodi was a paragon of all the virtues? There was no way that he could be wrong about her, was there?

But later on in the day as he drove back to his hotel he was aware of a small and very unwanted niggling doubt that somehow just would not be silenced. Was it realistic for him to believe that so many other people were wrong and that he was right? Common sense told him that it wasn't!

But nothing changed the fact that Jodi had still, most definitely, been in his bed!

Jodi forced herself to smile at the group of fathers gathered in a huddle outside the school gates, talking to one another whilst they kept a protective eye on their children.

The factory operated a shift system, which meant that quite a large proportion of the families where both parents worked split the task of delivering and collecting their offspring from school. Fathers for some reason seemed to favour afternoon school runs, and if Jodi hadn't still been preoccupied with her thoughts of Leo Jefferson she would have stopped for a chat.

As it was, whilst walking past she registered the fact that the men were discussing the possible closure of the factory, and how they intended to make their objections known.

'We should do something to stop the closure!' someone protested angrily. 'We can't just stand by and lose our jobs, our livelihood.'

'What we need to do is to stage a demonstration,' another man was insisting.

A demonstration! Well, Jodi couldn't blame them for wanting to make their feelings public; she would be tempted to do exactly the same thing if anyone was to threaten to close her beloved school.

A tiny frown creased her forehead. These parents were the very ones who had supported her unstintingly in her determination to keep the school open, and in her fund-raising to make sure that the school retained its adjacent playing field. The very least she could do, surely, was to support them in turn now. And her feelings about Leo Jefferson had nothing to do with it…

Retracing her footsteps, she walked back towards the small group.

'I couldn't help overhearing what you were just saying about demonstrating against the closure of the factory,' she began. 'If you do—' she took a deep breath '—you can certainly count on my support.'

'What, publicly?' one of them challenged her.

'Publicly!' Jodi confirmed firmly. As she spoke she had the clearest mental image of Leo Jefferson, watching her with icy-eyed contempt across Mary and Graham's dinner-table…

'Leo… Have you got a moment?'

Halfway across the hotel foyer, Leo stopped as Nigel Marsh came hurrying towards him.

'Look, I was wondering if we might have a word?'

Leo frowned as he looked at Jodi's cousin. The younger man looked both slightly uncomfortable and at the same time very determined.

Shooting back the cuff of his jacket, Leo glanced at his watch before telling him crisply, 'I can give you ten minutes.'

Nigel looked relieved.

'Thanks. I just wanted to have a word with you about Jodi…my cousin…you met her the other evening.'

He was speaking as though Leo might have forgotten just who Jodi was, Leo recognised, wondering just what Nigel Marsh would say if Leo was to tell him that Jodi was someone he would never be able to forget.

However, Leo had no intention of revealing any such

thing. Instead he replied with dry irony, 'You mean the schoolteacher.'

Nigel gave him a relieved look.

'Yes. Look, I know she must have come across to you as…as having a bit of a bee in her bonnet about your takeover—'

'She certainly has plenty of attitude,' Leo cut in coolly, causing Nigel to check himself. 'And a very hostile attitude where I'm concerned,' Leo continued crisply.

'It isn't anything personal,' Nigel denied immediately. 'It's just that the school means so much to her. She's worked damned hard to make it successful, and she's always been the kind of person who is attracted to lame dogs, lost causes… I remember when we were kids, she was always mothering something or someone. I know she went a little bit over-the-top the other night. But she wasn't expecting to see you there, and I suppose having hyped herself up to put her case to you at the hotel the night before and then having chickened out…'

He stopped suddenly, looking uncomfortably self-conscious, realising that he had said more than he should, but it was too late; Leo was already demanding sharply, 'Would you mind explaining that last comment, please?'

Even more uncomfortably Nigel did as he had been requested.

Leo waited until he had finished before asking him incredulously, 'You're saying that Jodi, your cousin, planned to approach me in person in my suite so that she could put the school's position to me and ask me to reconsider closing down the factory?'

'I know that technically I shouldn't have encouraged or helped her,' Nigel acknowledged, 'and Graham will probably read me the Riot Act if he finds out, but I just couldn't not do something. If you really knew her you'd understand that.'

Leo did, and he understood a hell of a lot more now too. Like just why Jodi had been in his room. His room, but not his bed! Had she ordered that nauseating alcoholic concoction to give herself some false courage? And then perhaps over-indulged in it? If so…

Nigel was still speaking and he forced himself to listen to what he was saying.

'Jodi deserves a break. She's battled so hard for the school. First to improve the teaching standards enough to get in more pupils, and then more recently against Jeremy Driscoll, to prevent him from acquiring the school's playing field.'

'I'd heard something about that,' Leo acknowledged.

'Jeremy wasn't at all pleased about the fact that he lost that piece of land. And, as I've already warned Jodi, she's made a dangerous enemy in him. It's no secret that he isn't at all well-liked locally.' Nigel gave a small grimace of distaste. 'Jodi can't stand him and I don't blame her.'

Leo started to frown, silently digesting what he was hearing. Nigel Marsh was the second person to tell him that Jodi didn't like Jeremy Driscoll.

Which meant…which meant that he had—perhaps—misjudged her on two counts. Yes, but that didn't explain away her extraordinary sensuality towards him in bed.

If he was to accept everyone else's opinion, such behaviour was totally out of character. As was his own, Leo was forced to acknowledge.

'I know that Jodi went a bit too far the other night,' Nigel was continuing, 'But in her defence I feel I have to say that she does have a point; without the factory—'

'Her precious school would be in danger of being closed down,' Leo interjected for him.

'We're a rural area, and it would be very hard to replace so many lost jobs,' Nigel said. 'That would mean that for people to find work they would have to move away, and so yes, ultimately the school could potentially be reduced to the position it was in when Jodi took over. But she's the kind of person who has always been sensitive to the feelings of others, and it is her concern for them that is motivating her far more than any concern she might have for her own career.'

He gave Leo a wry look.

'As a matter of fact, I happen to know that she's already been approached by a private school who are willing to pay her very well to go to them, and to include a package of perks that would include free education for her children were she to have any.'

'She isn't involved in a relationship with anyone, though, is she?' Leo couldn't stop himself from asking.

Fortunately Nigel did not seem to find anything odd in Leo's sudden question, shaking his head and informing him openly, 'Oh, no. She's one very picky lady, is my cousin. Casual relationships are just not her style, and as yet she hasn't met anyone she wants to become seriously involved with.'

'A career woman?' Leo hazarded.

'Well, she certainly loves her work,' Nigel conceded,

then changed the subject to tell Leo apologetically, 'Look, I've taken up enough of your time. I hope you don't mind me bending your ear on Jodi's behalf.'

'I'm half-Italian,' Leo responded with a brief shrug. 'Family loyalty is part of my heritage.'

It was the truth, and if he was honest Leo knew he would have to admit that he admired Nigel Marsh for his spirited defence of his cousin. But their conversation had left Leo with some questions only one person could answer—Jodi herself. But would she answer them? And would it really be wise of him to ask them and to risk becoming more involved with her?

More involved? Just how much more involved was it possible for two people to actually be? Leo wondered ironically.

Jodi closed her eyes and took a deep breath, filling her lungs with the soft, warm evening air. It was three days since she had last seen Leo Jefferson but he had never been far from her thoughts, even when she should, by rights, have been concentrating on other things. The committee meeting for the school's sports day, which she had attended two nights ago, for instance, and the impromptu and far less organised meeting she had attended last night to discuss the proposed demonstration outside the factory.

Feelings were running very high indeed with regard to the possible closure and, although Jodi had spoken to Nigel about it, he had not been able to tell her anything.

'Leo Jefferson has been in London, tied up in various meetings,' he had explained to her.

What he couldn't tell her, for professional reasons,

was that they had been informed there was a very real possibility that Jeremy Driscoll was going to be investigated with regard to anomalies in the stock records and accounts. It seemed there were considerable discrepancies involved for which no rational explanation had as yet been forthcoming.

Nigel had heard on the grapevine that Jeremy Driscoll was claiming the discrepancies had been caused by employee theft, and it was true that he had made insurance claims for such losses. However, the authorities were by no means convinced by his explanation, and it seemed that Leo Jefferson too was now questioning the validity of the accounts he had been provided with prior to buying the business.

Overhead, as Jodi climbed the narrow footpath that led to one of her favourite places, Ashton House—the beautiful Georgian manor house set in its own grounds outside the village—she could hear a blackbird trilling.

It had been agreed at last night's meeting that the workforce would start the demonstration tomorrow morning. Jodi was planning to join the demonstrators after school had finished for the day. As a student she had done her fair share of demonstrating, for both human- and animal-rights groups, and then, as now, as she had firmly explained to the committee, she was vehemently opposed to any kind of violence being used.

'I think we're all agreed on that point,' one of the mothers of Jodi's pupils had confirmed. 'I just wish it didn't have to come to this. We've tried to initiate talks with this Leo Jefferson, but he says that he doesn't consider it appropriate to meet with us at the moment.'

Leo!

Jodi closed her eyes and released her breath on a sigh. She might not have seen him for three days, but that did not mean… Hastily she opened her eyes. She wasn't going to think about those dreams she kept on having night after night, or what they might mean. Dreams in which she was back in his hotel suite…his bed…his arms. They were just dreams, that was all. They didn't mean that she wanted a repetition of what had happened between them. The fact that she had woken up last night just in time to hear herself moaning his name meant nothing at all…and neither did the shockingly physical ache that seemed to be constantly tormenting her body whenever she forgot to control it.

And as for those shockingly savage kisses she kept dreaming about… Well, those just had to be a product of her own fevered imagination, didn't they?

CHAPTER FIVE

LEO frowned as he heard the sound of someone walking along the footpath that skirted round the boundary to Ashton House. He had moved in officially that morning, having organised a cleaning team to go through the house ahead of him. He was now exploring the garden and coming to the conclusion that it was going to take a dedicated team of gardeners to restore it to anything like its former glory.

He had spent the last few days in London, locked in a variety of meetings concerning both his acquisition of the factories and their future. And now it seemed the authorities wanted to open enquiries into the financial workings of the Frampton factory, in particular whilst it had been under Jeremy Driscoll's management.

If he did decide to keep the factory going he would first of all need to make a decision about what to do with the other sites.

One of them housed the oldest factory, with an out-of-date production line and a depleted workforce, and was a natural choice to be closed down.

Of the other three…if he opted to keep Frampton in production he would have to either sell off the factory adjacent to the motorway system or change its usage to that of a distribution unit.

If he did that… Leo tensed as the walker drew level

with the gate in his walled garden that gave on to the path, and he had a clear view of her.

Jodi Marsh!

Jodi saw Leo at exactly the same time as he saw her. The sight of him froze her in her tracks. What was Leo Jefferson doing in the garden of Ashton House? Her house. The house she had secretly wanted from the first minute she had seen it!

Before she could gather herself together and hurry past he was opening the gate and coming towards her. He stood in front of her, blocking her path.

'I'd like to talk to you,' she heard him telling her coolly.

Jodi glared at him, praying that he couldn't hear the furious, racing thud of her heart or guess just what kind of effect he was having on her.

'Well, I certainly would not like to talk to you,' she retaliated.

Liar. Liar! her conscience tormented her silently. And you don't just want to talk to him either…

Horrified that he might somehow sense what she was feeling, Jodi tried to walk away, but he had already masterfully taken hold of her arm, and as she battled against the dizzying sensation of his touch somehow or other she found that she was being gently but firmly propelled through the gate and into the garden beyond.

She had been in the garden before—at the invitation of the old lady who had lived there who, like Leo, had happened to see her on the path one day.

She had ached then with sadness to see its neglect, and longed to be the one to restore both it and the house to their former glory. Of course that was an impossible dream. Jodi dreaded to imagine just how much money it would take to restore such a large house and so overgrown a garden. Far too much for her, but not, it seemed, too much for Leo Jefferson.

'Will you please stop manhandling me?' she demanded angrily as Leo closed the gate, and then her face burned a deep, betraying pink as she saw the way he was looking at her.

If he dared to say one word about anything she might have said to him under the influence of alcohol and desire she would… But to her relief he simply looked at her for several heart-stopping seconds before asking her quietly, 'What were you doing in my suite?'

Jodi gaped at him. It took her several precious moments to recover from the directness of his question, but finally she did so, rallying admirably to remind him firmly, 'Well, according to you, I was there because…' She stopped as he started to shake his head.

'I don't want you to tell me what I believed you were doing there, Jodi, I want to hear your version of events.'

Her version. Now he had surprised her. Stubbornly she looked away from him.

'It doesn't matter now, does it?' she challenged him.

'Doesn't it? According to your cousin, you were there to ask me to reconsider closing down the factory.'

Flustered, Jodi looked at him before demanding worriedly, 'You've been speaking to Nigel?'

Leo could tell that he had caught her off guard.

'I told him right from the start that it was a crazy idea, but he wouldn't listen.' Barely pausing for breath, she continued, 'I thought at first he meant that I should talk to you in the hotel foyer, but then he told me that he'd managed to borrow a key card.'

'And so you went up to the suite to wait for me and whilst you were there you ordered yourself a drink,' Leo supplied helpfully.

Jodi stared at him.

'No,' she denied vehemently, so vehemently that Leo knew immediately she was speaking the truth. Shaking her head, she told him angrily, 'I would never have ordered a drink without paying for it. No, I asked Nigel to arrange it for me. Nigel thought he'd ordered a soft drink, not—' She stopped abruptly, clamping her lips together and glowering at Leo.

'I can't see what possible relevance any of this has now,' she began, but Leo was determined to establish exactly what had happened—and why!

'So whilst you were waiting for me you drank the fruit punch, which was alcoholic, and then…'

Jodi had had enough.

'I don't want to talk about it,' she told him fiercely, 'and you can't make me.'

'You went to bed with me,' Leo reminded her softly. 'And from what I've learned about you, Jodi Marsh, that is something—'

'It was nothing,' Jodi denied sharply. 'And, anyway, you were the one who went to bed with me. I was already there, asleep.'

'In my bed…and you—' Leo stopped abruptly. This wasn't getting them anywhere and it wasn't what he wanted to say.

'Look,' he told her quietly, 'it seems that I misjudged the situation…made an error about the reasons for you being there,' he corrected himself. 'And, that being the case, I really think that we should discuss—'

'There isn't anything I want or need to discuss with you,' Jodi jumped in tensely.

The fact that he might have mistaken her reason for being in his suite, and even the fact that he was prepared to acknowledge as much, made no difference to what she had done or how she felt about it.

'What happened just isn't important enough to warrant discussing,' she added, determined to bring their conversation to an end, but to her consternation Leo was refusing to let the subject drop.

'Maybe not to you, but I happen to feel rather differently,' he said curtly. 'It is not, let me tell you, my habit to indulge in casual sex with a succession of unknown partners.'

Casual sex! Jodi had to struggle to prevent herself from physically cringing. Was there to be no end to the humiliation her behaviour was forcing her to suffer?

Before she could stop herself she was retorting passionately, 'For your information, I have not had a succession of partners, and in fact…'

Abruptly she fell silent, her face flushing. No, she must not tell him that! If she did he was bound to start asking even more questions than he already had, and there was absolutely no way she was going to tell him about that idiotic foolishness she had experienced when she had first seen him in the hotel foyer.

No doubt some might claim that she had fallen in love with him at first sight, and that was why…but she, Jodi, was made of sterner and far more realistic stuff. She was a modern-thinking woman and would not contemplate such nonsense!

What was it about her that infuriated him to the point where he itched to take hold of her and make her listen to him? Leo wondered distractedly, unable to stop himself from focusing on her mouth and remembering how hot and sweet it had tasted. He wanted to kiss her again now, right here. But she was already turning back towards the gate, and a sudden surge of common sense warned him against the folly of going after her and begging her to stay when it so plainly wasn't what she wanted. But she had wanted him that night. She had wanted him and he had wanted her right back. And for him the problem was that he still did.

'Jodi?' he began, making a last attempt to talk to her, but, as he had already known she would, she shook her head.

'No, I…'

She barely had time to give a disbelieving and indignant gasp before she was dragged unceremoniously and ruthlessly into Leo's arms, and held there tightly.

Against his ardent seeking mouth she tried to make a protest, but it was smothered immediately by the hot passion of his kiss…dizzying her, bemusing her, confusing her, so that somehow instead of repudiating him she was actually moving closer, reaching out to him…

Somewhere deep in her brain a warning bell started to ring, but Jodi ignored it, Leo was kissing her and there was no way she wanted anything, least of all some silly old warning bell, to come between her and the sheer intensity and excitement, the total bliss, of feeling his mouth moving possessively and passionately against her own.

'Mmm…'

Leo could feel the heavy, crazy thud of his heartbeat as Jodi suddenly dropped her defensive attitude and became so soft, so pliable, so bewitchingly and adorably warm in his arms that he was sorely tempted to pick her up and carry her straight to his bed.

But a bird calling overhead suddenly brought Jodi to her senses; white-faced and shaking, she pulled away from him. How on earth could she have allowed that to happen? Her mouth stung slightly and she had to resist the temptation to run her tongue-tip over it—to comfort it because it was missing the touch of Leo's? She ached from head to foot and she had started to tremble. Shocked to her heart by her lack of self-control, she cried out to him in a low tortured voice, 'Don't you ever touch me again…ever!'

And then she was gone, turning on her heel to flee in wretchedness, her heart throbbing with pain and self-contempt, refusing to stop as she heard Leo calling after her.

Jodi was still trembling when she reached the security of her own home. She had heard a rumour in the village that Ashton House had a tenant, but it had never occurred to her that it might be Leo Jefferson. Nigel had warned her that Leo had said that the negotiations over which of the factories he intended to close were likely to be protracted, but why did he have to move here to Frampton?

She felt as though there wasn't a single aspect of her life he hadn't now somehow penetrated and invaded.

Or a single aspect of herself?

Hurriedly she walked into her small kitchen and started to prepare her supper. Nigel had rung earlier and suggested they have dinner together, but Jodi had told him she was too busy, worried that if she saw him she might inadvertently betray the plans for the demonstration the following day.

Not that they were doing anything illegal, but she knew that Nigel would not entirely approve of her involvement in what was going to happen and would try his best to dissuade her.

She loved her cousin very much, they were in many ways as close as if they had been brother and sister, and she knew how shocked he would be if he was to learn how she had behaved with Leo Jefferson. She felt ashamed herself…but what was making her feel even worse were the dreadful dreams she kept having in which she relived what had happened—and enjoyed it.

Swallowing hard, Jodi tried to concentrate on what she was doing, but somehow she had lost her appetite. For food, that was. Standing in the garden earlier with Leo, there had been a moment when she had looked up at him, at his mouth, and she had never felt so hungry in her life…

Leo woke up with a start, wondering where he was at first, in the unfamiliarity of his new bedroom at Ashton House. He had been dreaming about Jodi and not for the first time. Reaching for the bedside lamp, he switched it on. The house had been repainted prior to being let and the smell of fresh paint still hung faintly on the air. Leo got out of bed and padded over to the window, pushing back the curtains to stare into the moonlit garden.

In his sleep he had remembered something about Jodi that disturbed him. Something he had not previously properly registered, but something that, knowing what he did now, made perfect sense!

Was it merely his imagination or had there really been a certain something about Jodi's body that might mean he had in fact been her first lover?

No, it was absurd that he should think any such thing. Totally absurd. She had been so uninhibited, so passionate…

But what if he was right? What if, in addition to having unwittingly drunk the alcoholic concoction supplied by her cousin and fallen asleep, she had been totally inexperienced?

Leo swallowed hard, aware of how very difficult he was finding it to use the word 'virgin', even in the privacy of his own thoughts.

But surely if that had been the case she would have said something.

Such as what? he derided himself. *Oh, by the way, before I went to bed with you I was a virgin.*

No, that would not be her style at all. She was far too independent, had far too much pride.

But if she had been a virgin…

At no point in the proceedings had she suggested that they should be thinking in terms of having safe sex, and he had certainly not been prepared either emotionally or practically to take on that responsibility, which meant…

There was no way Leo could sleep now. So far as

Jodi's sexual health was concerned, and his own, if he was right and she had been a virgin, he knew he need have no worries, but when it came to the risk of an unplanned pregnancy—that was a very different matter. And one surely that must be concerning Jodi herself.

He would very definitely have to talk to her now, and insist that she give him the answers to his questions.

Closing his eyes, he forced himself to recall every single second of the hours they had spent together—not that there was really any force involved, after all, his body and his senses had done precious little else other than relive the event ever since it had happened. But this time it was different, this time he was looking for clues, signs that he might have previously missed.

There had been that sweetly wonderful closeness between them in their most intimate moments, the feeling of her body being tightly wrapped around him. But she had said nothing. Given no indication that… What in hell's name had she been doing? he wondered, suddenly as angry for her as though she were his personal responsibility.

She was a schoolteacher, for heaven's sake. She was supposed to behave responsibly!

If she had been a virgin it put a completely different complexion on the whole situation. He was perhaps more Italian than he had ever previously realised, Leo recognised wryly as he felt an atavistic sense of male protectiveness engulf him, and with it an even more unexpected sense of pride. Because he had been her first lover? Because she might have accidentally conceived his child? Just how chauvinistic was he?

His mother, of course, would be overjoyed. A grandchild, and the kind of daughter-in-law she would wholly approve of and love showing off to her Italian relatives.

Whoa…Leo cautioned himself. These were very dangerous and foolish thoughts that had no business whatsoever clogging up his head.

For one insane moment he actually wondered if his mother might have gone ahead and got her village wise woman to put some kind of a love spell on him. Then reality resurfaced.

There was only one person to blame for the situation he was in and that one person was himself. He could, after all, have resisted Jodi. She was a woman, small and slender, weighing, he guessed, something around a hundred and twenty pounds, whilst he was a man, taller, heavier, and perfectly capable of having stopped her had he so wanted to.

Only he hadn't…

Have a heart, he protested to himself; she was there, warm, wanton, beddable, and totally and completely irresistible. It made him ache right through to the soles of his feet right now just to think about it.

Leo grimaced as he felt his body's unmistakable reaction to his thoughts.

He wanted her in a way that was totally alien to anything he had ever experienced before.

He wanted her. He wanted her. Oh, heavens, how he wanted her!

Jodi gave a tiny moan in her sleep, her lips forming Leo's name, and then abruptly she was awake, the reality of her situation blotting out the delicious pleasure of her lost dream.

She had felt so much safer when Leo Jefferson had not known who she was, when he had for some incomprehensible reason believed she was in cahoots with Jeremy Driscoll. Jeremy Driscoll! Jodi gave a brief shudder. Loathsome man!

One of the women who was going to be demonstrating had said at their committee meeting that she had seen Jeremy at the factory, coming out of a disused storeroom. He hadn't seen her and she had said that he had been behaving very furtively.

None of the workers liked Jeremy, and Jodi had wondered just exactly what he had been doing at the factory when it now belonged to Leo. Not that it was any concern of hers. No, her concern was much closer to home.

She had come so close to betraying herself this evening when Leo had been questioning her. The last thing she wanted was for him to realise that, far from being the experienced sensualist he obviously thought she was, she had, in fact, been a virgin before she had taken it into her idiotic head to go to bed with him.

And the reason she didn't want him to know the truth was because she was terrified that if he did he might start questioning just why she had been so compulsively attracted to him, so totally unable to resist the temptation he had represented.

She could, of course, always claim that, as a woman in her twenties, she had begun to see her virginity as a burden she wanted to free herself from, but somehow she doubted that he would believe her. He was too shrewd, too perceptive for that.

If he should ever find out just how she had felt about him when she had seen him in the hotel foyer Jodi knew that she would just die of embarrassment and humiliation.

But of course it was totally impossible that he should find out, wasn't it? Because only she knew.

And only she was going to know.

And only she knew that until she had met him she had been a virgin, and this evening she had as good as told him. That had been a mistake, yes, she allowed judiciously, but it was a mistake she had learned from. A mistake she most certainly was not going to be repeating.

She pulled the covers up more closely around herself. In the dream she had just woken from Leo had been wrapping her in his arms whilst he tenderly stroked her skin and even more tenderly kissed her lips…

What on earth was she? A born-again teenager indulging in a fantasy? She was not going to dream about him again, she told herself sternly. She was not!

The first Leo knew about the demonstration was when he received a phone call from a local radio station asking if he would like to comment on the situation.

Several other calls later he had elicited the information that the demonstration was non-violent, protesting against the factory being closed down.

Meetings he had already arranged with a large haulage group who were interested in potentially acquiring the site of the motorway-based factory meant that Leo was unable to go to Frampton himself until later on in the day, but he did speak with the leader of the group to set up a meeting with them to discuss the situation.

Although he was not prepared to say so at this stage,

Leo had virtually made up his mind that he would keep the Frampton factory open. This decision had nothing whatsoever to do with Jodi Marsh, of course.

Later in the day, when the police rang him to inform him that they intended to monitor the situation at the demonstration, Leo told them that he had every confidence that things would be resolved peacefully.

It was four o'clock, and there was no way he could leave London until at least five. His mind started to wander. What was Jodi doing now? He really did need to talk to her; if there was the remotest chance that she might have conceived his child then he needed to know about it.

Jodi glanced a little anxiously over her shoulder. She had joined the demo an hour ago, straight from school. At first things had been quiet and peaceful, and the leader had told her that Leo Jefferson had been in touch with him to organise a meeting for the following day. But then to everyone's surprise, half an hour ago Jeremy Driscoll had arrived. At first he had demanded that they open the factory gates to allow him access and when they had refused Jeremy had got out of the car. A small scuffle had ensued, but ultimately Jeremy had been allowed to walk into the office block.

He was still inside it, but ten minutes ago a police car had drawn up several yards away from the demonstrators, quickly followed by a reporter and a photographer from the local paper.

Now the original peaceful mood of the picketers had changed to one of hostile aggression as Jeremy emerged from the building, and one of the demonstrators to whom

Jeremy had been particularly verbally abusive on his way into the factory caught sight of him.

'You don't really think that this is going to make any difference to Jefferson's decision to close this place down, do you?' Jodi could hear Driscoll challenging her fellow demonstrator contemptuously.

'He's agreed to meet with us in the morning,' the other man was retaliating.

'And you think that means he's going to listen to what you have to say! More fool you. He's already decided that this place isn't viable and who can blame him, with a lazy, good-for-nothing workforce like you lot? It's because of you that we've had to sell the place. Everyone knows that...'

Jodi gave a small indignant gasp as she heard him.

'That's not true,' she interjected firmly, causing Jeremy to turn to look at her.

'My God, you!' he breathed. 'I suppose I should have guessed,' he sneered as he gave Jodi's jeans and T-shirt-clad body a deliberately lascivious stare. 'This isn't going to do you any favours with the school board, is it? But then, of course, your precious school will end up being closed down along with the factory, won't it? Looks as if I shall be getting my building land after all.' He smirked as he started to walk purposefully towards Jodi. People tried to stop him, but he was too quick for them.

As he moved towards Jodi one of the men started to step protectively between them. He was only a young man, nowhere near as heavily built as Jeremy, and Jodi winced as she saw the force with which Jeremy thrust him to one side.

The young man retaliated, and suddenly it seemed to Jodi as though all hell had broken loose; people were shouting, shoving, the police car doors were opening, and then before she could move, to her shock, Jeremy had suddenly taken hold of her and was dragging her across the factory forecourt.

Instinctively she tried to resist him, hitting out at him as he deliberately manhandled her; her panic was that of any woman fearing a man she knew to be her enemy, and had nothing whatsoever to do with her role in the demonstration. Jeremy dragged her towards one of the advancing police officers, claiming to them that she had deliberately assaulted him.

'I insist that you arrest her, officer,' Jodi could hear him saying as he gave her a nastily victorious look. 'I shall probably press charges for assault.'

Jodi tried to protest her innocence, but she was already being bundled towards the police van that had screamed to a halt alongside the car.

Jodi blinked in the light from the flashbulb as the hovering photographer took their picture.

The police station was busy. Jodi couldn't believe what was happening to her. A stern-looking sergeant she didn't recognise was beginning to charge them all. Jodi was feeling sick. Her head ached; she felt grubby and frightened. There was a bruise on her arm where Jeremy Driscoll had manhandled her.

'Name…'

Jodi flinched as she realised that the sergeant was speaking to her.

'Er—Jodi Marsh,' she began. Supporting the workforce by taking part in a peaceful demonstration was one thing. Ending up being charged and possibly thrown into a police cell was quite definitely another. She couldn't bear to think about what the more conservative parents of her pupils were going to say, never mind the school governors or the education authority.

'Excuse me, Officer.'

She was quite definitely going to faint, Jodi decided as she heard the unmistakable sound of Leo Jefferson's voice coming from immediately behind her.

Something about Leo's calm manner captured the sergeant's attention. Putting down his pen, he looked at him.

Leo had arrived at the factory gates just in time to hear from those who were still there what had happened.

'Yes, and they even took the schoolteacher away,' one of the onlookers had informed Leo with relish, wondering why on earth his comment should have caused his listener to turn round and head straight back to his car with such a grim look on his face.

'I'm Leo Jefferson,' Leo introduced himself to the sergeant. 'I own the factory.'

'You own it.' The sergeant was frowning now. 'According to our records, it was a Mr Jeremy Driscoll who reported that there was a problem.'

'Maybe he did, but I am quite definitely the owner of the factory,' Leo reiterated firmly. 'Can you tell me exactly what's happened, Officer. Only, as I understand it, the demonstrators were peaceful and I had in fact arranged to meet with them in the morning.'

'Well, that's as maybe, sir, but we were telephoned

from the factory by Mr Driscoll who said that he was not being allowed to leave and that both he and the property had been threatened with violence. Once we got there a bit of a scuffle broke out and this young lady here…' he indicated Jodi '…actually attempted to assault Mr Driscoll.'

Jodi could feel her face crimsoning with mortification as she leapt immediately to her own defence, denying it. 'I did no such thing. He was the one who attacked me…' To her horror, she could actually feel her eyes filling with childish tears.

'I think there must have been a mistake,' Leo Jefferson was saying. Although she couldn't bring herself to turn round and look at him, Jodi could feel him moving closer to her, and for some insane reason she felt that instinctively her body sought the warmth and protection of his.

'I happen to know Miss Marsh very well indeed. In fact she was at the factory on my behalf, as my representative,' Leo lied coolly. 'I cannot imagine for a second that she would have assaulted Mr Driscoll.'

The sergeant was frowning.

'Well, my officers have informed me that he was most insistent she be arrested,' he told Leo. 'He said that he intended to press charges against her for assault.'

Jodi gave a small, stifled sob.

'Indeed. Well, in that case I shall have to press charges against him for trespass,' Leo informed the sergeant. 'He quite definitely did not have my permission to enter the factory, and I rather imagine that the revenue authorities will be very interested to know what he was doing there. There are some account books missing that they are very anxious to see.'

Jodi gave a small start as she listened to him, impulsively turning round to tell Leo quickly, 'The mother of one of my pupils mentioned that she saw him coming out of one of the unused storerooms.' Her voice started to fade away as she saw the way Leo was looking at her arm.

'Is Driscoll responsible for that?' he demanded dangerously.

Without waiting for her to reply he turned to the desk sergeant and said with determined authority, 'I understand that you may have to charge Miss Marsh, but in the meantime, Officer, I wonder if you would be prepared to release her into my care. I promise that I won't let her out of my sight.'

The desk sergeant studied them both. He had a full custody suite and no spare cells, and he could see no real reason why Jodi shouldn't be allowed to leave if Leo Jefferson was prepared to vouch for her.

'Very well,' he acknowledged. 'But you will have to take full responsibility for her, and for ensuring that she returns here in the morning to be formally charged if Mr Driscoll insists on going ahead.'

'You have my word on it,' Leo responded promptly, and then before Jodi could say anything he had turned her round and was gently ushering her out into the summer night.

To her own chagrin, Jodi discovered that she was actually crying.

'It's the shock,' she heard Leo saying to her as he

guided her towards his car. 'Don't worry, you'll be OK once we get you home.'

'I want a bath...and some clean clothes,' Jodi told him in a voice she barely recognised as her own.

'The bath I can provide; the clothes we shall have to collect from your house on the way to mine,' Leo replied promptly.

'Yours!' Jodi's forehead creased as she allowed Leo to fasten the passenger seat belt around her. 'But I want to go to my own home.'

'You can't, I'm afraid,' Leo told her. 'The sergeant released you into my care, remember, and I have to produce you at the station in the morning.'

'But I can't stay with you,' Jodi protested.

'I'm sorry, Jodi.' Leo's voice was unexpectedly kind. 'You have to.'

'I didn't really assault Jeremy.' Jodi tried to defend herself. 'He was the one...' She stopped and bit her lip, her stomach clenching on a leap of nervous shock as she saw the ferocity in Leo's eyes as he turned to study her.

'If he hurt you... Did he, Jodi?'

When she looked away from him Leo cursed himself for the intensity of his own reaction. He had quite plainly shocked and frightened her, and she had already been frightened more than enough for one night.

'I thought the demonstration was supposed to be a peaceful one,' he commented as he drove back towards the village.

'It was,' Jodi acknowledged. 'But Jeremy was very confrontational and somehow things got out of hand. Is it true that he's being investigated?'

'Yes,' Leo told her briefly, 'but I shouldn't really have said so, I don't suppose.'

When they reached her cottage he insisted on going inside with her and waiting until she had packed a small case of necessities, and Jodi felt too disorientated to be able to have the strength to resist.

Jeremy Driscoll's manner towards her had left her feeling vulnerable, and she couldn't help remembering how when she had won her battle with him to retain the playing field for the school he had threatened to get even with her. He was a vengeful and dangerous man, and for tonight at least, loath though she was to admit it, she knew she would feel far safer sleeping under Leo Jefferson's roof than under her own.

CHAPTER SIX

'WHEN was the last time you had something to eat?'

Leo's prosaic question as he unlocked his front door and ushered Jodi into the hallway of the house made her give him an uncertain look.

She had been steeling herself for, if not his hostility, then certainly some sharply incisive questions. The fact that he seemed more worried about her personal welfare than anything else was thoroughly disconcerting—but nowhere near as disconcerting as the relief and sense of security it had given her to have him take charge in the way that he had done.

'Lunchtime.' She answered his question on autopilot, whilst most of her attention was given to what she was feeling at a much deeper level. 'But I'm not hungry.'

'That's because you're still in shock,' Leo told her gently. 'The kitchen is this way.'

At any other time Jodi knew that she would have been fascinated to see the inside of the house she had admired so much, but right now she felt as though her ability to take in anything was overwhelmed by the events of the evening.

As Leo had suggested, she suspected that she was suffering from shock. Otherwise, why would she be so apathetically allowing Leo to make all her decisions for her? She let him guide her firmly to a kitchen chair and urge her into it, whilst he busied himself opening cupboards and then the fridge door, insisting that the light supper he was going to make them both would help her to sleep.

'Which reminds me,' he added several minutes later as he served her with an impressively light plate of scrambled eggs, 'I'm afraid that you will have to sleep in my bedroom, since it's the only one that's properly furnished at the moment; I can sleep downstairs on a sofa.'

'No,' Jodi protested immediately, praying that he wouldn't guess the reason for the hot colour suddenly burning her face. The very thought of sleeping in his bed was bringing back memories she had no wish to have surfacing at any time, but most especially when the man responsible for them was seated opposite her.

To her consternation, Leo shook his head at her instinctive refusal, telling her calmly, 'It's all right, I can guess what you must be thinking, but you don't need to worry.'

Jodi tensed. How could he possibly know what she was thinking? And if he really did then how dared he treat it and her as though…?

As she tried to gather her thoughts into a logical enough order to challenge him she heard him continuing, 'The cleaning team came today, and they will have changed the bed linen.'

Jodi almost choked on her scrambled eggs as relief flooded through her. He hadn't realised what she was thinking after all; hadn't realised just what piercingly sensual and shocking images the mention of his bed had aroused for her.

But at least his comments had given her time to gain

some control of her thoughts, and for her to remember that she was supposed to be a sensible, mature adult.

'I can't possibly take your bed,' she informed Leo in what she hoped was a cool and businesslike voice.

'Why not?' Leo demanded, giving her a quizzical look, and then threw her into complete turmoil as he reminded her softly, 'After all, it isn't as though you haven't done so before.'

As the blood left her face and then rushed back to it in a wave of bright pink Jodi felt her hand trembling so much that she had to grip the mug of tea Leo had given her with both hands to prevent herself from spilling its contents.

She knew that she was overreacting, but somehow she just couldn't stop herself.

Leo's teasing comment had not just embarrassed her, it had left her feeling humiliated as well, Jodi recognised as she felt the unwanted prick of her tears threatening to expose her vulnerability to him.

But even as she struggled fiercely to blink them away, Leo was already apologising.

'I'm sorry,' he offered. 'I shouldn't have said that.' Leo paused, watching her, mentally berating himself for offending her. It amazed him how much discovering that he had been wrong in his earlier assessment of the situation had changed what he felt about her.

The last thing he wanted to do was to hurt her in any way, but there were still certain issues they needed to address—together—and, although he had not deliberately tried to lead up to them, now that the subject had been introduced perhaps he should seize the opportunity to discuss his concerns with her.

'I know that this perhaps isn't the best time in the world to say this,' he began quietly, 'but we really do need to talk, Jodi…'

Unsteadily Jodi put her mug down on the table.

'Is that why you brought me here?' she demanded as fiercely as she could. 'So that you could cross-examine me? If you think for one minute that just because you saved me from a night in prison I am going to repay you by betraying the others involved in the demonstration, I'm afraid you'd better take me back to the station right now—'

'Jodi.' Leo interrupted her passionate tirade as gently as he could. 'I don't want to talk to you about the problems at the factory, or the demonstration.'

As he watched her eyes shadow with suspicion Leo wondered what she would say if he was to tell her that right now there was only one person and one problem on his mind, and that was her!

'I've already arranged a meeting with representatives of the factory workforce for tomorrow, when I intend to discuss my proposals for the future of the factory with them,' he told her calmly.

'Yes, I heard.' Jodi suddenly felt totally exhausted, drained to the point where simply to think was a superhuman effort. 'Then what did you want to talk to me about?' she asked him warily.

Leo could see how tired she looked and he berated himself for his selfishness. She was still in shock. She needed to rest and recuperate, not be plagued by questions.

'It doesn't matter,' he told her gently. 'Look, why

don't you go to bed? You look completely done in...' Leo reached out to help her out of the chair.

Sensing that he was about to touch her, Jodi felt her defences leap into action, knowing all too well just how vulnerable she was likely to be to any kind of physical contact with him right now. She sprang up out of the chair, almost stumbling in her haste to avoid contact with him, and in doing so precipitated the very thing she had been so desperate to prevent. As Leo reached out to steady her his hands grasped her arms. As he took the weight of her fall against his body he closed the distance between them.

It was just a week since she had first seen him, a handful of days, that was all, so how on earth could it be that she was reacting to him as though she was starving for physical contact as though the sudden feel of him against her answered a craving that nothing else could hope to appease?

It was as if just the act of leaning against him fulfilled and completed her, made her feel whole again, made her feel both incredibly strong and helplessly weak. She felt that she had found the purpose in life for which she had been created and yet at the same time she hated herself for her neediness.

Mutely she pushed against his chest, demanding her release. Leo obeyed the demand of her body language, asking her gruffly, 'Are you OK?'

'Yes, I'm fine,' Jodi responded as she stepped back from him and turned away, ducking into the shadows so that he couldn't see the aching hunger in her expression.

How had things possibly come to this? How had she

come to this? Where had her feelings come from? They were totally alien in their intensity and their ferocity.

Leo held the kitchen door open for her. Shakily she walked out into the hallway.

Leo accompanied her to the bottom of the stairs. Jodi began to climb them, her heart bumping heavily against the wall of her chest. She dared not look at Leo, dared not do anything that might betray to him how she was feeling.

'It's the second door on the left along the landing,' she could hear him telling her. 'You'll find clean towels and everything in the bathroom. I'll go and get your bag for you and leave it outside the bedroom door.'

He was telling her as plainly as though he had used the words themselves that she need not fear a repetition of what had happened in his hotel bedroom, Jodi recognised. Which was surely very thoughtful and gentlemanly of him. So why wasn't she feeling more appreciative, more relieved? Why was she, to be blunt about it, actually feeling disappointed?

Wearily Jodi made her way to the top of the stairs.

As he stood watching the tiredness with which she moved Leo ached to be able to go after her, gather her up protectively in his arms. He deliberately forced himself to turn round and go out to the car to bring in Jodi's bag.

The look of confusion and despair he had seen on her face in the police station had prompted him into a course of action he now recognised as riven with potential hazards.

When he returned with Jodi's bag he took it upstairs, knocked briefly outside his closed bedroom door and went straight back downstairs again, shutting himself in the sitting room.

Jodi was standing staring out of the bedroom window when she heard Leo's knock. She deliberately made herself count to ten—very slowly—before going to open the door, and then told herself that she was relieved and not disappointed to find that the landing was empty and there was no sign of Leo.

Both the bedroom and the bathroom adjoining it were furnished so impersonally that they might almost have been hotel rooms; but thinking of hotel rooms in connection with Leo aroused thoughts and feelings for her that were far from impersonal. Jodi hastily tried to divert her thoughts to less dangerous channels as she went into the bathroom and prepared for bed.

Now that she was on her own she knew that she ought to be thinking about the morning and the possibility of having to face the charges that Jeremy Driscoll had threatened to bring against her—a daunting prospect indeed, but somehow nowhere near as daunting as having to acknowledge just how strong her feelings for Leo were.

That comment he had made to her earlier about her previous appropriation of his bed!

It had made her feel embarrassed and even humiliated, yes, but it had made her remember how wildly wonderful it had felt—she had felt—to be there in his arms. In his life? But she wasn't in his life, and he wasn't in hers, not really. All they had done was have sex together, and every woman—even a schoolteacher—knew that for men the act of sex could be enjoyed with less emotional involvement than they might feel consuming a bar of chocolate—nice at the time but quickly forgotten.

She crawled into Leo's bed—totally sober this time! The bed smelled of clean, fresh linen, as anonymous and bereft of any tangible sign of Leo as the room itself. Curling up in the centre of the large bed, she closed her eyes, but despite her exhaustion sleep evaded her.

She was almost too overtired to sleep, she recognised, the anxieties filling her thoughts, refusing to allow her to relax. She closed her eyes and started to breathe slowly and deeply.

Downstairs, Leo was finding sleep equally hard to come by. He had work to do that could have occupied his time and his thoughts, but instead he found that he was pacing the sitting-room floor, thinking about Jodi. Worrying about Jodi, and not just because he had now realised just what an awkward situation they could both be in because of their shared night together.

That bruise on her arm caused by Jeremy Driscoll had made him feel as though he could quite happily have torn the other man limb from limb and disposed of his carcass to the nearest hungry carnivore. The mere thought of him even touching Jodi…

Abruptly he stopped pacing. What the devil was happening to him? Did he really need to ask that? he mocked himself inwardly. He was in love. This was love. He was transformed into a man he could barely recognise. A man who behaved and thought illogically, a man driven by his emotions, a man who right now…

He froze as he heard a sound from upstairs, and then

strode towards the door, wrenching it open just in time to hear it again, a high-pitched sound of female misery.

Leo took the stairs two at a time, flinging open the bedroom door and striding across the floor to where Jodi lay in the middle of the bed.

She was awake; in the darkness he could see her eyes shining, but she was lying as silently still as though she dared not breathe, never mind move.

'Jodi, what is it?' he demanded.

A wash of shaky relief sluiced through Jodi as she heard and recognised Leo's voice. She had been dreaming about Jeremy Driscoll. A most awful dream, full of appalling and nameless nightmare terrors. It had been the sound of her own muffled scream of sheer panic that had woken her, and for a couple of heartbeats after Leo had thrown open the bedroom door she had actually believed that he was Jeremy.

Now, though, the sound of his voice had reassured her, banishing the nightmare completely.

Too relieved to think of anything else other than the fact that he had rescued her from the terror which had been pursuing her, she turned towards him, telling him, 'I was having the most horrid dream…about Jeremy Driscoll…'

Just saying his name was still enough to make her shudder violently as she struggled to sit up so that she could talk properly to Leo, who was now leaning over the bed towards her.

She could see the anxiety in his eyes now that her own had accustomed themselves to the night-time shadows of the room, their darkness softened by the summer moonlight outside.

'I'm sorry if I disturbed you.' She began to apologise and then checked as she saw that he was still fully dressed.

Was the sitting-room sofa so uncomfortable that he hadn't even bothered trying to sleep on it, or did the fact that he still had his clothes on have something to do with her presence here in his house? Was he afraid that she might try to seduce him a second time?

'What is it? What's wrong?'

The speed with which he had read her expression caught Jodi off guard. Her defences, already overloaded by the events of the day, gave up on her completely.

'You're still dressed,' she told him in a low voice. 'You haven't been to bed; if that's because—'

But before she could voice her fears Leo was interrupting her.

'It's because right now the only bed I want to be in is already occupied, and denied to me,' he told her huskily. 'Unless, of course, you're prepared to change your mind and share it with me?'

Leo knew that he was doing exactly what he had told himself he must not do under any kind of circumstances; that he was behaving like a predator, taking advantage of both Jodi's vulnerability and her current dependence on him, but he still couldn't stop himself. Just the sight of her sitting there in his bed, her slim bare arms wrapped around her hunched-up knees as she looked uncertainly up at him, was enough to make him know that he was prepared to be damned for this eternity and every eternity beyond it just to have her in his arms again, to be granted the opportunity to hold her, touch her, kiss her, caress her.

He wasn't still dressed because he didn't want her, Jodi realised, or because he was afraid that she might embarrass them both by coming on to him. She could feel her whole body starting to tremble beneath the onrush of wild excitement that was roaring through her.

Leo groaned her name, unable to hold back his longing for her. He reached for her, wrapping her in his arms, his mouth so passionately urgent that the sound of her name was lost beneath his kiss.

Jodi knew that she should resist him, that she should insist that he release her, so why instead of doing so was she clinging shamelessly to him? She opened her mouth eagerly to the demanding probe of his tongue, her whole body racked with a raw, aching hunger for him.

She had almost begun to convince herself that their previous lovemaking couldn't possibly have been as good as she remembered, that she had exaggerated it, romanticised it, turning it in her mind into an implausible state of perfection that was total fantasy. Now, shockingly, she knew her memory *had* been at fault, although not in the way that she expected!

Leo's lovemaking had not been as wonderful as she had remembered—it had been even better! More pleasurable, more intoxicating…

As her body relived the pleasure his had given her Jodi knew that there was no point in trying to stop herself from responding to him, no way she could stop herself from wanting him.

She heard the small, tortured groan that filled her own throat as she feasted greedily on his kiss. The touch of his mouth against hers was like receiving a life-giving transfusion, she told herself dizzily as Leo cupped her face in his hands and held her a willing captive and kissed her with an intimacy that almost stopped her heart.

Jodi trembled and then shuddered as the pleasure of being so close to him filled her, running through her nervous system like pure adrenalin.

'We shouldn't be doing this.' Jodi could hear the total lack of conviction in the longing-filled softness of her voice.

'I know,' Leo responded rawly. 'But I just can't stop myself.'

'I don't want you to stop!'

Had she really said that? Jodi was shocked by her own wanton lack of restraint, and shocked too by the discovery that somehow or other she had already managed to unfasten half of the buttons of Leo's shirt.

Beneath her explorative fingertips she could feel the soft silkiness of his body hair.

She leaned forward, breathing in the scent of his skin with deliberate sensuality.

A rush of sensation flooded her, a dizzying kaleidoscope of emotions, recognition—she would recognise his scent anywhere—exaltation, just to have the freedom to be so intimate, so possessively womanly with him. Inhaling his scent only served to remind her of just how many other ached-for intimacies she could enjoy with him. She felt a surge of power, of female strength, knowing that she was responsible for the acceleration of his breathing.

Leo felt himself shudder from top to toe, totally unable to control the fierceness of his response to Jodi. It felt as if every sensation he had ever experienced had just been intensified a thousandfold. Even the simple act of breathing seemed to fill his whole body, his every sense with a heart-rocking awareness of her and longing for her.

This wasn't, he recognised, mere lust, this was the big one; *the* one. She, Jodi, was his one and only. But, he knew instinctively, he couldn't tell her so, not now, not yet; what they were building between them was still too fragile.

He groaned out loud again as Jodi kissed his bared torso. His desire for her ran like fire through his body, the sweetest form of torture.

Swiftly Leo removed the rest of his clothes, never once losing eye contact with Jodi whilst he did so.

He warned himself that she might see in his eyes his love for her, but he couldn't make himself break the contact between them that seemed to be binding them so intimately close together.

In her eyes he could see wonderment, uncertainty, longing, and even a little old-fashioned female shock. Her body clenched when he cupped the tender ball of her shoulder with one hand whilst tugging off the last of his clothes with the other, but she didn't make any attempt to break the gaze that was locking them together.

Somehow the silent visual bonding between them was as sensually charged as touching.

His body ached intolerably for her, and so too did his heart, his entire being.

'Jodi.' He whispered her name again as he gathered her closer, finally breaking their eye contact to look down at her mouth and then up into her eyes again before slowly brushing his mouth against hers.

Jodi felt as though she was going to explode with the sheer force of the sensual tension building up inside her.

It was a good job she was not some impressionable teenager, she told herself, otherwise she would be in danger of deceiving herself that the way Leo was looking at her, as though he wanted to communicate something deeply meaningful, meant that he really cared about her.

She knew that she ought to bring what was happening between them to an end now, before things went any further, but Leo was taking hold of her, brushing his mouth against hers once more in a way that aroused in her such a sweetly aching desire.

Beneath his mouth Leo could feel Jodi's parting; he could taste the sweet exhaled breath, feel the soft little tremor that ran through her body as she nestled closer to him.

Leo was stroking her skin with his hands, making her ache and quiver, his mouth leaving hers to caress the vulnerable place where her shoulder joined her throat, nuzzling little kisses up to her ear whilst his tongue-tip investigated its delicate whorls. Each small sensation coalesced, melded together until she was on fire with the heat of the need he was creating inside her.

Her breasts, swelling, peaking, ached for the touch of his hands. As though he seemed to know it he shaped them, stroking the pads of his thumbs over the erect crests of her nipples.

Jodi trembled and moaned, closed her eyes, welcoming the velvet darkness that lapped protectively around her, and then opened them again on a gasp of piercingly sweet pleasure as she felt Leo's mouth against first one breast and then the other.

Her fingers dug into the hard muscles of his back, her body arching in an irresistible mixture of supplication and temptation.

Leo was kissing her belly, rimming her navel with his tongue. Her fingers clenched in his thick, dark hair. Her intention had been to push him away, but helplessly her hands stilled as he moved lower and then lower still.

Such intimacy was surely only for the most beloved of lovers, but Jodi couldn't find the strength to resist or deny what he was giving her; her body, like her emotions, clenched first against what was happening, and then gave in.

As he moved his body over hers and entered her Leo immediately felt the first fierce contraction of her release. His own body leapt to meet and complete it, his emotions as well as his senses taking hotly satisfying pleasure in knowing they were sharing this moment together.

Jodi cried out Leo's name, wrapping herself around him, holding him deep inside her, where she had so much wanted him to be. It felt so wondrously right to have him there, a part of her, now and for always.

'Leo.'

She sighed his name in exhausted pleasure as tears of fulfilment washed her eyes and flowed onto her face, to be tenderly licked away by Leo, before he reached out to wrap her in his arms.

She was asleep before they closed fully around her.

CHAPTER SEVEN

LEO allowed himself a small smile of satisfaction when he finally replaced the telephone receiver at the end of what had been a long half-hour of diplomatic discussion with the police.

He had earlier spent a very terse and determined five minutes on the telephone to Jeremy, informing him of the fact that he would most certainly be placing charges against *him* for unlawfully being on the company's premises if he was to go ahead and try to accuse Jodi of anything. Did he, Jeremy, Leo had asked grimly, possess the same physical evidence of this supposed assault that Jodi did of his unwarranted manhandling of her? Jeremy had blustered and tried to counter-threaten, but in the end he had given way.

The police had been rather less easy to negotiate with; for a start, as the superintendent had told Leo coolly, they did not take too kindly to the demands the demonstration at the factory had placed on their very limited financial budget, and they were certainly not about to give out a message to the public that acts of violence were something they were prepared to permit.

Leo had protested that the demonstration had been intended to be a peaceful one, citing the fact that he, as the owner of the factory, did not feel it necessary to make any kind of complaint against his workforce, so then surely the matter could be allowed to rest. As it transpired, Leo discovered that in the end none of the protesters had actually been held overnight at the police station, and that Jodi would have been the only one of them who might have faced the prospect of charges, and that only because of the assault incident claimed by Jeremy.

Ultimately the police had agreed, that since Jeremy was prepared to drop his accusation, there was no real case against her and she did not need to return to the station.

He had, Leo recognised, barely an hour left to go before he was due to talk with the factory's workforce, and there was still that vitally important and delicate issue he needed to discuss with Jodi!

Showered and dressed, Jodi hesitated at the top of staircase. Although she had pretended to be asleep, she had been fully aware of Leo getting out of bed and leaving her.

How was it possible for a supposedly intelligent woman to make the same mistake twice?

As anxious as she was about what might lie ahead of her when she returned to the police station, she was even more concerned about her feelings for Leo. Her feelings? When was she going to have the courage to give them their proper name?

Her love!

A tiny sound somewhere between a denial and a moan bubbled in her throat. If only last night hadn't been so…so perfect. So everything she had ever wanted the intimacy she shared with the man she loved to be. If only Leo had been different, if only he had done something, anything, that had made her want to distance herself from him.

As she started to make her way down the stairs Leo suddenly appeared in the hallway, standing watching her, making her feel breathless and shaky, weak with the sheer power of her love for him.

'I've just finished speaking with the police,' Leo began.

'Yes, I haven't forgotten that I've got to go back,' Jodi informed him quickly. Somehow she managed to force herself to give him a tight proud look, which she hoped would tell him that she was completely unfazed by the prospect. 'I'm not sure just what the formalities will be.' Her voice startled to wobble slightly, despite her efforts to control it. 'Presumably I shall have to contact a lawyer.'

'There wouldn't be any point in you doing that,' Leo began to inform her, and then stopped as he saw the look of white-faced anxiety she was trying so valiantly to conceal from him. 'Jodi. It's all right,' he told her urgently. 'I—that is, the police have decided that there's no need for you to go back.'

Leo wasn't entirely sure why he had decided not to tell Jodi of the role he had played in that decision; it just seemed like the right choice to make.

'I don't have to go back?'

It wasn't just her voice that was trembling now, Leo recognised as he watched the relief shake her body. The urge to go to her and wrap her in his arms whilst he told her that he would never allow anything to hurt or frighten her ever again was so powerful that he had taken several steps towards her before he managed to pull himself back.

Jodi was convinced she must have misunderstood what Leo was telling her.

'You mean I don't have to go right now, today?' she questioned him uncertainly.

'I mean you don't have to go back ever,' Leo corrected her. Adding in a softly liquid voice, 'It's over, Jodi. There isn't anything for you to worry about.'

'But what about Jeremy Driscoll?' Jodi protested.

'Apparently he's changed his mind,' Leo told her carelessly, turning away from her as he did so.

There was no way he wanted Jodi to feel that she was under any kind of obligation to him for speaking to Jeremy.

He was still aware that last night he had to some extent coerced her into making love with him, at least emotionally. And when the time came for him to tell her how he felt about her he didn't want her to feel pressured in any way at all.

He had a right, he believed, to explain how he felt now and how his own fight against his feelings had led, in part, to his original misjudgement of her. But he was not going to use any kind of emotional blackmail to compel Jodi into saying she felt the same.

When it came to whether or not they had created a new life together; well, that was a very different matter. Leo would use any means possible to make sure he would be a presence in that child's life.

'Look, Jodi, I have to go out shortly,' he told her. 'But before I do, there's something we have to discuss.'

Jodi felt her stomach lurch, a cold feeling of dread swilling through her veins.

She knew what was coming, of course; what he was going to say to her…

'Last night was a mistake. I'm sorry. But I hope you understand…'

Mentally she steeled herself for the blow she knew was about to fall.

'Let's go into the kitchen,' Leo began unexpectedly. 'I've made some coffee, and you must be hungry.'

Hungry!

'I thought you were in a rush to go out,' Jodi tried to protest as Leo ushered her towards the kitchen.

'I've got an appointment I have to keep,' Leo agreed, 'but I can talk whilst you eat.'

Eat! Jodi knew there was no way she could do that, but still she allowed Leo to fill her a bowl of cereal, and pour them both a mug of coffee before he began quietly, 'The first time we met I made a grave misjudgement, not just of the situation, Jodi, but of you as well.'

Leo paused, as though he was searching for the right words, and Jodi began to stiffen defensively.

'I'm concerned, Jodi, that because of the…the circumstances surrounding the intimacy we've shared we may both be guilty of having neglected to—er—think through the consequences of our actions and do something to ensure…' Leo stopped and shook his head.

'Look, what I'm trying to say, Jodi, is that if there's any chance that you might be pregnant…well, then something will have to be arranged. I wouldn't want you to…'

Pregnant. Jodi's heart bumped and thudded against

her ribcage as she stared at Leo in mute shock. '*Something will have to be arranged...*' She tried to absorb the meaning of his words. Did he think for one minute that if she was carrying his child she would allow that precious new life to be 'arranged' away? She would never agree to anything like that. Never!

Her blood ran cold. She had been expecting him to tell her that last night had been a mistake, an impulse he now regretted, a mere sexual encounter which she wasn't to take seriously nor read anything meaningful into. But to know that he had already thought as far ahead as wanting to dispose of any possible consequences of their intimacy hurt her more than she felt able to cope with and, at the same time, made her more angry than anything else he had either said or done.

What was it he was really worried about? Fathering a child he didn't want, or having her make any kind of financial or emotional claims on him on behalf of that child? What sort of a woman did he think she was?

Before she could even think about what she was saying she told him quickly and sharply, 'There is no chance of me being...of anything like that.'

Her heart was still thumping as she spoke, but her reactions were instinctive and immediate. How could she possibly continue to love him after this?

Jodi sounded so coldly positive that Leo started to frown. Had he been wrong to presume that just because she wasn't experienced that meant that she was unprotected from the risk of pregnancy?

Before he could stop himself Leo heard himself insisting fiercely, 'But that night in my suite was your first time, and—'

'How could you possibly know that?' she demanded, oblivious in her anger of the fact that she herself had just confirmed his gut feelings. Without waiting for him to answer her she continued emotionally, 'Well, just because I happened to be...because you were my first...' she amended hurriedly, 'that does not mean that I am going to get pregnant!'

As she spoke Jodi was getting up from the table and storming out of the kitchen, telling Leo acidly as she did so, 'I'm going to get my things and then I'm going home right now. And I never want to see you again! From the moment you arrived in Frampton you've caused misery and made life impossible for everyone. And just let me tell you that there's absolutely no way I would ever want to inflict on my child the burden of having you for a father.'

'Are you sure you'll be all right?'

Jodi glowered at Leo as he reached out to open the passenger door of his car. It had been galling in the extreme after her outburst to be forced to accept his offer of a lift home.

'Well, I shall certainly be far better here in my own home than I was last night in yours, won't I?' she demanded with pointed iciness as Leo insisted on carrying her bag to her front door for her and waiting to see her safely inside.

As she gave in to the unwanted temptation to watch him drive away Jodi felt sick with fear for her future, and anger against herself.

She was surely too adult, too mature for this kind of emotional folly!

* * *

As he drove away from Jodi's cottage Leo discovered that he was actually grinding his teeth. The last thing he felt like doing right now was sitting down at the negotiating table. The only thing he wanted to do was to take hold of Jodi Marsh and tell her in no uncertain terms just how he felt about her, and what his life was going to be without her…

So much for his earlier high-minded promise to himself not to use any kind of emotional blackmail to press his suit, Leo reflected grimly. But those comments Jodi had made about not wanting him as a father for her child had hurt—and badly—and he had been within a breath of telling her in no uncertain terms that if her body was allowed to speak for itself it might have a very different story to tell. 'Because make no mistake about it, Jodi Marsh, your body damned well wanted me!'

To Leo's consternation he suddenly realised as the sound of his own voice filled the car that he was talking to himself! No wonder they called love a form of madness!

More drained by everything that had happened than she wanted to admit, Jodi suddenly discovered that she was craving the escape of sleep. She normally had buckets of energy, but these last couple of days she had felt physically drained. On her return home she went upstairs, intending to collect some washing, and then she saw her bed, and one thing led to another and…

It was the sound of her doorbell ringing that finally woke her. Realising that she had fallen deeply asleep, still fully dressed, she made her way groggily downstairs, her heart leaping frantically as she wondered if her visitor was Leo.

It had hurt her so badly this morning, after the wonderful night they had spent together, to know how desperate he was to distance himself from her and to make sure she knew that he didn't want her.

However, her visitor wasn't Leo, but Nigel her cousin. As she let him in he was waving a newspaper in front of her.

'You're on the front page,' he told her. 'Have you seen the paper yet?'

The front page! Jodi took the newspaper from him and studied it, her face burning with consternation and embarrassment as she studied the photograph of the previous evening's arrests.

'I was half expecting I was going to have to bail my strait-laced cousin out of prison,' Nigel joked as he made his way towards her small kitchen.

'Only, as I understand it, Leo got there before me.'

He shot Jodi a wry look as she demanded, 'Who told you that?'

'I rang the police station,' Nigel informed her. 'Reading between the lines, it sounds as if Leo must have put one hell of a lot of pressure on Jeremy Driscoll to get him to back off from charging you.'

To back off? Jodi began to frown.

'But Leo said that Jeremy had changed his mind,' she protested shakily.

'Yeah, but probably only after Leo had told him that if he didn't he would change it for him, if my guess is correct,' Nigel agreed derisively. 'Apparently Leo was on the phone to the police for nearly half an hour this morning, insisting that he did not want charges pressed against you, or any of the workforce. It seems to me that Leo must think an awful lot of you, little cousin, to go to so much trouble on your behalf,' Nigel teased her. 'This wouldn't be the beginning of a classic tale of romance between two adversaries, would it?' He grinned, his smile fading when he saw the look of white-faced despair Jodi was giving him. 'Are you OK?' he asked in concern.

'I'm fine,' Jodi lied.

'Feel like going out for a meal tonight?' Nigel suggested.

Jodi shook her head. 'No; I've got some work I need to prepare for school on Monday,' she told him, 'but thanks for asking.'

Nigel was almost at the front door, when he turned round and told her, 'Leo was meeting with the representatives of the factory this morning. Did he drop any hints about what he was going to say to them?'

'No, why should he?' she asked Nigel primly.

He was, she could see, giving her a worried look.

'Something's wrong; you're not your normal self, Jodi. What—?'

'Nothing's wrong,' she lied grittily. 'I'm just tired, that's all.'

She felt guilty about lying to Nigel, who was practically her best friend as well as her cousin, but what alternative did she really have?

A small, uncomfortable silence followed her denial, before Nigel turned to open the front door.

Jodi watched him go. She had been unfairly sharp with him, she knew, and ultimately she would have to apologise and explain, but not right now. Right now she just wasn't capable of doing anything so rational! All she really wanted to do was to think about Leo, and what Nigel had told her.

It had confused her to learn that Leo had intervened with the authorities on her behalf. After all, he had allowed her to believe that they had been the ones to contact him, and not, as Nigel had implied, the other way around.

It galled Jodi to know that she was in his debt—not that that made a single scrap of difference to what she felt about what he had said to her earlier. No way! Those words were words she would never forgive him for uttering. Still, she knew she would have to thank him for what he had done, and the sooner she got that onerous task over with the better! Gritting her teeth, she went upstairs to shower and get changed.

Leo saw Jodi as she walked up the drive towards the front door of Ashton House. He was standing in the room he was using as an office, having just completed a telephone call with his new partner in the haulage and distribution business he intended to site at the motorway-based factory.

As he had informed the representatives of the Frampton workforce earlier, he had now decided to keep that factory open, but it would be up to them to prove to him that he had made the right decision, with an increased output to ensure his business kept its competitive edge over its overseas rivals.

Despite the fact that it was a hot summer's day, Jodi

was wearing a very formal-looking black trouser suit, its jacket open over a white T-shirt.

Leo, in contrast, had changed into a pair of casual chinos on his return from his meeting, but that did not prevent Jodi from thinking how formidable he looked as he opened the door just as she reached out to ring the bell.

Formidably male, that was, she admitted to herself as he invited her into the house.

Why, oh, why did she have to feel this way about him? Her pain at loving him was laced with her furious anger at his unbelievably callous words of the morning.

Perhaps to him, a high-powered businessman, an unplanned child was just a problem to be disposed of, but there was no way she could contemplate taking such an unemotional course.

If she thought for one moment that there was the slightest chance that she could be pregnant… After all, she had lied to Leo when she had intimated that she had taken precautions to ensure that she did not conceive.

Now she was deliberately trying to frighten herself, Jodi decided firmly, dismissing her uncomfortable anxiety. She was not pregnant. Totally, definitely not.

And, besides, didn't she have enough to worry about?

As she followed Leo inside the house she began with determination, 'Nigel's been to see me. He says that I have you to thank for the fact that I did not have to return to the police station this morning.'

The way she delivered the words, with an extremely militant look in her eyes, made Leo curse her cousin silently.

'Jodi—' he began, but she shook her head, refusing to let him continue.

'Is it true?' she demanded.

'The police agreed with me that there was no reason to take things any further with any of those concerned in what essentially had been a peaceful demonstration,' Leo palliated.

'So it is true,' Jodi announced baldly. 'Why did you do it?' she asked him bitterly.

'So that you could have me under some kind of obligation to you? Why would you want that, or can I guess?' she demanded sarcastically. 'So that you could demand that I—?'

'Stop right there.'

Now it was Jodi's turn to fall silent as Leo glared furiously at her. Did she really think that he would stoop so low as to try to demand that she make love with him?

Beneath his anger, running much, much deeper, Leo could feel the savage, ripping claws of pain.

Jodi told herself that she wasn't going to back down or allow him to make her feel she was in the wrong. After what he had said this morning it seemed perfectly logical to her that he would consider using the fact that he had negotiated her freedom to demand that she acquiesce to his demands over an accidental pregnancy.

All the anguish she was feeling welled up inside her. Ignoring the oxygen-destroying tension crackling between them, and the anger she could see glinting in Leo's eyes, Jodi protested, 'You just don't care, do you? Feelings, human life—they don't matter to you. You're quite happy to close down the factory and put people out of work…'

And quite happy, too, to deny his child the right to live, Jodi reflected inwardly, the pain of that knowledge twisting her insides like acid—not just for the child she was positive she had not conceived but also for the destruction of her own foolish dreams.

Somewhere deep down inside herself she had seen him as a hero, a truly special man, imbued with all the virtues that women universally loved, especially the instinct to protect those weaker and more vulnerable than himself. It hurt to know just how wrong she had been.

Leo had had enough. How dared she accuse him of not having feelings? If he was as callous, as uncaring as she was accusing him of being, right now she would be lying under him on his bed whilst he…

As Leo fought to control the surging shock of his fierce desire he couldn't stop himself from retaliating savagely, 'If this is your way of trying to persuade me to keep the factory open, let me tell you the tactics you employed in my hotel suite would be far more effective.'

Leo knew the moment the words were out of his mouth that they were a mistake, but it was too late to recall them.

Jodi was looking at him with an expression of contemptuous loathing in her eyes, whilst her mouth…!

Leo had to swallow—hard—as he saw that small, betraying tremble of her firmly compressed lips. The same lips he had not such a very long time ago teased open with his tongue before…

Was that actually a groan Leo had just uttered? Jodi wondered with furious female anger. Well, he certainly deserved to be in pain after what he had just said to her!

It was only the sheer force of her anger that was keeping her from bursting into either incoherent speech or helpless emotional tears.

How could he have stooped so low as to throw that at her?

Well, he would quickly learn that she could be equally offensive!

'If I thought that such tactics would work—and that you would not renege on any deal made in the heat of the moment—I might almost be prepared to risk them,' she told him with pseudo-sweetness, her tone changing completely as she added in a much colder and more authoritative voice, 'But if I were in your shoes…'

'You'd do things differently?' Leo supplied for her.

'Well, if I were you I'd make sure of my facts before I started throwing accusations around.' Jodi turned round, giving him one last furious look as she told him, 'I'm not listening to any more of this.'

And then she was gone before Leo had the chance to stop her, leaving him mentally cursing both her and himself.

Why on earth hadn't he simply told her that he had found a way of keeping the factory open?

Why? Because his damned stupid male pride wouldn't let him, that was why!

By the time she had walked home, Jodi was feeling both queasy and slightly light-headed. It was because of the heat of the sun and the fact that she had not really had very much to eat, Jodi told herself firmly—to even think of allowing herself to imagine anything else was completely and utterly silly.

Silly, yes, but still somehow she couldn't stop herself

from imagining, dreading that her foolish behaviour was now going to have dire consequences.

It wasn't that she didn't like children—she did, nor even that she didn't want to be a mother and have babies herself—she did. But not yet, and most certainly not like this.

No, she wanted her babies to be planned for with love, by two people equally committed to their relationship and their children's future.

She was, she told herself, panicking unnecessarily, deliberately blowing up a small feeling of nausea into something else. Easy to tell herself that, but far harder to believe it. Guilt was a terribly powerful force!

With her imagination running away from her at full speed and sending her harrowing images of single-parenthood, it was hard to think rationally.

Even if she was pregnant, it was far too soon for her to be suffering from morning sickness, surely, and if her nausea wasn't caused by that then how could she be pregnant?

But what if she was? What if? A woman in her position, a schoolteacher, pregnant after a one-night stand! She went cold at the thought, filled with repugnance for her own behaviour. Mentally she started counting the days until she could be sure that she was safe. And in the meantime… In the meantime she would just have to try not to panic!

CHAPTER EIGHT

Jodi could feel the buzz of excitement being generated by the group of parents gathered outside the school gates. Puzzled, she looked at them. Normally on a Monday parental exchanges were slightly subdued, but this morning's mood was quite obviously very upbeat—unlike her own, Jodi recognised, pausing as one of the parents called out to her.

'Have you heard the news—isn't it wonderful? I could hardly believe it when John came home on Saturday and told me that Leo Jefferson had announced he intended to keep the factory open.'

Jodi stared at her.

Leo had done that? But he had told her… Before she could sort out her confused thoughts another mother was joining in the conversation, chuckling warmly as she congratulated Jodi on her part in the previous week's demonstration at the factory.

'We were all really surprised and impressed by the way Mr Jefferson spoke up for you to the police, telling them that he had no intention of taking things any further. And then to learn that he's going to keep the factory open after all. It totally changes the way we all think about him.' She beamed, giving Jodi a look she didn't understand before continuing, 'Of course, you must have known what was going to happen before the rest of us!' Jodi's face started to burn.

The other parents were also looking at her with an unexpected degree of amused speculation, she recognised, although she had no idea why until suddenly she could hear Myra Fanshawe exclaiming vehemently, 'Well, personally I think it's absolutely disgraceful. A person in her position...a schoolteacher. A head teacher...indulging in a liaison of that nature. I must say, though, I'm not totally surprised. I've never approved of some of her teaching methods!'

Myra was talking to one of the other parents, her back to Jodi. As Jodi approached the other woman whispered something urgently to Myra, her face flushing with embarrassment.

But it seemed that her embarrassment was not shared by Myra, who tossed her head and then said even more loudly, 'Well, I'm sorry, but I don't really care if she does hear me. After all, she's the one at fault. Behaving like that... Openly spending the night in his hotel suite, and then trying to convince us all that she's Ms Virtue personified!'

Jodi felt her face burning even hotter as the group of parents surrounding Myra gave way and stood back as she approached.

Jodi's heart gave a sickening lurch as she saw the look of malicious triumph in the other woman's eyes. Myra had never liked her, she knew that. Jodi had to admit that she didn't particularly care for Myra either, but there was too much at stake here for her to be ruled by such feelings.

Reminding herself—not that she needed any reminding—of her position and her responsibilities as the school's head teacher, Jodi took a deep, calming breath and confronted the other woman.

'I assume that I am the subject of your discussion, and if that is the case—'

'You aren't going to try to deny it, I hope,' Myra interrupted her rudely before Jodi could finish speaking. 'It wouldn't do you any good if you did. Ellie, the receptionist who saw you at the hotel, both when you arrived and the next morning when you left, is my goddaughter, and she recognised you immediately from your photograph in the local paper. She couldn't believe it when she read that you had been demonstrating at the factory. Not when she knew that you'd spent the night with its owner.'

Jodi's heart sank. This was even worse than she had expected, and she could see from the varying expressions on the faces of the other parents that they were all shocked by Myra's disclosures.

What could she say in her own defence? What mitigating circumstances could she summon up to explain? Bleakly Jodi was aware that there was nothing she could say that would make the situation any better and, potentially, telling the truth would make things a whole lot worse!

'You do realise, don't you, that, given my position on the board of governors, it will be my duty to bring up the doubts your behaviour gives me as to your suitability to teach our children?'

'I haven't—'

Jodi tried to interrupt and defend herself, but Myra overrode her, stating loudly, 'And, on top of everything else, you were taken into custody by the police. It is my belief that the education authority should be told!' she said to Jodi with obvious relish. 'After all, as a parent, I have my child's moral welfare to think about,' Myra was continuing with a sanctimonious fervour that had some of the more impressionable parents watching her round-eyed. 'In your shoes…' she continued in an openly triumphant manner.

To Jodi's relief, the final bell summoning the children to their classrooms started to ring, giving her the perfect opportunity to escape from her tormentor.

From her tormentor maybe, she allowed half an hour later as she stood motionlessly staring out of the window of her small office, but not from the torment itself.

She had seen the looks—from pity right through to very unpleasant salacious curiosity—on the faces of the parents as they'd watched her reaction to Myra's disclosures. She knew that Myra had the power to make life very difficult and uncomfortable for her and for her family. The other members of the board were naturally going to be concerned about the probity and the moral standing of their school's head teacher, and, although Jodi did not think that any legal disciplinary action would be taken against her, naturally she did not relish the thought of being at odds with the governors or indeed of having her lifestyle bring disrepute on the school.

And as for Myra's remark about the education authority, well, Jodi suspected that had just been so much hot air, but she also knew that her own conscience would not allow her to stay on at the school against the wishes of the parents, or in a situation where they felt that she was not the right person to have charge of their children. Jodi's heart sank. If that was to happen…! If she was to be put in a position where she felt honour bound to step down from her post, after everything she had done, all her hard work. But what could she say in her own defence? she reminded herself bleakly. And that jibe Myra had made about her maternal concern for the moral welfare of her son had really hit a raw nerve.

Jodi's head was starting to ache. She had deliberately made herself eat a heavy breakfast this morning, just to prove to herself—not that she had needed it—that she most certainly was not suffering from the nauseous early-morning tummy of a newly pregnant woman. The meal was taking its natural toll on her now.

She felt distinctly queasy, but surely because she was so tense with anxiety and misery? She tried to reassure and comfort herself, but harrowing tales of members of her sex who had found themselves in exactly the position she was dreading kept being dredged up by her conscience to torment her. And the unfortunate thing was that she was prone to having an erratic cycle, especially when she was under stress.

Myra's comments had all but obliterated the original discomfort she had felt on learning that, contrary to what he had told her, Leo had actually decided to keep the factory open. Why had he let her accuse him like that?

It was almost lunchtime before Leo learned what was happening to Jodi.

He had been tied up with his accountants most of the morning, swiftly renegotiating finance packages to accommodate the changes he had made to his business plans for the factories he had taken over.

His bankers had shaken their heads over the discovery

that he intended to set up his own haulage and distribution business and then admitted ruefully that, being Leo, he was probably going to make a very profitable success of it.

But all morning what he'd really been thinking about, worrying about, had been Jodi and the row they had had the previous day. Why had he let her go like that?

He had a meeting at the factory, and when he arrived there he discovered that Jeremy Driscoll was waiting to see him.

Furiously angry, he confronted Leo, telling him, 'I want to collect some papers I left here, but the cretins you have left in charge have refused to allow me access to the storeroom. God knows on whose instructions.'

'On mine,' Leo told him equably.

There was a copy of the local paper on the desk, and Leo frowned as he caught sight of it and saw Jodi's photograph on the front page.

Jeremy had obviously seen it too, and he sneered as he commented, 'Little Miss Goody Two Shoes. Well, everyone's going to know what she is soon enough now.'

'What do you mean?' Leo demanded tersely as he recognised the malice glinting in Jeremy's pale blue eyes.

'What do you think I mean?' Jeremy grinned. 'She was spotted leaving your suite, creeping out of the hotel in the early hours of the morning. Good, was she?

'Well, you might have been impressed but somehow I doubt the parents of the brats she teaches are going to be when they learn what she was up to. Their head teacher, tricking her way into a man's hotel suite and not leaving until the morning...' Jeremy started to shake his head disapprovingly. 'I shouldn't be surprised if they demand her resignation.'

As he listened to him Leo's heart sank. Jeremy was too sure of himself, swaggeringly so, in fact, to simply be making a shot in the dark. Someone obviously *had* seen Jodi leaving his suite.

Leo's brain went into overdrive as he sought furiously for a way to protect her. There was only one thing he could think of doing that might help.

Fixing Jeremy with a cool, bored look, he told him calmly, 'Oh, I hardly think so; after all, what's so wrong about an engaged couple spending the night together?'

'An engaged couple?' Jeremy was staring nonplussed at him, but to Leo's relief he didn't immediately reject Leo's claim; instead he challenged, 'If that's true then why doesn't anyone know about it?'

'Because we've chosen to keep it to ourselves for the moment,' Leo responded distantly, 'not that it's any business of yours or anyone else's. Oh, and by the way,' he continued, giving Jeremy a nasty smile, 'I understand from my accountants that they've been approached by the tax authorities regarding some anomalies in the accounting system you put in place here after the fire that destroyed the previous records. Of course,' Leo continued smoothly, 'my accountants have assured the Revenue that we are prepared to give them all the help they might need.'

Miserably Jodi stared across her desk. As luck would have it, the school's parents had a meeting this evening at which she was supposed to be speaking about her plans to increase the range of extra-curricular activities provided for the children. Jodi gave a small shudder. She could guess what was going to be the hot topic of conversation at that meeting now!

And she could guess, too, just how much criticism and disapproval she was going to encounter—deservedly so, she told herself grimly.

Breaking into Leo's suite, getting drunk, falling asleep in his bed and then, as though all of that weren't enough…

She wasn't fit to be a teacher, or to hold the responsible position she did, Jodi decided wretchedly, and Myra Fanshawe had been right when she had warned Jodi that the parents would take a very dim view of what she had done.

If only that photograph of her had not appeared in the local paper. But it had, and— She tensed as she heard a soft knock on her door, her face colouring as Helen Riddings, the more senior of her co-teachers, popped her head round the door to ask uncertainly, 'Are you all right? Only…'

Only what? Jodi wondered defeatedly. Only you've heard the gossip and now you're wondering if it's true and, if it is, just what I'm going to do about it?

'I'm sorry, it's my turn for playground duty, isn't it?' Jodi answered her, avoiding the other woman's eyes, knowing perfectly well that her colleague had not really come to her office to remind her about that.

'Oh, but you haven't had any lunch,' Helen protested, obviously flustered. 'I can do the playground duty for you if you like.' She stopped and then looked acutely self-conscious as she told Jodi, 'Myra Fanshawe is in the playground with some of the other parents…'

'It's all right, Helen,' Jodi told her quietly when she broke off in embarrassment. 'I can guess what's going on. I expect that you and the other teachers will have heard the gossip by now…' Jodi could feel her courage starting to desert her.

'You don't look very well,' Helen commiserated, obviously genuinely concerned for her. 'Why don't you go home?'

Before the situation became so untenable that she had no option other than to retreat there—permanently? Was that what Helen meant? Jodi wondered bitterly.

'No, I can't do that,' she responded.

She was beginning to feel acutely ill. Gossip, especially this kind of gossip, spread like wildfire; she knew that. How long would it be before it reached the ears of her friends and family? Her cousin…his parents…her own parents…?

Jodi's stomach heaved. Her mother and father, enjoying their retirement, were on an extended trip around America, but they would not be away indefinitely. Her family were so proud of her. So proud of everything she had achieved for the school. What could she say to them when they asked her for an explanation? That she had seen Leo Jefferson in the hotel foyer and fallen immediately and helplessly in lust with him?

In lust. As Helen left her office and closed the door behind her Jodi made a small moan of self-disgust.

But it wasn't lust she felt for Leo Jefferson, was it? Lust did not affect the emotions the way her emotions had been affected. Lust did not bring a person out of their dreams at night, crying out in pain and loss because that person had discovered a cruel truth about the man they loved.

Her stomach churned even more fiercely.

She wasn't going to be sick, she wasn't. But suddenly, urgently, Jodi knew that she was!

It was tension, that was all, nothing else. Jodi assured herself later when she was on her way to take her first afternoon class.

She wondered if it was too soon to buy one of those test kits; that way she could be completely sure. Jodi flinched as she reflected on the effect it would have on the current gossip about her it she was to be observed buying a pregnancy-testing kit. No, she couldn't take such a risk!

Was it really only such a short time ago that she had been a model of virginal morality, basking in the approval of both the parents and the school authorities? And she'd been in receipt of an offer of employment from the area's most prestigious private school… She felt as though that Jodi belonged to another life! How could she have got herself into such a situation? She had heard that falling in love was akin to a form of madness.

Falling in love! Now she knew she was dangerously close to losing her grip on reality. No way did she still think she was in love with Leo Jefferson. No way!

Leo looked at his watch. He had been in meetings for the whole of the afternoon, but at last he was free.

He was acutely conscious of the fact that it might be politic for him to warn Jodi about their 'engagement', but after the way they had parted the last time they had met he doubted that trying to telephone her was going to be very successful.

School must be over for the day by now. He could drive over to the village and call on her at home, explain what had happened, tell her that once the furore had died down they could discreetly let it be known that the engagement was off.

Just the memory of the salacious look in Jeremy Driscoll's eyes when he had taunted Leo this morning about the gossip now circulating concerning Jodi was enough to make Leo feel murderous and to wish that he had the real right to protect Jodi in the way that he wanted to be able to protect her. And, so far as he was concerned, the best way to do that was for her to have his ring on her left hand—his wedding ring! He really was far more Italian than he had ever realised, he recognised grimly as he headed for his car, which reminded him—he ought to telephone his parents. The visit he had promised his mother he would make to see them again soon would have to be put back, at least until he was satisfied that Jodi was all right.

'I take it that you will be attending the meeting this evening?'

Jodi tensed warily as Myra Fanshawe stepped past the other parents grouped at the school gates to confront her.

'Only, now that you've got a wealthy fiancé to consider, I don't imagine you're going to be particularly concerned about the future of the school or its pupils, are you?'

A wealthy fiancé. Her? What on earth was Myra talking about? Jodi wondered wearily.

She couldn't remember ever feeling so drained at the end of a school day, but of course this had been no ordinary day, which no doubt explained why all she wanted to do was to go to sleep, but not until after she had had some delicious anchovies… For some reason she had been longing for some all afternoon! Which was most peculiar because they were not normally something she was very keen on!

Myra was standing in front of her now, her cold little eyes narrowing with hostility as she continued, 'I hope you don't think that just because you're engaged to Leo Jefferson it means that certain questions aren't going to be asked—by the parents if not the education authority,' she sniffed prissily. 'And—'

'Just a minute,' Jodi stopped her sharply, 'what exactly do you mean about me being engaged to Leo Jefferson?'

She was starting to feel light-headed again, Jodi recognised, her face burning hot and then cold as she wondered how on earth Myra could possibly have got hold of such an outrageous idea—and quite obviously spread it around as fast and as far as she could, Jodi guessed despairingly as she saw the other parents watching them.

'It's a little too late for you to assume either discretion or innocence now,' Myra told her disdainfully. 'Although I must say that, as a parent, I do think that someone in your position should have made more of an attempt to employ them both instead of acting in a way that could bring the school into disrepute.'

'Myra…' Jodi began grimly, and then stopped as the small knot of parents in front of the gates fell back to allow the large Mercedes to pull to a halt outside them.

'Well, here comes your fiancé,' Myra announced bitchily as Leo got out of the car. 'I just hope he doesn't think because he's bought Frampton at a ridiculous, knock-down price—virtually tricking the family into selling the business to him against their will, from what Jeremy has told us—it means that he's got any kind of position or authority locally! Jeremy was very highly thought-of by his workforce,' she continued, with such a blatant disregard for the truth that Jodi could hardly believe her ears.

Leo had reached them now, and for a reason she certainly was not going to analyse, Jodi discovered that a small part of her actually felt pleased to have him there.

Not that he had any right to be here, making a bad situation even worse by putting his hand proprietorily on Jodi's arm, before bending his head to brush his lips lightly against her cheek as he murmured into her ear, 'I'll explain when we're on our own.' Then he moved slightly away from her to say in a louder voice, 'Sorry I'm late, darling; I got held up.'

And then, without giving her an opportunity to say a word, he was guiding her towards his car, tucking her solicitously into the passenger seat, and then getting in the driver's seat beside her.

Jodi waited until she was sure that they were safely out of sight of the gathered watchers, before demanding shakily, 'Would you mind explaining to me just what is going on, and why Myra Fanshawe seems to think that we are engaged?'

'Myra Fanshawe?' Leo queried, puzzled.

'The woman with me as you drove up,' Jodi explained impatiently.

She felt tired and cross and very hungry, and the ridiculous temptation to beg Leo to stop the car so that she could lay her head on his shoulder and wallow in the cathartic pleasure of a really good cry was so strong that it was threatening to completely overwhelm her.

'She's a close friend of Jeremy Driscoll,' she offered casually, 'and—'

'Oh, is she?' Leo growled. 'Well, no doubt that explains how she knows about our engagement.'

'Our engagement?' Jodi checked him angrily. 'What engagement? We are not engaged…'

'Not officially—'

'Not in any way,' Jodi interrupted him fiercely.

'Jodi, I had no choice,' Leo told her quietly. 'Driscoll told me about the fact that you'd been seen leaving my suite early in the morning. He was…' Leo paused, not wanting to tell her just how unpleasant Jeremy's attitude and assumptions had been. 'Apparently—'

'I know what you're going to say.' Jodi stopped him hotly. 'I was seen leaving your room, so I must be some kind of fallen woman, totally unfit to teach school, to be involved with innocent children. For heaven's sake, all I've done is to go bed with you twice; that doesn't mean…'

To her own consternation her eyes filled with emotional tears, her voice becoming suspended by the sheer intensity of what she was feeling…

'Jodi, I know exactly what it does mean and what it doesn't mean,' Leo tried to reassure her. 'But that knowledge belongs only to the two of us. You do know what I'm saying, don't you?' he asked her gently.

When she made no response and instead looked studiedly away from him out of the passenger window he could see the deep pink colour burning her skin and his heart ached for her.

'I didn't think you'd particularly care for it if I were to take out a full-page advert in the local paper announcing that you were a virgin until that night in my suite.'

'That doesn't mean you have to claim that we're engaged,' Jodi protested.

'I did it to protect you,' Leo told her.

To protect her! How could he sit there and claim to want to protect her when he had already told her that he didn't want to keep their child? Or was that why he was doing this? Jodi wondered wretchedly. Was this just a cynical ploy to make her feel she could trust him, to keep her close enough to him for him to be able to control her, and act quickly, if necessary, to...?

'It isn't your responsibility to protect me.' Jodi told him fiercely.

'Maybe not in your eyes,' Leo retaliated, suddenly serious in a way that made her heart thud in pure female awareness of how very male and strong he was, and how she longed to be able to lean on that strength, and to feel she could turn to it and him for comfort and for protection and for love...

But of course she couldn't! Mustn't...

'But in mine, Jodi, I can assure you that I consider it very much my responsibility. You aren't the only one with a reputation to consider and protect, you know,' he told her. His voice was suddenly so hurtfully curt that Jodi turned to look at him—and then wished that she hadn't, as the mere sight of his profile caused a wave of helpless longing to pulse through her body, pushing every other emotion out of its way.

She must not feel like this about him, Jodi told herself in defensive panic. She must not want him, ache for him…love him…

A small sound somewhere between pain and despair constricted her throat.

'How do you think it is going to reflect on me once it becomes public knowledge that you and I—?'

'You mean, you're doing this for yourself and not for me?' Jodi challenged him.

This was more like it. Knowing that his behaviour was motivated by selfishness would surely help her to control and ultimately conquer her love for him?

'I'm doing it because right now it is the only option we have,' Leo told her firmly.

Jodi could feel herself weakening. It would be such a relief to simply let Leo take charge, to let him stand between her and the disapproval of public opinion.

To let the world at large believe that he loved her and that…

No. She could not do it. Because if she did she would be in grave danger of allowing herself to believe the same thing!

'No!' she told him fiercely, shaking her head in rejection. 'I'm not going to hide behind you, Leo, or lie, or pretend… What I did might have been wrong. Immoral in some people's eyes. But in my own eyes what would be even worse would be to lie about it. If people want to criticise or condemn me then I shall just have to accept that and be judged by them; accept the consequences of my behaviour.'

As he watched her and saw the fear fighting with the pride in her eyes Leo was filled with a mixture of admiration for her honesty and a helpless, aching tenderness for her vulnerability. She was so innocent, so naïve. He had to protect her from herself as much as from others.

As he swung his car into the drive to Ashton House he told her bluntly, 'You'll be crucified. Do you really want to throw away everything you've worked for, Jodi? The school, everything you've achieved there? Because I promise you that is what could happen.'

'There are other schools,' Jodi told him whilst she struggled to contain the pain his words were causing her.

He brought the car to a standstill and Jodi suddenly realised just where they were.

'Why have you brought me here?' she demanded indignantly. 'I wanted to go home.'

'You're my fiancée,' Leo told her silkily. 'This is your home.'

'No,' Jodi protested furiously. 'No... I...' She stopped and shook her head. 'We can't be engaged,' she told him helplessly. 'It isn't... We don't...'

'We have to be, Jodi,' Leo responded, shattering what was left of her composure by telling her, 'We can't afford not to be.'

'Take me home,' Jodi demanded wretchedly. 'To my home.' She added insistently, 'I've got a meeting tonight and if I don't go Myra Fanshawe is going to have a field-day.'

Jodi sank down onto her small sofa. The meeting had been every bit as bad as she had dreaded, with Myra

Fanshawe openly attempting to turn it into a debate on morality, plainly intent on embarrassing and humiliating Jodi just as much as she could.

Jodi had not been without her supporters, though; and several people had come up to her to congratulate her with genuine warmth on her engagement.

'It must have been very hard for both of you,' one of the parents had sympathised with her, 'with your fiancé potentially planning to close down the factory and you being committed to keeping it open. However,' she'd added with a smile, 'love, as they say, conquers all.'

Love might very well do so, Jodi reflected miserably now, but she was never likely to find out, since Leo quite plainly did not love her.

Her telephone rang, and this time, expecting Nigel, she picked up the receiver.

'You're a dark horse, aren't you?' were his opening words.

Jodi's heart sank.

'You've heard,' she guessed.

'Of course I've heard,' Nigel agreed wryly. 'The whole damned town has heard. Oh, and by the way, the parents have been on to me, wanting to know when they're going to get to meet your fiancé; I think my mother was on the phone to yours this afternoon.'

'What?' Jodi yelped in dismay. 'But I didn't want them to know…'

'What?' Nigel sounded confused.

'I mean I didn't want them to know yet,' Jodi hastily corrected herself. 'I mean I wanted to tell them myself and, what with everything happening so quickly…'

'Very quickly,' Nigel agreed with cousinly frankness

as he told her, 'I must say, I got a bit of a shock to learn that you'd spent the night with Leo at his hotel, especially in view of the fact that you treated him like public enemy number one at the dinner party.'

'Oh, Nigel…' Jodi began, and then stopped. How on earth could she explain to her cousin just what had happened? And how on earth could she explain to anyone else if she couldn't explain to Nigel?

When she had told Leo that she didn't want to involve herself in any kind of deceit or hide behind him she had meant what she had said, but now suddenly she realised that things were not quite so simple as that and that there were other people in her life whose views and feelings she had to take into account.

For several minutes after she had finished her call with Nigel she sat nibbling on her bottom lip before finally reaching for the phone.

She dialled Leo's number while her fingers trembled betrayingly.

When he answered just the sound of his voice was enough to make her stomach quiver in helpless reaction.

'It's Jodi,' she told him huskily. 'I've been thinking about what you said about our…about us being engaged and I…I agree…'

When Leo made no response her mouth went dry. What if he had changed his mind? What if he no longer cared about his own reputation or felt it was his responsibility, as he had put it, to protect hers?

And then she heard the click as the receiver was suddenly replaced and her heart lurched sickeningly. He *had* changed his mind!

Now what was she going to do?

Ten minutes later she curled herself up into her sofa in a forlorn little ball and then frowned as her front doorbell suddenly rang.

It would be Nigel again, no doubt, she decided wearily, getting up and padding barefoot to the door.

Only it wasn't Nigel, it was Leo, and as she stepped into her hallway she realised that he was carrying a bottle of champagne and two glasses.

'There's only one real way in my book an engaged couple should celebrate their commitment to one another,' Leo told her in a laconic drawl as she stared at him, 'and it involves privacy and a bed. Preferably a very large bed, and a very long period of privacy, but, since our engagement is not of the committed-for-life variety, this will have to be the alternative…'

As he finished speaking Leo looked at her, and Jodi knew that her face was burning—not with embarrassment or anger, she realised guiltily, but with the heat of the sheer longing his words had conjured up inside her.

'Of course,' Leo was suggesting softly, 'if you would prefer the first option…'

Jodi gave him an indignant look.

'What I'd prefer,' she told him, 'is not to be in this wretched situation at all.'

As she turned away from him Leo wondered what she would say if he told her just how dangerously close he was to picking her up in his arms and taking her somewhere very private and keeping her there until she was so full of the love he wanted to give her that…

That what? he asked himself in mental derision. That she would tell him that she loved him?

'How did the parents' meeting go?' he asked her

gently as he opened the champagne and poured them both a glass.

'Our engagement opened to mixed reviews,' Jodi told him wryly.

She wasn't going to tell him that Myra had informed her before she had left that she had decided it was her moral duty to inform the education authority of the situation.

'It's only a storm in a teacup.' Leo told her gently. 'Six months from now all this will be forgotten.'

That wasn't what he'd said earlier, Jodi thought, when he'd insisted that the only way to protect her job was for them to be engaged. Jodi bit her lip. Still, in six months' time Leo might have forgotten her but she would never be able to forget him.

Leo handed Jodi one of the glasses of champagne. Shaking her head, she refused to take it.

'No, I can't,' she told Leo bleakly.

To her relief he didn't press her, simply putting the glass down before asking her quietly, 'Because of the effect the cocktail at the hotel had on you? Jodi, from the smell of the jug, it contained the most lethal mixture of alcohol…'

Before he could finish Jodi was shaking her head. Oddly perhaps, in the circumstances, that had not been her reason for refusing the champagne.

'It isn't that,' she told him hollowly. 'It's that I hate having to pretend like this,' she told him simply. 'I abhor the deceit, and it just seems wrong somehow to celebrate in such a traditional and romantic way what is, after all, just a pretence…a fiction—'

'Jodi!'

Her honesty, so direct and unexpected, had brought a dangerous lump of emotion to Leo's throat. She looked so sad, so grave-eyed, so infinitely lovable that he wanted to take hold of her and…

'It doesn't…'

'Please, I don't want to discuss it any more.' Jodi told him, getting up and moving restlessly around the room.

She knew what he had been going to say. He had been going to say that under the circumstances their dishonesty didn't matter, and perhaps it didn't—to him, but it mattered to her. Most of all because there was something unbearably hurtful…something that was almost a desecration, about them cynically using a custom that should be so special and meaningful, and reserved only for those who truly loved each other and believed in that love, for their own practical ends.

'I…I'd like you to go now,' she told him chokily.

For a moment Leo hesitated. She looked so vulnerable, so fragile that he wanted to stay with her, to be with her, and she looked pale and tired as well…

Frowningly Leo checked and studied her again.

'Jodi. I know we've already been through this, but…if there is any chance that you could be wrong and you are pregnant, then I—'

'I am not pregnant,' Jodi interrupted him sharply.

If she had been wondering if perhaps she had misjudged him, her defences weakened by his unexpected sensitivity towards her and the situation she was in, then he had just given her the proof that she had not, she recognised bitterly.

If, too, she had been foolishly reading some kind of selfless and caring emotion into his arrival at her house tonight, and the things he had said to her, then she was certainly being made sharply aware of her error.

Of course there was only one reason he was here, only one reason he was concerned, and only one person he was concerned for! And that person certainly wasn't her, or the child he quite obviously did not want her to have.

'I'm tired,' she told him flatly. 'And I want you to go…'

As she spoke she was already heading for the front door.

Leo followed her.

As he got back in his car, he wondered what he had hoped to gain by his actions. Had he really thought that the simple act of calling to see her, bringing her champagne so that they could celebrate their fictitious engagement together, was in any way going to change her lack of love for him? How could it?

He might be a fool, he decided determinedly as he drove back to Ashton House, but he was still an honourable man and he damned well intended to make sure that both Jodi and her reputation were protected for just so long as they needed to be, whether she wanted it or not. As of now they were an engaged couple in the eyes of the outside world. And soon she would be wearing his ring to prove it!

CHAPTER NINE

UNABLE to stop herself, Jodi stared at the discreet, but flawlessly brilliant solitaire diamond engagement ring she was wearing.

She had protested long and loud against Leo's decision to buy her a ring, but he had refused to give in. In the end she had been the one to do that, partially out of sheer weariness and partially out of a cowardice she was loath to admit to.

Her aunt and uncle, Nigel's parents, had invited her and Leo to have dinner with them, and Jodi had known, as indeed Leo had warned her, that, being of an older generation, they would expect to see a newly engaged woman wearing a ring.

And it had been because of that and only because of that that she had allowed Leo to drive her to the city and buy her the diamond she was now wearing on her left hand.

At first she had tried to insist that she should wear something inexpensive and fake, but Leo had been so angered by her suggestion that she had been shocked into giving in.

She hadn't been allowed to know the price of the ring Leo had finally chosen for her. She had tried to opt for the smallest diamond the jeweller in the exclusive shop had shown her but Leo had simply insisted that she try on several rings before announcing that the one he liked best was the solitaire she was now wearing.

His choice had been another shock to Jodi, because it was in fact the very ring she would have chosen herself—under different circumstances. Now, as she sat next to him in his car, she couldn't help touching it a little self-consciously as the diamond caught the light and threw out a dazzling sparkle.

She wasn't exactly looking forward to this evening's dinner, much as she loved her aunt and uncle. They were a very traditional couple, especially her aunt, who was bound to ask all manner of difficult questions.

'You didn't have to do this,' she told Leo awkwardly as she gave him directions to their home. 'I could have come up with an excuse. After all, with the takeover...'

It was all over the village now that Jeremy Driscoll was being investigated by the revenue authorities, but even that gossip had not been enough to silence Myra Fanshawe's repeated references to her concern over Jodi's behaviour.

'You want to speak to Mr Jefferson?' Leo's new secretary at the factory asked the woman caller who had asked to speak to Leo. The woman had explained that she hadn't been able to get through to him on his mobile and that she hadn't heard from him in several days.

'Oh, I'm sorry, but he isn't here at the moment. And I expect he's switched off his mobile, because he's gone to meet his fiancée.'

On the other end of the line, Leo's mother, Luisa Jefferson, almost dropped her receiver.

'His fiancée,' she repeated. 'Oh, well, yes…of course.'

'Shall I tell him you called?' Leo's secretary asked her helpfully.

'Er—no…that won't be necessary,' Luisa informed her.

Replacing the receiver, she went in search of her husband, whom she found seated on a sun lounger beside their pool.

'I have to go to England to see Leonardo,' she informed him.

The evening had gone surprisingly well. Leo had laughed obligingly at her uncle's jokes and praised her aunt's cooking with such a genuineness that it was plain that they were both already ready to welcome him with open arms into the family.

Jodi, with the benefit of far more objectivity at her disposal, watched the proceedings with pardonable cynicism.

'So,' Jodi heard her aunt asking archly, once they were in her sitting room with their after-dinner coffee. 'what about the wedding? Have you made any plans as yet?'

'No—'

'Yes—'

As they both spoke at once her aunt looked from Leo's smiling face to Jodi's set one with an understandably baffled expression.

'We've only just got engaged,' Jodi defended her denial.

'I'd marry Jodi tomorrow if she'd agree,' Leo told her

aunt with a wicked, glinting smile in Jodi's direction that made her want to scream. He was enjoying this. She could tell.

'Well, of course Jodi will want to wait until her parents return,' her aunt said lovingly, before asking, 'And what about your parents, Leo?'

'I want to take Jodi out to Italy to meet them just as soon as I can,' Leo responded truthfully, 'but I already know that they will love her as much as I do.' And then, before Jodi could guess what he intended to do, he leaned towards her, taking one of her hands and enfolding it tenderly between both of his before bending his head to brush his mouth against hers.

Jodi could feel the quivering, out-of-control wanting begin deep down inside her the moment he touched her; it shocked and frightened her, and it made her feel very angry as well. She felt angry with Leo for making her love him, and angry with herself too, and yet she still couldn't stop herself from closing her eyes and wishing that all of this was real; that he did love her; that their futures really lay together.

Jodi's aunt and uncle said goodbye to them at their front door. Leo had placed his arm around Jodi as they walked to the door, and he kept it there whilst they walked to the car, even though it was parked out of direct sight of the house.

'You can let go of me now,' Jodi told him as they reached the car. 'No one can see us.'

'What if I don't want to let go of you?' Leo demanded softly.

There was just enough moonlight for Jodi to be able

to see the hot glint of desire that glittered in his eyes as he looked down at her.

Shakily she backed up against the car, her heart hammering against her ribs—but not with fear.

'Leo!' she protested, but he was already sliding his hands slowly up over the bare flesh of her arms. His touch made her tremble with desire, her emotions so tightly strung that she was afraid of what she might do. If just the casual caress of his hands could make her feel like this…

But she was so hungry for him. So very, very hungry!

'We're engaged,' Leo breathed against her ear. 'Remember…we're allowed to do this, expected to…and, God knows, I want to!' he told her, his voice suddenly changing and becoming so fiercely charged with sensuality that it made Jodi shiver all over again.

'But our engagement isn't real,' she told him.

'It may not be, but this most certainly is…' Leo growled.

And then he was holding her, one large hand on her waist, whilst the other cupped her face, tilting it, holding it. Jodi held her breath as she felt him looking at her, and then he was bending his head, and his mouth was on hers and…

When had she lifted her own hand towards his jaw? When had she parted her mouth for the hot, silent passion of his kiss? When had she closed that final tiny distance between them, her free hand gripping his arm, her fingers digging into its muscle as the ache inside her pounded down her defences?

'What is it about you that makes me feel like this?' Leo was demanding thickly, but Jodi knew that the words, raw with longing, helpless in the face of so much desire, might just as well have been her own.

She knew too that if Leo was to take her home with him now there was no way she would be able to resist the temptation he was offering her. Right now she wanted him more than she wanted her pride, her self-respect, or her sanity!

'Right now,' she heard Leo telling her thickly, 'I could…'

An owl hooted overhead, startling them both, and abruptly Leo was moving back from her, leaving her feeling cold and alone as he turned to unlock the car doors.

Jodi stared mutely at the package she was holding in her hand. She had bought it when she had been in the city with Leo, the day he had taken her there to get her engagement ring. She had seen the chemist's shop and had managed to slip away to get what she had begun to fear she needed.

That had been well over three weeks ago now and… Reluctantly she turned the package over and read the instructions. It was just a precaution, she told herself firmly, that was all.

It was practically impossible that her suspicions were anything more than simple guilty anxiety. Sometimes odd things happened to bodies, especially when their owners were under the kind of stress she was under right now.

Myra had informed her that her committee had felt that they had no option other than to report their concerns over her behaviour to the education authority, and that was exactly what they had done.

Jodi had already had to undergo an extremely difficult and worrying telephone interview, and now she was waiting to see what they were going to do.

At best, she would simply get a black mark against her for having been reported, and at worst… Jodi didn't want to think about what the worst-case scenario could be.

Jodi was under no delusions about the seriousness of the situation she was in, but right now…

She looked unhappily at the pregnancy-testing kit she was holding. She didn't really need to do it, did she? After all, it was only a matter of a few days late—well, a week or so—and she was one hundred per cent sure that that unwelcome feeling of nausea she had been experiencing recently was simply nerves and tension.

And the craving for anchovies?

She was careful about her health and followed a low-fat, low-salt diet. Her body had decided that it needed salt, obviously. Obviously!

Taking a deep breath, Jodi took the kit out of its packet. It was going to show negative, she knew that. She knew it.

Positive. Jodi stared at the testing kit, unable and unwilling to accept the result it was showing. Her hand shook as she picked it up for the tenth time and stared at it.

It must be wrong. A faulty kit, or she had done something wrong. Panic began to fill her. She couldn't be pregnant. She couldn't be!

Leo's baby! She was going to have Leo's baby! Why on earth was she smiling? Jodi wondered in disbelief as she saw her reflection in her bathroom mirror.

This was quite definitely not smiling territory…

Downstairs she heard her post coming through the letterbox. The school term had finally come to an end, so she did not have to rush to get to work. She finished dressing and went downstairs, collecting her letters on the way.

There was a card from her parents, and a whole bunch of unsolicited trash mail.

Jodi had to sit down before she could bring herself to look at it. Her parents. No need to ask herself how they would feel about what had happened. There would be gossip, there was bound to be, and she knew that life as an unmarried mother was not the life they had envisaged for her or for their grandchild. If she was honest it was not the life she had ever envisaged for herself either. Jodi's throat felt tight and dry.

She had asked her aunt and uncle not to say anything about her engagement to her parents if they spoke to them, explaining—quite truthfully—that she wanted to tell them herself, in person.

Then, knowing that they weren't due home for another two months at least, she had convinced herself that she had plenty of time to get her life back to some kind of normality before their return, but now…!

Her parents would love her and support her no matter what she did, she knew that, and her baby, their grandchild, no matter how unconventional its conception, would be welcomed and loved. But there would be gossip and disapproval, and, with Leo continuing to be a presence locally through the factory, Jodi knew there was no way that she could stay. How could she? How could she inflict such a situation on her family, and as for her baby…how could she allow him or her to grow up suffering the humiliation of knowing that he or she had been rejected by their father?

No, life would be much easier for all those she loved if she simply moved away.

After all, she decided proudly, it wasn't as though it was her teaching skills that were in question.

And as for the fact that she would be a single mother, well, a hundred or more miles away, just who was going to be concerned or interested in the malicious criticism of Myra Fanshawe?

'Mother!'

Stunned, Leo stared into the familiar face of his very unexpected visitor as he answered his front doorbell. He had told his parents that he had moved to a rented property in Frampton and that he would be living there until he had sorted out all the complications with the business. He knew he had not been able to keep his promise to go and visit his parents again, in Italy, but he had certainly not expected to have his mother turn up on his doorstep.

'Where's Dad?' he asked her, frowning as he watched her taxi disappearing down his drive.

'I have come on my own,' his mother told him. 'I cannot stay more than a few days,' she added, 'but I am sure if we apply ourselves that will be sufficient time for me to meet your fiancée.'

Leo, who had been in the act of picking up his mother's case, suddenly straightened up to look at her.

Several responses flashed son-like through his brain, but his mother was his mother, and one very astute woman, as he had had over thirty years to find out and appreciate.

'I think you'd better come inside,' he told her steadily as he took hold of her arm.

'I think I'd better,' his mother agreed wryly, pausing only to tell him, 'This house is a very good family house, Leonardo; it is well built and strong. Children will grow very well here, and I like the garden, although it needs much work. Is she a gardener, this fiancée of yours? I hope so, for a woman who nourishes her plants will nourish her husband and her children.'

His mother was the only person in the world who called him Leonardo with that particular emphasis on the second syllable of his name, Leo reflected as he ushered her into the hallway and saw her glance thoughtfully at the vase of flowers Jodi had arranged on the hall table earlier in the week.

Leo had taken her home with him prior to visiting her aunt and uncle so that he could drop off some business papers. His telephone had rung, and the consequent call had taken some time, and when he had finally rejoined her he had discovered that she had collected some wind-blown flowers from the garden and arranged them in a vase.

'It seems such a shame to just let them die unappreciated and unloved,' she had told him defensively.

'So, she is a home-maker, this fiancée of yours,' his mother pronounced, suddenly very Italian as she subjected Jodi's handiwork to a critical maternal examination. 'Does she cook for you?'

'Mamma!' Leo sighed, leading her into the kitchen. 'There is something that you need to know…and it is going to take quite some time for me to tell you.'

'There is,' Luisa Jefferson informed her son firmly, 'only one thing I need to know and it will take you very little time to tell me. Do you love her?'

For a moment she thought that he wasn't going to reply. He was a man, after all, she reminded herself ruefully, not a boy, but then he grimaced and pushed his hair back off his face in a gesture that reminded her of her own husband before he admitted, 'Unfortunately, yes, I do.'

'Unfortunately?' she queried delicately.

'There is a problem,' Leo told her.

His mother's unexpected arrival was a complication he had not foreseen, but now that she was here he was discovering to his own amusement and with a certain sense of humility that he actually wanted to talk to her about Jodi, to share with her not just his discovery of his love for Jodi but also his confusion and concern.

'In love there is always a problem,' his mother responded humorously. 'If there is not then it is not love. So, tell me what your particular problem is… Her father does not like you? That is how a father is with his daughter. I remember my own father—'

'Mamma, I haven't met Jodi's father yet, and anyway…I have told you that I love Jodi, but what I have not told you yet is that she does not love me.'

'Not love you? But you are engaged, and I must say, Leonardo, that I did not enjoy learning of your engagement from your secretary; however—'

'Mamma please,' Leo interrupted her firmly. 'Let me explain.'

When he did Leo was careful to edit his story so that his mother would not, as he had initially done, jump to any unfair or judgemental conclusions about Jodi, but he could tell that she was not entirely satisfied with his circumspect rendition of events.

'You love her and she does not love you, but she has agreed to become engaged to you to protect her reputation, since by accident she fell asleep in your hotel suite and was seen leaving early in the morning?'

Her eyebrows lifted in a manner that conveyed a whole range of emotions, most of which made Leo's heart sink.

'I am very interested to meet this fiancée of yours, Leonardo.'

Leo drew in his breath.

'Well, as to that, I cannot promise that you will,' he began. 'I have to go to London on business this afternoon, and I had planned to stay there for several days. You could come with me if you wish and do some shopping,' he offered coaxingly.

His mother gave him an old-fashioned look.

'I live in Italy now, Leonardo. We have Milan. I do not need to shop. No, whilst you are in London I shall stay here and wait for you to return,' she pronounced. 'Where does she live, this fiancée of yours?' she asked determinedly.

Leo sighed.

'She lives here in Frampton. Mamma, I know you mean well,' he told her gently. 'But please, I would ask you not to…to…'

'To interfere?' she supplied drily for him. 'I am your mother, Leonardo, and I am Italian…'

'I understand,' Leo told her gently. 'But I hope you will understand that, since I know that Jodi does not love me, it can only cause me a great deal of humiliation and unwanted embarrassment if it was to be brought to her attention that I love her, and quite naturally I do not wish to subject either of us to those emotions, which means…' He took a deep breath. 'What I have told you, Mamma, is for your ears only, and I would ask that it remains so, and that you do not seek Jodi out to discuss any of this with her. I do not want her to be upset or embarrassed in any way, by anyone.'

For a moment he thought that she was going to refuse, and then she took a deep breath herself and agreed.

'I shall not seek her out.'

'Thank you.'

As he leaned forward to kiss her Leo heard his mother complaining, 'When I prayed that you would fall in love I did not mean for something like this to happen!'

'You want grandchildren, I know.' Leo smiled, struggling to lighten the mood of their conversation.

'I want grandchildren,' his mother agreed, 'but what I want even more is to see you sharing your life with the person you love; I want to see your life being enriched and made complete by the same kind of love your father and I have shared. I want for you what every mother wants for her child,' she told him fiercely, her eyes darkening with maternal protection and love. 'I want you to be happy.'

* * *

His mother couldn't want those things she had described to him any more than he wanted them for himself, Leo acknowledged a couple of hours later as he drove towards Frampton *en route* for London. He had left his mother busily dead-heading roses, whilst refusing to listen to any suggestion he tried to make that, since he could not say categorically when he would be back, she might as well return home to Italy.

In the village the temptation to turn the car towards Jodi's cottage was so strong that Leo found he was forced to grip the steering wheel to control it.

His life would never be happy now, he reflected morosely.

Not without Jodi in it. Not without her love, her presence, her warmth; not without her!

Jodi stared at her computer screen, carefully reading the resignation letter she had been working on for the last three hours. Now it was done, and there was nothing to stop her from printing it off and posting it, but somehow she could not bring herself to do so—not yet.

She got up and paced the floor, and then on a sudden impulse she picked up her keys and headed for the door.

It was a beautiful, warm summer's day, and the gardens of the cottages that lined her part of the village street overflowed with flowers, creating an idyllic scene.

Normally just the sight of them would have been enough to lift her spirits and make her think how fortunate she was to live where she did and to be the person she was, a person who had a job she loved, a family she loved, a life she loved.

But not a man she loved... The man she loved... And not the job she loved either—soon. But, though the school and her work were important to her, they did not come anywhere near matching the intensity of the love she had for Leo.

Leo. Busy with her thoughts, Jodi had walked automatically towards the school.

There was a bench opposite it, outside the church, and Jodi sat down on it, looking across at the place that meant so much to her and which she had worked so hard for.

She was not so vain that she imagined that there were no other teachers who could teach as ably, if not more so, as she had done herself, but would another teacher love the school the way she had done? Would another woman love Leo the way she did?

Her eyes filled with tears, and as she reached hurriedly into her bag for a tissue she was aware of a woman sitting down on the bench next to her.

'Are you all right, only I could not help but notice that you are crying?'

The woman's comment caught Jodi off guard. It was, not, after all, a British national characteristic to comment on a stranger's grief, no matter how sympathetic towards them and curious about them one might be.

Proudly Jodi lifted her head and turned to look at the woman.

'I'm fine, thank you,' she told her, striving to sound both cool and dismissive, but to her horror fresh tears were filling her eyes, spilling down over her cheeks, and her voice had begun to wobble alarmingly. Jodi knew that any moment now she was going to start howling like a child with a skinned knee.

'No, you aren't. You are very upset and you are also very angry with me for saying so, but sometimes it can help to talk to a stranger,' the other woman was telling her gently, before adding, 'I saw you looking at the school…'

'Yes,' Jodi acknowledged. 'I…I teach there. At least, I did…but now…' She bit her lip.

'You have decided to leave,' her interlocuter guessed. 'You have perhaps fallen in love and are to move away and you are crying because you know you will miss this very beautiful place.'

Although her English was perfect, Jodi sensed that there was something about her questioner that said that she was not completely English. She must be a visitor, someone who was passing through the area, someone she, Jodi, would never, ever see again.

Suddenly, for some inexplicable reason Jodi discovered that she did want to talk to her, to unburden herself, and to seek if not an explanation for what was happening to her, then at least the understanding of another human being. Something told her that this woman would be understanding. It was written in the warmth of her eyes and the encouragement of her smile.

'I am in love,' Jodi admitted, 'but it is not… He…the man I love…he doesn't love me.'

'No? Then he is a fool,' the other woman pronounced firmly. 'Any man who does not love a woman who loves him is a fool.' She gave Jodi another smile and Jodi realised that she was older than she had first imagined from her elegant appearance, probably somewhere in her late fifties.

'Why does he not love you? Has he told you?'

Jodi found herself starting to smile.

'Sort of… He has indicated that…'

'But you are lovers?' the woman pressed Jodi with a shrewdness and perspicacity that took Jodi's breath away.

She could feel her colour starting to rise as she admitted, 'Yes, but…but he didn't… It was at my instigation… I…' She stopped and bit her lip again. There were some things she could just not bring herself to put into words, but her companion, it seemed, had no such hang-ups.

'You seduced him!'

She sounded more amused than shocked, and when Jodi looked at her she could actually see that there was laughter in the other woman's dark eyes.

'Well…I…sort of took him by surprise. I'd fallen asleep in his bed, you see, and he didn't know I was there, and when I woke up and realised that he was and…' Jodi paused. There was something cathartic about what she was doing, about being able to confide in another person, being able to explain for the first time just what she had felt and why she had felt it.

'I'd seen him earlier in the hotel foyer,' she began in a low voice. 'I didn't know who he was, not then, but I…'

She stopped.

'You were attracted to him?' the other woman offered helpfully.

Gratefully Jodi nodded.

'Yes,' she agreed vehemently. 'He affected me in a way that no other man had ever done. I just sort of looked at him and...' Her voice became low and strained. 'I know it sounds foolish, but I believe I fell in love with him there and then at first sight...and I suppose when I woke up and found myself in bed with him my...my body must have remembered how I'd felt then, earlier, and.... But he...well, he thought that I was there because... And then later, when he realised the truth, he told me... He asked me...' Her voice tailed off. 'I should never have done what I did, and I felt so ashamed.'

'For falling in love?' the older woman asked her, giving a small shrug. 'Why should you be ashamed of that? It is the most natural thing in the world.'

'Falling in love might be,' Jodi agreed, 'but my behaviour, the way I...' Jodi shook her head primly and had to swallow hard as she tried to blink away her threatening tears.

Her companion, though, was not deterred by her silence and demanded determinedly, 'So, you have met a man with whom you have fallen in love. You say he does not love you, but are you so sure?'

'Positive,' Jodi insisted equally determinedly.

'And now you sit here weeping because you cannot bear the thought of your life without him,' the older woman guessed.

'Yes, because of that, and...and for other reasons,' Jodi admitted.

'Other reasons?'

Jodi drew an unsteady breath.

'When...after...after he had realised that I was not as

he had first imagined, well, when he realised the truth about me he warned me that if…if by some mischance I…there should be…repercussions from our intimacy then he would expect me to…to…'

Jodi bit down on her lip and looked away as fresh tears welled in her eyes.

'I told myself that it was impossible for me to love a man like that, a man who would callously destroy the life of his child. How could I love him?'

She shook her head in bewilderment, whilst her companion demanded in a disbelieving voice, 'I cannot believe what you are saying. It is impossible; unthinkable…'

'I can assure you that it is the truth,' Jodi insisted shakily. 'I didn't want to believe it myself, but he told me. He said categorically that something would have to be arranged. Of course, then I really did believe that it was impossible that I could be—but now…'

As Jodi wrapped her arms protectively around her still slender body her companion questioned sharply, 'You are pregnant? You are to have…this man's child?'

Numbly Jodi nodded. 'Yes. And I am also facing an enquiry because I was seen leaving his hotel suite, and other things. And, as a head teacher, it is of course expected that I should… That was why he said we should get engaged, because of the gossip and to protect me.'

As she spoke Jodi raised her left hand, where Leo's diamond glistened in the sunlight nearly as brightly as Jodi's own falling tears. 'But how can he offer to protect me and yet want to destroy his own child?'

'What will you do?' the other woman was asking her quietly.

Jodi drew a deep breath.

'I plan to move away and start a fresh life somewhere else.'

'Without telling your lover about his child?'

After everything she, Jodi, had told her, how could she sound so disapproving? Jodi wondered.

'How can I tell him when he has already told me that he doesn't want it? ''Something will have to be arranged''—that is what he said to me, and I can imagine what kind of arrangement he meant. But I would rather die myself than do anything to hurt my baby.' Jodi was getting angry now, all her protective maternal instincts coming to the fore.

She had no idea how long she had been sitting on the bench confiding in this stranger, but now she felt so tired and drained that she longed to go home and lie down.

As she got up she gave her unknown companion a tired smile.

'Thank you for listening to me.' She turned to go, but as she did so the other woman stood up too, and to Jodi's shock took hold of her in a warm embrace, hugging her almost tenderly.

'Have courage,' she told her. 'All will be well. I am sure of it.'

As she smiled comfortingly at her, Jodi had the oddest feeling that there was something about the woman that was somehow familiar, but that, of course, was ridiculous. Jodi knew that she had never seen her before.

CHAPTER TEN

'LEONARDO, you are to drive back to Frampton right now.'

'Mamma,' Leo protested.

'Right now, Leonardo!' Luisa Jefferson insisted. 'And before you do, could you please explain to me how it is that poor Jodi believes that you wish not only to deny yourself as a father the child you have created with her, but that you wish to deny it the right to life as well?'

'What...what child? Jodi told me there would be no child.'

'And she told me that there will be, not that I needed telling; I could see it in her eyes...her face. You have hurt her very badly. She truly believes that you do not love her and she is hurting because she thinks she loves a man who would destroy her child.'

'I cannot understand how she could possibly think that!' Leo protested. 'I would never—'

'I know that, of course,' his mother interrupted him, 'but your Jodi, it seems, does not. "Something will have to be arranged", is apparently what you told her.'

'What...? Yes...of course...but I meant...I meant that if she was pregnant we would have to get married,' Leo told his mother grimly. 'How on earth could she interpret that as...?'

'She is the one you should be speaking to, Leonardo,

and not me. And you had better be quick. She plans to leave, and once she does…'

'I'm on my way,' Leo announced. 'If you dare to say anything to her until I get there you will be banned from seeing your grandchild until he or she is at least a day old.'

When she replaced her telephone receiver Luisa Jefferson was smiling beatifically.

Picking it up again, she dialled the number of her home in Italy. When her husband, Leo's father, answered she greeted him, 'Hello, Grandpapa!'

'Oh, come on, Jodi, I'm starving and I hate going out for dinner on my own.'

'But, Nigel, I'm tired,' Jodi had protested when Nigel had rung her unexpectedly, demanding that she go out to eat with him, 'and surely you could ask one of your many girlfriends.'

But in the end she had given in and she had even managed not to protest when, having picked her up in his car, he had suddenly realised that he must have dropped his wallet on her footpath and gone back to pick it up.

Now, though, at barely ten o'clock, she was exhausted, and yawning, and she couldn't blame Nigel for glancing surreptitiously at his watch.

She hadn't been the most entertaining of companions.

Even so, his brisk, 'Right, let's go,' after he had checked his watch a second time made her blink a little.

'Don't you want to finish your coffee?' she asked him.

'What? Oh, no…I can see you're tired,' he offered.

He had been in an odd mood all evening, Jodi recognised, on edge and avoiding looking directly at her. But she was too tired to ask him what was wrong, instead allowing him to bustle her out into the car park and into his car.

Once they reached her house, Jodi asked him if he wanted to come in, but rather to her surprise he shook his head.

As she heard him drive away Jodi decided that she might as well go straight upstairs to bed.

In Jodi's sitting room the light from her computer screen lit up the small space around it, but Jodi was too exhausted to bother glancing into the room, and so she didn't see the smiling babies tumbling in somersaults all over her computer screen around the large typed message that read, 'I love ya, baby, and your mamma too!'

Once upstairs, she went straight to the bathroom, cleaning off her make-up and showering before padding naked into the darkened bedroom she was too familiar with to need to switch on the light.

She was already virtually asleep before she even pulled back the duvet and crawled into the longed-for comfort of her bed—the good old-fashioned king-size bed that almost filled the room and which Nigel had wickedly insisted on buying her as a cousinly moving-in gift. It was a bed that no one other than her had ever slept in—though someone was quite definitely sleeping in it now!

It was a someone she would have known anywhere, even without the benefit of being able to see his face. She would have known him simply by his scent, by the subtle air of Leo-ness that enfolded her whenever she was in his presence.

Leo! Leo was here, fast asleep in her bed! No, that just wasn't possible! She was going mad. She was day-dreaming…fantasising!

'Mmm.' Jodi gasped as a decidedly realistic pair of warm arms wrapped themselves firmly around her body, imprisoning it against their owner's wonderfully familiar maleness.

'Leo!' Jodi whispered his name weakly, her voice shot through with the rainbow colours of what she was feeling.

'How could you possibly believe that I don't love you?' she heard him demanding thickly. 'I'm mad about you! Crazily, insanely, irredeemably and forever in love with you. I thought you were the one who didn't love me. But then they do say that pregnancy affects a woman's ability to reason logically…'

'Leo!' Jodi protested, her voice even weaker. She couldn't take in what was happening and, even more importantly, had no idea how it had come about. 'How? What?' she began, but Leo was in no mood to answer questions.

His lips were feathering distracting little kisses all along her jaw, her throat, her neck. He was whispering words of love and praise in her ear; he was smoothing a tender hand over the still flat plane of her belly, whilst his voice thickened openly with emotion as he whispered to her, 'How could you think I didn't want our child, Jodi?'

She tried to answer him but the seeking urgency of his mouth on hers prevented her, and, anyway, what did questions, words matter when there was this, and Leo, and the wonderful private world of tender loving they were creating between them?

'The first time we met you stole your way into my bed and my heart,' Leo said to her as he touched her with gentle, adoring hands, the true extent of his passion only burning through when he kissed her mouth. 'And there hasn't been a single day, a single hour since then when I haven't ached for you, longed for you,' he groaned. 'Not a single minute when my love for you hasn't tormented and tortured me!'

Jodi could see as well as feel the tension pulsing through his nerve-endings as he reined in his sensual hunger for her.

'Now it's my turn,' he told her. 'Thanks to Nigel, I have stolen my way into your bed, and I warn you, Jodi, I do not intend to leave it until I have stolen my way into your heart as well, and heard from your own lips that you intend to let me stay there, in your heart, in your life and the life of our child—for ever!'

'For ever,' Jodi whispered back in wonder as she touched the damp stains on his face that betrayed the intensity of his emotions.

'I might have thought that loving you was torture,' Leo told her rawly, 'but now I know that real torture would be to lose you. Do you know what it was like finding you in my bed, having you reach out and touch me, love me?' Leo was groaning achingly. 'Shall I show you?'

Hadn't her mother always warned her against the danger of playing with fire?

Right now, did she care?

'Show me!' she encouraged him boldly.

She could hear the maleness in his voice as well as feel it in his body as he told her triumphantly, 'Right.'

They made love softly and gently, aware of and awed by their role as new parents-to-be, and then fiercely and passionately as they claimed for themselves the right to be lovers for themselves.

They made love in all the ways Jodi had dreamed in her most private and secret thoughts—and then in some ways she had never imagined.

And then, as it started to become light, after Leo had told her over and over how much he loved her, how much he loved both of them, and insisted that she tell him that she returned his feelings, Jodi demanded, 'Explain to me what has happened... How...?' She stopped and shook her head in mute bewilderment. 'It's almost as though a fairy godmother has waved her wand and...'

Propping himself up one elbow, Leo looked tenderly down at her.

'That was no fairy godmother,' he quipped ruefully. 'That was my mother!'

'What?' Jodi sat bolt upright in bed, taking the duvet with her, only momentarily diverted by the magnificent sight of Leo's naked body. Long enough, though, to heave a blissful sigh of pleasure and run her fingertip lazily down the length of him, before finally playfully teasing it through the silky thickness of his body hair whilst watching with awed fascination as his body showed an unexpectedly vigorous response to her attentions.

'Don't go there,' Leo warned her humorously. 'Not unless you mean it.'

Hastily removing her hand, Jodi insisted, 'I want to hear what's been going on.'

Leo heaved a sigh of mock-disappointment.

'My mother flew over from Italy to see me. She'd heard about our engagement from my new secretary and not unnaturally, I suppose, given the nature of mothers, she decided that she wanted to meet my fiancée—the girl who had answered her prayers and those of the village wise woman, whose skills she had commissioned on my behalf. No, don't ask, not yet,' he warned Jodi, shaking his head.

'She wanted to know all about you, and I naturally obliged—well, up to a point. I told her that I'd fallen totally and completely in love with you,' he admitted to Jodi, his voice and demeanour suddenly wholly serious. 'And I told her too that you did not return my feelings. As you know, I had to go to London on business, so I invited her to go with me but she refused. She said she preferred to stay where she was until she was due to take up her return flight. I had my suspicions then, knowing her as I do, and so I made her promise that she would not under any circumstances attempt to seek you out—and she promised me that she wouldn't, but it seems from what she has told me that fate intervened.

'She had gone for a walk in the village, when, as she put it, she saw a young woman in distress. Naturally she wanted to help, so she sat down beside you and—'

'That was your mother?' Jodi interrupted. Now she began to understand!

'I felt that there was something familiar about her,' she admitted, 'but I just couldn't put my finger on what it was.

'Mmm.' She smiled lovingly as Leo broke off from his explanations to kiss her with slow thoroughness. 'Mmm…' she repeated. 'Go on.'

'With what?' Leo teased her. 'The kisses or the explanation?'

'Both!' Jodi answered him promptly.

'But the rest of the explanation first, please, otherwise…'

Laughing, Leo continued, 'Just as soon as she had left you she rang me in London, demanding to know what on earth I had said to you to give you the impression that I wouldn't want our child! Jodi…' Gravely Leo looked at her, his eyes dark with pain. 'How could you have thought that I…?'

'You said something would have to be arranged,' Jodi defended herself firmly.

'Yes, but the arrangement I had in mind was not a visit to—' He broke off, so patently unable to even say the words that Jodi instinctively wrapped her arms tightly around him, as filled with a desire to protect him as she had been to protect their unborn child.

'The place I had in mind for you to visit was a church so that we could be married,' Leo told her hoarsely. 'That was what I was talking about. Even if I had not loved you I could never, would never… Thank heavens my mother knows me better than you seem to! Still, at least that puts us on an equal footing now. I originally misjudged you and now you have misjudged me, and, that being the case, I suggest that we draw a line beneath it and start again.'

He took a deep breath. 'I love you, Jodi Marsh, and I want to marry you.'

Jodi began to smile.

'I love you too, Leo Jefferson,' she responded, 'and I want to marry you…'

'Now, getting back to the matter of those kisses…' Leo told her wickedly as he drew her back down against his body, and rolled her gently beneath him.

Several hours later, Jodi smiled a very special smile to herself. 'And so Nigel left his key for you to find under the flowerpot by the front door?' she questioned Leo as she licked the jam from her toast off her fingers and looked across the bedroom at him as he walked out of the bathroom, freshly showered, smiling as he watched her eating her toast hungrily.

'Yes; he took a considerable amount of persuading, though, and he was terrified that you might suspect that something was going on.'

'I probably would have done if I hadn't been so tired,' Jodi admitted.

Watching her, Leo could feel his love for her filling him. It had been a tremendous risk, short-circuiting things by installing himself in her bed, but thankfully it had worked, allowing them to talk openly and honestly to one another.

As Jodi finished her late breakfast he reached for her again, drawing her towards him, burying his face against her body before wrapping his arms around her and kissing her tenderly.

When his mobile rang he cursed and reached for it, starting to switch it off and then stopping as he murmured to Jodi, 'It's my mother.'

'Hello, Mamma.' He answered the call and from

where she was standing Jodi could hear his mother quite plainly, 'Leonardo, it is not you I wish to speak to but my daughter-in-law-to-be, your delightful Jodi. You have had her to yourself for quite long enough. Put her on the phone to me this minute, if you please, whilst I tell her about this wonderful shop for all things *bambino* in Milan.'

EPILOGUE

'AND you still intend to teach at your school?'

Over her mother-in-law's head Jodi smiled into Leo's eyes as Luisa Jefferson cooed ecstatically over the bundle that was her baby grandson.

It was Leo and Jodi's wedding anniversary and they had flown out to Italy to stay with Leo's parents.

'For the time being, but only on a part-time basis,' Jodi replied.

All the letters of support she had received from her pupils' parents had thrilled Jodi, and, as she and Leo had agreed, she owed it to everyone who had supported her to stay on at the school until the right kind of replacement for her had been found.

'After all,' she had smiled to Leo, 'our own children will be going there.'

Leo had bought Ashton House, and Jodi had spent all her free time in the months before baby Nicholas Lorenzo's birth organising its renovation and redecoration.

Leo's parents had flown over to Frampton from Italy for the baby's birth, and a special extra guest had been invited to the large family christening, much to Leo's wry amusement and his mother's open delight.

'Her name is Maria, and she says that she will make a special potion for you to drink that will guarantee the happiness of you and Leonardo and your children,' Luisa

Jefferson had whispered to Jodi when she had introduced her village's wise woman to her.

'My happiness is already guaranteed,' Jodi had responded with a shining smile of trust and love in her husband's direction. 'Just so long as I have Leo!'

* * * *

Look out for Penny Jordan's
latest Modern romance in March 2006
with *The Italian Duke's Wife.*

THE ENGLISH BRIDE

by

Margaret Way

CHAPTER ONE

IT WAS getting on towards late afternoon when Grant Cameron set the chopper down on the rear lawn of Kimbara as sweetly as a pelican setting down on a lagoon. Winds created by the whirling fanlike rotor stirred up a mini dust storm mixed with grass clippings and a sea of spent blossom from the nearby bauhinias but that quickly abated as the long blades wound to a standstill. Grant completed his interior checks and took off his headset, preparatory to jumping down onto the grass.

This was historic Kimbara Station, desert stronghold of the Kinross family since the early days of settlement; the nearest neighbour to his own family station, Opal Downs, some hundred miles to the north-east.

His older brother, Rafe, much loved and much respected, was currently on honeymoon in the United States with his new bride and love of his life, Alison Cameron, nee Kinross. Rafe ran the station. He, Grant, was making a very successful business out of his own aerial mustering service, operating out of Opal. It had suited both brothers well. Rafe was the cattleman. He was the pilot.

He'd always been mad about aircraft even since he'd been a kid. Even the inconsolable grief of losing their beloved parents to a light aircraft crash hadn't killed his love of flying. With an outback so vast flying was a way of life in Australia. The tragedy had to be survived.

Grant reached for his akubra and slung it on at an unconsciously rakish angle. The sun still had a powerful kick in it and he couldn't altogether forget his tawny colouring, a Cameron trademark. ''A pride of lions'' was the way people used to describe his dad, Douglas Cameron, and his two sons, Rafe and Grant.

A pride of lions!

For a moment a terrible sadness constricted his chest. He wished with all his heart his dad was still alive. Mum and Dad. They never got to see him make such a success of himself. They would have been proud. He had always been the younger brother, a bit of a wildcat trying to develop in his brother's shadow. Rafe was born responsible, ready to take over from their father.

Out of the helicopter Grant made a quick circuit of the aircraft, his eyes always checking for the slightest sign of possible trouble though the fleet was scrupulously maintained. The yellow fuselage with its broad blue stripe and company logo in blue and gold gave off a crackle as the metal cooled down. He patted the insignia with satisfaction and made off for the house.

It had been an exhausting day driving a whole heap of cantankerous, overheated cattle in from the isolated Sixty Mile out near Jarajara, a single huge sentinel granite dome that marked Kimbara's western border to the camp Brod's men had set up out near Mareeba Waters with its winding water courses. Camp would be shifted as the muster went on. The men were expected to be out for the best past of three weeks. What he needed now was a long cold beer and to feast his tired eyes on a beautiful woman.

Francesca

Not necessarily in that order he thought dryly. Francesca was occupying far too many of his thoughts these days. Lady Francesca de Lyle, first cousin to Brod Kinross, master of Kimbara and brother to Ally, his new sister-in-law. Cameron and Kinross were legendary names in this part of the world, pioneering giants.

Now with the marriage of Rafe and Alison the two families were finally united to everyone's great satisfaction except maybe Lainie Rhodes of Victoria Springs who had nurtured an outsize crush on Rafe since puberty struck her. Not that Lainie wasn't good marriage material but there had never been anyone else for Rafe but his Ally.

The unbreakable bond between them had been forged in their childhood out of tempered steel. Now they were man and wife, deliriously happy from all accounts but Grant realised full well he had better start making plans.

Big as Opal's homestead was he had no intention of intruding on his brother's and Ally's privacy. They would want the homestead to themselves no matter how much they tried to reassure him Opal was as much his home as theirs. A big *share* of Opal Station maybe, which had financed his aerial muster business, but the homestead was for the newlyweds. He was determined on that. Besides Ally had lots of plans for doing the place up and he guessed it needed it.

What would it be like to be married? Grant mused as he strode past the original old kitchens and servants' quarters. Long out-of-date they were perfectly maintained for their historic value. Shrubs surrounded these outbuildings, light filtering trees, the whole linked to the Big House by the long covered walkway he now took.

What would it be like to come home each night to

a woman he could take to his heart, to his bed? A woman to share his hopes and dreams, his profoundest inner expectations. A woman he belonged with as surely as she belonged with him.

The first time he met Francesca de Lyle when he was in his teens he had felt an instant click, a deep rapport, now years later he was well into fantasising about her. Why then was he so persuaded an intimate relationship with Francesca could only bring danger to them both? Maybe he wasn't ready for any deep relationship after all. Hell, wasn't he too damned busy to commit. Nothing should be on his mind but work. Building up the business. He had such ideas.

A branch of Cameron Airways was now carrying mail and freight but he'd had recent discussions in Brisbane the state capital a good thousand miles away, with Drew Forsythe of Trans Continental Resources regarding building a helicopter fleet for use in minerals, oil and natural gas exploration.

He'd met the very high profile Forsythe and his beautiful wife, Eve, on several occasions but that was the first time they'd ever got into really talking business. And he had Francesca of all people to thank for that.

Never one, apparently, to let a good public relations opportunity go by, Francesca who had struck an immediate chord with the Forsythes when they had all been seated together at a charity banquet had brought up the idea in the course of an enjoyable evening.

Beautiful blue eyes sparkling she put it to Forsythe: "Doesn't this make good sense to you? Grant knows the Interior like the back of his hand and he's absolutely committed to the big picture, isn't that right, Grant?" She had leaned back towards him then, so heart stoppingly graceful in her strapless satin gown, her lovely cool, clear English voice, full of support and encouragement. Ah, the bright aura of breeding and privilege!

And she was clever. If some sort of a deal ever came off, and he was working on it right now, he owed her. A glorious romantic weekend away together, he fantasised. One of those jewel-like Barrier Reef islands that had those luxurious little self-contained bungalows down near the beach. Though he would have to watch her in the hot Queensland sun. She had the flawless porcelain complexion that so often set off Titian hair. How strange she should want to fit into his background on the fringe of the great desert heart. It was almost like trying to grow an exquisite pink rosebush on the banks of a dried-up clay pan. For all his deep and immediate attraction to her they were an impossible match. And he better not lose sight of it.

He lost sight of it less than two minutes later when Francesca herself appeared, running down the side verandah and leaning over the white wrought-iron balustrade wreathed with a prolific lilac trumpeted vine that gave off a seductive fragrance in the golden heat.

"Grant!" she called, waving happily. "How lovely to see you. Of course I heard the chopper." A singing sweetness showed in every line of her body. Sweetness and excitement.

"Come here," he ordered very gently as he came alongside, reaching up a long arm to pull her lovely head down to him. Despite all the little lectures he gave himself, despite all natural caution, every atom of his being was focused on kissing her. He even murmured her name unknowingly as he put his mouth over hers, sensation beating through him like the powerful whoosh of a rotor. What in hell made him do it? But he was a man and keenly physical.

When he let her go she was breathless, trying not to tremble, a deep pink colour running across the fine skin of her cheeks, sparkling lights in the depths of her eyes. Her beautiful flame-coloured hair had come loose from its clasp and spilled around her face and over her shoulders. "That's some greeting!" Her voice was little more than a soft tremble.

"You shouldn't look at me that way," he warned, still feeling ripples of pleasure moving down through his body, pooling in his loins.

"What way?" She gave a shaky laugh, feeling enslaved by his enormous dash, moving back along the wide verandah as he resumed his journey to the front of the house.

"*You* know, Francesca," he half growled, half mocked. "Lord are you a sight for sore eyes!" He ran his gaze over her, from the tip of her radiant head to her toes. His hazel eyes, which could turn grey or green according to his mood, were now a clear green beneath the brim of his black akubra. They scanned her face, her swan's neck, the slender body with its willow waist, her light limbs, a muscle in his hard jaw lightly flicking.

It was impossible to cast his glance away so caught up was he in her feminine beauty, the soft ravishing prettiness he found irresistible. She was wearing riding gear. Such riding gear! The aristocratic young English lady from the grand stately home and one of the most egalitarian young women he had ever known.

Her short-sleeved cream silk blouse lightly skimmed her delicate breasts and was tucked into tight-fitting cream jodhpurs. Highly polished, very expensive, tan coloured riding boots adorned her small feet. There wasn't an ounce of excess weight on her. She had the neatest, sleekest little butt and good straight legs. It nearly mesmerised him just to see her move along the verandah, near dancing to keep up with him. To his overheated mind, and body, make no mistake about it it thrummed like electricity, she appeared to be floating, so lightly were her feet touching the timber floorboards.

"A hard day?" Francesca asked him as he mounted the short flight of stone steps to the verandah, excited, not her usual calm, contained self at all.

He leaned against the rail with slouching elegance, smiling at her with the unblinking cat's eyes she found so wildly attractive. "I'm over it now I've seen you," he drawled. He was, too. "What have you been doing with yourself all day?"

"Come and I'll tell you." She indicated the comfortable white wicker furniture. "I expect you'd like a cold beer? Brod always does."

He nodded and took off his hat using it like a Frisbee to skim unerringly onto the head of a wooden sculpture.

"Rebecca will be here in a moment," Francesca slid into the chair he held out for her. Rebecca was mistress of Kimbara, Brod's new wife. "We've been organising a picnic race meeting for most of the day. We thought it would be a change from the usual polo. Rebecca worries about Brod when he plays. He's such a daredevil. For that matter so are you." She actually shivered at some of her recollections. Polo was a dangerous game. Especially the way these fellows played it.

"So you worry about me as well?" He held her with his eyes.

"I worry about you *all,*" she returned lightly before she drowned in his expression. It struck her more than ever how physically alike Grant and his brother Rafe were. The rangy height, the golden good looks, though Grant was tawnier.

Both had great presence. Both wore achievement like a badge. If there were a difference, Rafe had a kind of courtliness about him. There was no other word for it. Grant showed more "temper" a high mettled energy and determination that didn't sit all that comfortably with everyone. To put it in a nutshell Grant Cameron could be difficult. Add to that, he had a habit of speaking his mind, without holding back. He was full of energy and had a macho quality, an absolute manliness that characterised these men of the outback. In some respects he even seemed like a creature from another world. A creature of vast open spaces with no boundaries. The image of a splendid young lion sat easily on him. He was her first taste of a thrilling excitement that contained a kernel of caution. She knew her feelings for Grant Cameron were getting right out of hand.

Now he knit his dark golden brows together, staring across at her, his strong brown arms on the circular glass-topped table steely with muscle. He was wearing the uniform of his company in serviceable khaki the blue and gold logo on the breast pocket. He looked great, the afternoon breeze ruffling his thick tawny hair with its pronounced deep wave.

"So what's the verdict, my lady?" He came closer to grasping her hand. Never letting her go.

She laughed and blushed at the same time. "Was I staring? Sorry. I was just thinking how much alike you and Rafe are. Growing more so as you—"

"Mature?" he cut in swiftly, his relaxed easy drawl taking on a faint glittery edge.

"Oh, Grant," she said in gentle reproach. Francesca knew the brothers were devoted to each other, but Grant a couple of years younger must have chafed often under Rafe's authority. With both parents dead Rafe had had to take on almost a parental role from an early age. Grant still had a tendency to chafe if only because of his driving ambition to prove himself, to be the man his father always said he would be. Grant fairly pulsed with raw ambition, undischarged energy. "Actually I was going to say, as you grow older," she told him mildly, watching his tall, super lean body with its athlete's muscles relax.

"Of course you were," he agreed with his charming, slightly crooked smile that revealed perfect white teeth. "Sometimes, Francesca, I've got a perverse devil in me."

"Yes, I know," she told him gently.

"I love Rafe as much as any brother could."

"I know you do," she said with understanding, "and I know what you mean so don't bother explaining." The best of relationships were fraught with little tensions. Like mother and daughter. She turned her head as footsteps sounded in the front hall. "That'll be Rebecca."

A moment later Rebecca appeared like a summer breeze, all smiles, touching Francesca affectionately on the shoulder before speaking directly to Grant who came swiftly to his feet. "Don't bother to get up, Grant," she said, realising he must be tired. "All over for the day?"

"Thank the Lord." He gave a wry grin.

"Then you could probably do with a cold beer?"

He laughed aloud and resumed his seat. ''Brod sure has his womenfolk trained. Francesca has just offered me one, too. That'd be great, Rebecca. I have to admit it was long, hard and dusty. I'm parched.'' He was struck again at how much Rebecca had changed from the enigmatic young woman who had first come to Kimbara to write Fee Kinross's biography. Fee, Francesca's mother, had had a brilliant career on the London stage. The biography was due out any day.

Since her marriage to Brod, Rebecca was all friendliness and warmth, happiness and contentment shining out of her quite extraordinary grey eyes. This was a marriage that would work, he thought with great satisfaction. God knows Brod and Ally had one hell of a childhood with their arrogant bastard of a father. Such was Rafe's persona even Stewart Kinross had approved of Rafe, though he hadn't lived to see Rafe and his only daughter, Alison, married.

Grant was certain Kinross would never have approved of him. ''Too much the hothead!'' Kinross had once described him, ''with the intolerable habit of expressing his quite juvenile opinions.'' Opinions, of course, that ran counter to the lordly Kinross. Still the two families, Cameron and Kinross had always been entwined. Almost kin. Now they were.

When Rebecca returned with his cold beer, just the one—he was too responsible a pilot to consider another—and an iced tea for herself and Francesca, they talked family matters, their latest communications from Rafe and Ally, local gossip, what Fee and David Westbury, the visiting first cousin to Francesca'a aristocratic father, were up to. The two had become inseparable to the extent Francesca told them she wouldn't be surprised to get a phone call to say they'd popped into the register office that very day. Which would make Fee's third attempt at making a go of marriage.

They were still talking about Fee and the important cameo role she was to play in a new Australian movie, when they were interrupted by the shrilling of the phone, the latest miracle for the outback that had depended for so long on radio communication. Rebecca went to answer it, returning with an expression that wiped all the laughter from her luminous grey eyes. "It's for you, Grant, Bob Carlton." She named his second-in-charge. "One of the fleet hasn't reached base camp or called in, either. Bob sounded a bit concerned. Take it in Brod's study."

"Thanks, Rebecca." Grant rose to his impressive lean height. "Did he say which station?"

"Oh I'm sorry!" Rebecca touched her creamy forehead in self-reproach. "I should have told you at once. It's Bunnerong."

The station was even more remote than they were. About sixty miles to the north-west. Grant made his way through the Kinross homestead, familiar to him from childhood. It was amazingly grand in contrast to the Cameron stronghold with its quietly fading Victorian gentility. Ally, of course, would change all that. Ally the whirlwind but for now his mind was on what Bob had to say.

Bob, in his mid-fifties, was a great bloke. A great organiser, a great mechanic, well liked by everyone. Grant relied on him, but Bob was a born worrier, a firm believer in Murphy's Law, whereby anything that could go wrong, would. Equally Bob was determined no harm would come to any of "his boys."

On the phone Grant received Bob's assurance all necessary checks had been made and the chopper had passed the mandatory 100-hour service. The helicopter was to have set down when the stockmen were camped at Bunnerong's out station at approximately four o'clock. The pilot, a good one with plenty of experience in aerial muster had not arrived by four forty-five when Bunnerong contacted Bob by radio. Bob in turn had not been able to contact the pilot by company radio frequency.

"I wouldn't worry too much about it." Grant wasn't overly concerned at that point.

"You know me, Grant, I'm going to," Bob answered. "It's not like Curly. He runs by an inbuilt timetable."

"Sure," Grant acknowledged. "But you know as well as I do things can go wrong with the radio. It's not all that unusual. It's happened to me. Besides it's almost dusk. Curly would have put down somewhere and made camp for the night. He's got all he needs to make himself comfortable. He'd resume again at first light. If he's anything like me he's dog-tired. Besides, he's not actually due to start the muster until morning anyway."

All of which was true. "There's an hour or so of light left," Grant said at length breaking in on Bob. "I'll take the chopper up and have a look around, though I'm coming from another direction. I need to refuel on Kimbara, if I'm going to get close in to Bunnerong."

"I suppose we might as well wait for morning," Bob sighed. "Curly could still turn up. Bunnerong can get a message to us and I'll relay it to you."

So it was decided. "Curly" to all because of a single wisp of hair that curled like a baby's on his bald patch, was a pro. He had food with him. A swag. He'd probably put down near a bush lagoon and set up camp for the night. Nevertheless Grant felt the responsibility to take his chopper up. Initiate a bit of a search before night fell.

Bob's mood had affected him, he thought wryly. Experience told him Curly, though obviously having problems with his radio was most likely safe and sound setting up camp on the ground. Still he liked to know *exactly* where every one of his pilots and helicopters in service were.

Grant walked swiftly back through the house, telling the two young women of his intentions the moment he set foot on the verandah.

"Why don't you let me come with you?" Francesca asked quickly, keen to help if she could. "You know what they say, two pairs of eyes are better than one."

Rebecca nodded in agreement. "I was able to help Brod once on a search and rescue. You remember?"

"That was from the Beech Baron," Grant told her, a shade repressively. "Francesca isn't used to helicopters. The way they fly, the heat and the noise. She could very easily get airsick."

Francesca stood away from her chair. "I don't suffer from motion sickness at all, Grant. In the air. On the water. Please take me. I want to help if I can."

His response wasn't all that she hoped. The expression in his hazel eyes suggested there was a decided possibility she could become a liability. But in the end he nodded in laconic permission. "All right, lady! Let's go."

Minutes later the rotor was roaring and they were lifting vertically from the lawn, rising well above the line of trees, climbing, then steering away for the desert fringe. Francesca like Grant was strapped into her co-pilot seat, wearing earphones that at least made the loud noise of the swishing blades tolerable. Still she found it a thrilling experience to be up in the air looking down at the vast wilderness with all the rock formations undergoing another change in their astonishing colour display. Even when they flew through thermal cross-winds over the desert she kept her cool as the winds took hold of the small aircraft and shook it so it plunged into a short, sickening dive.

"O.K.?" Grant spoke through the headphones, a deep frown of concern between his eyes.

"Aye, aye, skipper!" She lifted her right hand in a parody of a smart salute. Did he really think she was going to go to pieces like the ladies of old? Have the vapours? She had pioneering blood in her veins as well. Her maternal ancestor had been Ewan Kinross, a legendary cattle king. The fact that she had been reared in the ordered calm of the beautiful English countryside and her exclusive boarding school didn't mean she hadn't inherited the capacity to face a far more dangerous way of life. Besides it was as she'd told him. She had a cast iron stomach and she was too excited for nerves. She wanted to learn this way of life. She wanted to learn all about Grant Cameron's life.

They searched until it got to the point when they had to turn back. When they landed Brod was waiting for them in the brief mauve dusk that in moments would turn to a darkness that was literally pitch black.

"No luck?" Brod asked as Grant jumped out onto the grass turning to catch Francesca by the waist and swing her down like the featherweight she was.

"If Curly doesn't turn up on Bunnerong first thing

in the morning we're looking at another search. Bob report in?"

"No news. Nothing." Brod shook his head. "You'll stay the night." It wasn't a question but a statement of fact. "Better you're here anyway. We're closer to Bunnerong if there's any need of a search. I expect your man is boiling the billy now moaning his radio is out of order."

"I shouldn't be surprised," Grant responded to Brod's good spirits. "It's Francesca here who's the real surprise."

"How so?" Brod turned to smile down on his English cousin, as dark with his raven hair and tanned skin as Grant was tawny gold.

"I think he thought I was going to go into a panic when we hit some thermals," Francesca explained lightly, striking Grant's arm in reproach.

"I wouldn't have blamed you if you did," he answered with a faintly teasing smile, enjoying fending her off. "I've always said you're much more than a pretty face." A ravishingly pretty face.

"It would take a lot to put Fran in a tizzy," Brod said with affection. "We've learnt over the years this little piece of English china has plenty of spunk."

Up at the homestead Rebecca smilingly allotted him a guest room overlooking the rear of the house. The meandering creek that ran near and encircled the home compound revealed itself in a silver line as the moon turned on its radiance. Brod walked in a few minutes later with a pile of clean, soap-smelling clothes from his own wardrobe.

"Here, these should fit," he announced, placing the clothes neatly on the bed, a blue-and-white striped cotton shirt on top, cotton beige trousers and underwear that hadn't even come out of its packet by the look of it. Both men were much the same height a few inches over six feet with the lean, powerful physique of the super active.

"Am I glad of them. Thanks a lot," Grant answered, turning away from his own speculation of the night to smile at his brother's best friend. With Rafe and Brod those few years older he'd always been the one trying to catch up, trying to catch them, trying to emulate their achievements, academically and on the sports field. All in all he hadn't done too badly.

"No problem." There was an answering smile in Brod's eyes. "You've saved me dozens of times. I'm for a long, hot shower. I expect you are, too. It's been a thoroughly tiring day." He started to move off then stopped briefly at the door. "By the way I don't think I thanked you properly for doing such a great job," he said with evident approval. "It's not just the way you handle the chopper, which is brilliant, you're a cattleman as well. The combination makes you extraordinarily good."

"Thanks, mate." Grant grinned. "I aim to offer the very best service. And it doesn't come cheap as you're due to find out. What time are we off in the morning always supposing Curly gets a message through he's okay?"

Brod frowned, answering a little vaguely for him. "Not as early as today, that's for sure. The men have their orders. They'll have plenty to do. We'll wait and see what the morning brings. I know bush logic tells us Curly has landed safely, but I'd like to stick around until we're sure."

"I appreciate that, Brod." Grant accepted his friend's support. "A land search in such a huge area would be out of the question. It will take aircraft to find him if he's in any kind of trouble.''

''Not that it's odd having problems with the radio,'' Brod echoed Grant's own previous words, obviously trying to offer reassurance mixed in with the voice of long experience. Brod's expression brightened. ''Now, what about a barbeque? I feel like eating outdoors tonight and it gives me the opportunity to show off. I cook a great steak if I say so myself. We can throw in a few roast potatoes. The girls can whip up a salad. What more could a man want?''

Grant smiled broadly. ''Go for it! I'm hungry enough to eat the best steak Kimbara can offer.''

''You're going to get it,'' Brod assured him.

A long, hot shower was a wonderful luxury after the heat and uproar of the day. The bellowing of the cattle as they were herded into doing what they clearly didn't want to do; leave the familiar surroundings of the scrub was still in his ears. More of the same tomorrow. And the day after. But he planned on getting right out of fieldwork. He wanted to concentrate on expanding the business. He'd go on building up the fleet and the team but his mind was firmly on extending the range of services.

With time on his hands and glad of the company of such good friends, he used some of the shampoo he found in the cupboard beneath the basin. Kinross sure knew how to look after its guests, he thought with wry admiration. There was an impressive array of stuff to make a guest feel good. Fancy soaps, bath gels, shower gels, body lotion, talc, toothbrushes, toothpaste, hair dryer, electric shaver. Lots of good, big absorbent towels. Man-size. Brilliant!

He stepped out of the shower and wrapped one

around himself, feeling the exhaustions of the day slip away. His hair needed cutting as usual. Barbers weren't all that easy to come by in the desert. He shook his wet, darkened hair like a seal deciding he'd better use the dryer if he wanted to look presentable.

Which he did. He was intensely aware of his attraction to Francesca, her marvellous drawing power though he knew how ill advised it was. The Camerons and the Kinrosses had always lived like desert lords but their world was beyond "civilisation" as Lady Francesca de Lyle knew it. No question the call of the outback had reached her. After all she had an Australian mother born in this very house but Francesca was on holiday, taking the rose-coloured holiday view. It was impossible for her to realise the day-to-day isolation, the terrible battles that were fought against drought, flood and heat, accident, tragic deaths. Men could bear the loneliness, the struggles and frustrations, the crushing workload. He knew in his heart an English rose like Francesca would find it all unbearable no matter how adaptable she claimed she was. She simply had no experience of the bush and the hazards it presented.

Grant threw down the hair dryer, thinking he shouldn't have used it. It made his hair look positively *wild.* He turned to dressing, pulling out the belt of his uniform to thread it through the cotton trousers. No difficulty with sizing. The fit was perfect. If only he were certain Curly was safe and sound he could really look forward to enjoying this evening.

It had been lonely at home with Rafe away on honeymoon. He was looking forward to a letter from them or maybe another phone call. Ally had been so full of their stay in New York. She adored it. The excitement she felt as she ''hit the sidewalk'' the ''thrum'' of the place more electric than any other city on earth. ''And we've got you some wonderful presents,'' she'd added. ''Really special!'' That was Ally and she had the money.

The Camerons had never kept pace with the Kinrosses in the generation of great wealth, though Opal was an industry leader and Rafe was dead set on expansion, building up a chain, just as he, himself, was determined on making his mark in aviation.

The pride of lions! Well he and Rafe had tasted tragedy as had Brod and Ally. At least some things were now working out. Brod had found real love, much rarer than people thought. As for Rafe and Ally! They were like two sides of the same coin. Allowing himself to fall in love with Francesca had to make him downright crazy. Easy enough to get led astray, though, he reasoned. Finding the path back might prove very, very, difficult.

Francesca was crossing through the front hall when Grant descended the stairs. She looked up feeling a sudden rush of blood to her face. He looked marvellous, his strong, handsome features relaxed, hazel eyes sparkling, his full, thick head of hair, obviously freshly washed, settling into the deep natural waves women paid a fortune to achieve. She was astonished at her own desire, so sweet, so primitive like a woman staring at the man she wanted for her perfect mate.

''Hi!'' His voice was pitched thrillingly low, stirring her further.

She had to force a flippant tone in case he read what was on her mind and man-like backed off. ''You look *cool.*''

"Courtesy Brod." He grinned. "He rustled up some gear."

"It suits you." She spoke with a nice balance of admiration and teasing.

"Actually you look very sweet yourself." His eyes gently mocked. She was wearing a sapphire-blue full skirt with a matching strappy little top, the fabric printed with white hibiscus. Blue sandals almost the same shade were on her feet, her Titian hair wound into some braided coil that suited her beautifully. He saw the apricot flush on her creamy skin. He knew it was there because he was coming close.

How did it happen? This longing for a woman that sent a man reeling? He'd been making love to her in his mind at least three times a week for some time now, seriously considering it *had* to happen, shocked because he couldn't seem to come to his senses. But what did sense have to do with sexual attraction? He felt compelled to have an affair. He couldn't make the wider choice, yet he moved right up to her, surprising her and himself by moving her into an impromptu tango, remembering how they had danced and danced at Brod's then Rafe's wedding.

There was music in him, Francesca thought. Music, rhythm, a sensuality that was reducing her limbs to jelly. This man was taking her over utterly, making all her senses bloom like a flower.

"I'm in perfect company right now," he murmured in her ear, just barely resisting the temptation to take the pink earlobe into his mouth.

"Me, too." The words just slipped out, very soft but not concealing her intensity. She hadn't made a conscious decision to fall in love with him surely, but his effect on her was so pervasive she could hardly bear to contemplate her holiday on Kimbara coming to an end.

Rebecca, coming to find them, burst into spontaneous applause at the considerable panache of their dance. "You're naturals, both of you," she cried. "I've never thought of it before but this is a terrific dance floor." She looked around the very spacious front hall, speculation in her eyes.

"Why would you need it when you've got the old ballroom?" Francesca asked, catching her breath as Grant whirled her into a very close stop.

"I mean for Brod and me," Rebecca smiled, still very much the bride. "Come and join us for a drink. I've chilled a seriously good Riesling. It's beautiful out on the back verandah. The air is filled with the scent of boronia. How I love it. The stars are out in their zillions." She came forward very happily to link her arm through Francesca's, her long, gleaming dark ribbon of hair falling softly from a centre parting the way her husband loved it, the skirt of her summery white dress fluttering in the breeze that blew through the open doorway.

They found Brod wrapped in a professional-looking apron, the large brick barbeque well alight, the potatoes in foil already cooking. Ratatouille kebabs prepared by Rebecca lay ready for the grill plate, a leafy green walnut and mushroom salad prepared by Francesca waiting for the dressing.

Grant was given the enjoyable task of opening the wine, and pouring it into the tulip-shaped glasses set out on the long table, while Francesca passed around the crackers spread with a smoked salmon paté she had processed a half hour before. It was light and luscious and the conversation began to flow. These were people, interconnected through family, who genuinely enjoyed one another's company. The steaks, prime Kimbara beef, were set to sizzle over the hot coals and Rebecca decided she'd like a tarragon wine sauce so went to the kitchen to fetch it. While they were waiting, Grant walked Francesca to the very edge of the verandah so they could see the moon reflected in the glassy-smooth surface of the creek.

"Such a heavenly night," she breathed, lifting her head from contemplation of the silvery waters to the glittering heavens. "The Southern Cross is always over the tip of the house. It's so easy to pick out."

Grant nodded. "Rafe and Ally won't see it in the United States. The cross is gradually shifting southward in the sky."

"Is it really?" Francesca turned her head to stare up at him, thrilled because he was so *tall.*

"It is, my lady." He gave a mocking bow. "A result of the earth's precession or the circular motion of the earth's axis. The Southern Cross was known to the people of the ancient world, Babylonians and Greeks. They thought it part of the constellation Centaurus. See the star furthest to the south?" He pointed it out.

"The brightest?"

He nodded. "A star of the first magnitude. It points to the South Pole. The aborigines have wonderful Dreamtime legends about the Milky Way and stars. I'll tell you some of them one of these days. Maybe nights when we're camping out."

"Are you serious?"

A short silence. "I suppose it could be arranged." His voice sounded sardonic. "Do you think it would be a good idea, the two of us camping out under the stars?"

"I think it could be wonderful." Francesca drew a breath of sheer excitement.

"What about when the dingoes started to howl?" he mocked.

"Mournful not to say eerie cries, I know—" she shivered a little remembering "—but I'd have you to protect me."

"And who's going to protect me?" Suddenly he put a finger beneath her chin, turning up her face to him.

"Am I so much to worry about?" She cut to the very heart of the matter.

"I think so, yes," he answered slowly. "You're out of reach, Francesca."

"And I thought you were a man who aimed for the stars?" she taunted him very gently.

"Aircraft are safer than women," he countered dryly. "They don't preoccupy a man's mind."

"So that makes harmless little me a great danger?" Her voice was low-pitched but uniquely intense.

"Except in the realm of my secret dreams," he surprised himself by admitting.

It was a tremendous turn-on, causing Francesca's body to quiver like a plucked string. "That's very revealing, Grant. Why would you reveal so much of yourself to me?" she asked in some frustration.

"Because in many ways we're intensely compatible. I think we knew that very early on."

"When we were just teenagers?" There was simply no way she could deny it. "And now we're to assume a different relationship?"

"Not assume, my lady." His voice deepened, became somewhat combative. "You were born to grandeur. The daughter of an earl. Journeying to the outback is in lots of ways an escape for you, maybe even an escape from reality. An attempt to avoid much of the pressure from your position in life. I'd expect your father will confidently expect you to marry a man from within your own ranks. A member of the English aristocracy. At the very least a scion of one of the established families.''

It was perfectly true. Her father had certain hopes of her. Even two possible suitors. ''I'm Fee's daughter, too.'' She tried to stave the issue off. ''That makes me half Australian. Fee only wants me to be happy.''

''Which means I'm right. Your father has high expectations of you. He wouldn't want to lose you.''

Francesca shook her head almost pleadingly. ''Daddy will never lose me. I love him. But he has his own life you know.''

''But no grandchildren.'' Grant pointed out bluntly. ''You have to give him them. Such a child, a male child, would become his heir. The future Earl of Moray. Inescapably a fact.''

''Oh don't let's take that all on yet, Grant,'' Francesca burst out. She wanted them to be together, with no conflicts between them.

But Grant had other ideas, seeing where it was taking them. ''I have to. You know as well as I do we're becoming increasingly involved. Hell what am *I* sacrificing here? I could fall in love with you then you'd go off home to Daddy, back to your own world, leaving me to profound wretchedness.''

Somehow she didn't associate him with becoming any woman's victim. He was too much the self-contained *man.* ''I think you have what it takes to resist me.''

''Darn right!'' Abruptly he bent his head and gave her a hard kiss. ''I've seen these patterns before.''

''So what's the solution?'' She was compelled to clutch him for support.

''Neither of us allows ourselves to get carried away,'' he said brusquely.

''So much for your behaviour then. Why do you have to kiss me?''

He laughed, a low, attractive sound with a hint of self-disgust. ''That's the hell of it, Francesca. Reconciling sexual desire with the need for good sense.''

''So sadly there are to be no more kisses?'' she challenged with a little note of scepticism.

He looked down into her light filled eyes, aware of the complexity of his feelings. She looked so lovely, very much a piece of porcelain, a woman to be cherished, protected from damage. ''Can I help it if I'm continually at war?'' he asked ironically. ''You're so beautiful, aren't you? You moved into my path like a princess from a fairy tale. I know dozens of eligible, available women. Wouldn't I be the world's biggest fool to pick on someone like you? A young woman who has lived a charmed life? Equally well I don't think your father would get a big kick out of knowing you were dallying with a rough-around-the-edges man from the outback.''

It in no way described him. ''Rugged, Grant. Never rough. You're a lot more edgy than Rafe, but he's very much your brother and one of the most courteous men I've ever met.''

''Free from my aggression, you mean.'' Grant nodded in wry amusement. ''It's an inborn grace, Francesca, he inherited from our father. I'm nowhere near as simpatico.''

Her normally sweet voice was a little tart in her

throat, like citrus peel in chocolate. "Well don't feel too badly. *I* like you. Temper and all. I like the way you hit on an idea and go for it. I like your breadth of vision. I like the way you make big plans. I even like your strong sense of competitiveness. What I don't like is the way you see me as a threat."

He could see the hurt in her eyes but he was compelled to speak. "Because you *are* a threat, Francesca. A real threat. To us both."

"That's awful." She looked away abruptly over the moon-drenched home gardens.

"I know," he muttered sombrely, "but it makes sense."

Unlike a lot of men let loose at a barbeque, Brod cooked the steaks to perfection, each to their requirements from medium rare to well done. For all her whirring feelings Francesca enjoyed herself, eating a good meal, warming to the conversation, and afterwards offering to make coffee.

"I'll help you." Impulsively Grant moved back his chair, willing the pleasure of the evening to go on. Brod and Rebecca had shifted seats and were now holding hands. The younger couple wouldn't be missed for a while.

In the huge kitchen outfitted for feeding an army, Grant thought, Francesca set him to grinding the coffee beans, the marvellous aroma rising and flowing out towards them. Francesca was busy setting out cups and saucers then assembling plates for the slices of chocolate torte she'd already cut. All very deftly, he noticed. She was very organised, very methodical, with quick, neat hands.

"You're managing very well," he drawled.

''What is that supposed to mean?'' The overhead light turned her glorious hair to flame, giving him a great wave of pleasure.

''Have you ever actually cooked a meal?'' he smiled.

''I made the salad,'' she pointed out collectedly.

''And it was very good, but I can't think you ever have any need to go into a kitchen and start cooking the supper.''

She scarcely remembered being allowed in the kitchen except at Christmas to stir the pudding. ''Not at Ormond, no.'' She named her father's stately home. ''We always had a housekeeper, Mrs. Lincoln. She was pretty fierce. Nothing casual about her and she had staff, just as Brod's father did, only Brod and Rebecca have decided they want to be on their own. At least for a while. Once I shifted to London to start work I managed to get all my own meals. It truly isn't difficult,'' she added dryly.

''When you weren't going out?'' He poured boiling water into the plunger. ''You must accept lots and lots of invitations?''

''I have a full social life.'' She flashed him a blue, sparkling look. ''But it's not an obsession.''

''No love affairs?'' He found he couldn't bear the thought of her with another man.

''One or two romantic involvements. Like *you.*'' Grant Cameron didn't lack female admirers.

''No one serious?'' he persisted as though the thought was gnawing away at him.

''I've yet to meet my perfect man,'' she answered sweetly.

''Which brings me to why you have designs on me.''

His effrontery took her breath away. ''You can haul

yourself out when the going gets tough. Because I'm only following my own instincts. You do have a certain emotional pull and physically you're extraordinarily attractive.''

He gave a mock bow, surprisingly elegant. ''Thank you, Francesca. That makes my heart swell.''

''As long as it's not your *head,*'' she retorted crisply.

''My head has the high ground at the moment,'' he drawled. ''But I've enjoyed tonight. Brod and Rebecca are such good company and you are *you.*''

It was so disconcerting, the swings from sarcastic to sizzling emotion. An acknowledgment, perhaps, that their connection was powerful, though he was going to fight it all the way.

''That's good I've done something right,'' Francesca said in response, trying to keep her tone light, but she was utterly confounded when tears came into her eyes. Being with him made her more sensitive, more womanly with a much bigger capacity for being hurt. For all the calmness of her voice, Grant was instantly alerted. He glanced up swiftly, catching her the moment before she blinked furiously.

''Francesca!'' Heart drumming with dismay and desire he reached for her, pulling her into his arms. ''What is it? Have I hurt you? I'm a brute. I'm sorry.'' He could see the pulse beating in her creamy throat answering the pulses that were beating in him. ''I'm trying to see what's best for both of us. Surely you can understand that?''

''Of course.'' Her voice was a husky whisper. She dashed her hand across her eyes. Just like a little girl. Grace under fire.

An immense wave of passion tied to a deep sense of protectiveness broke across him, causing him to mould her into him more tightly, achingly aware of the feel of her delicate breasts against the wall of his chest. He was on the verge of losing it. It was terrible. But good. Better than good. Ravishing.

She attempted to speak but he was seized by the urgent need to kiss her, to take the crushed strawberry sweetness of her mouth, to find her tongue, to move it back and forth against his in the age-old mating ritual. This incredible delight in a woman was something new to him. Something well beyond his former sexual experiences. He wanted her. Needed her like a man needs water.

There was tremendous passion in his kiss, a touch of fierceness that thrilled her because she knew she meant more to him than he dared acknowledge. His hand held her nape, cupped it, holding her head to him. She was almost lying back in his arms, allowing him to take his intense pleasure, and something deep, deep inside her started to melt. She was almost fainting under the tumult of sensation, her own ardent response. She had never known such intimacy, never before revelled in it, knowing it could be a cause of much unhappiness but she was too needy or too stupid to care.

What bright spirit impelled towards delight was ever known to figure out the cost?

They broke apart, both of them momentarily disorientated as though they had been beamed down from another world. Grant, for his part, was profoundly conscious his moods, attitudes and thoughts about this woman were vacillating wildly like a geiger counter exposed to radiation. She set his blood on fire, which greatly complicated their relationship. How could one think calmly, rationally when he was continually longing to make love to her? She might even see his masculine drive as excessive, a kind of male sexual aggression. She was so small, so light limbed, so fragile in his arms, the perfume of her, of her very skin, a potent trigger to desire.

By contrast she seemed shaken, deprived of speech, unusually pale.

"I'm sorry, Francesca." Remorse was in his voice. "I never meant to be rough with you. I got carried away. Forgive me. It's as you say, I lack the courtly touch."

She could have and perhaps should have told him how she felt, how she welcomed his advances with all her heart, but the tide of emotion was too dangerously high. She stood away, putting a trembling hand to her hair, realising a few long, silky strands had worked their way loose. "You didn't hurt me, Grant," she managed to say. "Appearances can be deceptive. I'm a lot tougher than I look."

His low laugh was spontaneous. "You could have fooled me." He watched her trying to fix her hair, wanting to pull it free of its braided coils. What fascination long, beautiful hair had for a man. He could even imagine himself brushing it. God he had to be mad! He forced a grin, the smile not going with the look in his eyes. "I suppose we'd better take the coffee out. It'll be getting cold." He reached around and set the glass plunger on the tray. "I'll carry it out. You relax. Get the colour back in your cheeks." A tall order when he had reduced her to a breathless quivering receptacle of sensation, naked in her clothes.

CHAPTER TWO

FRANCESCA woke with a start knowing before she even looked at the clock she had slept in. She had set the alarm for five in the morning, now it was six-ten.

"Damn!" This was too awful. She wanted to go with Grant. Francesca flung herself out of bed, glancing through the open French doors that gave onto the verandah. Sun-up four-thirty. The sky was now a bright blue, the air redolent with the wonderful smell of heat. She had even missed the morning symphony of birds, the combined voices so powerful, so swelling they regularly woke her at dawn. Sometimes the kookaburras started up their unique cackling din in predawn and she was awake to hear them, lying in bed enjoying their laughter. But she had slept deeply, exhausted by the chaos of emotion that was in her.

Still she planned to go with Grant and he'd agreed, if somewhat reluctantly. Grant had told them all before retiring he intended to wait an hour for a message to be relayed in from Bunnerong. All stations operated from dawn. Perhaps his pilot had already called in or Bunnerong had notified Kimbara of his arrival? That was the way they did it in the bush.

Hastily she splashed her face with cold water to wake herself up, cleaned her teeth and dressed in the clothes she had laid out the night before to save time. Cotton shirt, cotton jeans, sneakers. She put the brush through her hair, caught up a scarf to tie it back and rushed out into the silent hallway, padding along it until she reached the central staircase. She was almost at the bottom, when Brod came through the front door, surprise on his handsome face. "Fran? We thought we'd better let you sleep in."

Dismay hit her and she sent him a sparkling glance. "You don't mean to tell me Grant has gone without me?" Her emotions were so close to the surface she felt betrayed.

"I think he *intends* to go without you," Brod admitted wryly. "He has the firm idea you're not really up to it. Bunnerong has called in, as expected. Curly still hasn't arrived. Grant has delayed taking off for as long as he can. He's down at the airstrip refuelling."

"So he hasn't taken off yet?" Hope flashed in her eyes.

"No." Brod heaved a sigh, beginning to think Grant was right not to take her. This was his little cousin from England. He valued her highly but she wasn't used to confronting potentially dangerous situations. With no makeup and her long hair floating all around her, her cheeks pink with indignation she looked little more than a child.

"Get me down there," she said, racing towards him and taking him firmly by the arm. Literally a fire head.

Brod resisted momentarily, even though his expression was affectionate and understanding. "Fran, think about this. There's a possibility the pilot has come to some harm. That could be very distressing for you. Believe me, I *know*."

She looked up at him with her flower-blue eyes. "I won't screw up, Brod, I promise. I want to be of help. I completed a first-aid course."

Brod gave a sigh and ran his hand through his raven hair. "I don't want to be alarmist but out here accidents aren't something that happen to other people, Fran. We don't read about it in the newspapers or see it on television. They happen to *us*. All the time. Curly might be beyond first-aid. Think of that. No matter how game you are, how much you want to help, you've led a protected life.''

''Most people do. But I'm ready to *learn*, Brod.'' Francesca caught his stare and held it. ''Stop treating me like a pampered little girl. I've had my tough times as well. Now, get in and drive.'' She ran to the waiting Jeep ahead of him, almost dancing in her desire to get down to the airstrip. ''Grant promised he'd take me,'' she called over her shoulder. ''I know it mightn't be good but I'm not going to cave in. I'm half Kinross.''

She was, too, he thought with some admiration. Used as a buffer between warring parents. ''It sounds to me like you have something to prove, love,'' Brod said as he started the engine.

''Yes, I have.'' The great thing about her cousins, Brod and Ally, was they wanted to listen.

''To Grant?'' He looked at her with his all-seeing eyes, encouraging her.

''Who else?'' she flashed him her smile.

Brod nodded, his expression wry. ''He's a helluva guy, Fran, a genuinely exciting personality. He'll go far, but he's very stubborn. Once he makes up his mind you won't change it. Princess that you are you won't wind him around your little finger so be warned. Grant has very strong views. A quick pride. Strength and energy to burn. But he has lots to learn like the rest of us. We know he's deeply attracted to you but you could get hurt. Rebecca and I don't want to see that because we care about you too much.''

Francesca's delicately arching brows drew together.

"I know and I love you for it but I have to take my own chances in life, Brod. Make all my own mistakes. That's as it should be. My friendship with Grant *has* gone a step further. Everyone is aware of it. We're more involved and as a consequence we're coming increasingly into conflict."

"You know what they say. Life isn't meant to be easy. I can see it happening, Fran." Brod accelerated away from the compound. "Grant has never felt a woman's power. He's had casual affairs but they never burned him. What happens when you go back to Sydney? Have you thought of that?"

"Of course I have!" Francesca exclaimed, trying to push the thought away. "I don't want this time with you and Rebecca to end. I'm longing to see Ally when she gets home. Rafe, too, though I know he has reservations about my friendship with his 'little brother.'"

Brod chose his words carefully, knowing what she said was quite true. "Responsibility is Rafe's middle name, Fran. He damned near had to father Grant when their parents were killed. In his shock and grief Grant went more than a little wild. He was always getting into trouble, always trying to bring some daredevil prank off. That tragedy has shaped him. Put fear in him. Showed him about loss. It might well be to remember it. Grant mightn't let a woman get too close to him. His grief at the loss of his parents was enormous. He was very close to his mother as the youngest.

"They were wonderful people, the Camerons. They took pity on Ally and me and our chaotic home life. They as good as fostered us. Rafe is as close to me as a brother. Come to that I always thought of Grant as a younger brother. To love is to lose. Grant learned that early."

When they arrived at the airstrip Grant was close to taking off. He saw them coming and jumped down again onto the tarmac. There was Francesca looking like someone who should be scattering rose petals at a wedding, Titian hair flying all around her lovely head. He tried to keep a sudden anger down, wondering why he was feeling so angry at all. He didn't want her hurt. That was it. He didn't want her exposed to danger. In short he didn't want her to come.

She was running towards him, crying out in reproach. "You surely weren't going to leave without me?"

He nodded more curtly than he intended. "I don't have a real good feeling about this, Francesca. It might be better if you stay home."

"But you promised me last night." Her churning emotions sounded in her voice.

"You agree with me don't you, Brod?" Grant shot his friend a near imploring glance.

Brod considered a while. "I figure she'll come to no harm with you, Grant. She may see something she's not prepared for but knowing her I'd say she is adult enough to handle it. There may not be much wrong at all. A choke in the fuel pipe, or running too low on petrol to reach the scheduled landing."

"Which places him fair and square in a difficult and potentially dangerous situation," Grant said, feeling the pressure. "The sun is generating a lot of heat." Both men knew a lost man could dehydrate and die within forty-eight hours in the excessively dry atmosphere.

"We're all praying, Grant," Brod said.

"I know." There was tremendous mateship in the bush. Grant turned to see Francesca tying her hair back with a blue scarf for all the world as if she was donning a nurse's cap. She looked achingly young. Adolescent. No make-up. She didn't need it. No lipstick, her soft, cushiony mouth had its own natural colour. What was he to do with this magical creature? But she was game.

A few minutes later they were airborne, heading in the direction of Curly's flight path. Grant pointed to various landmarks along the way, their flight level low enough for Francesca to marvel at the primeval beauty of the timeless land.

Beneath them was lightly timbered cattle country, with sections of Kimbara's mighty herd. Silver glinted off the interlocking system of watercourses that gave the Channel Country its name. Arrows of green in the rust-red plains. Monolithic rocks of vivid orange stone thrust up from the desert floor, thickly embroidered with the burnt gold of the spinifex. The aerial view was fantastic.

Kimbara stockmen quenching their thirst with billy tea waved from the shade of the red river gums along a crescent-shaped billabong. This was vast territory. Francesca could well see how a man could be lost forever.

While Grant spoke to Bob Carlton on Opal, Francesca looked away to a distant oasis of waterholes supporting a lot of greenery in the otherwise stark desert landscape. The sky was a brilliant cloudless enamelled blue and the heat was beginning to affect her.

This wasn't the super aeroplane, the great jet she was used to on her long hauls from London to Sydney. This was a single rotor helicopter she knew little about except it could fly straight up or straight down, forwards, backwards, hover in one spot, or turn completely around. It could do jobs no other vehicle of any kind could do like land in a small clearing or on a flat roof. In many ways, a helicopter was pretty much like a magic carpet and Grant was known as a brilliant pilot. That gave her a great deal of confidence.

A lot of time passed and they saw nothing to indicate closer inspection. Francesca's eyes were moving constantly, trying not to concentrate on the extraordinary surrealistic beauty of the great wilderness, but on spotting a yellow helicopter. Huge flocks of budgerigar, the phenomenon of the outback often passed beneath them, the sunlight striking a rich emerald from their wings. She could see wild camels moving across the red sand beneath them and looking east a great outcrop of huge seemingly perfect round boulders for all the world like an ancient god's marbles.

They were now within the boundaries of Bunnerong with several large lagoons coming up. Fifteen minutes on, Grant pointed downwards then proceeded to tilt the rotary wings in that direction.

They both spotted the company helicopter at the same time. It had come to rest on a small claypan that was probably baked so hard it was like cement and virtually waterproof. Dead trees supporting colonies of white corellas like a million flowers ringed the shallow depression. A short distance off was one of the loveliest of all desert plants the casuarina, a mature desert oak with its foliage spreading out to form a graceful canopy. Beneath the oak Francesca could plainly see the body of a prone man, his face covered by the broad brim of his hat. He didn't rise at the sound of the helicopter. He didn't lift the hat away from his face. He didn't wave. He kept on lying there like a man dead.

Dear God! Francesca felt a moment of sheer terror. She had never seen death before.

In a very short time they were down on the fairly light landing pad, Grant on the radio again to let Bob Carlton back on Opal know he'd found Curly grounded, the helicopter apparently safe. More news would follow.

Outside the helicopter Francesca looked to Grant for instructions.

''Stay here,'' he ordered, just as she knew he would. ''And take this and put it on.'' He handed her his akubra knowing it was much too big but it would have to do. ''You go nowhere without a hat. Nowhere. And you the redhead!''

She took the reprimand meekly because she knew she deserved it. If she hadn't slept in she would have brought one of her wide-brimmed akubras. ''Do what I say now,'' Grant further cautioned. ''Stay put until I see what's going on.''

It seemed sensible to obey. The birds outraged by the descent of the helicopter into their peaceful territory were wheeling in the sky, screeching a deafening protest before flying off.

She looked at Grant's broad back as he moved off, sharply aware he felt deeply responsible for this pilot. The moment he called back to her, ''He's alive!'' was to stay bright in Francesca's memory. She ran without thinking towards them, even though he stood up abruptly, holding up his hand.

She hadn't seen the blood. It had dried very dark, almost dyeing the pilot's shirt.

''What's happened. What is it?'' she asked in considerable alarm.

''I don't know. It looks like something has attacked him.'' Grant strode off to the helicopter, returning with a rifle just in case. Wild boars. Bound to be plenty about. Dingo attack. He didn't think so. Then what? God forbid the attack was human. ''Poor old fella! Poor Curly!'' he found himself saying.

Francesca went to the unconscious man and fell to her knees. ''He needs attention quite urgently. Whatever's done this to him?'' Very gingerly she began to unbutton the pilot's blood-soaked shirt and as she did so he started to moan, beginning to come around.

''Here, let me take a look,'' Grant said urgently, gazing down at the fallen man with perplexity. ''He landed the chopper quite okay. He must have become ill. Maybe he's had a heart attack. But those wounds!'' Grant looked closer as Francesca working deftly peeled the shirt away. ''God!'' Grant exclaimed, ''It's like claw marks. Feral cats.''

''Could they do so much damage?'' Francesca asked dubiously, used to the adorable home variety.

''They could slash you to pieces,'' Grant said grimly. ''So many introduced animals do terrible damage to native wildlife and habitats. The camels, brumbies, foxes, wild pigs, rabbits, you name them. I've seen a man gutted by a wild boar. Feral cats aren't like your domestic tabbies. They're ferocious. More like miniature lions.''

''They must be if they've done this.'' Francesca turned her head briefly. ''Why don't you get the kit from the chopper,'' she urged. ''I'm okay here. These wounds need to be cleaned. A lot of them seem to be fairly superficial although he's bled a great deal. Others are deep.''

''They could start bleeding again,'' Grant warned, looking at her closely. In the shade of the casuarina she had discarded his hat, which in any case had fallen down over her eyes. She had gone very pale but her hands were rock steady.

''I'll be very careful,'' she said. ''Blood is horrible but I won't faint if that's what's bothering you.'' In fact she was willing herself to remain in control. ''Hello there,'' she said in gentle amazement as Curly opened his eyes. ''Lie there quietly,'' she bid him swiftly, fearful his wounds would reopen. ''You're fine. Fine.''

Curly's alarmingly grey face took on the faintest colour. ''Have I died and gone to heaven?'' His voice was little more than a rusty croak.

Grant moved so he was in Curly's sights. ''Hi there, Curly. I'm not paying you to rest easy under a tree.''

This time Curly tried a smile. ''Hi, boss. I wondered when you'd get here.''

''Don't try to speak, Curly. Save your strength,'' Grant urged, perturbed his man looked terrible. He'd get onto the flying doctor right away. Curly could be airlifted to Bunnerong, which had its own airstrip. The Royal Flying Doctor's Cessna could land there.

''Bloody cats, would you believe it,'' Curly groaned. ''Bloody feral cats, savage little bastards. A whole pack of them came at me out of nowhere while I was off balance being as sick as a dog. Never had such a thing happen to me before. Must have scared them somehow. Reckon I passed a kidney stone I was in so much pain. The radio is out. Needs an expert. I had to land. Just made it before I passed out. Agony I tell ya! Hell wouldn't be too strong a word for it. Now I open my eyes to an angel with eyes like the sky and hair like the sunset.''

''Don't talk, Curly.'' Francesca smiled, knowing it was taking too much out of him. ''You've had a very bad experience. I'll try not to hurt you but those scratches need attention.''

Curly gave the ghost of a cheeky grin. ''Whatever you do to me, I'll love it.''

Come to think of it she could pass for a celestial creature, Grant thought as he walked back to the helicopter to put through his calls. She could be counted on, too, to keep her head in an emergency as well. He had to admit he was impressed with her quiet efficiency.

A day later Curly was sleeping peacefully in hospital minus his gall bladder, lamenting the fact the ''angel'' who had tended his lacerations so tenderly had been replaced by a burly male nurse.

The following week saw the return of Fee and David Westbury, arms full of presents, looking wonderfully rested and increasingly affectionate after a fortnight on a small exclusive Great Barrier Reef island. Both wore becoming golden tans, Fee telling all and sundry she wasn't in the least afraid of the sun, it was ''absolutely'' essential. Of course Fee was blessed with a good olive skin, well hydrated, well cared for and she'd spent nearly all of her adult life in misty England.

''I'm not like you, my darling!'' She looked across worriedly at Francesca. ''You've got to watch yourself with that red hair and de Lyle skin. You'd shrivel up if you lived out here,'' she said innocently.

Well thank you, Mamma, Francesca heaved a small inner sigh. Thank you for confirming Grant's worst fears.

They were all at dinner in Kimbara's truly beautiful formal dining room, Brod, their host at the head of the long, gleaming mahogany table, Rebecca in a lovely aquamarine silk shift with a slightly ruffled hemline facing him at the opposite end. Fee, with David beside her was to Brod's right, ever glamorous in some kind of sophisticated tiger stripe drapery with a deep cowl neck. Facing them Francesca wore a simple shift dress similar in style to Rebecca's but a glowing midnight-blue, with Grant beside her. Their bright colouring was startling under the light from twin chandeliers. Francesca all rosy apricot reds and golds, individual strands of hair glittering like jewellery, Grant tawny bronze, hair and skin.

Brod, sensing Francesca's discomfit, and aware of Grant's misgivings about her, decided to weigh in. ''Fee's just having fun, Fran,'' he told her lightly. ''It's simply a question of taking care. Rebecca has perfect skin.'' Brod raised his wineglass to his beautiful wife in salute, his eyes full of admiration.

''Of course she has, darling.'' Fee reached out to pat his hand. ''But it's that thick, creamy magnolia skin. My darling girl's is eggshell thin.''

''Does that mean it can't wait to crack?'' Francesca gave a little wail, her cheeks catching colour as they always did when she was upset. ''Anyway eggshell may be delicate, but it's *strong.*''

''The answer is as Brod says,'' Rebecca intervened gently. ''Good sun protection and protective clothing plus the essential, wide-brimmed hat. I think Fran could not only survive but flourish out here,'' she added, earning Francesca's gratitude.

''Becky, darling.'' Fee finished her wine with amazing speed and no apparent effect. ''Don't give Francesca any ideas. She's all but promised to Jimmy Waddington. That's the Honourable James Waddington. His father Peregrine is de Lyle's closest friend. Jimmy was distraught when Francesca quit her job to come to Oz. He's fully expecting her to return. As is her father. Believe me I know my daughter loves it here, but England is her real world.''

''What a pity nobody told me.'' Francesca tried to smile, wishing for the ten thousandth time her mother wouldn't volunteer so much information. But then no one could stop Fee. She had a terrible habit of letting the cat out of the bag and if that didn't go off too well to shove it back in.

''Just knew she'd left a boyfriend behind.'' Grant turned his head to give Francesca a direct look. ''Jimmy Waddington. The Honourable James Waddington. That sounds just about right.''

''Breach of privacy, Fee.'' Brod tapped his aunt's magnificently beringed hand. ''Now let's hear Fran's version.''

Oh, thank you, Brod, Francesca thought, diving into an explanation. ''I think of Jimmy as my friend. I've known him all my life. I love him in that way because he's a truly lovable person. He's decent and kind and he's very intelligent.''

''In short someone you ought to marry,'' Grant inserted in a voice like dark polished silk.

''Except I don't love him in any romantic way. I forgot to mention that.'' Francesca returned his gem-hard gaze.

''Believe me, darling, liking is much better.'' Fee of the fantastic love affairs pronounced without turning a hair. ''You simply must have things in common. Have the same friends, share the same tastes, the same background. Passion is all very well but unless a man and a woman have similar views of life, things can become very quickly unstuck. Your father for instance was madly in love with me but he should never have married me.''

''I can't imagine why he did.'' Brod gave a brief laugh. ''Obviously you were much too hard to resist, Fee, let alone control.''

''Well, as they say, it seemed like a good idea at the time,'' Fee replied. ''I desperately want my girl to be happy. I don't want her to make an awful mistake, like me. One should approach marriage in a cool and rational manner.''

''That's why you did just the opposite,'' Francesca pointed out with less than her usual tolerance, causing David to chuckle out loud.

''Fee often says things she doesn't mean,'' he told Francesca soothingly. ''Being in love is the grandest feeling of all. It makes one come alive. It makes one whole. Which brings me to my announcement of this evening.'' David tapped his crystal wineglass with a spoon and looked around the table. ''Fee and I have something to tell you and we hope you'll be as happy about it as we are. We have decided to get married.''

Brod was the first to respond, ''Now why doesn't that surprise me?'' Then everyone stood up at once. Francesca running around the table to kiss her mother, followed by Rebecca, while the men shook hands.

''Congratulations!''

''We're both so happy.'' A very becoming blush spread over Fee's golden cheeks. ''Life is wonderful with David around. Of course he's the man I should have married.''

Brod, catching David's eyes gave a sardonic little grin, but didn't point out David was married at the time. ''I think this calls for champagne.'' He looked to his wife, loving her madly, this woman who was making him extraordinarily happy. "Would it be too much to hope we've got something really good in the frig?"

"If you're into Bollinger." She smiled into his eyes. "Some little instinct told me to put it in."

Afterwards Francesca and Grant chose to walk off the effects of the celebration, leaving Fee to talk further about her plans. The air was filled with all the clean, dry aromatic scents of the bush, the purplish black sky palpitating with the glittering white fire of countless stars. It should have been exciting but there was a kind of estrangement between them.

"So is marriage going to interfere with this movie part Fee's been offered?" Grant asked, more to break the awkward silence than anything else.

"I'm sure Mamma and David have talked it through," Francesca said. "It's not a big role. A cameo they call it. Mamma's thinking of it as a last hurrah."

"Her swan song?" Grant's deep voice sounded sceptical.

"God knows she has enormous energy and a great deal to offer. Anyway David's used to Mamma," Francesca said. "She's right about one thing. They're two of a kind. David has always led a full life, a pivotal member of a very glamorous group, the theatre, the art aficionados. He's very different from Daddy. My father likes the companionship of a few lifelong friends and his own peaceful world of Ormond. He hates leaving it even for a day."

"I expect it's very beautiful."

"One of the most beautiful places on earth." Francesca felt her heart swelling with pride.

"But you won't inherit it?" Grant countered with a kind of disbelief.

Francesca plucked a waxy flower then twirled it under her nose. ‘‘No.’’

‘‘Good Lord!’’ Grant stared up at the pulsing stars. ‘‘Don't you mind, this male of the line stuff?’’

‘‘Perhaps.’’ She nodded, in reality deeply attached to her ancestral home. ‘‘But I grew up knowing I wouldn't inherit Ormond, just as Ally knew Kimbara would be Brod's.’’

‘‘A bit of a difference there, I'd say.’’ Grant sounded as if he didn't appreciate the parallel. ‘‘The business of running a cattle chain is all hard slog. Backbreaking work, stoic resilience, lots of responsibility. I wouldn't wish the load on any woman's shoulders. The outback is a man's world, Francesca, for all we need our women's love and devotion. You would be in perfect harmony with your ancestral home.’’

She'd been counting on him to say that. ‘‘Only it's *not* mine,’’ she repeated wryly. Hadn't she already moved out, not at all close to her father's second wife, not able to help making comparisons with a beautiful, brilliant Fee.

‘‘That's too damned bad,’’ Grant was saying. ‘‘If I were your father I'd have changed things.’’

‘‘I'm very glad you're not my father,’’ she offered dryly, deeply conscious of his tall, powerful figure beside her, whipcord lean.

He laughed, then suddenly began to croon, taking her by surprise. ‘‘You must have been a beautiful baby. You must have been a beautiful child. When you were only startin' to go to kindergarten, I bet you drove the little boys wild....’’

Perfect tune. Smooth as honey baritone. It sounded great with a considerable degree of seductiveness.

"I didn't know you could sing," she said delightedly.

"Of course I can sing." The ice broken he pulled her against him, wrapping an arm around her waist. "You should hear me when I'm out riding. When I was a kid I used to sing to the cattle. It used to calm them every time."

"Are you serious?" she laughed.

"Ask Rafe." He launched smoothly into another song. "Home, home on the range…"

His voice came back to them on the wind and Francesca clapped in appreciation. "From now on you're going to have to serenade *me.*"

"Am I?" He turned her, his hands spanning her narrow waist. "So what about this Jimmy?"

She dipped her head. "Daddy's choice, Grant. Not mine."

"You're not running away from them, are you?" he asked as if he were resolved to find out. Holding her, touching her, desire rippling deep inside him.

"In what way?"

"Unwillingness to commit maybe. Your father is concerned with marrying you off properly. He doesn't trust your mother in that regard."

"He doesn't trust Fee at all," Francesca confessed wryly. "He may have loved her madly once but all I can remember is his finding fault. It's not very nice being the child in the middle of a fault-finding divorce and the long aftermath. The physical separation from Mamma. It was like being deprived of the sun. The actor Fee was having an affair with and later married was remarkably handsome and when he wasn't drunk he could be very nice but Daddy *hated* him. He refused to allow me to visit if Fee's 'new man' was anywhere around.''

''Well he wasn't around long, thank the Lord.'' Grant gave a deep sigh. Fee's exploits over the years were well known to all of them. He had a vivid picture, too, of how it must have been for one sad and solitary little girl.

''I can give you some lyrics à la Cole Porter,'' Francesca offered half in fun, half serious. '''It was just one of those things. One of those crazy things.' Fee can't be without a man.''

''Now she's got David, so cheer up.'' Grant turned her gently so they could walk on.

''And my dear cousin, David, will keep Mamma in line,'' Francesca said with a note of satisfaction. ''He may look and act the perfect gentleman with the Eton accent but he's steel at the core. If he'd been married to Fee in the first place she'd never have shared anyone else's bed.''

''Her time with your father could scarcely have been wasted,'' Grant reminded her. ''She had *you.* That alone was a great gift. Anyway she adores you.''

''I know.'' Forgiving by nature Francesca's anger and bewilderment at her mother's abandonment had long since dried up.

''And you're going back to Sydney for her book launch.'' It was obviously a statement, not a question.

''Of course I have to and I want to. Rebecca as the biographer is going as a matter of course. It's just a pity Ally won't be home. I want to be here when she gets back.''

''And I need to be *out!*'' Grant startled her by saying.

Anxiety sounded in her voice. ''What does that mean?''

He gave a little amused growl low in his throat. ''Why, Francesca, do I really have to spell it out? Two's company, three's a crowd. Especially when you're newly married.''

She stood stock-still to stare up at him. ''But the homestead is so big!''

''What's wrong, love?'' Very lightly he pinched that delicately determined little chin. ''Don't you like it? Rafe and Ally will want to be on their own.''

Privately she thought Rafe and Ally would be very upset if he left. ''But where will you go?'' she questioned. ''I never thought for a minute you'd leave Opal. Apart from the fact it's your home, it's the base for Cameron Airways.''

''That can be changed.'' He sounded as if he'd thought it all out.

''You're serious then?'' She was totally distracted.

''Absolutely.''

''Do Rafe and Ally know of your plans?'' she persisted, so nearly giving herself away.

''Not as yet. Needless to say they assure me Opal is my home as well.''

''I should think so.'' Francesca felt like she was in some trance of non-acceptance. She couldn't lose contact with this man she'd fallen helplessly, probably hopelessly in love with. ''Where would you go?''

Grant took her hand and walked on. ''Somewhere more central. Even Darwin.''

''In the Territory?'' She was shaken by the thought. He was talking a thousand miles away and more.

''Gateway to Australia.'' Grant nodded. ''I know of a fine property that could come on the market.''

Francesca gave him a dismayed look, unaware her expression was easily readable by the moon. ''You've taken my breath away,'' she told him unnecessarily. ''Everyone will miss you terribly.'' *Me* most of all.

For a long moment he was mad with wanting her. Wanting to crush her to him, feel the softness and smallness of her body against his. Inhale her scents. Instead with force of will he pressed his thumb into her palm, feeling her heat, caressing it with a deep circular motion. What stopped him from making love to this young woman as he was wild to? Other times, other places, other girls, he had felt none of this anguish over lovemaking. The answer was he cared too damned much about her. He couldn't force a potentially disastrous situation. She was Lady Francesca de Lyle, daughter of an English earl and the internationally famous stage actress, Fiona Kinross. If she were any other girl, a young woman of his own circle, he'd have raced her to the altar. Francesca's background reeked of centuries old tradition, a high place in one of the most privileged societies on earth. Even Fee had pushed the fact Francesca was meant for better things.

Finally he managed to say, ''I'm not going that far away. Not as a plane flies. I don't aim to stick to helicopters. Dad left me a fair share of Opal even if I'm not Numero Uno.''

You are to me, Francesca thought, blindly turning her face away. ''Why don't you build a homestead of your own on Opal?'' she frowned. ''There's plenty of room in a couple of thousand square miles.''

His spirits lifted unaccountably. Why hadn't he come around to that? ''Opal has only ever had one homestead,'' he pointed out as if it was written in stone.

She shot him a quick look, aware of his change of mood. ''Two Cameron sons who love each other and don't want to be parted? Even if they don't want to share the same house, I would have thought building another homestead would be the obvious solution. And I'll tell you exactly where you should do it.''

He was halfway to laughing now, loving the sweet sound of her voice and the surprising authority in it. ''Go on. Tell me,'' he invited, taking the path that led to the walled garden with its pond and winged nymph, glorious scents of roses, jasmine and boronia, herbs crushed underfoot, soft little night wind like music and two carved garden seats.

Peace and harmony by day. Powerfully seductive by moonlight. Maybe he'd been worrying so much he'd suddenly got to the point where he couldn't care anymore. Whatever the reason he led her to one of the benches, sending a few fallen leaves and spent blossoms flying with a lick of the handkerchief from his trouser pocket. Protecting her pretty deep blue dress was a priority. The short skirt showed her lovely legs. The deep oval neck descended onto her breasts, delicate, tantalising, the skin of the upper slopes smooth as silk, white as milk. The rosy nipples he just knew would be like luscious little berries in his mouth, the taste more exquisite than any known fruit.

God the only thing that saved him from ravishing her was he knew right from wrong. Even so his breath seemed to be rasping in his chest. Desire was the very devil. It made an utter fool of a man.

''I would have thought you'd guess,'' Francesca was saying, making room for him on the bench, mercifully unaware of his unsettled state. ''It's extraordinary country and it's only about a mile or more from Opal homestead. Grassy flats, bordered by spinifex and mulga country, then in the distance the rippling slopes of the desert dunes. But what makes it all fascinating is that very strange hill with the perfectly flat top, except for three little peaks around the border for all the world like some ancient crown. It's full of magic. Every time I've seen it, from the distance or the air, it seems to be floating in an amethyst mirage."

Of course he identified the site right away. Francesca was right. There was something about it. "Francesca, you're talking about Myora," he said, referring to the landmark. "There are all kinds of legends attached to it."

"Which makes it all that more delightful," she said happily. "As hills go it isn't high. What would it be…a couple of hundred feet? But it has such an *aura!*" Then she suddenly asked, "It's not a sacred site?" She knew that could change things with aboriginal tribes currently focusing on regaining their sacred sites.

"No—" Grant shook his head, instantly following her line of thought "—but it has associations from the Dreamtime."

"Does that mean you can't build there?" She felt unaccountably disappointed.

"I can build anywhere I want," he told her firmly. "This is Cameron land. We feel we have as much kinship with the land as our aboriginal brothers. The Camerons have always treated tribal people well. We came as protectors as well as pastoralists. As a courtesy I would discuss my plans with the tribal elders. But, Francesca, Myora is even more isolated than Opal homestead."

"You mean the difficulty of getting building materials, etc., to the site?'' Immediately Francesca was overwhelmed by the challenges of the job.

''No, I don't,'' Grant said surprisingly. ''Our forebears performed fantastic feats. I mean—'' he broke off, rubbing his neck. ''Hell I don't know what I mean.'' When every other thought was given over to placing Francesca, like a jewel, in her proper setting. The middle of the Never Never, for all its fascination, didn't seem the right spot.

''You could *think* about it,'' Francesca suggested, looking up at his strong profile.

''Wouldn't you be terrified on your own out there?'' he countered.

Another rejection. ''What should I be terrified of?'' She kept her voice composed. ''There aren't any bushrangers anymore. No stockman would dream of causing me harm.''

''You know nothing about utter isolation,'' he said, leaning a little away from her. ''When you come out here you stay at one of the grandest homesteads in the country. Kimbara. You're safe and cushioned at all times. I love the bush, Francesca, I have great respect for it but I can tell you even hardened stockmen can get spooked on their own. There are some areas, some places, that have an atmosphere, that can make the hair on the back of your neck stand up. We've all experienced it. This is an incredibly ancient land. We're by way of being very recent newcomers.''

Francesca gave a delicious little shiver. ''Are we talking ghosts?''

''I'm not talking ballyhoo, my lady,'' he retorted, giving a lock of her long hair a slight tug. ''What I say isn't to be taken lightly. There are certain places even the aborigines won't go.''

"On Opal?" She felt as if she was drowning in mysteries.

"Of course on Opal." Grant's voice was matter-of-fact. "Kimbara, too. It's *strange* country in many ways. Our country and not our country. Not the white man's country if you know what I mean. Our ancestors came from elsewhere. The Camerons and the Kinrosses hailed from Scotland. In certain places the Interior seems to be not exactly hostile but not welcoming, either."

"You can't mean Myora?" She'd always thought the land welcomed her on all her visits.

Grant's voice was level. "*I've* never felt it there. But *you've* never actually been there, have you?"

"I'd like to go." She lifted a delicate brow.

"Then this is your chance," he surprised her by answering. "I have a few days all to myself. I can take you tomorrow, though the odds are against my ever building there."

"You might change your mind." She attempted lightness when she was feeling utterly emotional.

"Wishful thinking, Francesca." He turned his hazel eyes on her.

"*What* am I thinking?" Suddenly she could barely breathe. There was humour in his voice but something else that sent a deep pulsing, quiver right through her body.

"An impossible dream."

"What dream," she challenged, softly. "What am I dreaming?"

For answer he bent his head and pressed his mouth to the creamy flesh of her throat.

"Grant!" Even to her own ears she sounded startled.

"You don't really know what you're trying to get yourself into," he said, a shade harshly.

"Can't you see you surprised me?" In fact she was more frightened of her own reactions than anything he might do to her. He was the most beautiful man. Full of a man's powers. Just the touch of his lips against her throat made her head swim.

"You're safe with me, Francesca," he said in a dry voice and stood up, his height exaggerated in the silver moonlight. "As safe as if you were sitting in church."

She, too, came to her feet, humming with tension. "Now I've made you angry, why?"

"I'm not angry with you at all," he said, not really meaning it and not knowing why. "I just don't want you to forget who *you* are and who *I* am."

"Now that's a *message,*" Francesca said.

"Yes, it is." Even he grimaced, thinking himself as much a victim of circumstances as Francesca.

"Why can't you get through your head I'm a *woman* not a figurine," Francesca suddenly exploded.

That somehow inflamed him to the point he felt he was burning up. *He* didn't appreciate she was a woman? How could she say such a ridiculous thing, this miracle of femininity.

Before she could take a breath he held her lovely face and kissed her hard and fast. Just seconds to be ravenous. He wanted to plunge his hand into the low, tempting oval of her dress and take hold of her small creamy breasts. Just the thought of it made him wild, but he couldn't do this to her. It was all so damned confusing. One might have thought she was some kind of family, or a little Titian-haired, blue-eyed saint on a pedestal. He should have avoided her right from the start. She was so hopelessly out of reach.

Francesca's own confusion was immense. Grant was breathing heavily. So was she. Both of them filled with a terrible unrequited desire. More than that. Love. She was certain he loved her but instead of helping her it was somehow making him feel guilty. She could have wept.

"Grant, I really care about you," she said, moving close, gripping onto his shirtsleeve with her hand. "Why are you pushing me away?"

"You know very well." That high mettled note came into his voice. "I care about you, too, Francesca. Too much to want to cause you real unhappiness. I can see to the end of this if you can't?"

It was obvious his concerns were real. "You mean you think it inevitable I'll go back to England."

"You'll leave me before I'll ever leave you. England *is* your home. You have a certain position in life. It's not outback wife. Even the heat of the sun can be killing."

She was nearly crying with frustration. "So Rebecca can survive it. So can Ally, so can my mother. Every other woman it seems but me."

He looked down at her, she was totally enchanting and anguish edged his voice. "It's the way you look."

"You think I'm an ice cream that might melt." She made a little sound of exasperation.

"Hell I'm afraid of just that. Look, Francesca, I'm not trying to insult you—" he stroked her cheek "—or anything like that. I'm trying to decide what's best for both of us."

"Which of course is as good as saying *I'm* stupid." She shimmered with sudden temper.

"Far from it." He knew he shouldn't but he laughed, loving the sparkle in her star-struck eyes.

"Then why don't you let me decide what *I* want," she challenged, her blue gaze riveted to his strong handsome face.

"Because it's too dangerous." He bent his head and just brushed the corner of her mouth with his lips. "You're hell bent on a holiday romance."

She heard the teasing note in his voice...of course she did, yet she flinched. "Then it's really astonishing the way *you* keep kissing *me*."

He grinned at her, his teeth flashing very white. "That's what's called turning the tables. I'm sorry, Francesca, you might have started up the saying, you're adorable when you're angry, but I don't want to hurt you. You make me feel as protective as a big brother."

"Oh Lord!" She inhaled the jasmine-boronia filled night air. "So we don't get to take our trip tomorrow?"

He smiled slightly. "Hell you can't go around disappointing me. Of course we will. I wouldn't forego it for the world. You're going to show me where to build my dream house."

"Why should I?" she questioned, turning up her face to him. Why? When he would take to it some other woman as his bride.

"Because you're Lady Francesca de Lyle," he explained in a voice like dark velvet. "And it's your gift to me."

CHAPTER THREE

"YOU'RE going to do what?" Fee burst out, turning from the French doors and walking back into Francesca's bedroom.

"You heard, Mamma," Francesca continued, brushing her hair at the mirror. It was crackling with electricity, red, amber, rose and gold strands sparkling and flashing. "I'm going over to Opal with Grant. I'm going to help him pick out a home site."

"I don't believe it." Fee's dramatic face wore a worried frown. She slumped into a comfortable armchair imagining she was having a nervous breakdown. "I must ask you darling, is this wise?"

"Of course it's wise, Mamma," Francesca responded respectfully, firmly.

"But you know, darling, your father has big plans for you," Fee reminded her. "I might have embodied his biggest nightmare but you're his dream child. He loves you. He wants to see you happy in your own setting. Married to one of your childhood friends."

"Like good old Jimmy, my ex-boyfriend," Francesca asked wryly, waiting for her hair to settle so she could braid it.

"Not Jimmy if you don't think you could come to love him," Fee told her, reasonably. "But there are others, darling. Roger and Sebastian to name just two."

"Except I don't love them, either. Daddy didn't ask my permission to marry Holly. He just mentioned to me he was thinking of remarrying."

"How extraordinary when he hated every minute of being married to me," Fee said, gazing at her lovely daughter tenderly, maternally.

"No, he didn't, Mamma," Francesca corrected, ever loyal to her father. "He loved you. He would have stayed married to you forever if you hadn't run off."

"It must have been Springtime," Fee said, her face reflective. "Actually I was terribly misled but I was always hotly desired."

"You won't run away from David," Francesca warned.

"Darling, as if I'd want to!" Fee protested going quite pink. "At long last I've got it right. Best thing I've ever done. Anyway it's not me we're talking about, it's you. Don't think for a minute I have anything against Grant. He's a splendid young man, so sexy, he even gives your dear Mamma a funny feeling, but he has his own vision in life. Why only last night he was telling us his plans. His commitment is *here*. The Australian outback."

"Don't you think you're running too far ahead?" Francesca said, making little braids of her front hair.

Fee snorted. "Come on, darling, I know everything there is to know about love affairs. The air literally crackles around you two."

"Holiday affair?" Francesca asked.

"Well if you have to get him out of your system," Fee considered. "I don't see you two together, my darling. I can only see heartache and separation. I know it's not easy but one must try to be wise."

Francesca raised a delicate brow. "Yes, of course, Mamma, but I'm only going over to help him pick out a possible site for a new homestead. Grant doesn't want to intrude on Rafe and Ally."

"Goodness how nice of him," Fee said. "But the place is *huge*. Besides, why couldn't he buy a property? Douglas would have left his sons very well provided for."

"I'm certain Rafe doesn't want to lose his brother," Francesca said. "They're very close. Closer than most because of the sad circumstances of their life. Why buy another property when Grant could build a second homestead on Opal. Lord knows they've got a whole world to themselves as Brod has here."

"A kingdom at the very least," Fee agreed complacently. "My friends used to find it fascinating listening to stories from my childhood on Kimbara. But don't try to distract me. I'm doing my best to play Mamma. In short, I'm trying to warn you, my darling. You could get badly hurt. So could Grant. I should tell you, too, the Camerons are men of strong passions. And proud. Fiercely proud. You'll have to live with that."

"Actually I like it," Francesca said, her eyes going dreamy.

Fee fell back, unable to keep the genuine worry out of her voice. "Darling, normally I wouldn't interfere but I have a feeling this could be very serious. What have you really got on your mind? Surely as your mother I'm entitled to know?"

Francesca found herself sinking into the armchair opposite her mother. "I've never felt like this before, Mamma," she explained. "I feel like I'm lit up inside."

"You're in love." Fee nodded. "It's just rotten luck you had to fall for Grant."

Instantly Francesca jumped up, outraged. "That's not funny, Mamma."

Fee, too, hauled herself to her feet. "I'm not trying

to be funny, darling. For heaven's sake! I'm worried where this might lead. You have *everything* at home in England.''

''Except Grant,'' Francesca said with a touch of fire.

''Maybe so.'' Fee started to sound doubtful. ''But this life couldn't be more *different,* Fran. You've never seen Kimbara under drought. In times of flood. You can't possibly know. You haven't been around when the tragedies happen. Let's face it, darling, do you really want this lifestyle? Can you cope with it?''

''Rebecca is blooming,'' Francesca told her.

''Rebecca isn't *you* and I expect she'll take up her writing again. She'll have something engrossing to do. She and Brod will start a family. Kimbara needs its heirs.''

''What about Ally then?'' Francesca challenged, feeling like everyone was against her. ''Ally could have had a huge movie career. She knocked it all back for Rafe.''

''Oh, darling.'' Fee returned to her chair looking at her daughter with pity in her eyes. ''Ally is that little bit older than you, and she's had longer to consider what she really wants out of life. Then there's the fact, good actress that she is, Ally wasn't really dedicated as one has to be. The theatre was *everything* to me. That's the difference.'' But there had been a devastation to it, Francesca thought, but was too tender-hearted to mention. Her mother had been a wonderful actress but she hadn't been the best of mothers.

''A career isn't the only way to happiness and fulfilment, Mamma,'' she said quietly, sitting on the edge of the four-poster bed. ''It's a big job raising a family and I want children. I'd rather find Mr. Right than be a huge success in the business world though most people would tell you I was very effective at P.R.''

''And it didn't hurt to have an earl for a father,'' Fee pointed out dryly.

''That doesn't give me a warm glow, Mamma.'' Francesca couldn't help but speak a little sharply. ''In many ways your view of me seems to be as a *child.*''

It was true. ''Ah well, you are very young, darling,'' Fee sighed. ''Moreover you're the bearer of your father's dream. You're bright, beautiful, charming, so clearly destined for big things. You must realise, too, your son could become your father's heir.''

Francesca looked at her mother levelly. ''Even Grant has pointed that out to me.''

Fee nodded. ''I'm sure it concerns him. Whatever his feelings for you he must be aware of the situation.''

''*What* situation,'' Francesca burst out in pure frustration. ''Anyone would think I was a member of the Royal Family. Grant and I are equals. Come to that you always had more money than Daddy. I know you helped extensively at Ormond.''

''You can say that again!'' Fee breathed. ''But I don't feel at all bitter about it. It's as I say, one day my grandson might occupy it. I don't want to be disagreeable, darling. I don't want to upset you. I know the wonderful feelings that come with thinking oneself in love but I have to help you to look steadily to your future. I feel a great affection for the Camerons, Rafe and Grant. Grant is an admirable young man. There's no question he's going places. He's masterful, aggressive, assertive and very hot-headed from time to time. You may find it exciting now but as he develops I think he'll turn into a real dynamo. Dynamos in a way are dangerous people. They're high risk.''

"I'm not afraid of anything about Grant, Mamma," Francesca said very seriously, twining her arms around the polished mahogany bedpost, all rose and cream and blue sheened eyes. "I think he'd die rather than hurt me. What makes me fearful is the thought he could turn me away thinking it was for my own good."

Fee gave an uncomfortable little laugh. "Darling, have you considered he might be right?" Breeding showed in every line of her daughter's petite, slender body, breeding and what Fee interpreted as a certain fragility, an inability to withstand rigours.

Her mother's seeming opposition was like little barbs to the heart. Francesca moved off the bed so quickly her thick braid swung against her cheek. "Except if I lost him I know I'd be sorry for the rest of my life."

They landed on Opal's front lawn while the hot humming earth sent up spirals of dried grass, bleached bronze and gold leaves. When the air was still they alighted, Francesca looking with great pleasure towards the huge, rambling old homestead with its gables and verandah bays, the pedimented porch and the white wrought-iron lacework that matched the timber fretwork. Opal lacked Kimbara's conscious grandeur but it was a fine colonial homestead by anyone's standards. Cascading bright red bougainvillea made a glorious show falling from the slate roof of the east wing, down the white pillars to the ground, as did the deep hardy border of agapanthus with huge hyacinth and white heads right along the front of the house, but it was evident not a great deal of time had been spent on the once extensive home gardens. The lawn not shaded by a giant magnolia and a row of classic gums, was yellowed by the heat of the sun and the central three tiered fountain that once had played was now dry and dusty. Nevertheless it was an amazingly attractive building and Francesca knew Ally would have the most wonderful time bringing the homestead and its home grounds back to their former glory.

''Come up and look around,'' Grant said, taking her by her silky arm, feeling the sizzle in his fingers. ''It's very quiet with no one around. As you can see, the gardens of my mother's day have gone, neither Rafe nor I have had the time to look after them. Not that either of us know much about gardening but we surely miss what it was like with Mum around. That wonderful feminine grace went out of everything. But Ally will bring it back.''

Francesca looked up to smile into his face, feeling so happy it was like her blood was filled with bubbles. ''And have a marvellous time doing it. I *love* the homestead.'' Her eyes shone. ''It's extraordinarily picturesque. As a matter of fact now I look at it, it would be the ideal outback setting for Mamma's new movie?''

''What are you saying here?'' Grant cocked a brow. ''I thought the woman director was coming out to take a look at Kimbara? Surely Fee said so at dinner last night?''

''Actually, Mamma did that without asking,'' Francesca confessed. ''Something she has a tendency to do. Not that Brod would refuse her and Rebecca would take pleasure in it but I've read the screenplay and Kimbara homestead is too...too...'' She sought the right word.

''Teetering on grand?'' he suggested dryly.

''In every way. Uncle Stewart spent a fortune on its upkeep and it shows.''

"While the Camerons did not." He looked her straight in the eyes, loving her sudden flush, a rosy pinkness that wasn't there a moment ago.

"I don't mean that." Francesca shook her head. "I mean Opal has a soft well lived in..."

"Faded charm?"

"Are you going to finish all my sentences for me?" she demanded.

"If we want to get to the nitty gritty." He grinned, moving her into the shade of the verandah.

"If you read the screenplay you'd know what I mean."

"Francesca, I'm one up on you." His smile mocked her. "I've read the book."

"*Have* you?" She sounded delighted.

"Outback people are great readers," he told her. "Didn't you know?"

"As a matter of fact I do." Reading was a big part of entertainment. "Opal homestead is really what they're after."

"Maybe, but who would need all those film people around?" He opened the front door, turning to look at her in her simple cotton shirt and jeans. Who said a redhead couldn't wear pink? He'd never seen a pink shirt look so good.

"You said yourself it was very lonely on your own." Her eyes were alive with ideas. "I expect the outback scenes could be shot in a month. Riversleigh, the Sydney colonial mansion is the setting for most of the action. Anyway it's just a thought."

"Then why are those blue eyes so bright and alive?" he retorted with amusement. "The last time they sparkled just like that you were doing an excellent P.R. job on Drew Forsythe from TCR."

"I'm always full of ideas," Francesca said, moving into the spacious hallway and looking around.

"I can see that," he commented, captivated by her presence.

"So am I allowed to discuss it with Mamma?" She twirled her small supple body. "The director and script writer will be here in a couple of days."

"You're kidding?" In a way he was utterly taken aback.

"No," she answered simply. "It would be lovely to see Opal up on the big screen. It's not the first time a colonial mansion has been used in an Australian movie. I think it would be brilliant! Moreover you have such enormous interest in everything you'd probably enjoy it."

"Well I might," he admitted, "but, Francesca, I'm not around much during the day. I have a business."

"All right. So no one would bother you. There would be good company for dinner. You would want to speak to Rafe and Ally?"

He laughed. A mocking sound, slightly awry. "Darling, are you reminding me of my obligations?"

The way he called her "darling" nearly took her breath away. "Really I'm just having a bit of fun," she wavered.

"No, you're not." The laugh turned indulgent. "You want me to take this seriously."

"I swear I never thought of it until five minutes ago," she said sincerely. "I looked up at the homestead and there it was! The setting right under my nose, so to speak."

"They pay well I imagine?" Grant the business man was considering.

"I'm sure they would."

"In that case Rafe is involved in a programme for rehabilitation for troubled youth, a kind of bush rescue scheme. I'm interested, too, but as Rafe runs the station it's mainly his concern. The Trust could do with the money."

"What a good idea." She felt a real flutter of excitement. "I've heard about the scheme from Ally. I can see, too, the bush has great healing powers.

"Nature's cathedral," Grant said. "God can speak very clearly here. But hang on, Francesca, your mother has other ideas."

"Not by the time I've spoken to her." Francesca gave her lovely endearing smile.

"I believe you, but you'll have to hang on until I speak to Rafe and Ally. They mightn't want any part of it."

Francesca lifted her face to him. "I'm not exactly sure about Rafe, but I know Ally will be intrigued. She might even want to be home when they shoot the scenes. We'll all enjoy watching Fee. She becomes so much the part she's playing, it's shivery. As soon as the makeup goes on, the dress, she's that person."

Grant could well believe it. He'd seen Fee transform herself into any number of people in the space of telling a story. "You've never thought of acting yourself?" he asked Francesca.

"Believe it or not I was considered quite good at school."

"So did Fee go along to see you? Tell you how wonderful you were?"

The smile faltered slightly. "She was so busy at the time she missed all of my performances, but Daddy came."

"Hell I put my foot in it," he groaned, so much in empathy with her he felt her old pain.

"It doesn't hurt anymore."

"Sure?" He badly wanted to kiss her, hold her in his arms, comfort her, only he was too keenly aware it could all get out of hand. She made his blood soar, this exquisitely fashioned young woman. Not a figurine. She had far too much intelligence, humour, radiance to be that.

"I don't think I could love Mamma any more than I do. I *know* she's not ordinary but I have missed her terribly many times in my life." Read years, Francesca thought but would never say. Not now when the estrangement was over.

"It could have ruined your relationship forever," Grant considered broodingly, "but you're far too compassionate for that. Fee was perfectly charming to me when we left, but I got the feeling she's afraid of something."

"Oh, Grant, don't talk about it." She came to him and took his hand, trying to distract his attention. "I feel like a cup of coffee and I want to look over the homestead."

"You know you're safe with me, don't you," he said, not to be deflected.

She stared right into his eyes. "To me you're the most honourable man on the face of the earth."

"Francesca!" He couldn't help it, he pulled her into his arms as his emotions took control. "I have to tell you I'm suffering for it." His tone was self-mocking and dry.

"What could be wrong about falling in love?" she whispered rejoicing in being within the circle of his arms.

"Falling in love is wonderful, Francesca," he agreed in a low feeling voice. "The world is a lovely, romantic place, but there's no question falling in love with the wrong person can wreck lives."

"Then why don't you let me go," she taunted him very gently, lifting her head.

His expression was wry. "It seems my arms have a life of their own."

"So you are happy to hold me?"

"I love holding you," he said and meant it. "I could hold you like this forever. I could spend eternity looking into your eyes. I could run my mouth over that little pulse in your throat. I could open that pink shirt and caress your breasts. I could topple you into my bed. But that wouldn't get the coffee made." Determinedly he bent his head, kissed her cheek and swiftly turned her about. "Do you like it black or white?"

"You're a devil," she said. So he was for tempting her so richly.

"There's a devil in every man," he warned her, his eyes glinting," but depend on it I'll keep him well hidden around you."

They took the horses along the long, twisting trail of gullies and billabongs that led to the ancient flat-topped hill the aborigines named Myora. At intervals they came across stockmen leading herds of cattle to camp, stopping briefly to watch an aboriginal stockman breaking in a silver-grey brumby obviously descended from station stock. The stockman's movements were filled with a kind of exquisite grace and Francesca was reminded Australian aborigines were among the finest natural dancers in the world. Overhead legions of birds flew like bright flags in the sky and there was music, too, from thousands and thousands of tiny throats with occasionally a wonderful cello solo from some bell-toned bird in the furthermost branch of a towering gum, or deep in the swamp.

There were kangaroos of all sizes, a marvellous sight when they bounded away across the flats, endearing standing stock-still by the water as they picked up their scent, ears pricked, pointed noses quivering, a curious look in their large, bright eyes. Through all this wonderful ride, Grant kept exclusively to the shade, following the tree-lined creeks that were scented with acacia and some kind of little lilies that grew thickly guarded by grand old coolabahs and ghost gums. At one of the many reed fringed billabongs they saw masses of waterfowl, and several times the wonderful blue cranes, the brolgas, making a striking picture as they fished among the waterlilies. Pink in this lagoon, blue in another, sometimes a mixture of blue and cream. Francesca, the nature lover, was utterly enchanted, thinking as she always did, the bush was a place of great magic. Her mother's blood truly spoke to her. She had absorbed it into her soul.

By the time they reached Myora there was a taut expectancy in the air. Because of the extreme flatness of the vast open plains even an elevation of a few hundred feet took on a considerable aura. Today as she had seen it from the air Myora's base was floating in a sea of amethyst mirage giving the impression the ancient eroded mesa was anchored to a cloud. To north, south, east and west the plains ran on for endless miles. In fruitful years wildflowers bloomed in their countless millions, way out to the far horizon but even in the Dry it was a magnificent sight.

"You're really enjoying yourself, aren't you?" Grant said with immense satisfaction, keeping a sharp look out for anything to startle her, a large goanna, a prowling dingo, the frilled lizards that came at a lightning rush but were harmless, some slight movement at the base of a bush that could only be a snake trying to escape.

"This is a special place," Francesca breathed, watching as Grant hitched the horses to a huge fallen tree limb for all the world like a massive sculpture. "This is where you should build your house. Right in the middle of the sweeping plain with Myora as a backdrop. It must be an incredible sight when the great inland blooms. I've missed it on every visit."

"You'll have to come back when the time is right," Grant managed to say in a casual voice, at the same time feeling a deep ache that took a moment or two to pass. "Flowers as far as the eye can see," he continued. "Mile after mile, the flowers go on. Over the graves of the pioneers. Over the graves of the lost explorers. The flowers are fragrant as well so the air might be blown in from heaven. Last year after the winter rains the country around here was smothered in yellow and white paper daisies, golden craspedia, green pussy tails, poppies and firebush, hopbush saltbush, yellow top carpet of snow, you name it. Though I've witnessed the flowering of the desert gardens all my life in times of drought even I can't believe the flowers will ever rise again. Yet they always do."

"A miracle," Francesca said quietly, still badly shaken by his casual acceptance she would be returning home.

He walked towards her, tall and powerful. "It sure seems like it. Experiments have been done on the remarkable desert seeds. Apparently they contain chemicals that prevent germination until the optimum time. Nature's green light. They don't spring to life for example after a brief shower only to quickly die back. The right timing ensures the seed crop for future generations." He pointed upwards to the ancient glowing hill.

"At the right times, there are beautiful blooms hidden away up there on Myora. Tucked into all sorts of places where the wind has blown the seeds. Fan flowers, wild hibiscus, little lilies, Lilac Lamb's Tails literally covering the rubble down the hillside, all waving in the breeze. Anyway, come along." He took hold of her hand. "I've something special to show you. Something we don't talk about a great deal on Opal mainly for protection."

"That's exciting! What is it?" She stared up into his golden-skinned face, his iridescent eyes shadowed by the broad brim of his akubra.

"All in good time." He stopped, touching a gentle forefinger to her chin. "God, you're beautiful!" He truly didn't mean to say it but it just popped out. Why was he sending out all these dangerous, conflicting, messages? Only her lovely face looked so rapt.

"I'm happy," she told him.

"That's what I want you to be." He spoke quietly but something in his voice turned hard. "Let's climb to the summit." He drew her on. "It's not that far and it's amazing the view of the surrounding countryside.

Despite his contradictions, a not to be denied exhilaration took hold of Francesca. It lent wings to her small feet. She was like a gazelle going up the rocky slope, foot sure, keeping hold of his hand but making her own confident ascent.

"Oh, this is marvellous!" she announced, when they finally reached the plateau.

"Get your breath," he advised, knowing he was being overprotective.

"I'm not out of breath." She showed a radiant smile to him.

"No, you're not," he admitted.

"It's all so vast!" She turned away from him and threw up her arms. "Overwhelming. I love the colours of the inland. All the ochres. They're so deep and weathered yet they *vibrate.* And the sky's so blue. Not a cloud in sight. The European explorers must have thought they'd ventured onto another planet. Thousands of square miles with not a soul in it except for nomadic tribes. And that sea of red sand dunes on the horizon sweeping on and on forever."

He went to her and checked her progress towards the rim. "Deserts are powerful landscapes. They're also death traps, so don't forget it. Knowledge is the thing. Modern transport, equipment. Even then things go wrong."

"Hey, Grant, you can't put me off," she warned gently.

"I can see that."

"Besides the Channel Country is a riverine desert," she pointed out. "All this wonderful network of interlocking rivers and creeks. The billabongs and lagoons."

"In drought except for the permanent billabongs they go dry," Grant told her. "In flood the rivers run for miles across. That's what the Channel Country *is,* a vast flooded plain. It covers a good five percent of the continent. During the monsoonal months the deserts to the north and here can be hit by fierce electrical storms. One claimed Stewart Kinross's life. Almost claimed Rebecca's. The roars of thunder are quite terrifying and they're accompanied by tremendous flashes of lightning. When lightning hits the inflammable spinifex we can have grass fires for days.''

''So you're telling me it's a beautiful savage land.''

''One has to remember that at all times.''

''Yet it's so incredibly peaceful.'' Francesca looked out over the endless open vista. ''Man needs the wilderness. These vast, open plains. There's such dignity about the outback. So much character. When one loves city life, cities are the place to be. I've always been a country girl at heart. I'm like my father. I love the land.''

''This is a far cry from what you're used to, Francesca.'' He felt driven to keep repeating it.

''Certainly,'' she agreed. ''Sheer *size* alone. It's a strange beauty. Primeval. One is constantly aware of the land's great antiquity but it's not alien to me. Don't you see that?''

''Francesca, you're classic English,'' he pointed out bluntly.

''And you just could be a classic stubborn Scot,'' she returned with a touch of fire.

He inclined his head in wry acknowledgment. ''Anyway I love your company. I love your calm, your patrician elegance and that little fiery streak that shows itself now and again.''

''But you're discouraging anything beyond close friendship?''

''Actually I think I'm behaving impeccably while we sort something out.''

"I'll remind you of that when you're married, secure and settled." She managed a smile. "But you haven't told me. What do you think of my idea of Myora for a homesite? It's spellbinding country."

"Don't you think I should consult my future bride?" he asked, a sardonic note in his voice.

"Not necessarily. Opal homestead has been lived in for generations. I'm part of everything. I'm descended from Cecilia Kinross who married her kinsman Ewan Kinross when she really loved Charles Cameron."

Grant groaned. "That story has been around for a long time."

"It must have been true. What do you think? There must have been some reason for Cecilia to turn her back on the man she loved? Then there was the famous opal-and-diamond necklace. Cecilia's Necklace. Both men Kinross and Cameron gave it to her."

"I love your accent." He digressed knowing where this was heading.

"I love yours, too." She barely paused. "The deep drawl until it gets very clipped. Anyway to continue the conversation maybe your ancestor allowed my ancestor to outmanoeuvre him. Maybe your ancestor tried to talk Cecilia out of staying in this country. It would have been hard indeed in the early days. He must have felt obliged to warn. He may have even urged her to go back to Scotland for her own good."

"Now why aren't I surprised you'd get around to saying that?" he asked a little caustically.

"I wonder what did happen?" She moved away a few feet, staring down at the spinifex-covered plains. The mirage was abroad, creating phantom hills, lakes and tall, sticklike nomads.

"My family believes there was a trick," Grant admitted after a pause. ''Kinross managed to convince Cecilia his friend was promised to another woman, a woman far more suited to his way of life. The woman, in fact, Charles Cameron eventually married. But what does it matter now? Eventually the two families were reunited but the two men were never close again. It happens like that with betrayal. God knows a man like Stewart Kinross could have played that role.'' The accusation surged out, borne of many old resentments and griefs.

''But my grandfather wasn't like that,'' Francesca protested, recognising the hard kernel of truth in what Grant had said of her uncle Stewart. ''Sir Andrew was greatly loved and respected.''

It was perfectly true. ''Sorry. I'm sorry, Francesca,'' Grant apologised. ''Sir Andy was a fine man. Don't let's talk about ancient history anymore.''

''It seems to me it has repercussions to this day,'' Francesca sighed. ''Everyone gets stirred up when they talk about that old love affair.''

''A love affair gone wrong.'' He spoke briskly. ''Come back from that edge, there's a lot of loose shale.''

''I'm no daredevil.'' She obeyed at once. ''But it does have a compelling fascination.''

''Tell me have you seen enough?'' He was moved by her reactions, the great pleasure she had taken in their trip.

''For now. But you promised me a surprise.''

''And I'm going to show it to you.'' He captured her hand again, so small in his, fingers so delicate. ''We'll take another route down.''

She would have missed the dome-shaped entrance to

the cave guarded as it was by a desert grevillea in full orange flower that appeared to grow out of sheer rock.

"We're here." Grant steadied her, though the ledge was fairly wide.

"Oh my goodness!" She felt a surge of excitement and anticipation. "Don't tell me, rock paintings?" She looked at him, willing him to say "yes!"

"This isn't a recorded site." He smiled at her enthusiasm. "There must be thousands all over the country. We like to keep ours a secret. It's not an important site but it's fascinating and it's been here since God knows when. The aborigines love to give colour and life to all of their shelters and caves. Inland hills, rocky outcrops, anywhere they can execute their art. A great many are in inaccessible places. It would be very easy to miss this. The family didn't know about this particular cave until fairly recently. Of course the local aborigines knew of its existence. Apparently they decided by my grandfather's time the Camerons had sufficient respect for traditional aboriginal culture to be told of its location."

"Why haven't I heard of this?" Francesca's expression was a mixture of awe and animation.

"You might have repeated the story all over." Grant drew back a large sage-green branch with its long, slender spines and masses of curly orange brushes exposing the wide, shallow entrance.

"Heavens you could have trusted me," Francesca said, peering in.

"I'm trusting you now," Grant's tone was dry. "I also want that ribbon you've got in your hair."

"Really?" She turned in surprise, standing stockstill as he reached out and pulled the ribbon from her thick upturned braid. Immediately the plait began to unravel and he smiled in beguilement, thinking she had the most wonderful hair he had ever seen. ''Don't worry, Francesca, I'll give it back. For now I want to tie up this branch and let a bit of sun into the cave otherwise we won't have sufficient light.''

''Keep the ribbon. A memento.'' It was a throwaway line but she found herself quivering at the look in his eyes, utterly brilliant, utterly desirous. She could not look away. She felt powerless to move. He tied the branch back, then he took her arm, moving her away from the neck of the cave. ''Just stand out of harm's way for a moment while I check the interior. Some animal might have made the cave its home.''

''As long as we're not talking bats.'' She gave a little shudder.

A moment more and he returned, so masculine, so vibrant, he stirred every deep feeling in her. ''All clear. Actually I've forgotten how marvellous it is.''

The instant they were inside the sandy-floored cave Francesca straightened up. Her eyes flashed around the ancient gallery that was covered in drawings. So many! The stone mass of the rear wall displayed highly stylised designs Francesca couldn't understand but found very attractive, executed in ochres, red, yellow, charcoal, black and white. On the ceiling, the highest point of the dome some eight feet, the designs were quite different. She understood immediately that they were male and delicate female figures in different aspects of making love watched over by what appeared to be totem beings or spirit figures. On the end walls were drawings of kangaroos, emus, mammals, reptiles, fish, birds and what seemed to be giant insects. Simple linear drawings but accurate and charming, the whole framed by impressions of human hands like a decoration.

"I can't possibly see this all in one day," she said her voice instinctively pitched low in deference to all these ancient symbols and ancestral beings. For all the drawings' simplicity this wasn't doodling in any shape or form. The rock paintings had a definite mystical power. The paintings relating directly to sex were even bringing the hot blood to her cheeks.

"So what do you suggest?" Grant's voice too was quiet with a faint shivery ring caused by the acoustics of the cave.

"Oh, God, I don't know! These are wonderful. Who else have you brought here?" She was aching for him to touch her, as sensations flashed through her body like so much sorcery. Weren't all those paintings supposed to mean love magic? Now there was a light wind blowing through the neck of the cave, adding its own hollow drumming, deep, soft notes reminiscent of the native didgeridoo, the wind's movements rippling the burnished sandy floor that she now saw had delicate, unusual patterns all over it. Spiders or little dragon lizards, she thought. Tracks recorded on the fine sand. Their tracks as well. Hers and Grant's. Her foot so much smaller.

"I expect a hundred girls," Grant said with a faint rasp.

"All of them in love with you?" She turned quickly, knowing without being told that she was the first woman outside family, except she was sure her cousin Ally, who had ever been brought here.

"I've never been in love in my life," he said, "except I'm afraid with *you,*" he admitted almost roughly, a certain tension coming into his high-mettled face.

She had to clear her throat to speak. "And that's taboo?"

"That's how it is, Francesca."

One hand unconsciously went up to lie between her breasts. "You mean my title is a terrible constraint?"

"Your title is the smallest part of it," he said. "The *implications* of your title stronger, but overriding everything the near impossibility of transporting someone as delicate as you into a baked, red-glowing soil. It would take a miracle for you to survive."

His rejection was shattering. "So falling in love isn't enough?"

He groaned. "Think about it, Francesca. I beg you. Falling in love is agony. Allowing a woman to reach far into your mind and your body would be to give her all the power in the world."

She looked at him out of sparkling eyes. "So it hasn't happened yet?"

"I'm not going to let it get the better of me, Francesca," he warned.

Her heart was beating swiftly, to the point of pain. "So you think rules apply to people like me and you're not going to break them?"

He held up his hands, palms forward like a suppliant warding her off, yet his glance was magnetic, luring her on. "Don't look at me like that."

"Do you think I wanted this to happen, willed it to happen?"

"You couldn't have." He shook his head. "It happened all at once. Years ago when you were just a sweet little teenager."

"We were close then." Nostalgia was reflected in her voice.

"Aren't we closer now?" His own tone was regretful.

"But you want me to go?"

"As things are—" He broke off, intensely confused. On the one hand he was trying to do the right thing, on the other he was mad to take this woman and make her his. It had got to the point when he couldn't imagine life without her. It wasn't meant to happen like this. Not at all.

She gave a little cry that startled him. Then she was flinging herself backwards as a small brightly patterned dragon lizard lifted itself out of the deep sand, every spine on its head and back upraised, a fearsome little harmless thing, still with the ability to give an unsuspecting person a fright. It dashed at breakneck speed, across Francesca's foot and outside the cave.

"God, Fran, here." He caught her as she stumbled, sinking, sliding to the cave floor. "It's only a lizard. It can't hurt you." But he could. The fragrance of her body, that unique rose scent was everywhere. He thought constantly about making love to her. Now here she was in his arms, a featherweight, so utterly beautiful inside and out.

"I'm sorry. Sorry." She gave a little laugh that wasn't a laugh at all. More like a sob because it was all so sad, so ridiculous, so cruel.

Desperate for her now, Grant caught her up strongly, experiencing such passion he was drawn to cover her mouth fiercely, voluptuously, feeling it open…open, her breath as sweet as the desert breeze. The tip of her small tongue, barely lapping, danced around his, inciting him until he felt he couldn't stand it. He was hard with desire, bearing her slender body down onto the soft sand as if he had been waiting for this all his life.

''Francesca!'' Everything about him was doing a slow, sizzling burn.

''Don't talk.'' Her white fingers came up to his lips. ''Don't talk at all.''

She allowed him to slip open the small pearly buttons of her pink shirt. He had never known such exquisite anticipation. He moved his hands over her small breasts, the rosy nipples already bunched tight to his touch. She was wearing some kind of white lacy thing like a little singlet beneath her shirt. Nothing else. Her breasts were perfect, small, taut, high, the skin like satin. He lowered his head and took first one nipple then the other into his mouth, hearing her soft, urgent moans, the most exciting and dangerous little sounds in the world.

Exactly what he feared was happening. He could get her pregnant. This beautiful creature. Yet his hand found the zip of her cotton jeans, drawing it down. His fingers moved in desperate caressing patterns over her velvet stomach to the apex of her body, a point he knew he shouldn't cross, but he did because he couldn't summon enough will to turn back.

Wonder. It was wonderful. And now he was quite, quite certain of what he had only suspected.

All the while he caressed her, his ministrations causing her to writhe, he studied her lovely face. Her eyes were closed, her head turned sideways, her hair a fiery bolt of silk across the sand.

Take her, he thought. Just take her. Give in to your greatest desire. You're both young and so much alive. So much in love. He couldn't deny it. She was too honest to try.

''Francesca, Francesca,'' he muttered in a mindless ecstasy, his mouth closing over hers again. She was extraordinary. A dream. He never imagined a woman could be so beautiful. He wanted to cover every inch of her with kisses. Kisses like little indelible marks that would stay on her body forever.

He smoothed his palm across her satin-smooth stomach. So flat. He imagined her having a child. His beautiful child. Boy or girl he wouldn't care. Such a child would surely have red-gold hair. A little innocent. Perfect in their eyes.

But seeing that child in his mind's eye brought him back to his senses at a powerful rush. Her slender white arms were thrown back, fingers digging into the sand. She couldn't stop that soft, little moan as his hunger had taken him deeper and deeper into exploring her body.

His hesitation was minimal but deeply painful as if he was gripped by cramps, but by sheer force of will he managed to move, retrieving the pink shirt he had thrown away, getting a handle on the deep clashing tumults inside of him.

"Francesca. Please. Come on." He coaxed her urgently but she kept her eyes shut, not responding. Somehow, unaided, he fixed the little singlet, got her shirt back on and buttoned, rezipped her jeans.

She didn't help him at all as if she had loved the way she was, half-naked and lost to him.

"You don't think this is easy for me, do you?" he pleaded, half-cursing his own principles. "This is harder than you'll ever know. But I have to stop, Francesca."

At last she showed some reaction by shaking her head. "Why?"

"How can you ask? How can I possibly know if the

time is right for you?'' he asked tautly. ''Are you on the pill or don't you care if you fall pregnant?''

She sat up immediately, clenching her small white teeth. ''I'm going to get a prescription right away.'' She was howling inside. Full of frustration.

''You have your virginity to bring to a man as a gift,'' he pointed out quietly.

''Damnation to that!''

He had to laugh, though the laugh went awry. ''I like it. It's pretty unusual these days.''

''It's the way I've chosen to live,'' she said, averting her head. ''I've never cared enough about anyone to let them get to the stage where they *know* me.''

He held her face between his hands and kissed her. ''So whatever happens some part of you will always be mine. Could I have made you pregnant today?''

A wild rose flush mounted her cheeks. She looked across the silent cave, her blue gaze falling on ancient couplings. ''I was too far gone to make notes.'' She tried a sad little joke. ''I suppose you expected better of me?''

Her expression was so poignant he reacted strongly. ''*I'm* the guilty one here, Francesca. I found the way to seduce you.''

''And you would have only you're blessed with an exceptionally strong will.''

''A year from now you might thank me.'' He stared into her face intently, committing every single feature to memory.

''I don't think so.'' She shook her head firmly, pushing her long hair back over her shoulders. ''I don't regret any of this, Grant Cameron. What I feel for you is in very short supply.''

CHAPTER FOUR

For days after Grant drove himself so hard, Brod, all his life honorary big brother, began to feel a niggling concern. There was no question Grant was splendidly fit, physically very strong, with nerves of steel, but it seemed to Brod he was putting himself under too much pressure without a safety valve. Cameron Airways now had sufficient pilots able and experienced enough to take over the big mustering jobs, but Grant was handling too much himself. It was a day in day out, dawn to dusk routine and not without its dangers especially for the helicopter pilot manoeuvring in difficult situations.

There was an undercurrent to all this. Brod was sure he knew what it was. *Francesca.* Grant had fallen very deeply in love with her but it was obvious to anyone who knew Grant well, he was taking it hard. It wasn't just a question of a young man used to a high level of self-sufficiency and freedom, fighting love's lasso. Grant seemed to be in genuine fear of hurting both of them by allowing their relationship to deepen.

Whatever happened the day he took Francesca off to Opal to see the cave—both had confided in him and of course as Rafe's best friend he had seen it—had been pivotal in their relationship. Of that Brod felt all but certain. There was a kind of shining innocence about Francesca, a definable purity that remained. But something fairly traumatic had happened.

Midafternoon when the men were relaxing over billy

tea and fresh damper, hot from the coals, Brod drew Grant aside.

"Why don't we go down there?" He indicated a fallen log like a giant bonsai on the sandy shore of the creek, with its spreading green signifying the return of the good seasons.

Grant followed him gratefully. Rarely tired, he found himself curiously drained. "All right with you if Jock McFadden finishes tomorrow?" he asked, as soon as they were settled, a fragrant mug of tea in hand, a couple of the cattle dogs, Bluey and Rusty, curled at their feet.

"No problem at all." Brod pushed his akubra back on his head, turning to look at his friend. "Is everything okay?"

Grant smiled wryly. "Now why do you sound like Rafe?"

"Do I?" Brod's grin displayed his beautiful white teeth. "Well, Rafe's away."

"So you're his deputy. Anyway I meant to tell you—" Grant swallowed a mouthful "—had a phone call from them last night. Early hours of the morning actually."

"Both well?" Brod watched him expectantly.

"On top of the world. They're on the West Coast now. Los Angeles. And guess who they met up with in the street?" His hazel eyes sparkled with amusement and pleasure.

"Any clues?"

"One." Grant nodded. "When we were kids he was considered an even bigger rebel than me."

Brod laughed. "In that case it would have to be your cousin, Rory."

"Got it in one." Grant took another deep gulp, realising he was parched. "Rory Cameron."

"Would have been at Rafe's wedding only he was taking a little hike up Everest wasn't he?" Brod asked.

Grant nodded. "What words can you use to describe that? He's fearless, Rory. I'd love to do it myself. He went up with a New Zealand party. Rory's a real adventurer. There's nowhere he hasn't been from the Himalayas to the Amazonian jungle. His dad thinks he'll never settle down."

Sammy Lee, part aboriginal part Chinese camp cook arrived with slices of damper and jam, which both took.

"It's a good thing then Rory has an elder brother to take over the running of Rivoli," Brod remarked dryly after Sammy had gone. Rivoli was one of the Northern Territory's biggest cattle stations owned and run by Grant's uncle, stepbrother to his late father.

"Josh is a great guy," Grant agreed, "but he hasn't got Rory's enormous *zest.* There's a guy who's brimming over with life. Anyway would you believe it, he's coming home?"

"Lord, he's been away years. He's going to find it tame, settling in the one place, if that's what he intends to do."

"Don't spread it around but I aim to talk him into joining me," Grant told Brod confidentially. "I got to thinking about it last night after the call. Rory's a great pilot. Every last Cameron has a head for business. I could use a man like Rory."

Brod shook his head doubtfully. "No way he'd come into anything without being a full partner."

"You're not wrong! But no harm in discussing it. Rory's my cousin, a Cameron. I know for a fact he got all old Digby Cameron's money. That makes him a rich man. Anyway we'll see. Needless to say Rafe and Ally send you and Rebecca their love. I spoke to Rafe too about Francesca's idea of doing those outback location shots on Opal.''

Brod finished off his mug of tea and signalled for another. ''What did he say?''

''He doesn't mind. In fact he supports it if I negotiate a good deal and the money goes to the Bush Rescue trust.''

Brod nodded his approval. ''Rafe's doing a wonderful job with that. Now that Dad's gone Kimbara will enter the scheme. Rafe and I discussed it. Even if we save one kid and put them on the right path it's worth it.''

''Well it's working.'' Grant paused to thank Sammy who was back pouring fresh tea.

''So what are you going to do tomorrow?'' Brod returned to his main concern. ''Take some time off. It seems to me you've hit a cracking pace.''

''I won't have Francesca over to visit if that's what you mean.'' Grant shot him a sidelong glance.

''What's the problem?'' Brod was equally direct. ''Aren't you two in love?''

''God, love! What *is* love?'' Grant muttered in a kind of anguish.

''I'd say what *you feel,*'' Brod responded. ''You're not just in love with my cousin. You love her. You're tormenting yourself with what you consider is appropriate.''

''It shows?'' asked Grant, not smiling.

''Hell, Grant, I've known you all your life. I know how a man feels, when he's faced with a big emotional decision. I know you're a man of integrity. I know I can trust you with Francesca. I know you would never consciously hurt her.''

Grant gestured wearily. ''I'm wrong for her, Brod.''

''Why?'' Brod damned nearly shouted. ''The consensus of opinion is you're an exceptional young man. You have real standing in the outback community. That's not all that easy to earn.''

''Down here. Down here, I'm worried.'' Grant struck his chest. ''If she were any other girl! I want her as much as it's possible to want a woman, but she's like some enchanting creature from another planet. Even her colouring scares me.''

Brod shook his head, halfway between disbelief and understanding. ''Grant, get a balance here. Your own father had red hair. Your mother was very blonde. Look at you and Rafe. Don't all the girls call you the golden boys?''

Grant studied the glint of hair on his forearms. ''We've had generations to acclimatise. We've grown hardy. We're *natives.* Francesca is like some rare exotic no one in their right mind would plant here. She can't survive. The big heat is ahead. You know as well as I do, Brod, the mercury can hit forty-eight degrees!''

Brod looked up at the cloudless, peacock-blue sky. ''We don't expect our womenfolk to go out in the midday sun, whatever Noel Coward had to say. Times have changed greatly. We have so much now, so many aids we've never had before. It's been a technological revolution.''

''Maybe. But the fact remains no one is going to be able to change the desert environment.''

''Between the two of us,'' Brod said wryly, ''I don't want to change it. I love my home like no other place on earth.''

Grant responded with a sudden spurt of passion. ''Don't get me wrong. I love it, too. We've learned to love it. We thrive on it. But Francesca is a very special person. I'm determined to protect her.''

''Hell, Grant, if you keep this up you'll drive her away,'' Brod warned. ''You'll lose her. Are you prepared to risk that?''

Grant's handsome, determined features tautened. ''I'd rather lose her now than lose her later on. That would kill me. What if we were married and she decided one day she longed for everything she had lost? Everything she had ever known and understood? She's no *ordinary* girl.''

''An ordinary girl wouldn't suit you, Grant. Have you thought of that?'' Brod suggested dryly.

Grant shook his head. ''I don't know any other girl of her particular background. Surely it couldn't be more different from ours?''

''So you don't think she's adult enough to make up her own mind?'' Irony crackled in Brod's tone.

''You realise any son she may have could be her father's heir?''

Brod gave a faint smile. ''So what? As far as I know, Francesca's father is having the devil of a job trying to keep Ormond intact. The upkeep must be crippling. Especially without Fee's money. Fee was the heiress. For that matter, still is.''

''You don't see anything tremendously threatening about our relationship?'' Grant asked, realising this conversation was going some way to easing his mind.

Brod took his time replying. Then he spoke very seriously, from the depths of his soul. ''I think when you find someone you truly love you never let them go.''

* * *

In amongst all his thinking, and he had lots on his mind—an upcoming meeting with Drew Forsythe of Trans Continental Resources for one—he kept drawing mental plans of his dream homestead. Of course he'd need an architect to walk the site, gauge just the right spot for the house to go. There were vast, sweeping views from everywhere nevertheless siting the homestead properly would present a challenge. Without fully realising it his mind was extraordinarily visual so his intermittent daydreams really came alive. He wanted the house set on low pylons like Opal but there the similarity ended, except for the mandatory wide verandahs to shelter the core of the house from the heat and sun at the same time as providing deep shade and cooling breezes.

He wanted his homestead radically different. He wanted a completely contemporary structure using a mix of materials: stone, glass—lots of glass, floor to ceiling—steel to support the long spans of verandah, the polished timbers he loved, local stone with all its wonderful ochres, especially for the fireplaces. The really hard thing would be to come up with a design worthy of the great wilderness bounded as it was by the great rolling parallel waves of the desert, unobstructed views over the plains to the horizon with the legendary Myora for a background. How many people had an awe-inspiring prehistoric monolithic rock in their backyard. A backyard that ran on forever.

He had visited the island of Bali many times, loved it, and found Balinese influences creeping into his thinking, though the lush jungle settings could scarcely be more different from Opal. But the harmonious feeling of timbers, open spaces, high tentlike ceilings, open pavilions was the same. Like Bali, too, nights in the

Dry could be surprisingly cold as the desert sands lost their heat. He would need those couple of huge, inviting fireplaces. In every room he saw Francesca, however much he tried to picture some other woman.

Lord knows he knew enough attractive girls. They swarmed to the polo meets. There was a time he felt quite happy with Jennie Irvine. Her father, Tom Irvine, the well-known pastoralist, had been a good friend to his own father. Jennie was good-looking, well educated, easygoing, fun to be with. He knew he could get Jennie to marry him. He knew her parents would be really happy about it but someone called Francesca de Lyle had put paid to that. By Brod's wedding he had really known Francesca had stolen his heart.

She was like some irresistible fragrance. All those silly ads he had seen about perfume and the way they enticed a man weren't so silly after all. Francesca was a rose, to him the most beautiful, the most fragrant of all flowers.

Even his dreams were set at this homestead that had yet to be built. Vividly he saw Francesca at the breakfast table, having a cup of coffee with him. Francesca in the glowing panelled dining room playing hostess to family and friends. Francesca in the study reading over his shoulder as he drafted an important letter, welcoming her input because he valued her opinion and good business sense. Most of all he saw her in the bedroom, lying on top of their huge bed, a modern four-poster hung with curtains of white netting against any little insects that might fly through all the open doorways. For some reason he never saw his Francesca naked. She was always wearing the prettiest, beribboned, most feminine nightgown, a swirl of peach silk, he would lovingly peel off.

What a fool! At this point he always woke himself up. Falling in love with Francesca was bliss and despair. Her destiny like his was already written. Dreams had little to do with real life. That was the unpalatable fact. The reality of the situation was, he was acting out a fantasy and heading for disaster. Love had to be matched by other factors that would make a marriage survive.

Francesca was a beautiful, bright superior creature, carefully guarded by her father and clearly destined for a privileged life similar to the one she had led. How could he hold such a woman in isolation? The polar caps could melt before he tired of her but what if she found his way of life far too lonely and distant from all she had known? Despite his conversation with Brod he still was deeply affected by practical constraints as a man who was making a decision that would affect his whole life had to be.

He didn't need to be a mind-reader, either, to guess Francesca's father would be utterly and completely against such a marriage and why not? It would take his only beloved child away from him. Halfway across the world. As far away as she could go. Shatter his plans. Fee had all but admitted that. So problems continued to beset his euphoria. Women seemed conditioned by nature to take great leaps into the unknown. For a man it was different. A man's duty was to keep his feet on the ground.

The film people arrived at the weekend, staying over at Kimbara, which with its many guest rooms at the ready was far better suited to accommodating guests than Opal; Ngaire Bell, the New Zealand born director, who was making quite a name for herself internationally, accompanied by long-time associate and script writer, Glenn Richards. Grant was kept busy all day Saturday working out schedules for incoming jobs, double-checking maintenance, arranging freight pick-ups, a workload that kept him on Opal but sunset found him landing on Kimbara preparatory to meeting Brod and Rebecca's guests at dinner.

Francesca was there to greet him, dressed in jeans and a yellow T-shirt, her hair burning like flame in the incandescent light.

"Hi, this is nice!" He bent to kiss her cheek, thinking "nice" was a ridiculous word. He was just plain thrilled to see her. She made his heart run hot.

"It's lovely to see you, too," she responded. "It's been a very long week."

"Lots to do." He spoke casually, throwing his hold-all in the back seat of the Jeep, not mentioning he had found the time away from her a near eternity. "So what are the guests like?" he asked as they got under way, Francesca at the wheel, small hands but capable and confident.

"I know you're going to like them." Francesca turned her head half-laughing now with pleasure. "Ngaire is a very interesting woman. She and Fee are getting along famously. Glenn is good company, too. Rebecca and he have a lot in common."

"And what about you?"

"I'm happy. I'm really happy," she said, eyes alight. "We're all getting along well but of course the others have special interests in common."

"How old, I wonder?" He spoke lightly, companionably when all he wanted to do was wrap her in his arms.

''Ngaire, late thirties, early forties. Naturally I didn't ask. Glenn would be around thirty-five.''

''Married?'' He wanted this guy married. He refused to confront why.

''Neither of them are married,'' Francesca said. ''They're great friends and colleagues but I wouldn't think they were romantically involved. Of course I could be wrong. You didn't want to kiss me?''

Because if I did I wouldn't stop. ''Kissed your cheek, didn't I?'' he said.

''So you did. It was nice, too. How glorious the sunsets are out here,'' she said, examining the sky.

''Like your hair.'' He successfully resisted touching it. ''If you want to see a sight, cut off the track now and head north-west for about a mile. The black swans should be heading in for their roosting sites at dusk.''

''So where are we going?'' Where the heck *is* north-east, she thought. She'd have to ask him to show her.

''Here, let me.''

They stopped to swop positions, Grant driving, Francesca in the passenger seat of the open Jeep. ''Kingurra. You must know it,'' Grant said a few moments later, the Jeep exploding into action.

''Lake Kingurra?'' She cast a glance at his golden profile. Like Rafe he had a cleft chin, the cleft not so deep but vertical.

''The very one,'' he teased. ''Kingurra means black swan. Didn't you know that?''

She shook her head. ''The straight answer is no. There's so much *to* know. It would take a lifetime. Even learning all the aboriginal names.''

''They're the ones I like best. Our aboriginal brothers have been custodians of this country for over sixty thousand years. Kingurra is a very old lake, a real oasis of wildlife.''

''Of course I've seen it,'' Francesca said. ''It's astonishingly beautiful especially with the area all around it so arid.''

''Listen *now.*'' Grant leant towards her, his expression full of the pleasure of sharing.

They heard the birds before they saw them, the sound carried on the sweet evening breeze. The dark shadows became hundreds of black swans skeining across the darkening mauve sky still banded with the brilliant rose, gold and scarlet of the desert sunset.

''What a sight!'' Francesca lifted her head, staring, fascinated by the pure white underwings of the ebony birds, the little band of turquoise, the red beaks. The *S* bends of their beautiful necks were fully outstretched, straight as arrows.

''We've got time to take a walk down to the water,'' Grant said, picking up speed and heading away from the mulga scrub to the lake.

A little bit of excitement went a long way. ''It might sound extraordinary but I'm rarely away from the homestead at this hour,'' Francesca explained, her cheeks pink. ''If I go riding or driving around the property Brod likes me home before dusk.''

Grant shot her a shimmering glance. ''So would I if you were on your own. Night falls as dramatically as a black curtain. But this is worth seeing and I'm with you.''

He held her hand all the while they descended the sandy track crisscrossed with the prints of kangaroos and smaller creatures. Quietly, quietly, they kept to the cover of the trees so as not disturb the birds.

There were hundreds of them! Squadrons splashing

down on the silver lake, while others circled just like aircraft waiting for landing. Two hundred or more stately pelicans had congregated at the far end of the lake, keeping their distance from the common ducks, the cormorants, egrets, banded stilts and so many species Francesca couldn't possibly identify them. As the swans landed, they sealed off their white underwings, bending their long necks into the beautiful curves of legends. They remained, united by their great pleasure in the scene, familiar to Grant all his life, though he never tired of it, a rare enchantment for Francesca.

The outback *was* birds. She adored watching the great flights of budgerigar, the parrots and galahs, the flocks of white corellas that literally covered the trees, but she had never seen so many water birds congregated in the one place. It was like some wonderful harbour, the waters that swirled with birds gradually blanketed in feathers.

"This is wonderful!" she whispered.

"I agree." His head was bent over hers, his breath warm against her ear.

"Thank you for bringing me here."

"I'm amazed you've missed it on your visits."

Not so many, she thought with regret. She'd first come to Kimbara at the age of ten. Her father didn't want her to come. He told her Australia was a far country. *Strange.* He told her her mother's people lived in the desert. Were barely civilised. Yet her mother was the most beautiful most glamorous creature she had ever seen.

When she arrived on Kimbara it was like coming home. She wasn't drawn to it. It didn't take time. She loved it at once. It was almost like her spirit had been unleashed. She was a very lonely little girl. Although her father tried to do everything he could, when she wasn't away at boarding school, she was left to her own devices a great deal.

"Coming to Australia was the greatest adventure of my life," she murmured aloud. "Still is for that matter."

"What about the heat, little Titian head?" he gently mocked.

"The heat could never exhaust my excitement. Not now. Not then. It's *dry* heat, isn't it? Not steamy, enervating heat."

It was true she always looked as cool as a lily. "Well, I'm glad you enjoyed your visit," he said lightly, "but we'd better go." Before I give in to the desire to kiss you until you're panting and incoherent.

They crouched low beneath some overhanging branches, finding their way back up the slope, Francesca forging ahead with a buoyant step. They almost arrived at the top when suddenly Grant grasped her firmly from behind, locking an arm around her waist, stopping her short.

"What is it?" Now he lifted her clean off the ground, holding her with one arm as though she were still a ten-year-old.

He didn't answer for a moment, then he set her down again with a nonchalant, "Nothing!"

She had to lean back against him momentarily unsteady. "You gave me such a fright."

"Better that than let you tread on a snake," he drawled. "There it goes. Off by the rocks."

"Lord!" Her expression sharpened with dread, as she strained back against him.

"Harmless, that one," Grant told her. "It was only

trying to get across the track. Snakes flee man in general. It doesn't do to step on one all the same.''

She gave a little shudder, turning within the circle of his arm, banging him on his chest in an instinctive response to fright. ''I suppose you think I'm silly?''

He slipped his hand around her wrist and felt the delicate bones. ''No, I think you're enormously brave.'' He gazed down into her eyes, eyes that seemed to see further into him than anyone else. ''I'm sorry I scared you.''

''I'm not scared,'' she breathed. And now she wasn't. ''I'm here with you.''

Inside he fought a violent struggle but he lost it. He lowered his head blindly, ravenously, taking her sweet gorgeous mouth, devouring it deeply, hungrily, luscious as a peach.

My God, I love her! he thought, abandoning himself to the ecstasy. Why the hell didn't he just hang on to that instead of making a terror out of all their difference.

''At least we've got one thing in common,'' he muttered, when he found the strength to lift his head.

''Lots!'' She could only manage one word, her heart hammering, her breath drowned in her throat.

After a minute she was able to open her eyes. ''We've got lots of things in common,'' she protested with soft vehemence. ''Don't push me away, Grant,'' she warned, and he had never seen her more serious. ''I've been pushed away all my life.''

The next moment she turned, straightened the T-shirt his caressing hands had somehow pulled askew, and ran from him leaving him utterly sobered, staring after her.

Pushed away all her life! How was that possible?

From all accounts her father adored her. He had big plans for her. Fee was Fee. Not the most maternal of women but it couldn't be plainer she loved her beautiful daughter. It struck him like an actual blow Francesca could ever feel rejected. Francesca was a miracle. She touched his mind, his body, his heart with her exquisite grace.

They all came together in the very grand drawing room for a predinner drink, Brod introducing Grant to his guests.

"My God!" Ngaire Bell thought as they shook hands. These cattle kings are something else! A distinct breed. To begin with they had such an aura of masculinity they really made a woman *feel* like a woman. Moreover they made direct eye contact with far-seeing, delightfully sun-crinkled eyes. Broderick Kinross was an extraordinarily handsome man. She truly hadn't expected anyone else to match him yet here was this fabulous-looking man with the rarest of colourings.

On their looks alone she could make stars of them, she thought wryly, only it couldn't have been more obvious they exactly matched their setting. They were outback men yet they lived in great style.

Kimbara homestead was splendid, meticulously maintained, but too grandly furnished for the homestead of her new movie. It had been suggested to her by Fee Kinross's beautiful daughter, Francesca, the homestead at Opal Downs would fit readily the description of the sprawling, elegant old homestead of the novel, its Victorian furnishings still largely in place, the atmosphere retained. She was dying to see it. Couldn't wait. This wasn't the first historic mansion she had been invited to but this was the furthest into the continent's Wild Heart. It fired her already fertile imagination.

Glenn Richards, drink in hand, was thinking much the same thing as his friend and colleague. These Kinross-Camerons were an extraordinarily good-looking bunch. He had to put it down to the desert air. Even Fiona Kinross, who had to be in her sixties, looked marvellous. In the flattering light no more than forty-five. Of course she could have had cosmetic surgery, but he didn't think so. Nevertheless her skin was unlined, her jawline firm, her figure in a neat jade knee-length dress, excellent. She cut a glamorous figure as did they all, including Fiona's brand-new fiancé, David Westbury, tall, distinguished, pewter haired, very upper class English. As far as Glenn could make out, Westbury was a relative of sorts, and he was a touch overawed, trying to click in all his various impressions.

But the one who really took his eye and had from the very first moment, was the Lady Francesca. As far as he was concerned she was quite lovely. He adored her soft, dreamy looks, the uncontrived sensuality that made a man drool. And that colouring. He couldn't think of a more heavenly combination than red-gold hair and sky-blue eyes. Not a freckle in sight. Not even a gold dusting across her nose.

It struck him she would be perfect in the movie as the hero's tragic first wife. What made it even better was she had the authentic English accent. Maybe a bit too cut glass but that could be modified slightly. It was only a small part. They had more or less settled on Paige Macauly but he was certain if the girl could act at all she would be perfect in the role. And why wouldn't she be able to act with Fiona Kinross for a mother, let alone her cousin, Ally, who proved she didn't have what it took to make the big time by going off and getting married. What a waste!

Still, their leading lady Caro Halliday, wife number two in the film, who didn't feature in the early outback scenes, was beautiful, talented and almost as charismatic. As they went into dinner, Glenn began to turn over ideas in his mind. He'd put a lot of hard work into the screenplay. A lot of his own money went into the backing. It was crucial the film do well not only as an ''art'' film but as entertainment for the masses. The English rose, Francesca was enormously appealing, beautiful but nonthreatening. She had as much appeal as her far more exotic mother.

Grant, as sensitive to Francesca as it was possible to be, honed in immediately on Richards's interest in her. It was all managed with charm and a certain suavity but Richards couldn't keep his eyes off her. Not that Grant could blame him no matter how it made him inwardly bristle. Francesca looked ethereal in a delicate lace dress, the soft apricot of his dreams. She had left her hair out, too, in the way he loved it, long and flowing.

It wasn't the first time he had seen Francesca capture a whole lot of male attention but it was the first time another man had provoked his male aggression. Francesca was *his.* Immediately, as he thought it, he was forced to confront his own contradictions. He had no rights where Francesca was concerned. She was a free agent. As was he and apparently Glenn Richards. But no question about it, Richards's eyes on Francesca had set him off. Richards wasn't even being terribly discreet, his dark eyes savouring Francesca's appearance and the quality of her conversation. Which seemed reasonable enough given Francesca showed her intelligence and breeding, but he was starting to fill Grant with an odd hostility he tried to fight down.

Richards was an attractive man—dark curly hair, deep brown eyes, quirky eyebrows, an easy, friendly smile, midheight, well dressed, well-travelled, clever and articulate. Nothing there to dislike except he was taking far too much interest in Francesca. Grant felt a need to sort out his emotions before they got out of hand. He knew he had an aggressive streak. He knew he had to keep it under control.

They were seated in the formal dining room with its fine paintings and furnishings. Ngaire started out by commenting on the exquisite floral arrangement at the centre of the table, and reached to stroke a petal. Rebecca smiled her pleasure. ''Francesca must take the credit. We spent some time over the arrangements, experimenting with containers and the various shapes for the flowers.''

''Yes, I noticed,'' Ngaire said as indeed she had. ''The arrangement in the main hall is quite dramatic.''

''I'm afraid we robbed the Golden Shower tree.'' Francesca smiled. ''A few palms, gold ribbon. A wonderful big Chinese vase. We had a lot of fun.''

''Ikebana isn't it?'' Ngaire asked, thinking how beautiful and stylish all the arrangements through the house were.

''I actually took a course with a master teacher a few years back,'' Rebecca said. ''I must say Fran is an apt pupil. The centrepiece is inspirational.''

''I agree.'' Brod looked like he thought his wife and cousin could do anything they turned their hand to.

''A mangrove root, dracena and a couple of sprays of white butterfly orchids, plus some red wire for a bit of dash,'' Francesca said, identifying the materials she had used. ''It means something, too. I quote from I don't know where. Probably anonymous. 'Happiness is like a butterfly. The more you chase it the more it will elude you, but if you turn your attention to other things, it will come and softly sit on your shoulder.''' Somehow it seemed appropriate. Her gaze met Grant's enigmatically across the table. ''Of course, too, it's a symbol of welcome.''

''Yes, indeed. Welcome to Kimbara, Ngaire and Glenn.'' Brod raised his wineglass and the others followed suit. ''Tomorrow you'll see Opal, my sister Ally's new home. It has its own wonderful appeal as you're due to find out. In our childhood Opal was Ally's and my second home.''

''In fact we were all so close we were family.'' Grant gave a truly illuminating smile. ''Now we are family. The Camerons and the Kinrosses united at last.''

''There's such a fascination about your stories,'' Ngaire said. ''Two great pioneering dynasties. I can't wait to read your biography, Fee.''

''Don't worry, darling,'' Fee said in her deep sexy voice. ''You and Glenn are invited to our preview party. It was a brainwave on Fran's part thinking of Opal for the colonial outback scenes. I was re-reading *The Immigrant* last night. The station is close to perfect for Bruce Templeton's book.''

Grant nodded. ''I've read the novel as well and thoroughly enjoyed it. With a few minor changes the homestead will serve you well. You're lucky Ally hadn't got started on all her refurbishing. My mother intended to make them but never got the chance.''

''I'm so sorry, Grant,'' Ngaire murmured, aware his

parents had been tragically killed in an air crash. "I can't wait to visit tomorrow," she added gently.

The meal Rebecca and Francesca had worked on for a couple of days before the guests arrived, progressed splendidly with help in the kitchen: crab cream for starters, with crisp fried vermicelli followed by tournedos of Kimbarra beef with roast parsnips and potatoes, fresh green beans and two sauces, madeira and béarnaise. The conversation flowed over a wide range of subjects: the movie, Fee's role in it, Fee's and David's impending nuptials, Grant's vision for Cameron Airways, outback life, Rafe and Ally's overseas honeymoon, domestic politics, world politics, a smattering of gossip, books that had not made an easy transition into movies.

Everyone took part, full of animated interest as the wineglasses quickly emptied. Francesca, as usual, limited herself to two. She noticed Rebecca did the same, but Fee sipped her wine quickly, glass after glass, showing no effects except her beautiful, slender hands moved even more expressively and her green eyes glittered with great good humour. This was an area where Fee shone, and David looked on, his heart swelling with pride. After the last few sad years Fee was a positive joy to him.

There was a choice for dessert—chocolate sorbet and orange ice-cream or an Old English apple pie, richly flavoured with dark brown sugar, nutmeg, cinnamon, orange and lemon zest, raisins and sultanas, served with double cream. This was David's contribution to the meal from a family recipe he had enjoyed from childhood. He knew all the ingredients, even if he didn't know exact quantities. He even stood beside

Francesca in the kitchen while she made it saying he always liked his with cheddar cheese.

Mellowed by such a wonderful meal, Glenn took the opportunity to say what he'd been thinking for the past two hours.

''It was a wonderful coup securing you for a pivotal role, Fiona—'' he deferred to her ''—you'll bring great presence and credibility to the role, but I can't help thinking your beautiful daughter, Francesca, would make a marvellous Lucinda.''

''Hey, that's amazing!'' Ngaire burst out, but Fee stared at Glenn in astonishment, her spoon frozen in midair.

''Fran doesn't *act,* Glenn,'' she said as though it were completely out of character. ''She's had no training whatsoever. Ally is the only other actress in the family.''

''And she's marvellous, too,'' Glenn said, still getting over his disappointment Ally Kinross had rejected the lead.

But Ngaire waved a hand. ''Training is important, of course, Fee, but I know for a fact some people are naturals. The fourteen-year-old I had in my last movie was sensational. Straight from school though she was learning drama and art of speech.''

''But Fran has no interest in acting, have you, darling?'' Fee looked down the table, clearly unable to picture her daughter as an actress. ''She's much happier with her drawing and her music. She's very good at both. Francesca is the product of a very good school.''

Grant turned his iridescent eyes on Francesca. ''I didn't know that,'' he said, sounding like he wished he had.

"Now that we've settled down I'll get a good piano sent out here," Brod said briskly.

"Make it a Steinway." Francesca smiled at him.

"Then a Steinway it is." Brod was quite serious. "I know you *draw* extremely well."

"What about acting?" Glenn persisted, fingering his wineglass. The sauterne was wonderful. "Surely they put on plays at your very good school?"

Francesca nodded her head. "Of course they did. Mamma's going to be amazed but I was very much in demand. A lot of Shakespeare. I was a fabulous Juliet," she joked, "to my friend, Dinah Phillip's Romeo. Pity you didn't see us."

"*Why* didn't I see you?" Fee demanded.

"Ah, Mamma," Francesca murmured, rolling her eyes.

"You mean I wasn't around?" Fee gazed off into the middle distance remembering how it was.

"You were lighting up the London stage," Francesca reminded her.

"Now I think about it you *could* play Lucinda." Grant's voice had gathered conviction.

"I agree," Ngaire murmured.

"You really think Francesca could handle it?" Fee stared at Ngaire as though she had gone mad.

"I'd love to," Francesca said

"You could handle it, I know you could." Grant looked across the table at Francesca thinking Fee was the last straw. "It would be good for you. A bit of fun, widen your horizons."

"Surely, darling, you wouldn't entertain the idea of acting as a career?" Grant might as well have suggested prostitution.

"No, Mamma, I wouldn't." Francesca shook her

head, her manner gentle but firm. ''It's more as Grant says. A bit part. A bit of fun.''

''A challenge.'' Grant smiled, always one for a challenge, good, too, at encouraging others. ''You're full of surprises, Francesca. Full of refinements. I'd *love* to hear you play the piano.'' No wonder he always heard music flow around her.

''So you shall,'' Brod promised. ''There was a grand piano here in my mother's day. She played beautifully, but my father got rid of it. He wouldn't let Ally learn, either,'' he added a trifle bleakly, ''though she wanted to.''

''I expect it was too painful,'' Ngaire murmured, not knowing the full story.

''But surely you have that NADA graduate, what's her name, Paige something?'' Fee carried on with her objections.

''Paige Macauly,'' Glenn supplied. ''Yes, Paige was well in the running but we've made no final decision, have we, Ngaire.''

''I thought we had, dear,'' Ngaire said wryly. ''But I quite share your vision of Francesca as Lucinda. One can see her in the part.''

''I get killed off early,'' Francesca said. ''I could do a good job of pining away. Isn't that what I'm supposed to do. Pine away in a strange new country?''

Glenn smiled. ''Of course your character was never very strong. Physically you suggest fragility, sensitivity.''

Francesca didn't see herself as quite the marshmallow. ''Ballerinas are very fragile looking,'' she pointed out, ''but they're very strong. I'll have you know I play an excellent game of tennis. There was a time I was good at archery. I'm a very good rider, aren't I, Brod?''

She appealed to her cousin who was always on her side.

"A lovely seat on a horse. Sweet hands," Brod agreed. "A woman's looks can belie her strengths."

"So what about reading for the part?" Glenn pressed on as keen to get to know Francesca better as to have her in a role that would keep her in daily contact.

"I must say, Glenn, I think you're going too fast," Fee protested. "Francesca's father wouldn't be at all happy about another actress in the family. One was more than enough."

"It's only a bit part, Mamma," Francesca said reassuringly.

"Yes, but you might get the bug."

It was hard to say what was really bothering Fee, David thought. Fear Francesca could cause herself some embarrassment? He couldn't see *how*. Or fear of de Lyle's wrath. As far as he was concerned his cousin was of an age she could do as she pleased. Probably very well.

It was difficult for Grant to get Francesca alone until well after eleven when Brod excused himself from the conversation saying he had a dawn start. Station work went on seven days a week and though the staff had a roster Brod did not. Rebecca, too, excused herself with a charming smile leaving Fee to carry on with the conversation, which reverted to an in-depth discussion of the film, characterisation and so forth.

It was time to grab Francesca and run, Grant thought, aware of Richards's acute disappointment when she left the charmed circle, though Fee talked on, her chain of thought unbroken.

"I think you've won yourself a heart," Grant commented dryly as they walked down the front steps to take a short stroll.

Francesca ignored that, picking up on what really concerned her. ''Mamma didn't sound too pleased with Glenn's suggestion,'' she said, her own pleasure eroded by her mother's reaction.

''I think you're going to be brilliant,'' Grant said, mutually upset by Fee. ''You're vibrantly artistic. I don't like to say it but Fee seems to be devoid of sensitivity sometimes.''

''She isn't always tactful,'' Francesca was forced to agree. ''Maybe she thinks I'm going to make a goose of myself. Or worse a goose of her.''

He drew her to him, one arm lightly around her waist. ''You want to do it, don't you?''

Francesca felt a lot easier in his company. ''Yes, but not if Mamma would rather I didn't.''

''You're a big girl now, Francesca,'' he pointed out, his voice oddly tender.

''I've never been much good at upsetting people.''

''Don't feel guilty about Fee,'' he warned.

''So what do you think I should do?'' she spoke softly, but sounding pained.

''I've told you. Go for it. You'll enjoy it.'' His arm tightened in a hug.

''And what if I get bitten by the bug as Mamma seems to think?'' She knew she wouldn't. Her priorities had been long since fixed.

''If you get hooked, you get hooked,'' Grant answered lightly, thinking it unlikely. ''It's your life. Just don't move away too far. I'd miss you too much.''

''So you don't care if I turned into another Fee?'' she stopped dead, rounding on him, heart high.

''You won't, Francesca.'' He couldn't resist it. He

bent his head and briefly brushed her velvet mouth. Fast and light, still consumed by the pleasure of it. "Remember all the heart-to-heart talks we used to have when we were kids. You want home and family. A man who loves you. A man who is fully committed to you to share your life. And what was it? Four children. That's a full-time job," he added with a sympathetic laugh.

"That's what comes of being an only child," she said as he steered her onwards. "My growing up was painful. I'm not going to let that happen to my children."

"But you still need your mother's encouragement and approval?"

"That's normal isn't it? It's what we all hope for. Parental approval?"

He nodded gravely. "Our parents were one hundred percent behind Rafe and me. Brod and Ally endured a kind of hell. I didn't fully appreciate how deeply your parents' separation affected you until recently. While we're on the subject, what about your father? Would he object so strenuously to your becoming an actress if it ever turned out that was what you wanted?"

"Wow!" Francesca's exclamation said it all. "Actually he'd be *shocked.* Depend on it."

"Because he has big plans for you?" Definitely. It was an inexorable fact.

"They won't work, Grant, if they're the opposite to mine," Francesca murmured, in the fierce grip of sexual longing. "I don't want to disappoint either of my parents but as you've just pointed out my life is my own. That's what makes your pushing me away so peculiar."

"For pity's sake, Francesca. That's not what I meant

at all.'' He stared down at her, her beautiful skin silvered by the moonlight.

''But you won't allow I know my own mind?'' Her response was swift.

''What *is* your mind, Francesca?'' He made a little grimace, taking her firmly by the shoulders and turning her to him.

''Are we allowed to use the word love here?'' A flush of colour had appeared on her cheeks. Even by moonlight he was able to see it. ''You hold so much back.''

He was haunted by the truth. ''There's no way ever, Francesca, I'd hurt you. I'm in love with you,'' he admitted freely. ''You know that. You're in my mind all the time, let alone my dreams.'' How intoxicatingly erotic he didn't tell her.

''You care a lot but you won't take me seriously.'' She couldn't control the wave of resentment that welled up.

''That's ridiculous and you know it.''

Her chin came up. ''Then maybe there's some part of you you don't want me to share. A man like you would worry about loss of liberty, loss of freedom.''

He was shocked she thought that. ''So what do you want me to do? *Marry* you?'' he demanded of the embodiment of his dreams.

''I'm sorry, sorry.'' Suddenly Francesca broke away feeling utterly humiliated. Where was her pride? Did she really have to force his hand?

''Francesca.'' He came after her, wrapping his arms around her. ''It's never been like this for me with *anyone.* I want you desperately. So desperately I can't really understand myself. That day in the cave, I wanted to take you then. I was a hair's-breadth away from messing up your life. My life. It's not as easy as you're saying. You can't know what's involved."

"And you won't let me learn?" The strong passion in him communicated itself to her.

"I'm trying to think what's best for both of us. God, do you think I'm so utterly selfish I'd trap you in a cage?"

She broke away again, moving like a shadow into the swaying sheltering trees. "I don't want to hear it."

"You've got to hear what I'm saying." He found her easily in the velvet dark, following her fragrance. "I take the idea of marriage as a very serious business. I'm like the black swans. I'm going to mate for life. If you'd had my own kind of background I wouldn't hesitate for a minute but you were reared to the high life. Do you really think I'd ever let you run off? Do you think I'd ever let you get away from me with another man?

Tears sprang to her eyes at his forcefulness. Didn't he know she loved him? "I don't know what you're talking about," she said, her agitation apparent.

"But it happens, Francesca," he groaned, trying to get a handle on an emotional situation that was gaining swiftly in intensity. "It happens all the time. Not every woman can stand the isolation, the lack of entertainment, theatre, ballet, concerts, art showings, all the things you've been used to, being on your own when your man's away. I have to point out these things. I'd be painting a false picture if I didn't."

Even as he spoke, trying to warn her, prepare her, he didn't know which, shards of desire were piercing him through, sharper and sharper as she stood quietly under his hands, her long hair rippling over them like skeins of silk. He was desperately afraid of his own driving male hunger so fierce it could frighten her. ''Hell I'd take the all-for-love gamble if you could pay the price. If I married you I'd never let you go,'' he exploded. ''Can't you understand all this loving, this passion is dangerous?''

His hands were sending electric currents through her. She loved his hands, the shape of them. Hands were important to her.

Francesca bowed her head in acknowledgment, knowing her feeling for him had not only coloured her world, but turned it on its head. There was a Before Grant and After Grant. What else was Fate for? Nevertheless she turned away saying poignantly. ''I won't bother you again.''

''Francesca!'' he moaned aloud his frustration, torn between stifling her mouth with kisses and letting his ardour cool. Love. This kind of love was like jumping off a cliff.

''It's depressing coming down to earth with a crash.'' She made a gallant attempt at humour, almost reading his mind. ''You're quite right, Grant. We don't have enough in common.''

Nothing would work without a solid base of trust and hope.

CHAPTER FIVE

THE week the film people moved into Opal, Grant had to fly to Brisbane for a meeting with Drew Forsythe, set up some time back. A meeting that went so well, it spun out to intensive discussion over a period of three days as Forsythe found time out of his hectic schedule. Both men clicked, sons of dynasties, full of vision, energy and ambition with the brain power to make it all work. So it was working out deals by day, getting the go-ahead from his own financial advisers and at night Drew and his beautiful wife, Eve, made it their business to see Grant enjoyed himself.

They organised a dinner party one evening, and tickets to "Pavarotti and Friends" in concert, the next. They even rustled up a very attractive young woman called Annabel to make up the numbers, dark brown hair, big brown eyes, a head-turner in her own right, but Grant couldn't get Francesca out of his mind. Such was the depth of his feeling for her, she was a constant "presence." Before he'd left she had already been accepted for the role of Lucinda despite Fee's stated qualms. Ngaire Bell and Glenn Richards had swept Fee before them after hearing Francesca read.

"No shortage of talent in this family" was Ngaire's comment, breaking into a big smile. "With Francesca's looks and voice she would never be out of work. With no experience at all she understands the part thoroughly."

"Audiences will weep for her," Glenn Richards

added, looking spellbound. Francesca got such ''agony'' out of his lines. It was very gratifying.

It struck Grant as ironic Francesca was playing a part that had some relevance to their own situation, however slight. The character in the book, Lucinda, a gently bred English girl migrates to Australia with her handsome, vital, adventurer husband, loving him so deeply she is prepared to give up everything, homeland, family, friends to share his life. Eventually the rigours of trying to survive, let alone cope in a harsh new land with no one outside her husband who thrives in his new environment, to turn to for comfort or advice, wears her down. Never strong, painfully aware of her husband's disappointment in her, his expectations so much more than she can give, her inability to conceive, Lucinda sinks into a depression that ends in tragedy.

''Don't come without a box of tissues,'' Ngaire warned, using one herself. She was enormously encouraged by Francesca's ability to win sympathy for her character without portraying her as in any way wimpish. Francesca delivered her lines movingly, and with great sincerity bettering the very talented Paige Macauly.

Even Fee had been impressed, in fact her little girl took her breath away. Perversely Fee was hurt. Francesca hadn't asked her to run through her lines with her, or even offer a few words of expert advice.

''Brought it all on your own head, Fifi,'' David told her. ''Francesca wants to contribute. Let her.''

Whilst he was in Brisbane, Grant decided to take the opportunity to speak to an architect about his proposed homestead. Drew recommended an excellent man and an appointment was set up by Drew's secretary. The homesteads of Opal Downs and Kimbara appeared in a number of editions of *Historic Homesteads of Australia* and when Grant arrived at the architect's office he found the best coffee table edition lying open on the desk. They talked for quite a while about family influence and inheritance, the marriage between architecture and environment, while Grant revealed the sort of thing he wanted.

He expected the architect, Hugh Madison, a handsome clever-looking man in his late forties to pick up a pencil and tracing paper, instead he went to the computer and immediately began drawing up concepts. It was fascinating watching a wonderful kaleidoscope of graphics, but Grant still preferred drawings like the framed architectural drawings that hung on the walls of Opal. Drawings he had loved all his life. It was agreed Madison should visit the proposed site and a tentative date was set towards the end of the month. Madison would travel to the nearest outback domestic terminal and Grant would pick him up from there and ferry him back to Opal.

"I feel quite excited by the prospect," the architect told Grant as they parted. "It will be a joy! It's not often one gets the chance to design a major contemporary homestead. The powerful mystique of the outback will be inspirational. It will fully test what gift I have." As it would have to, Madison privately thought. This young man radiated purpose and energy. He was also very definite about what he wanted. He would be an exacting client but a very appreciative one if Madison could deliver his dream. Madison was confident on both scores.

* * *

Back at the Opal homestead, Francesca was finding filming wasn't as easy as she supposed. As a novice she had so much to learn, even how to turn her head but Ngaire, the guiding hand, was very patient with her, taking her steadily over her scenes. They didn't amount to many—Lucinda disappeared early—but they were essential to the story. They were shot to surprisingly few takes, sometimes four or five, never as many as Francesca feared might be necessary given her inexperience. But she made sure she came well-prepared—as well-prepared as Fee, who continued to show her amazement at this new side to her daughter.

Ngaire seemed delighted by both their work. She even listened to Francesca's input regarding her own character, a delicate young woman but still possessed of courage, struggling to survive in a world radically different from everything she had known. For all Ngaire's demonstrated brilliance, Francesca found she was remarkably kind and easy to get on with, never once giving way to temper when sometimes, as could be expected, things went quite wrong.

The lights were hot, cords trailed all over the floors. The make-up was just awful. It took such an age to put it on let alone get it off. Wearing the costumes in the sweltering heat. But Francesca found herself having a very good time. The trick was to forget Francesca de Lyle completely. She was Lucinda who loved her husband desperately, knowing each day she was losing him to forces outside her control. A young woman's dreams shattered. A young man's vision rewarded. Francesca was stunned to finish a particularly poignant scene only to see her mother and Ngaire bunched together with tears pouring down their cheeks.

"Oh my God, darling, you could make your mark!"

Fee cried emotionally, neatly evading a whole lot of equipment to take Francesca in her arms. "You do have a lot of your mother in you after all."

Each night when they watched the day's scenes reeled off, Francesca couldn't believe it was herself she was seeing on the screen. It gave her an actual frisson seeing her own face as she had never seen it before. She couldn't help but know her looks were out of the ordinary but the young woman on the screen was lovely in a way she hadn't fully appreciated and she had a way of speaking with her eyes and her hands. It cheered Francesca enormously to know she was acquitting herself rather well. It affirmed her value, reinforced her confidence in herself.

"And with absolutely no experience!" Fee exclaimed, still struggling to come to terms with this unexpected side to her daughter. "Just goes to show the power of the gene. Ally will marvel at this when she sees it."

Except Ally always knew I was a closet actress, Francesca thought. It was different with her mother who viewed her as much more a de Lyle than a Kinross.

Glenn was always there at her shoulder, ready to offer help if she needed it, ready to explain, to instruct, to admire. Glenn was very much part of everything, not only the screenwriter, but Ngaire's much valued colleague. Ngaire and Glenn took their lunch break together, heads close as they got into intense discussion about how things were progressing. In the evening Glen had taken to asking Francesca to go for an after-dinner stroll with him. Francesca didn't know quite how it happened. Certainly she hadn't initiated anything but she found Glenn attractive, his personality easy yet stimulating. There was a depth to him she liked and they had the film in common as a constant subject of conversation.

"So when is Grant coming home?" Glenn slid the question in neatly the third night out.

"I don't really know." Francesca shook her head desperate for Grant to return home.

"Really? I thought you two were very close." Glenn stared down at her, attracted to her strongly but unsure how to proceed. It wouldn't take a rocket scientist to discern something intangible but very powerful between Cameron and Francesca.

Yet Francesca was startled by the question, not thinking herself and Grant so transparent. It wasn't as though there was any kissing or touching or telling conversation in front of other people. "Surely you've had very little time to see us together?" she parried.

He gave a faint laugh. "I'm someone who notices things, Francesca. I'm a writer. It's my training and my nature."

"So what have you noticed?" She tried to speak lightly.

"I would say you two had a special understanding."

Francesca stopped to shake a tiny pebble from her sandal. "I'm not sure what you're getting at, Glenn?"

His voice was wry. "I suppose what I really want to know is are you spoken for?"

She knew she blushed, grateful he couldn't see it. "A writer must be noted for getting to the point."

"It's not every day I meet someone like you, Francesca," he said. "I don't think it's a secret, either, that I find you very attractive. I would like to get to know you better. But maybe that's not possible?"

How to frame a response? As though it were any of his business anyway. ''Grant and I are very good friends.'' Francesca lifted her head to stare up at the glittering desert stars. Friends? When he filled her with the most wonderful sensation of ''coming home.''

Glenn evidently wasn't impressed. ''Don't you just hate that,'' he mocked. ''Very good friends.''

''Well that's all I'm prepared to say.''

''Actually I am rushing it,'' Glenn apologised, shaking his head ruefully. ''But a man's a fool if he lets someone wonderful like you pass him by. You're beautiful, Francesca. You're also very talented.''

''I'm sure Mamma's surprised,'' Francesca answered lightly, trying to turn the conversation. She did find Glenn attractive. In some ways he charmed her but there was only one man she wanted and perversely he was trying to push her away.

''Would you think of repeating your experience?'' Glenn asked, warmed by the silken brush of her arm.

''You mean consider acting as a serious career?'' She sensed he was very interested in her answer.

''There would be much to learn, Francesca, but there's no doubt you're a natural and the cameras love you. It doesn't love everyone no matter how good-looking. I've seen beautiful people film as quite ordinary.''

''Strange, isn't it?'' Francesca mused. ''I suppose it's all about photography. I've always taken a good picture. But to answer your question, I don't want to be a film star, Glenn. That's not my dream at all.''

It was absurd to feel such disappointment. ''And what is your dream?'' he asked, looking down at her silken head.

''In some ways the hardest thing of all,'' Francesca

responded. ''To have a happy, lasting marriage. To raise a family. Bring all my children up with the right values. Help them to become people of confidence and accomplishment. I want to *love* them. Have them love me. I never want discord or alienation. I fear conflict.''

This girl had been hurt. Deeply hurt, Glenn thought.

''No easy ambition,'' he murmured

''I know.'' She looked back at the purple sky. ''But I want to focus all my energies on family. If one is in the fortunate financial position to do so being a wife and mother is a full-time job.''

''Fee's career would have taken her a lot away from you?'' he said with sudden realisation.

''Yes.'' Francesca nodded not wanting to discuss the breakdown of her parent's marriage, her father's custody of her which Glenn didn't know.

''But I understand from Rebecca that you had a first-class P.R. job in London?''

''That's true. I was competent but I've said my goodbyes. It didn't make me feel I was doing anything terribly important. There was no *charge.* I wanted to have a musical career at one time but my father vetoed that. It wasn't quite the thing.''

''I expect your father wants what you want. For you to marry well and happily.''

Though Francesca laughed, it sounded a little hollow. ''He has my future husband lined up.''

''Good grief you're surely not going to let your father pick your future husband?'' That would ruin everything, Glenn thought.

''Of course not,'' Francesca answered calmly. ''But there's been a bit of pressure there. From my side of the family and his.''

''Your suitor's?'' Glenn was totally distracted.

"It's a class thing, Glenn, being an Australian you mightn't understand. I'm a 'today' person. My father definitely isn't. Being an earl has a lot of implications."

"I would imagine," Glenn agreed dryly, his quirky eyebrows going up. "And being an earl's daughter has its responsibilities, I take it?"

"They do have an effect on me." Francesca remembered all the times she had suffered inner qualms and discomforts, aware of her father's plan for her. "I can't overlook them but my parents had their life. Surely I must have mine."

"I should jolly well say so." Glenn was thinking too much parental involvement was a terrible intrusion on a person's life. "Surely this chap knows you don't love him?"

Francesca's voice was gentle, almost resigned. "I do love him. I've known him all my life. He's counting on that. But it's not that kind of love. That *one* person."

That one person! It sounded very much like she'd found him. "Does Cameron have any idea about all this?" Glenn asked. Cameron was in love with her. He was quite sure of his own radar.

Francesca answered with some irony. "Grant seems to be on side with my father's master plan."

Glenn turned his keen, intelligent brown eyes on her. "I find that very hard to believe. I see Grant Cameron as a tough, very determined young man in a man's world. He wouldn't knuckle down to anyone."

"Except maybe himself," said Francesca.

His father had always told him, especially when he was a headstrong kid. "Don't *do* things, Grant, without thinking them through. Hell, hadn't he learnt? Yet he couldn't wait to get back to her, every day bringing him closer to asking her to marry him and to hell with the rest. Why not let it out? Let his feelings go free? Tell her exactly what he felt for her. Why didn't he simply cry out, "Now I've found you I'll never let you go!" *Why!* Did his love for her run to self-sacrifice? Was that what love was? Putting the loved one's welfare before one's own?

In his business he had grown into the habit of setting down all his concerns, identifying them by putting them in print. Then working out solutions from there. Even as he was hiring an architect to draw up plans for the new homestead his mind was ranging over other options. Other places from where he could operate.

Places where Francesca wouldn't feel quite so isolated and the climate would be kinder. Maybe most of the Camerons from the beginning had been blondes or redheads? They'd had time to acclimatise over the generations. He was as genuinely fearful for Francesca's beautiful skin as a collector would be fearful of hanging a fine painting where it received too much strong daylight. Francesca was taking up so much of his head space he felt he was never without her.

He was flying in over Opal, on a hot clear day, looking down at the great maze of interlocking billabongs and creeks, marked by narrow bands of verdant green on both sides of the water channels. The mulga, the vast region where acacias predominated, spread away to the horizon, bridging the gap between the hardiest eucalypt country and the true desert with its golden plains of pungent, pointed, spinifex and saltbush, its glittering gibber-stones and rolling dark red sand-dunes.

How he loved it! His home. It called to him as it always did when he went beyond its boundaries. The Dead Heart. Only it wasn't dead at all. It was beating, magnificent, unique; the flora without parallel for its adaptation to such a harsh environment. Even the ghost gums grew out of sheer rock where occasional storm waters had flowed and the barren interior became an ocean of wildflowers that gloried in its short, breathtaking tide.

Flowers! The fragrant flowers of the inland. Blazing on and on. Mile after mile. In such a harsh land none had thorns. Neither did the trees and bushes of the desert. Nothing to protect themselves. The exquisite roses had thorns to protect them. In other parts of the world thorns were the rule rather than the exception. Grant went with his stream of consciousness, which always carried images of Francesca. She might have been the only girl left in the world so obsessed was he with the thought of her.

The fair Francesca! A pink rose with satin petals. A rose in the wilderness. Once this wilderness, this great savage land, the parched deserts and plains formed the bed of the Great Inland Sea of prehistory. Twenty thousand years ago the vast Interior had been clothed in luxuriant vegetation to rival the paradise of the wild, the tropical rainforests of the Far North. Crocodiles had once thrived as they still did north of Capricorn. There were many drawings of crocodiles recorded by the aborigines in the rock paintings in and around the Wild Heart. A remarkable witness to the length of time the aborigines had roamed Australia. One of the rarest trees in the world, the Livistona, a tall, graceful tropical "cabbage" palm he had seen growing in pockets in the heat of the desert. A microclimate created by a river gorge.

An oasis in the desert. Ferns and palms and the ancient cycads, their emerald-greens contrasting with the fiery red walls of the cliffs and the deep sapphire sky.

An oasis. Lushness in the arid spinifex plains.

It mightn't be the natural environment for a rose but roses survived and flourished in the sheltered gardens of Kimbara, which relied on bores that had been sunk deep in the Great Artesian Basin. It had taken generations for the gardens at Kimbara to flourish. Generations, a great deal of time and money, a dedication that had filled Kimbara's women's souls.

In his grandfather's day the gardens at Opal had been significant though they had never rivalled Kimbara's. He remembered his mother working hard to keep the gardens going. He remembered her talking about the difficulties. It had taken such a short time for Opal's gardens to die after their mother had been taken so cruelly from them. But Ally would bring them back. Ally was a doer. Ally and Francesca. Cousins. And great friends.

He began to imagine Francesca walking through the gardens love would create in the desert. Francesca in a microclimate. In an oasis of fragrant flowers. Surely if he could create an oasis for her she could not only survive but thrive. Go forward, a voice in his head told him. You can only go forward. You can't go back.

The cast and crew were taking a break from filming when he arrived at the homestead early midafternoon. All these strange people in his family home. But they were paying well and Bush Rescue would get a very welcome injection of funds. Fee saw him first as he pulled the Jeep off the circular driveway into the shade of the trees, waiting for him at the top of the steps.

"Hello there, Grant, darling," she called, the incomparable Fee completely at home in her elaborate get-up that had to be stifling in the heat. "We've missed you. How did it go?"

He bent to kiss the cheek she extended to him, a thin layer of the heavy make-up used for filming smearing his lips. "Sorry, darling." Fee produced a handkerchief from somewhere in her deep violet costume, dabbing at his mouth.

"It's all right, Fee," he reassured her casually. "It'll come off. In answer to your question, things went well. TCR and Cameron Airways are not far away from signing a deal. The lawyers will work it out. Where's everybody?"

Fee gestured gracefully towards the house. "Taking a break. It's hot work as you can imagine, consequently tempers are getting a little frayed. I came out to catch whatever breeze there is. Apart from that things are moving along nicely. Francesca has been the truly big surprise. She's amazingly good."

"Why wouldn't she be?" Grant countered breezily, feeling Fee hadn't been giving Francesca enough credit. "She *is* your daughter."

They were all over the main reception rooms so Grant decided on going immediately to his room, changing his clothes, then looking in on Francesca and Ngaire on his way back. He sent a searching glance through the drawing room nevertheless hoping to catch a glimpse of Francesca. He wondered what she would look like in period costume. That tiny waist his hands could span, her beautiful hair dressed in unfamiliar fashion. He couldn't wait to see her on the footage they had shot. It was a pity he'd had to go off as shooting started but he couldn't have cancelled his meeting with Drew. It was too important.

They were sitting side by side on an old Victorian love seat. Richards obviously feeling the need to hold Francesca's hands in his. He had his dark head bent to her, speaking earnestly, while she listened as attentive as any man could possibly wish. She was the embodiment of Lucinda in her dark grey gown, the bodice tightly buttoned, a show of cream near the throat, the heavy full skirt spread out across the rose velvet. Her glorious Titian hair was drawn back severely from her face from a centre parting with some kind of thick roll at the back. The hair style and get-up reminded him of how they had tried to make Olivia de Havilland plain for the part of Melanie in *Gone with the Wind.* Never succeeding. Both de Havilland and Francesca had such sweetness of expression quite apart from the lovely features that could never be denied.

And just because he was the screenwriter did that give Richards the right to go into a huddle with Francesca? Surely Ngaire, who was nowhere to be seen, should be handling the direction? Grant had thought he would be overjoyed to see Francesca again, thought they would greet each other like they'd been parted for years. Instead here she was lifting her head to stare soulfully into Richards's eyes while Richards stared back at her, clearly under her spell.

What the hell was going on? Grant fumed. Whatever it was it ripped the heart out of him. He broke his glance, striding off towards his bedroom, his earlier mood of excitement and anticipation replaced by one he barely recognised as jealousy. Not that he had time for any of it, he thought grimly. He had work to do.

Bob Carlton was a tower of strength to him but he couldn't leave him carrying the load. Also Bob would be anxious to hear all about his meeting with Forsythe.

Dressed in his everyday uniform of khaki bush shirt and trousers, he went back through the house, hearing voices from the formal dining room he and Rafe never used while they were on their own. Obviously they were back at work. Not that he was about to interrupt. Not now. In his absence he had arranged for one of his men to ferry Francesca, Fee, Ngaire and Richards back to Kimbara at the end of the day's shoot and the leading man when he arrived—he could have for all Grant knew. The male film crew elected to stay close to their equipment, bunking down in the stockmen's quarters, and taking their meals there.

The women, four in all, wardrobe and make-up had taken over a bungalow, which had been made as comfortable as possible by a couple of the station wives. Over the period of time it took to finish the outback scenes, the wives were assisting the camp cook who could produce dishes every bit as good as those many city chefs could offer. Opal staff worked very hard. Opal staff deserved to be fed very well. It was essential to keep up their energy level and good spirits. It was mandatory as well, to ensure station guests were well catered for.

Grant stalked off realising he had to return before sunset if he wanted to see Francesca at all. He had planned on ferrying them back to Kimbara himself but something about Richards's proprietorial attitude and Francesca's seeming quiescence had set him off. It shamed him and made him angry he could be so jealous. A feeling entirely new to him and something he didn't want to accept. He realised with a kind of despair this was another thing that went along with passion. He didn't like Richards's intimacy with *his* girl!

Fee waited until she and Francesca were getting out of their heavy costumes, handing them over to Liz Forbes, from wardrobe, before she mentioned Grant had arrived home.

"You mean he never came in to say hello?" Francesca turned sharply towards her mother, feeling a clutch of dismay on two accounts: Fee had neglected to tell her and Grant hadn't called in.

"I thought he would," said Fee taking off her wig and placing it carefully on the dummy.

"Perhaps he didn't want to interrupt us," Francesca suggested, trying to rid herself of the notion Grant hadn't missed her as much as she had missed him.

"We were taking a break at the time," Fee protested. "Don't be upset, darling." Fee began to brush her own hair out. "He's probably had lots to attend to. The meeting in Brisbane went well."

"Couldn't you have told me earlier, Mamma?" Francesca asked reproachfully, not appreciating the fact Fee seemed to be working underground to drive a wedge between herself and Grant.

Fee shook her head. "Darling girl when you're in character it's best not to have any outside distractions. I'm proud of what you're doing. You're very good you know."

But Francesca wasn't to be diverted. "I think you planned it, Mamma." She looked her mother in the eye, seeing no sign of apology on Fee's still stunning face. "You like Grant. At least I thought you did but you're doing your level best to create divisions."

"Darling girl, I'm not the enemy here," Fee exclaimed. "I don't want you to ruin your life." Tears suddenly filled Fee's eyes and she made no attempt to blink them away. "I *do* like Grant. He's an admirable young man but I just can't see he's for you."

"Okay so who is?" Francesca challenged, more aware than anyone her mother could call up tears at will. "Don't leave it up in the air. *Who?*"

"Jimmy," Fee's response was instantaneous as though she'd come up with a crucial piece of information. "Jimmy Waddington. Surely you can't have forgotten him? Jimmy will make you happy."

Francesca concentrated hard on not getting angry. "How's that?"

"Darling, he knows you so well," Francesca cried with more than a touch of theatre. "He *understands* you. You've been great friends since you were children. Be honest now, weren't you in love with him?"

"I didn't know what love was." Francesca shook her head. "I'm very fond of Jimmy but fondness isn't what changes your life."

"Maybe not," Fee admitted. "Being in love is wonderful at the time but it doesn't last. Lord, child I should know."

It had to be said. "I'm not frivolous like you, Mamma."

Fee opened her eyes wide. Francesca didn't realise it but she sounded exactly like her father. "Darling, couldn't you be more respectful?"

"I'm surprised you don't agree. Anyway Jimmy *doesn't* understand me. He doesn't think I have a serious thought in my head."

"What nonsense!" Fee gave the impression she was shocked. "You know perfectly well he thinks you're a wonderful girl. More importantly you have the same background. Your father has hand-picked Jimmy for your husband.''

''Father's not the expert on marriage, either,'' Francesca said. ''Anyway fathers have no right to do that.''

''You can face him with that?'' Fee challenged, locking her daughter's gaze.

''It wouldn't be easy, but yes.'' Francesca gave a long-suffering sigh. ''What are you trying to suggest anyway, Mamma? In refusing Jimmy I'm betraying Father. Is that what you're saying?''

Fee stared off for a moment. ''Please don't raise your voice, darling. Ngaire and Glenn are still about. I'm the last person in the world to want to upset you. I love you, but I must point out Grant in many respects is an unknown entity.''

''After all these years?'' Francesca gave a wry little laugh.

''Darling, you met him briefly when you came for visits,'' Fee pointed out. ''You didn't really get to know one another until recent times.''

''So you don't recommend him as a husband?'' Francesca said. ''Be frank.''

Fee reached into her handbag and pulled out her eau de cologne. ''I'm sure he'll make a delightful husband but maybe a difficult one, too. He's very ambitious. Hungry for success.''

''He's a success already, Mamma,'' Francesca said in a pained voice. ''Grant told me he wants to give something to his country, to his community. I believe him. The Camerons have money already. Money isn't the motivating factor with Grant.''

''Don't be ridiculous, darling,'' Fee said with hard irony.

"I'm not being ridiculous." Francesca shook her head. "Money is fine. Everyone welcomes it but I know Grant means what he says. He wants to do things. He has a vision. Don't please tell me Jimmy has one."

"At least you'll be able to handle him," Fee said in a voice that suggested Francesca wouldn't be able to handle Grant. "Come on, darling," she coaxed as Francesca turned away from her. "I'm sorry if I'm upsetting you but I'm trying to do the right thing. At least give yourself *time.* I know all about dynamic men. They sweep you off your feet, but before you know where you are—"

"Please, Mamma." Francesca signalled she had had enough. "You're so used to thinking of me as your little girl…you can't see I'm an adult. I can't depend on you or Father to make my decisions for me."

"Even when there's so much at stake?" Fee pleaded, using her full voice. "Your happiness? Your well-being?"

"May I speak now, Mamma?" Francesca asked. "Even then. This is the most serious relationship of my life. If I'm ready to take the leap Grant is reflecting on things long and hard. In fact it might ease your mind to know he, too, is considering our relationship might be dead wrong."

Fee frowned deeply as though no one was permitted to think such a thing of her daughter. "My darling, don't you see you could fight about everything! I see a huge contrast between you two," she said.

"Then you don't know Grant or me as well as you think," said Francesca.

* * *

Grant did return to ferry them home but Grant and Francesca never had the chance of a private word until they reached Kimbara homestead and the others had gone inside.

''Couldn't you stay, Grant?'' Rebecca, who had been standing with them on the verandah asked. ''Do you have to rush away?''

''Actually I do, Rebecca.'' Grant softened his refusal with a smile. ''I have to be ready for a big job on Laura tomorrow. Thanks anyway. Give my best to Brod when he comes in. Tell him everything went well.''

''That's great. I know he'll be thrilled for you.'' Rebecca smiled, a sparkle in her eyes. ''I'll leave you two to catch up. You're coming to Fee's book launch aren't you?''

''Well I'm thinking about it,'' Grant said.

''You *have* to!'' Rebecca insisted. ''It'll be lovely for the four of us to go out together one night while we're in Sydney. You and Fran. Brod and I. See if you can pull out all the stops.''

''I'll try!'' Grant sketched her a salute. ''Rebecca is looking radiant,'' he said, when he and Francesca were alone.

Francesca raised a delicate eyebrow. ''Is that really so surprising? She's head over heels in love with her husband.''

''Then she has excellent taste.'' Grant allowed his eyes to dwell on her. The slant of her blue eyes, the curve of the lid, the line of her cheek, the clean cut of her jaw, the exquisite shape of her mouth. She'd creamed off all the heavy film make-up and her beautiful skin had a slightly shiny lustre. ''How are you?'' he asked, wanting to tilt her face to him and kiss it. Amazed he didn't.

"A bit down in the dumps," Francesca admitted. "Why didn't you come in and say hello when you arrived?"

He raised a sardonic eyebrow. "Because I didn't want to interrupt your little coaching session with Richards."

"You're kidding!" Whatever she imagined, it wasn't that.

"Never more serious actually. I glanced into the drawing room only to find the two of you on that old love seat, tenderly holding hands."

"Could it be your eyes were deceiving you?"

"No."

Francesca glanced up at him quickly, her eyes searching out his mood. "If it were anyone else but you I'd say you were jealous."

"Not overly. You don't think I'm capable of being jealous?" he asked, iridescent eyes narrowing over her.

"You wouldn't allow yourself to go so far. Now let's see. We were sitting on the love seat. I'm trying to cast my mind back."

"Cocooned in your own little world," he prompted. "Richards has his head bent to you. You were staring up soulfully at him. It was one hell of a scene!"

It must have been to cause such a reaction. "Now I remember. I'm just a beginner, Grant," she explained patiently. "Green as they come. There's so much I don't know. Practically all of it. Glenn has been very kind to me."

"Kinder than Ngaire?" he asked suavely. "I thought she was the director. Isn't it her task to correct any mistakes? Smooth over all the little rough bits."

"Ngaire helps me as well," she told him briskly. "Everyone does. They give me all the support I need."

"So you're loving it then?" Because I missed you like hell.

"I think I'll look back on it as a very worthwhile experience," Francesca said. "But I'm not taking it too seriously. And what about you? I want to hear all about your meetings with Drew. How's Eve by the way? Did you manage to see her?"

He nodded. "Eve's fine. She sent her best regards. They entertained me royally. Two nights. A dinner party at their beautiful home. Then Pavarotti and Friends in Concert. Our meetings went very well. Drew and I are on the same wavelength. Let's walk down to the chopper?" He took her arm, wondering how things could go so easily wrong, when he desperately wanted to hold her close. "I called in on an architect while I was there. Drew recommended him."

Her head seemed to explode with stars. "Really? Now you know something funny? I dreamt that you did."

He squeezed her delicate upper arm. "Francesca you're not *acting?*"

"No I'm not. I don't tell fibs. I actually did dream w—" she could hardly give herself away "—you and an architect were speaking together. It was quite a vivid dream. I've thought about it a lot. As a matter of fact I've had a lot of fun sketching some designs. You might like to see them some time."

"Run and get them now," he said. "I'll wait."

The high colour of excitement came into her cheeks. "I want us to look at them *together.*"

"Then come back to Opal with me tonight," he said with quiet intensity. "I want to be near you. Make love to you. Open all the doors and curtains so the moonlight will fall on your beautiful, luminous skin."

She hesitated, half-poised to run back to the homestead. ''Sometimes you're crazy.''

He gave her an ironic look. ''You don't want to come?''

''You know I do.'' Her breathing softly rasped. ''I missed you terribly.''

''Did you?''

''Yes.''

He took her chin and tilted her mouth. ''Poor, poor, Francesca,'' he said very softly. ''It was no different for me.''

She stood very still while he kissed her, feeling the force of his desire held on a tight leash. ''What is it you want?'' she whispered into his mouth, half-closing her eyes.

He wanted to slide his hand down over her swan's neck, cup her smooth, creamy breast, feel it swell to the tenderness of his fingers. He wanted to let his hand descend…

''Just one word, Francesca,'' he said huskily. ''*You.* There's so much I want to tell you.''

''So much I want to hear.''

Anything might have happened next, so closely were they drawn together in heart and mind, only Fee chose that very moment to come hurrying out onto the verandah, walking to the balustrade. ''Darling, Ngaire wants to show us today's rushes. Sure you can't stay and see them, Grant?''

Grant's smile was openly mocking. ''I really have to get away, Fee.'' Of course she knew he did, if he wanted to be on Opal by nightfall. ''You'd better go, Francesca,'' he told her dryly. ''Fee's full of surprises. Now she's applying a bit of maternal pressure.''

Goddammit, yes, Francesca thought in amazement.

The phantom mother of her childhood, the brilliant shooting star, was now siding of all things with the ex-husband she had so capriciously cut out of her life. Nevertheless Francesca sprang to Fee's defence so deeply was the habit ingrained. "Mamma only intends to be..."

"Please don't say kind," Grant warned, his strong, handsome face showing its high mettle. "I think Fee could be a ruthless opponent. What she doesn't intend is for you to be buried away in the wilds. Not that I blame her. God knows I can see both sides."

Gently, conciliatory, Francesca touched his hand. "I'll bring my sketchbook over tomorrow. I so much want to show it to you. Another part of my dream—" the *same* part...she didn't tell him in her dream the homestead and the garden merged "—we were planning an oasis in the vast landscape. It would be impossible to conquer such immensity but one could devise a sort of sweeping Australian garden landscape. Something on the grand scale to live in harmony with the unique environment and survive drought. I suppose it's far too ambitious, but one could landscape some of the watercourses. Indigenous trees of course but massed plantings. And there could be a polo field with lots of shade for the ponies, the spectators and their cars. It would be an enormous challenge, probably daunting, but so exciting. We could create our own vision rather than going along with existing..."

He interrupted her almost fiercely. "We? You did say *we,* didn't you?"

Francesca didn't falter, even with her mother waiting anxiously for her up on the verandah. "Yes," she answered, her heart in her eyes.

CHAPTER SIX

NEXT day he couldn't get away from Laura Station until after the midafternoon break. He had a new recruit on roster, a man the same age as himself, Rick Wallace—an excellent helicopter pilot with more than enough qualifications and flying hours to warrant his inclusion in the team, but a mite short on actual experience in aerial mustering. It was his first priority as boss of the team to make sure Wallace was handling the job properly. He always conducted a premuster briefing, always took aerial shots, pointing out possible dangers on the site, sometimes acting as copilot to continue with the first-hand instruction. By smoko he was sure he was leaving the rest of the day's work in Rick's gifted hands. Rick was well on the way to having the same sort of skills as himself and he, too, was mad on flying. They would be friends.

When he arrived back on Opal it was to find the leading man had arrived to film his scenes; Ngaire introduced them, pleasure in her eyes. Her hero was an up-and-coming young English actor unconventionally handsome, dark-haired, light-eyed, with reputed considerable sex appeal for women and the ability to get male audiences onside. Grant knew the role called for a genuine English accent rather than an assumed one, which could slip from time to time, as well as a male lead with an international ''name.'' The name was Marc Fordham. He had a friendly manner and a firm hand shake. Grant liked him.

Marc was dressed in part in a stained and dusty rather billowy white shirt and tight dark brown trousers and a wide silver buckled belt. His dark curly hair was shoulder-length and tousled, a few days growth of beard on his face. He looked great, every inch the dynamic hero of the novel. The women wouldn't be able to take their eyes off him, Grant thought, amused the dark tan—dark as Brod's that went so extraordinarily well with light eyes—was courtesy of the make-up department. Someone would have to warn him of the dangers of the outback sun. Though he tried not to make it too obvious his own eyes were going in search of Francesca. Finally when she didn't appear and he couldn't sight her, he was forced to ask Ngaire where she was.

''Out riding,'' Ngaire volunteered, as though it was her own greatest pleasure to be in the saddle. ''With Marc here we thought we'd go ahead with his scenes with Fee.'' Fee played the hero's distant relative, the wife of a powerful Sydney landowner keen to recruit the hero to his interests. ''Francesca wasn't needed so she and Glenn decided to go for a ride. Glenn is a weekend rider,'' Ngaire laughed indulgently. ''Francesca, I believe is a brilliant horsewoman. One of the many reasons she got the part of Lucinda. She has that mad, suicidal ride in her final scene. We'll leave that to the last days of shooting. We were even going to ask you if you could line someone up for the long shoots. Someone who could pass for Marc. Marc has had to learn to ride a horse of course, but he's no expert. If you could come up with a stand-in?'' Ngaire looked winsome, clearly hoping or counting on, either he or Brod would do it. But he couldn't answer for either of them.

Instead he nodded noncommittally. "Any idea where they're headed?"

"Oh, not too far I would imagine." Ngaire started to lose interest, keen to get on with filming. "Francesca said you liked her to stay close to the home. I think she left a note for you." She cast her eyes around, saw nothing, fluttered a hand. "She was sitting out on the side verandah, sketching as I recall. Maybe it's out there."

No note. A number of sketchbooks tidily stacked on the circular table, a leather case full of pencils, charcoal sticks close beside. He was finding out something new about her all the time. It was absurd to be jealous of Richards. Beautiful as she was, Francesca as a femme fatale he couldn't buy. Francesca was honest and true. She had gone for a ride and she would be back soon. Grant sat down taking the sketchbook from the top of the pile, conscious of a swift emotional response as his eye fell on a drawing of…

Himself. Or himself as Francesca saw him. He stared at it for a long time thinking she had made him look a whole lot better looking than he was, maybe a touch arrogant with the lift of his chin and the angle of his head. But it was undeniably him and it was very good. He turned more pages marvelling at the drawings. Himself again and again. Members of the family. There was Brod, a genuinely handsome devil. Beautifully lily cool Rebecca in any number of poses. Fee in an armchair, Fee reading a script, Fee and David, numerous sketches of Ally, a few of Rafe looking like a medieval knight. Perhaps that was the way she saw him.

Other books were devoted to animals, beautiful drawings of horses, cattle, kangaroos, emus, brolgas, swans, pages of the giant wedge-tailed eagle with detailed inserts of wings. She was wonderful at capturing animals in action. She must have sketched at the instant it happened. Other sketchbooks contained Kimbara landscapes, with stockmen at rest, or driving herds of cattle. There were innumerable little sketches of wildflowers, lilies, ground orchids, boronia, flowering vines.

Another couple of sketchbooks were devoted to studies in anatomy the structure of the human body. They appeared to be absolutely accurate. Other exercises fleshed out the skeleton. Obviously Francesca had received a good deal of training. He'd no idea she was so talented in this way. He wondered if she painted in other media—watercolours, pastels, oils? He would love to see what she could do. Talent like this deserved the greatest encouragement.

The very last book in the pile, almost hidden, contained what he was so desperate to see. Francesca's visions of his dream homestead. The first sketch was front on. So real he felt he could reach out and open the front door.

Francesca! He loved what he saw. She drew effortlessly as if she loved it. The facade was completely modern, huge areas of glass that could be opened to the desert air. The central core of the homestead enclosed front and sides by sweeping verandahs, no flamboyant classical columns but representations of narrow steel supports running the entire length of the facade. A concession to tradition a double height entrance but what totally blew him away rising behind it a three-story open bell-tower, modelled on a Spanish mission tower from where bells would call and one would have a fantastic view of the desert landscape.

Other drawings followed, different aspects, different

angled facets, various sketches of the tower, all a little different, open views down into the interior with the layout of open-plan rooms and an enclosed central courtyard with a tall fluid water sculpture instead of the traditional fountain. But what was so fascinating was Francesca had put splashes of colours—yellow ochre, burnt umber, raw sienna, ultramarine blue, cobalt blue, cadmium yellow and red, lamp black, he read them off—down the side of the pages along with specified materials, stone, glass, steel, richly grained timbers, different shades and textures of granite.

Obviously their minds worked in the same way. Working quite independent of him, with her own background of a jewel-like English country home, she had come up with a design structure little different from his own except for the novel addition of a tower.

It was downright uncanny. Her vision reflected his own. A graceful house for all its modernist approach. She had even sketched entrance gates to the main compound. Not high to restrict the uninterrupted views but substantial, making a statement, two low pillars of desert rocks anchoring bronze gates depicting two magnificent rearing horses, the whole shaded by an A-framed roof from which hung the legend, Myora-Opal Station.

There weren't words for what he felt. He only knew he wanted to live there. With the girl of his dreams, Francesca.

This was the kind of thing he had wanted from the architect but he realised in that he was being too simplistic. Madison had picked up on all his basic cues, his vision a striking contemporary version of the traditional homestead but Francesca with her knowledge of the site had worked from the imagination. Clever, clever, girl.

From his vantage point on the verandah he was the first to see the grey gelding come in, disconsolate, head down, reins trailing.

God!

Grant vaulted up from his chair, taking the steps at a single leap, running across the garden to the open grasslands. The horse heard his repeated whistles, carried on the wind. It pricked its ears in the direction from whence they had come, then adjusted its direction. Minutes later Grant had it by the reins. The grey's coat was covered in sweat. It was obvious it had bolted, only slowing its flight when it was in sight and sound of the homestead. It gave Grant considerable comfort to know Francesca was a fine horsewoman with hands like silk. But Richards, according to Ngaire, was an inexperienced rider. He only hoped if it was Richards who had become unseated he'd been wearing one of the light weight helmets the station insisted their guests wear. Galloping across the plains with only an akubra to protect a fragile skull was only a romantic notion for anyone but a skilled rider.

A young aboriginal boy came running as he approached the stables complex, taking the grey's reins. "What'sa matter, boss?" Bunny so called because of his prominent but dazzlingly white, front teeth stared up at him with black, liquid eyes. "Where this one come from?"

"You tell me, Bunny," Grant responded grimly. "Were you on hand when Miss Francesca and her friend went out?"

"Sure was, boss." Bunny was happy to confirm it. "Saddled up for them. Miss Francesca picked out

Gypsy. A bit frisky but I reckon she can handle 'im. The guy settled for Spook. Nice and quiet." Bunny ran an ebony hand over Spook's side. "Though with a horse you never to know. Reckon he's come a way. Sweatin'."

Grant looked as if he was about to curse but didn't. "So someone has taken a tumble I just hope to God, Bunny, you gave him a hard hat?"

Bunny looked him straight in the eye. "I was goin' to, boss, but Miss Francesca insisted on it right away. Wore an akubra herself like the rest of us. Talk about bushie!"

"You know she's half Australian. Get the saddle off him, Bunny," Grant said. "Any idea where they headed?"

Bunny waved a hand. "Miss Francesca didn't say and I didn't think it my place to ask."

"That's okay," Grant said. "See ya, kid. From now on you have my permission to ask everybody where they're headed. So don't have any qualms. I'll go back to the house and check. Miss Francesca was supposed to have left a note."

Fee as it turned out had it, which struck Grant as odd, given Fee appeared to be against his and Francesca's deepening involvement. She apologised profusely when Grant told her crisply she should have handed it over once he returned.

"One of the horses has returned without a rider," he told her, grey-green eyes glinting. He took the note from its unsealed envelope and opened it. "Don't panic, it's not Francesca's horse," he had the grace to reassure Fee. "She was riding Gypsy. Richards was riding the grey gelding, Spook. It's a quiet work horse, but like all horses it's unpredictable." As he was speaking he was reading swiftly. "They've headed out to Blue Lady Lagoon. An easy trail. I'll get going."

"I do hope it's nothing serious." Fee was looking unaccustomedly chastened. "I understand Glenn was little more than a beginner. He couldn't handle anything at all lively. And Francesca! I know she's got a lot of common sense but I hope she gave that serious consideration."

"I only hope we're not looking at broken bones. Just in case I'll have to put out a call to the Royal Flying Doctor."

"Glenn wouldn't have a clue about roughing it," Fee said.

"Would Francesca?" Grant countered briskly. "Anyway I must go. There's only so much daylight left."

He took the four-wheel drive, heading out across the plains country to a favourite haven for all the station, black and white. Blue Lady Lagoon. All the stations in the Channel Country had similar flowering waterholes, filled with beautiful waterlilies, the sacred blue lotus, the pink, the cream, the rarer red lotus and the giant blue waterlily of Blue Lady Lagoon with its spectacular flowers growing up to a foot across. No matter how hot it was Blue Lady Lagoon with its tall trees, numerous golden grevilleas and native hibiscus, its understorey of mosses, vines and ground orchids offered an almost junglelike cool. He could understand why Francesca had headed there. He didn't realise it but he had tightened his jaw until it ached. He wouldn't accept Francesca was perfectly all right until he laid eyes on her. At least they couldn't get lost. They had only to follow the chain of billabongs home.

Ten minutes out he was confronted by an extraordinary sight. In the shimmering, dancing light of the atmosphere a small figure appeared out of the near distant mulga. The figure was on foot leading a black horse that could only be Gypsy. Hunkered down over the horse's back was a far more substantial figure. Richards.

Without further ado Grant tore off across country, angered beyond words—Francesca was walking in the heat. No way to travel! God she could have been walking for miles! If so she would be parched. A wave of hostility towards Richards swept through him, rivalled by his great sense of relief. Richards had to be in a bad way if he had consented to do the riding while Francesca walked.

Closer he saw Francesca had come to a standstill, holding firmly to Gypsy's reins, looking up at Richards probably asking him how he was. Moments more and he brought the Jeep to a halt, jumped out and moved towards them with all the speed and purpose of a big cat.

"What's happened here?" His intense scrutiny devoured Francesca as he checked to see if she was all right. Only then did it move on to Richards as he tried to neutralise his anger. "Are you okay there, Glenn?" he asked, moving alongside Gypsy soothing him.

Richards managed a smile, trying to straighten. "Afraid I took a tumble." That was clear from all the grazing down one side of his face and the condition of his clothes.

"No bones broken." Francesca came to stand at Grant's shoulder. "He's concussed, I imagine. Very groggy."

"So you let him up on your horse?" He all but accused her in a display of perverse male emotion.

"Come off it, Grant. I had to," she answered in a mild voice. "He's in no condition to walk."

"And *you* are?" He stared down into her lovely, sensitive face. She was wearing her wide-brimmed akubra with a light blue bandanna protecting her nape, but her face was very flushed and beads of sweat had gathered across her forehead at her temples and beneath her eyes. Sensibly she had let down her long hair as a curtain and had rolled down the long sleeves of her yellow cotton shirt but he could plainly see a runnel of sweat moving down between her breasts with damp patches all over the blouse and waistline. "The first thing we've got to do is get you a drink of water," he said harshly, starting back to the four-wheel drive.

"It's all right." She came after him to lay a reassuring hand on his arm. "I made sure we didn't set off without water. I stopped to give us a drink just before we moved out of the scrub."

"So you can drink some more now," he said, making short work of pouring out some water from the supply in the vehicle.

"You're not going to stand over me while I drink it?" Francesca asked wryly.

"Yes, I am," he answered firmly. "Something else I want you to do while I get Richards is put this towel over your face and neck." He started to saturate a small hand towel with water, not content with handing it to her but taking charge himself. He swept her akubra off then began sponging her hot face with the cool, clean water easing part of it around her throat. "What boots have you got on?" he demanded next, his brow knotted.

"Good ones," she gasped as he ceased mopping her

up. But her sense of being dreadfully overheated had eased.

"So get in the vehicle," he ordered briefly. "I'll attend to Richards."

Francesca did so gratefully, making a real effort to appear sprightly though it cost her a lot. Glenn might be very gifted in his own area but a man of action he wasn't. The last hour had been fairly ghastly as she made their way out of the rough country where the gelding's startled gallop had ended, and found a track through the mulga until they reached the open plain. Nothing had spooked the grey gelding outside its rider. Glenn simply didn't have sympathetic contact with the horse. In fact he had all the common faults, especially with his hands. A horse's mouth was soft and sensitive. Glenn's handling harsh and unencouraging. She'd even been giving Glenn riding instructions as they went, realising he'd never been taught, much less got to the point where he understood horses. Nearing the lagoon despite her objection, he had resorted to force instead of hands to change the gelding's direction, kicking the heel of his boots into its side.

Spook didn't like that. Francesca the horse lover didn't blame him. With Glenn's armchair seat and his bad leg position it was inevitable he would be thrown. To make matters worse he had complained about wearing the helmet from the outset saying he found it much too hot when he really wanted the breeze through his hair. Somehow she had persuaded him to keep it on until they reached the green shade of the red river gums. There he had whipped the helmet off with a kind of bravado, ignoring her pleas to keep it on.

The miracle was she didn't have to pick up the pieces after he'd been thrown. Some facial grazing where he'd hit the ground hard. A large lump on his head, all the symptoms of concussion, blurred vision, grogginess, some retching. She'd had the devil's own job getting him up on Gypsy, finding the right boulder to use as a mounting block, then using her own weight on the other side to counteract his. Finally it had all come together without strain to the horse. Gypsy, the ex-racehorse, had been very, very good while the inferior hack, Spook had taken the rare occasion to play up.

Her clothes felt terribly damp and heavy on her, her shirt soaked from Grant's ministrations, her hair slick with sweat in need of a shampoo. She turned back the cuffs of her shirt, rolled them up then she whipped off the wet blue bandanna. Her heart was still thudding in her chest after her long walk but she just had to grit her teeth and bear it until she could get under a lovely cold shower. Originally she had wanted to ride to the homestead for help but Glenn though disorientated had been adamant she didn't leave him. She might be getting used to vast distances and life in the wild but Glenn appeared to be genuinely intimidated by the bush. In his altered state he gave the impression he really believed if she left him he'd never be found again or dehydration would claim him.

With Glenn comfortable in the back of the vehicle, Francesca wasn't surprised when Grant shot her a rapier glance. "Why didn't you ride for help, Francesca? You made it so hard for yourself walking in." He noted with relief the high colour of exertion had faded a little from her face. In fact though she was uncharacteristically dishevelled she was looking remarkably calm and composed.

"My fault, I'm afraid," Glenn mumbled from the

back. "I wouldn't let her go. I don't mind telling you I find the bush extremely intimidating. It's great size! A man doesn't realise until he gets out here."

"You're sounding better, Glenn," Francesca said with satisfaction, turning her head with its dark curtain.

"What a fool you must think me."

Why not? Grant thought with strong disapproval.

"I have to say you did give me the impression you were a better rider," Francesca pointed out in a wry voice.

"But, Francesca, I thought I *was*. Just goes to show how much I'm out of my element here. I've been on horse riding trails. Come to think of it, it was mostly in a straight line and always with a party."

"And what became of your helmet?" Grant asked gratingly, trying to push his extreme irritation with Richards to the back of his mind. Not only had Richards expected Francesca to sit and hold his hand, he had expected her to lead him seated on the horse across the spinifex belt in the heat of the afternoon. He'd never have allowed a woman to undertake such a long, hot trek. This was rough open country not a jaunt through a tree-filled city park.

"It came off in the fall." Francesca aware of Grant's anger risked a fib. "The safety harness must have worked loose."

Grant sighed. "Tell me another one."

"Sorry. I'm ashamed of myself. Glenn was feeling the heat. He took it off briefly to cool down."

"And what spooked the gelding?" His eyes sparkled. "Make my day and give me a straight answer."

"It was the darnedest thing." Glenn found his voice from the back. "Such a tame horse yet it cut up a treat. I gave it a little bit of a kick in the sides to make it change direction and ended hanging on for dear life. It bolted into the scrub. I felt a branch might take off my head.''

''Especially without your helmet,'' Grant murmured dryly. ''They say all's well that ends well, but I don't suppose you'll be interested in going riding again.'' He mightn't have put it into words but *not with Francesca* came over loud and clear.

By the time they got back to the house everyone had been alerted to the situation, swarming out onto the verandah as Grant drew the four-wheel drive up at the base of the front steps. There were hugs and kisses all round. As the injured party, however self-inflicted, Glenn came in for the lion's share of attention but as Fee drew her daughter away her face revealed the strain of the past half hour.

''My darling!'' One good look was enough for Fee. Embarking on a horse ride with Glenn Richards had not paid off. She could see Francesca's pink shirt was drying quickly in the heat otherwise she looked as if she'd been dunked, her beautiful long hair pressed flat against her skull her face carrying an expression Fee remembered down the years. Francesca trying very hard indeed to be a good little girl and not cause any fuss.

''It's all right, Mamma,'' she was saying now, anxious to offer reassurance. ''Glenn took a tumble but no bones broken. A bump on the head and a modicum of hurt pride.''

''To hell with that!'' Fee laughed shortly, looking back over her shoulder to where Glenn was seated on a verandah chair with Ngaire and the crew in attendance. ''I don't know why you took him in the first place. All Glenn knows about horses is what he's learned in the movies.''

Grant pondered that. ''I've never seen the hero look for the little lady's help. He *rode. She* walked,'' he said, trying with some difficulty to lighten his own expression.

''For crying out loud.'' Fee shook her head in a flurry of ringlets. ''Look, I've got to have that out with him.'' She made to stalk off with a considerable air of majesty, only Francesca caught at her arm pleadingly.

''Please don't, Mamma. It wasn't as though Glenn was himself. He'd taken a tumble. I expect quite a lot of bumps and grazes will appear overnight. ''He was far too groggy to walk. The gelding simply bolted for home.''

Outback-bred Fee stared at her perplexed. ''But my darling child, why didn't you simply leave him there and ride for help?''

''Because he got quite agitated when I tried to leave.''

''A case of a city man behaving rather badly in the bush,'' Grant offered in a sardonic voice. ''Leave it, Fee. Glenn has a nice little story for after dessert. Right now Francesca should get under the shower and cool off. She had quite a trek in the heat.''

Fee knitted her brow very delicately to lessen the chance of wrinkles. ''There are things that *need* saying, Grant.''

''Don't be upset. Forget it, Mamma,'' Francesca begged, hearing another wave of laughter at Glenn's droll account of his tumble. ''It was all my fault. I knew almost from the outset Glenn had little experience. I should have abandoned the ride altogether.''

Grant agreed with a single, very definite nod. ''By

the same token a man of sense would have told you how little experience he'd had.'' He reached out and encircled Francesca's fragile wrist. ''I can find you a clean shirt of mine to put on. Sorry about the jeans. You can use either the bath or the shower in the master bedroom. I'll find you some clean towels. Richards can use the shower room off the storeroom at the rear of the house. There are clean towels there. I'll get Myra up to take a look at him.'' Grant referred to the wife of Opal's overseer, for years a qualified nursing sister. ''I don't think there's much the matter with him if he can sit around spinning yarns.''

''I'm going to make it my business to put them all straight later,'' Fee promised. ''I'll come with you, darling,'' she said to Francesca, feeling for once extraordinarily useless.

''No, Mamma, I'm fine!'' Francesca shook her head. ''I just want to cool down. Thank the Lord I was wearing a good sun block. Glenn will find himself with a bad case of sunburn, but I'm afraid he was too careless for comfort.'' She glanced at her watch, then back to her mother. ''You're not finished for the day are you?''

''We'll see, darling.'' Fee glanced around. ''We were doing some lighting set-ups when that wretched horse came in. But now that you're both home safely I expect Ngaire will want to finish the scene. Marc and I are ready. He's a pleasure to work with. So professional.''

''Can you pass on that message to Richards, Fee?'' Grant asked, as Fee started to move off. ''I'll put a call through for Myra to come up to the house and take a look at him. She'll find him a good spray for that sunburn. It doesn't matter how many times you warn people of conditions out here they don't seem to take much notice.''

All the rooms at Opal were of a generous size but the master bedroom was huge, dominated by a beautiful satinwood four-poster the floral pelmet of the elegantly decorated canopy matching the chintz of the ruffled bed valance that fell to the carpeted floor. All the furnishings were instantly familiar to Francesca's English eyes, the George III giltwood mirror, the mahogany chests, the scrolled day bed near the French doors, a pair of Regency chairs. All of it could have come from Ormond even to the side cabinet painted Chinoiserie panels and the English needlepoint carpet. Obviously the Camerons had gone ''Home'' to do their buying or had the furnishings and all that went with it shipped out.

''The bathroom is through here,'' Grant said, leading her through the dressing room to a very large bathroom, which had been modernised without losing its sense of the traditional.

''You wouldn't have anything like shampoo?'' Francesca asked hopefully, realising the master suite hadn't been used for some time.

''I wouldn't think here,'' Grant said doubtfully, looking towards a wall of handsome timber cabinets and matching wall cabinets complemented with brass fittings. ''But let's see, Rafe and I didn't want a live-in housekeeper like the old days. A couple of the station wives, headed by Myra, keep an eye on the place for us.'' As he was speaking, Grant walked to the line of cabinets trying the wall fixtures first.

''It's your lucky day,'' he announced, full of satisfaction. ''There's a whole range of stuff here. There could even be towels in the linen press. Myra must be anticipating the day Rafe and Ally get home.''

That was evident judging by the contents of the tall linen press that flanked the cabinets. Francesca saw two of the deep shelves held bed linen, others a selection of towels in three colours: white, pale yellow and apple-green.

''I don't know what we'd do without Myra and her crew,'' Grant said gratefully. ''They're downright motherly. I expect Ally will change things but she'll always have their support. So what's it to be.'' He turned to Francesca as she stood staring around her.'' Bath or shower? I can run the bath for you if you like? You might relish a soak.''

Francesca raised her eyes to his, finding them electric, sparkling with erotic fantasies that rivalled her own. ''I would but I think I'd better settle for a shower,'' she said as calmly as she could. ''Easier to shampoo my hair. Besides you'll want to get everyone home before sunset.''

''I find I'm more concerned about you,'' he said, still gazing at her with those gold-flecked eyes.

''The shower is fine, Grant.'' It shook her that she was wishing he could join her, her whole body, tired as it was, vibrating with awareness, her pulses speeded up.

''All right I'll leave you to it.'' Grant moved abruptly, prey to his own wishful thinking. ''Thanks to Myra everything you need is there down to new combs. Take your time. Some of those towels would be bath sheets. Rafe and I hate those little bits of things that would only go once around you. You'll be able to wrap yourself up.''

Without a backwards glance he moved off, closing

the bedroom door after him with a soft thud. Alone Francesca shook her head, trying to clear it. It was truly extraordinary the way he affected her. She had never in her life believed herself to be highly sexed. Now she realised it was only because she had never met the man who could deeply stir her. The master musician who could play her like golden sounds.

Quickly Francesca stripped off her clothes and wrapped herself in a huge yellow towel. Then she walked out to the enclosed verandah off the bedroom where she lay her clothes over a couple of chairs that still received hot rays of sunshine. That should dry them off! Back in the bathroom she flung off the towel stepping into the large shower enclosure that would easily accommodate two people with its frameless translucent walls and porcelain fittings. She turned on the taps, keeping the temperature initially lukewarm. The shower cascaded like a waterfall from a very effective wide nozzle producing a wonderfully, sensual, soothing effect. She held up her face to it letting it splash all over her skin. She really needed this. She had come over really rough terrain on foot and no one could understand the effects of the blazing outback sun, the dazzling quality of the *light* unless they had experienced it.

She reached for the shampoo and conditioner in one, lathering her hair twice then rinsing off. Only then did she start to feel the effects of her trek or maybe it was the alternate play of warm then cold water. A faint mist, like a veil, seemed to rise before her eyes and the legs that had pumped so strongly across the spinifex plains began to feel extraordinarily weak. She made a big effort to pull herself together, lurching forward to grasp the porcelain controls. The mist wasn't clearing.

It was turning into a fog. Surely she wasn't going to do something silly and faint? She hadn't done that since childhood when she had taken a nasty fall from her pony.

Moaning aloud, Francesca made another attempt to get out of the shower enclosure, only barely aware of a tall figure that loomed up outside the glass door.

In the west wing of the house, Grant had put a call through to the overseer's bungalow, glad Myra was around to pick it up. Quickly he explained what had happened to Richards asking her to come up to the homestead and check him over. That out of the way he thanked her for looking after the homestead so well, particularly for stocking the bathroom in the master suite. It had proved a godsend.

Afterwards, with Myra's bubbly, pleased laugh still in his ears, he hunted up a fresh shirt for Francesca to put on. He understood she would be the most fastidious of young women. Of course he was a good foot taller and maybe four stone heavier but the shirt would be clean and fresh and she could turn up the sleeves, tie up the tails, whatever women did with men's shirts. Difficult to fit her out with jeans, he thought with a wry grin, but her pink shirt had taken the worst of it.

A soft collared white cotton sports shirt with a blue stripe through it came to hand. He couldn't remember the last time he had worn it if he'd worn it at all. Either way it looked pretty new or it had been beautifully laundered and pressed. It would do nicely. He had a clear mental picture of how Francesca would look in it. *Only* it. An image that caused him to take a deep, whistling breath. He tapped on the master bedroom door and received no reply. Unless she'd been very slick about it, Francesca would still be washing her hair. The shirt over his arm he trod quickly to the foot of the canopied bed, intending to lay the shirt on the quilted damask coverlet before beating a retreat when he heard to his alarm the most piteous low moan.

The hair on the back of his neck literally stood up, his stomach muscles contracting sickeningly. For God's sake what was the matter? He shouldn't have left her. He should have sat right outside the door.

''Francesca?'' Grant strode to the entrance of the dressing room, noting the sliding door to the bathroom wasn't fully shut. ''Francesca?'' His voice had picked up considerably in volume and intensity. What the hell *was* this? She had to hear him.

No answer but he could hear the water running. He called her name one more time coming right to the sliding door. Another of those moans saw him flinging it back so hard it rocked in its tracks.

Her naked body was even more beautiful than his imaginings, the curves and the contours, the breasts like fruit. She was hunched over the taps, slender arms extended to turn them off, fingers tightening but ineffectually.

''All right, I'm here!'' Grant moved with speed, opening the shower enclosure, catching the spray, grasping her with one arm while the other made short work of turning off the taps. ''Francesca!''

She slumped against him causing a great surge of desire he couldn't possibly control, her lovely creamy flesh under his hands, breasts so pretty they left him breathless, the lick of red-gold at the base of her body. Desire he was immediately ashamed of. She was fainting right under his eyes.

A long arm with its whipcord muscles shot out and

grabbed a yellow towel. With the utmost dexterity he wound it around her as carefully as if she were a newborn babe, cradling her, before he lifted her completely into his arms, carrying her back to the bedroom where he sat her upright on the side of the bed.

"Francesca, sweetheart!" Quickly he pushed her head to her knees, one arm around her strongly and within moments he was rewarded by the little sounds she made as she came around fully.

"I nearly fainted." Her voice was weak and husky.

"Don't talk." A few moments more and he let her head come up slowly, her long hair hanging in dripping coils. "I'm furious with myself for leaving you," he admitted. "Thank God I came back. How do you feel?"

The first shock over, Francesca started to realise her situation. "Still a bit giddy."

"Hell!" he said quietly. Now that she was recovering he was back to being excruciatingly aware of her nakedness, trying to keep his eyes on her beautifully shaped legs, imagining his hands stroking their satin length. Petite, she was perfectly proportioned, the most graceful nude a master such as Renoir might have painted, though there was far less of her than his usual voluptuous young models. But the red-gold hair, the extraordinary luminescent flesh, the rose tips of her breasts gave off the same erotic charge. The yellow towel had slipped almost to her waist and he pulled it back up with great delicacy, his sense of touch never more pronounced, never more sensuous, her free-flowing hair fell forward over her shoulders and down in the curve of her back, so richly coloured it lit her skin.

"Myra is coming up to the house to take a look at

Richards,'' he told her gently. ''I think I'll ask her to also take a look at you.''

She was trembling slightly, a mixture of emotions spiralling through her, not able to handle any of them. ''I'm all right,'' she protested, shaking her head a little so spray fell on him.

''I'll get her to come all the same. It won't hurt.'' Grant stood up and walked through to the bathroom coming back with a fresh towel. ''Here, let me dry your hair.''

She held the towel tight against her breasts. ''I'm dripping all over the coverlet.''

''Who cares! You don't suppose Ally is going to leave any of this intact?'' he asked wryly. ''Sing out if I'm hurting you.''

Hurting her? Every sexual nerve end was screaming into life.

Yet she sat quietly, the yellow bath sheet wrapped tight around her while Grant drew her hair back over her shoulder and mopped up the long ends. Then he applied the towel with a more vigorous motion until it was ready to comb. He might have been doing this all his life so efficiently he went to work drawing the wide-toothed tortoiseshell comb down the full length of the strands until the job was done.

''Have you any idea how young you look?'' He forgot everything and put his mouth to her tender nape.

Her whole body began to tingle, responding irresistibly, causing her to lean in against his lean powerful frame.

''What are we doing here?'' he whispered into her ear, one hand coming down to cup the delicate mound of her breast. ''You should be getting dressed. I should be going for Myra.'' His head dipped further, his mouth against her ear, the top of his tongue flickering over its shell-like shape. ''Francesca!'' He began whispering things, endearments that turned her heart over, his breath warm and clean going deeper and deeper into her, like a tunnel that reached into her soul. ''You taste of fruit,'' he marvelled. ''A delicious white peach.''

She thought she would faint again with the pleasure of it. The ravishment.

''God, what's the matter with me?'' he whispered hoarsely something about the attitude of her body concerned him. He lifted his mouth away from her with a remarkable effort. ''I'm sorry, you need care not hungry kisses.'' His voice was so low and seductive before it turned brisk and businesslike. ''If you hold the towel around you I'll help you get into my shirt. That's what I came for. Here, Francesca.'' He reached for his white shirt, slid it on one slender arm, fixed it around her back, then pushed her arm into the other sleeve.

She didn't feel able to help him and he seized her hand and kissed it. Then he went down on his haunches in front of her, beginning to do up the buttons, hazel eyes smouldering as his hands skimmed her breasts, slid along the smoothness of the fine cotton, lingered in her lap, the warmth of her, the place where he wanted to be.

''Well that's done!'' Her weakened physical condition was the only thing that saved him. He wanted her so much he could feel his own head swimming. Only then did she make eye contact.

''I love you, Grant,'' she said, more sweetly he thought than any other woman would have said it before.

''Will you say that when you're ready to say your goodbyes to me?'' he asked her tenderly, his whole soul crying out for her. "I bet you never even told your father about me."

It was true. It never seemed to be the right time when she rang home. Her letters contained a lot of news: people, places, families, her own family the Kinrosses, and their neighbours the Camerons. But unless her father was excellent at reading between the lines he would have little idea she had fallen madly in love with Grant Cameron. Why didn't she tell him? Was she a coward? She only knew her father had always been there for her when her mother wasn't. She dreaded the thought of hurting him, a beloved parent, shattering his dreams.

"Somebody ought to tell him, Francesca," Grant warned. "Tell him straight, you owe him that. If you can't. *I* can. Then you'll really know what to expect."

Her delicate fingers touched his face, tracing the cleft in his chin. "How would you tell him?" Was he offering a magical solution?

He made a little sardonic grimace. "What do you think, flower face, I'd hop on a plane."

"Just like that?" His decision seemed to galvanise her.

"Why not?" Your father doesn't bother me. He bothers *you.* He even bothers Fee who doesn't give a damn about anyone. I suppose that's what comes of being a belted earl." Grant stood up determinedly. "Now I'm going to get Myra to take a look at you. Why don't you lie down while I'm gone."

"I'll take the daybed near the door." Francesca made an attempt to stand up, Grant assisting her until she was upright. Her feet were aching, she realised without surprise. But what about her neck and her back? How had she hurt herself? The answer was obvious, struggling with Glenn, first to get him off the ground then mounted on Gypsy. Strangely she hadn't felt much of anything at the time. She was going to have to suffer for it now. But she had no intention of complaining. It wasn't her way and she had brought a lot of it on herself. She should have left Glenn to go for help. Even as she thought it she knew she would do the same thing all over again. Ally always told her she was a softie.

She looked utterly adorable in his shirt. It was miles too big for her, but for all that or maybe because of it she looked as innocent as a child. Yet incredibly sexy. The flame-coloured mane he had combed back from her face and over her shoulders was drying in the late-afternoon sun. It radiated light, the perfect foil for the creaminess of her skin. She touched every part of him, the sight of her an actual hand squeezing his heart.

He took her chin between his fingers, tilting her face to him, staring into those starry eyes with a very serious expression. A total acceptance of his role. "I want you more than I've wanted anything in my whole life," he told her, his voice harsh with emotion, but reverent. "I've dreamed about you. Night after night after night. I want you in my bed. I want to take your precious gift of virginity. And it is a gift, Francesca. I want to be the only man in your life. *Ever.*"

The whole room seemed to be filled with the fabulous colours of the sunset. Tears came from a deep place inside of her. "And I'm yours to keep. To have and to hold."

Triumph blazed in his eyes. His arms closed around her so strongly they almost lifted her from the floor. He found her upturned mouth, a smile of utter bliss at its corners, her tongue feverish to mate with his. The kiss went on forever. ''Do you love me?'' she whispered frantically, twisting away from him for a few seconds. ''Say it. Say it.''

''*Say* it? I'll show you.'' His whole body was reverberating with passion. There was no alternative left in the world for them but marriage. And God how he wanted it. He would do anything for her. Fly to England. Seek out her father. Speak to him. Ask for his approval. He owed him that courtesy. With Francesca by his side he could build something of great value. She needn't jettison her old life altogether. He would always allow her to visit her father, her homeland, her friends. Hell he'd find time to go with her. She was the only woman who would make his life right and he was drunk on her love.

Fee calling in to see how her daughter was, found her and Grant locked in a kiss so passionate she felt no one had the right to intrude on such intimacy. But disturb them she must, discovering in herself a great rush of regrets. Although she had known Francesca and Grant were in love she'd had no real inkling of the depth of their feelings.

What she was witnessing was something irrevocable. Something that would work. A cataclysm of desire the likes of which she had never thought her lovely young daughter capable. Francesca was so young, so inexperienced, sheltered all her life. Now it seemed Grant Cameron had taught her all about her own sensuality. This wasn't the holiday affair she had feared. Francesca's loyalty lay with Grant Cameron when Fee genuinely believed it lay elsewhere.

While Fee stood rigid, unable to move, Grant and Francesca finally became aware of her presence. They didn't spring apart. They didn't act in the least guilty.

They broke apart slowly. Francesca shook her long hair back from her face and Grant gave his white mocking smile.

"Fee, you've made an art form of exits and entrances."

If she'd been thirty years younger Fee would have blushed. "Sorry, I didn't mean to intrude but I thought at least Francesca you'd be lying down. And what on earth have you got on?" She peered at her daughter's petite figure, astonishment on her face.

"Goodness, Mamma, can't you see?" Francesca came forward for inspection, the most beautiful smile blooming on her face. "It's a man's shirt. Grant's."

"And it looks very fetching," Grant remarked, reaching for Francesca's hand, a unity of two. "Actually, Fee, we made a mistake leaving Francesca. She all but fainted under the shower."

Fee who couldn't even remember all her lovers' names looked and sounded aghast. "And you rescued her?"

"Thank God I was on the spot," Grant answered very seriously. "I returned with the shirt and heard Francesca's moans."

If it hadn't been her own daughter, Fee would have come out with something possibly caustic, instead she rushed to Francesca's side. "Is this true, darling? You're such a delicate creature."

"Even Ally might have fainted after a trek like that," Grant offered dryly.

"I don't think so, dear," Fee said. "Ally wouldn't have been fool enough to take pity on the man."

"Lucky Ally to get your approval, Mamma," Francesca said with a gentle touch of censure.

"Oh, you know what I mean!" Fee cried. "Don't

be miffed at me, darling. You're such a tender-hearted little thing.''

A wry smile spread across Grant's face. ''And there is the shining fact, she makes no fuss. None of us have heard a word of complaint from her. Francesca may be tender-hearted and I love her for it, but she knows how to handle herself. Tell you what. You two have a talk. I'll go fetch Myra. Francesca is looking a vision at the moment but we can't overlook the fact she did go into a faint.''

''For a girl who nearly passed out you're looking the vision Grant said,'' Fee commented, looking into her daughter's eyes. ''You've come to an important decision, haven't you?''

''I knew right from the beginning,'' Francesca answered simply. ''Grant had certain fears for me. As you did, Mamma, and probably still have. But ours won't be a marriage between two very different people. A marriage between two cultures, two different lands. Grant and I are soul mates. We agree on mostly everything. All the important things anyway. Now he's finally realised I will be able to adapt to his world. Something I've known for years. I've loved my mother's country since I was ten. It speaks to me, too.''

Fee thought for a long time. ''I should have seen that, darling,'' she said, ''but as usual I was too self-engrossed.''

''I know in my heart, Mamma, this is right. Grant and I will aid each other. He trusts me. He respects me. He knows I can help him. That's the way of a real marriage.''

Fee touched her daughter's cheek with love and uncharacteristic humility. ''Do you realise how lucky you are, darling? It's taken me half a lifetime to find my other half. David loves me just the way I am. Your father desperately wanted me to change. Still he mattered a great deal to me at one time.''

''He loved you, Mamma,'' Francesca pointed out gently, ever loyal to her father.

''They all did, darling,'' Fee argued, juggling all her memories, ''if I say so myself I was very hotly desired.''

''So am I.'' Francesca gave her enchanting smile, moving over to the daybed near the French doors and sinking back on it. ''I want Father to give me away. I want to go forward to my new life with my hand on my father's arm.''

''Of course, darling,'' Fee agreed. ''But you must tell him about Grant without delay. Once he sees how happy you are I'm sure there will be no anger, no pressure.'' Fee sincerely hoped not, finding solace in the knowledge the earl doted on his daughter. Besides, stacked up against Jimmy Waddington, Grant would emerge the overwhelming winner.

''As it happens, Grant wants to fly home to see Father,'' Francesca was saying, sounding as though her own resolve had firmed considerably. ''He wants to speak to Father himself. I'm not afraid they won't get on. In many ways Father and I are very much alike.''

''You do show your lineage,'' Fee agreed. ''Little bits of us both you carry around with you.''

''And I'm going with him,'' Francesca said. ''There are many things I want to explain to Father. Many things to thank him for. As for Father and Grant! I think they'll find plenty to talk about,'' Francesca said prophetically. ''There's nothing to stop him coming to see us from time to time.''

"My darling, count on it," Fee said. "Especially when you have your first baby."

Both women laughed, a wonderful companionable sound.

When had her daughter turned from a charming child into a woman ready to take on the biggest challenge in life, Fee thought. Quite obviously when I wasn't looking.

CHAPTER SEVEN

TEN days later with the outback location shots completed and Francesca's small part in the film over, Ngaire, Glenn and the crew, returned to Sydney taking Fee and David with them. Fee still had some scenes, shot in and around Sydney, to go and she needed to prepare for the big party she was throwing to launch her biography. That was set for the end of the month.

"Thank you for saving my life, Francesca," Glenn exaggerated suavely on departure, taking her hand and pressing a lingering warm kiss on it. "I can't wait to see you again at Fee's party. You were absolutely perfect as Lucinda. The best we could have hoped for."

Ngaire agreed with a hug and a kiss. "Let's face it, darling, you could have a career if you wanted it."

Not when I have a better one in mind, Francesca thought, keeping her own big news for the time quiet.

Grant watching Richards turn on the charm had the satisfaction of knowing by the next time Richards saw Francesca she would be very much engaged. He had the ring in his pocket. It had only arrived the day before. And it was breathtaking! Fit for a princess. He'd faxed the family jeweller over a week ago, listing his requirements. 18ct white gold set with a finest quality diamond. Maybe 1.5 or 1.6cts—he left it to them—thinking a 2ct central stone would be too big for Francesca's small, elegant hand. The central diamond was to be flanked by something different. Rare pink diamonds? Perhaps pear-shaped? He drew a sketch of what he wanted, the cost coming in as a secondary consideration. His gift to her had to be just right. The ring was to be exquisite. As flowerlike as Francesca herself.

The jeweller lost no time at all sending a return fax with two detailed sketches featuring a classic central stone, one oval, one round, flanked by the finest quality Argyle pink diamonds. In the second sketch the pink diamonds were pave set. He knew immediately which one he wanted. It all but fitted his own design except for the oval-shaped central stone, which looked better than his own idea of a round cut, the flanking pink diamonds set like leaves. He felt charged to the hilt, desperate to slide it on her finger.

"Rebecca has asked me to stay to lunch," he told her as they watched the charter flight lift into the peacock-blue sky. "After that I have to get back to Opal to supervise a maintenance check." He lowered his head, his eyes beneath the wide brim of his akubra, glittering like gemstones. "What if we take a quick run out to Myora? I want to show you something."

She looked at him with pleasure. "That will be lovely! I've been meaning and meaning to show you my sketchbooks but with all the rush of the filming there hasn't been much time. Fee kept them hard at it. She wanted it all over before the book launch. And you haven't really answered the question. Are you coming?"

"I insist on coming," he said dryly. "What with Richards still acting loverlike. Who said he could press kisses into your hand?"

"Didn't mean a thing," she teased.

"I hope so, I'm amazed by his cheek."

* * *

Ten minutes out on their cross-country drive they stopped to watch a pair of roaming emus, one of the world's largest birds, conducting a comic mating dance. The male was acting up so crazily, kicking up its long legs, crossing them, lifting itself off the ground, Francesca couldn't stop laughing. The female on the other hand was displaying a considerable hauteur that could have passed as indifference, stalking about the male or preening her mass of feathers, the assumed indifference as it turned out far from the case.

"Just giving him the run-around." Grant grinned. "Emus are remarkable creatures and not only for their speed. They can find a living in the most arid parts of the run but they seek shelter in thick scrub when they're nesting. The eggs are huge as you know. They require more than two months incubation."

"That's a long time for poor Mum."

"Poor dad don't you mean? The male undertakes that task."

"Well, good for him. Mother kangaroo at least carries her little ones in her pouch. They're just adorable, the joeys. It's absolutely fascinating watching a herd of kangaroos bounding across open country on their long hind legs yet when they walk slowly they use their forefeet and their tail to steady them rather like a tripod, as the hind legs come forward."

"You've made quite a study of them." He didn't tell her he had seen her wonderful sketchbooks. Not yet. She had the eye of the artist. The capacity for acute observation.

When they arrived at the site for his proposed homestead, they could see in the distance a large herd of cattle feeding on the purple flowering succulent, the parakeelya, peculiar to the sandhills. The stock could live on this or other succulents for months without water.

"Rafe and Ally will be home soon," Grant said quietly, still sitting behind the wheel of the Jeep.

"They're disappointed they're going to miss Mamma's party," Francesca said, "but she put the launch off long enough to fit in with filming."

"*And* her marriage," Grant drawled.

"She and David don't want to tie the knot without Ally present." Francesca gave him a quick smile. "Mamma and Ally are very close."

"Does it bother you?" he asked gently, relieved when she shook her head.

"Not really, I love them both. Mamma understands Ally better than she does me. I'll have to get married to convince her I've grown up."

"As long as you don't make it *three* times." Grant had a wry joke at Fee's expense. "Let's get out." He moved swiftly around the vehicle to help her, taking her hand, loving the way she twined her fingers through his. In front of them Myora glowed a fiery red under the hot sun, the breeze that seemed to have sprung up out of nowhere causing a strange sighing sound to emanate from its hollowed out cavities and caves.

"Voice of the spirits," Grant said, looking down at her. "Are you scared?"

"Why wouldn't there be spirits," she said. "This is an old old land, full of Dreamtime significance."

It was time to tell her. Here in this place so close to their hearts.

"I saw your sketchbooks."

She lifted her head, blue eyes surprised. "Why didn't you tell me?"

"I think I was too moved by them," he answered

simply. ''I didn't want anyone else to look at them. Or your sketches of *our* homestead. That's something uniquely ours.''

''You liked them?'' She stared back at him steadily.

''I loved them, Francesca,'' he said, his dark voice deep. ''As I love you. I can't possibly draw like you but you read my mind. Your sketchbooks finally convinced me you truly love this country. The flowers and the animals you've drawn so accurately. Your idea of an oasis in isolation proves how closely our minds work.''

She touched his golden face tenderly, in absolute love. ''It means everything to me, Grant, you feel like that.''

''I do.'' His strong arms encircled her. ''Forgive me for ever doubting you couldn't adapt to a strange land. It isn't strange at all. It's part of the richness of your inheritance. And now I have something for you.'' He cast his eyes around, settling on a large boulder, mainly rust-red in colouring but with thick yellow ochre veins. ''Come sit over here.''

''What is this all about?'' She let him lead her, feeling unbelievably precious to him. It was wonderful. Intoxicating. As necessary to her as the air she breathed.

''You'll see,'' he promised.

When she was seated he went down theatrically on one knee before her, flashing her his brilliant smile. ''Lady Francesca de Lyle I beg you to marry me. I adore every hair of your Titian head. I'm even prepared to beard your father, the earl, in his den. I want his consent for us to marry. I want his blessing. I want everything that's going to make you happy. We can be married in England if that's what you want. I know you'll want your father to give you away. I'm certain it would please him. I'm equally sure he'll want it that way. I'll risk the grey skies and the cold of your winter. I'll risk everything if only you'll marry me. And just so you won't keep me on my knees too much longer I'd be honoured if, in the meantime, you'd wear my ring." He took a small navy case from his pocket, opened it and withdrew the ring. "Your hand, my lady." His smile deepened as he registered the joyous anticipation on her lovely face.

"Take it," she breathed, feeling her hand nerveless.

He did so, slipping the diamond engagement ring down over the satiny skin of her finger. "Not bad! A perfect fit. I love you, Francesca. I'll love you always."

"Oh, Grant!" she whispered, extending her hand to the sun, watching all the brilliant flashing lights. *Pink* diamonds! So beautiful.

"You're not going to cry, dear love?" Grant asked very tenderly, feeling extraordinarily emotional himself.

"Of course I'm going to cry. It's obligatory on these occasions. Tears of joy!" She flung herself forward, against his chest, his arms closing around her before he lost his balance. They both rolled on the pure clean sand that was covered in parts by a broad-leafed vine.

Now she was gurgling with laughter.

"Stay still. I want to kiss you." He arched over her.

"I haven't told you if I'm going to marry you yet."

"Tell me *after.*" He moved with big cat grace, bringing his hands in tightly to hold her body captive, riveted by its *female* suppleness. Then he lowered his head.

"Ah, Grant...."

The laughter died. There was such burning desire in

his voice and in his eyes she felt an answering flame lick her veins.

He kissed her into breathless submission, pressing the length of his body against hers. "Anyway I'm not going to take no for an answer." His fingers tripped the pearly buttons of her shirt and slipped inside, shaping and caressing her naked breast. He was utterly sure of her, the dominant male, but she loved it. Her arms slid around his neck, her fingers digging into the tawny hair that curved thickly into his nape. He was a beautiful man. Beautiful!

"I love you."

"I thought you did," he said passionately.

"I can't wait to marry you."

"I can't wait to marry *you,*" he groaned, falling back on the sand beside her. "We have to see your father. We have to make him delighted with our news. A wedding has to be arranged. How the hell am I going to be able to manage all that without ravishing you?"

"But I *want* you to." Her voice choked on emotion. She ached for him to take her.

"And I going to." He was breathing harshly, his handsome, high cheek-boned face taut and hungry but with a strength that confounded her. "But not like this, my love. The first time we're together is going to be very, very, precious. The first time I lower myself into your body. The time and place will be right. No hurry."

"You're too sure of yourself, Grant Cameron."

He turned and kissed her again, brushing back the hair that fell about her face in wild disarray. "I have some news for you that you will like," he told her as they eventually lay back entwined. A small grin crooked the corners of his shapely mouth. "I'm having that architect I saw come out here to walk over the site. It's all organised. We'll show him your sketches. Let him work with them. I'll order it so we can have a three-month honeymoon. Anywhere in the world you want to go. Fiji, Patagonia, Antarctica, the Swiss Alps. By the time we get back, our dream home will be built.''

EPILOGUE

THE Cameron-de Lyle wedding took place in England in June of the following year. The ceremony was held in the centuries-old village church of St. Thomas, adjoining the bride's father, the earl of Moray's splendid country estate in the rolling hills of Hampshire; the reception for two hundred people held in giant white marquees erected in the grounds of Ormond Hall the de Lyle ancestral seat, which at that time of the year were breathtakingly beautiful, a landscape gardener's dream and inspiration. The wedding said to be one of the most beautiful of the decade was covered by *Tatler, Harpers & Queen* and the *Australian Woman's Weekly,* so there were plenty of photographs for those who followed the social pages and weren't fortunate enough to get an invitation.

A marvellous shot of bride and groom looking gloriously happy appeared on the cover of the Australian magazine. Although the bride Lady Francesca de Lyle, dubbed by the Australian press, "The English Bride," was indeed English on her illustrious father's side, her mother was the internationally known Australian born actress Fiona Kinross who had had a brilliant career on the London stage, spanning some thirty years. Fiona Kinross, Mrs. David Westbury, was a member of the prominent landed Kinross family, daughter of the late Sir Andrew Kinross, a legendary Australian cattle king, whose forebears had pioneered the industry in colonial days.

There were colour photographs of the bride on her own, looking exquisitely romantic in delustred duchess satin, the sweetheart neckline and bodice decorated with beautiful corded lace that ran down the full skirt. On her head she wore a flaring waist-length tulle veil held in place by a delicately beautiful family tiara of diamonds and pearls. Pearls with a diamond pendant at her throat, a small posy of beautiful white roses in her hands.

There were photographs of the bride with her two small flower girls, an enchanting shot; the bride with her attendants, the stunning Alison Cameron, nee Kinross, matron of honour, first cousin to the bride on the mother's side, Lady Georgina Lamb and Miss Serena Strickland, the bride's friends from childhood, all in harmonious shades of pink silk. There were photographs of the groom with his attendants, the best man, elder brother, Rafe, master of the Australian historic cattle station, Opal Downs, their close friend and recent brother-in-law by virtue of Rafe's marriage to the stunning matron of honour, and *her* brother, Broderick, master of the equally famous Kimbara Station. Mr. Kinross's beautiful wife, Rebecca, was clearly from the photographs some months pregnant but radiant in a simple, elegant blue dress with a gorgeous blue hat.

There was a lovely photograph of the bride with her father, the earl of Moray, both beaming with delight. A photograph of Mr. and Mrs. David Westbury, Mrs. Westbury wearing the most fabulous emerald hat and silk two-piece suit, shoes and handbag precisely matched. No photographs of the bride's father and mother together. But one of the earl with his present countess, Holly. Some photographs of people the

English side of the family didn't know at all. Among them Miss Lainie Rhodes from Victoria Springs, a cascade of blonde hair and an irresistible big smile wore an elegant white-and-navy suit with a rather wonderful confection in navy with a huge navy-and-white bow on her head. ''It's wonderful! The best fun!'' Miss Rhodes went on record as saying. Seated beside her, a rakish grin on his mouth, a strikingly handsome young man who bore a decided resemblance to the tawny haired groom and his ''golden'' brother. Family, of course—Mr. Rory Cameron, world traveller.

The honeymoon, which included a flight over Antarctica said to be ''truly awesome'' in the true sense of the word, would take the happy couple to places as far away as Scandinavia and Canada where the groom wanted to look up members of the Cameron clan who had migrated there in the early days.

It was the perfect day for a perfect wedding, all three magazines reported. Sky-blue and golden the sun pushing its way through a few early-morning clouds to shine down on the happy couple. Everyone who was there and those who devoured the magazine photographs afterwards, agreed it was plainly a love match.

Wasn't that just wonderful!

* * * *

RESCUING DR RYAN

by

Caroline Anderson

CHAPTER ONE

'AH, NO!'

Will rammed his hands through his hair and stared disbelievingly at the wide, wet stain on the mattress. Cocking his head a little, he looked up at the ceiling, and winced. Yup, there was a corresponding stain, right over the middle of the bed. The new bed.

Great. There must be a missing tile on the roof, just over the bedroom, and, of course, as luck would have it, it had been the wettest March on record.

He sniffed experimentally, and sighed. Mildew. Lovely. Probably soaked right through the bed and rotted the carpet underneath. He said something his grandmother wouldn't have understood, and stomped out, slamming the door behind him.

Before anyone could use the little cottage, it would need a new bed—another one—and a new carpet—and Lucie Compton, their new GP registrar, was due in two hours. He crossed the yard, turned and squinted up into the sun. Yes, there it was—or wasn't. A neat hole in the middle of the roof slope. Still, it could have been worse. The tile was sitting in the gutter and hadn't smashed on the ground—although if it had smashed at least he would have stood a chance of noticing it sooner.

He gave a hefty sigh and fetched the ladder and some tools from the barn. Within moments he'd put the tile back and secured it, and checked the others around it. All looked fine.

Good. He put the tools away and came back for the ladder, and as he carried it round the end of the little converted barn he noticed Minnie, the tiny little Siamese kitten, running across the roof and crying.

'Oh, Minnie, how did you get up there?' he asked, exasperated.

'Mreouw—rrr,' she replied.

'Did you? Well, that'll teach me to leave the ladder there for you, won't it?'

'Mreow.'

'OK, I'm coming,' he said. He glanced at his watch. One hour seventeen minutes and counting. Hell.

He stuck the ladder up against the side of the barn, checked that it was steady and gave the sloping ground a dubious look. Oh, dammit. He didn't have time to tie it. He rattled it again, just to make sure it was secure, and climbed carefully to the top.

'Come on, Minnie. Come here.'

The kitten came almost within reach, sat down and cried piteously.

'Well, come here, then!' he coaxed with the last shred of his patience. He held out his fingers and she brushed against them. If he could just reach out…

The ladder jolted, lurching slightly to the side, and he grabbed the rungs and hung on, freezing for a moment.

Hmm. Now what? Minnie came to the top, within reach, and rubbed herself against the top rung. 'Damn cat,' he said with affection, and reached for her cautiously.

There was another lurch, and he felt the ladder sliding out from under him. He grabbed the top rung and prayed, but God was either elsewhere or had decided it was time Will was taught a lesson.

It was, he thought with strange detachment, almost like watching something in slow motion. The ladder skidded, dropped below the guttering and then slid down the side of the barn, gathering speed as it neared the ground.

Oh, hell, he thought. I really don't need this.

Then he hit the deck.

Everything hurt. His head hurt, his legs hurt, his ribs felt crushed, but it was his arms that were really, really giving him stick.

He rested his forehead on the rung in front of him and instantly regretted it. He shifted, finding a bit that wasn't bruised, and lay still for a moment, waiting for his chest to reinflate and his heart to slow down.

He was also waiting for the pain to recede, but he was a realist. Five minutes later his breathing and heart rate were back to normal, and he decided that two out of three weren't bad. Given a choice, he would have gone for a different two, of course.

The kitten rubbed herself against his head, and he cracked open an eye and glared at her balefully.

'I am going to kill you,' he said slowly and clearly. 'Just as soon as I work out how to get out of here.'

Unabashed, she sat down just inches away and washed herself.

Will ignored her. He had other problems more immediate than a bit of cathartic blood-letting. He shifted experimentally, and gasped. OK. Not a good idea to press down on his right arm. What about the left?

Nope.

Knees? Better. And shoulders were OK. Now, if he could just roll over…

He bit back a string of choice epithets, and rolled onto his back, falling with a sickening jolt to the ground beside the ladder.

Phase one completed. Now all he had to do was get to his feet, go inside and call for help.

Hah!

He lifted his head a fraction, and stifled a groan. Damn. Headache. He persisted, peering at his arms which lay awkwardly across his chest.

No doubt about the right one, he thought in disgust. He'd be lucky to get away without pinning and plating. And the left?

His wrist was swelling before his eyes, and if it got much bigger his watch was going to cut off the circulation to his hand. Wonderful. He closed his eyes with a sigh and laid his head back down carefully on the ground. He'd just have to wait for Lucie Compton to arrive and rescue him.

There was a lump of something hard sticking into his spine, but it was beyond him to shift himself away from it. It was just one more small pain amongst many. If he were a philosopher, he'd welcome the pain as proof that he was alive. However, he wasn't, and at that particular moment he wouldn't have minded being dead.

And then, just as if survival itself wasn't a big enough bundle of laughs, he felt the first heavy splash of rain hit his face.…

Lucie was late. Lucie was usually late, but she really, really hadn't needed Fergus giving her the third degree on the way out.

He *knew* she had to do this, *knew* that spending time in a general practice was part of her GP training, *knew* that it was only temporary.

Well, not any more. Not the separation, at any rate, although her sojourn into the countryside would be as brief as she could get away with. Six months tops. That, on top of the six months she'd already spent in her inner-city practice, would see her qualified to practise as a GP, and then she'd be back in the city like a rat out of a trap.

Of course, she didn't *have* to spend the time in the country. She could quite easily have found another London practice but, to be honest, Fergus was one of the reasons she'd wanted to get away, at least just for a while, to put some distance between them and see if what they had was a forever thing or just a temporary habit that needed breaking.

Well, she'd broken it, in words of one syllable.

YOU DO NOT OWN ME. GO AWAY. LEAVE ME ALONE.

OK, mostly one syllable. He'd understood, anyway. He'd flounced off, slamming the door of his car and roaring off into the sunset—except it had been some time after sunrise and he hadn't roared anywhere very much in the traffic off the Fulham Road.

She pulled over to the side of the road and checked her map. It was raining, of course, blurring everything and making it harder to read the signs.

'"Pass the turning to High Corner and take the next track on the right. Follow to the end. It's a bit rough in places." Hmm.' She peered at the sandy track ahead. Could that be it? It didn't seem to have a sign, and looked like nothing more than a farm track, but the address was Ferryview Farm, so it was possible.

With a resigned shrug, she turned onto the track and followed it. Some of it was sandy, some stony, some just downright boggy. It *was* a bit rough in places, she thought, and then lurched into a pothole.

Make that very rough, she corrected herself, and picked her way carefully through the next few puddles. Of course, without the rain—

There was a lurch, a nasty crunching grinding noise and her car came to rest on the centre of the track, its wheels dangling in matched potholes.

She put it in reverse and tried to drive out, but it was stuck fast, teetering on a high point. Damn.

Damn, damn, damn.

She got out, straight into a puddle that went over her ankle, and slammed her car door with a wail of frustration. Just let Dr Ryan wait until she caught up with him!

Pulling her coat close around her shoulders and hitching the collar up against the driving rain, she headed up the track. It couldn't be far, surely?

Not that it mattered if it was miles. She had no choice, not until she could get a breakdown truck to come and drag her car off the track.

Always assuming, of course, that she hadn't shattered the sump!

'Look on the bright side, Lucie,' she told herself, scraping a muddy hand through her rapidly frizzling hair. 'It could be snowing.'

Ten seconds later a little flurry of sleet plastered itself against her face. 'I didn't say that!' she wailed, and hitched the collar higher. The moment she caught up with Dr William 'it's a bit rough in places' Ryan, she was going to kill him!

She was late. Typical bloody woman, she was late, just when he needed her. He thought again of struggling to his feet and trying to get inside, but after the effort of sitting up and shuffling back into the lee of the barn, he thought it would probably kill him. Besides, the house keys were in his pocket, and he knew getting them out was beyond him.

So he sat, and he waited, and he fumed.

Still, he had Minnie for company—Minnie, the cause of all his grief. He might have known the damn cat was perfectly capable of getting herself down off the roof. If he'd thought about it at all, which, of course, he hadn't, he would have realised she could jump down on the top of the oil storage tank at the back and thence down to the ground. It was probably the way she'd got up in the first place.

He dropped his head back against the side of the barn and closed his eyes. The sun was out now—typical of April, sleet and driving rain one minute, glorious sunshine the next—and where he was sitting in the shelter of the barn, he was facing directly into it.

Good. It might warm him up, stop him shivering uncontrollably. He was in shock, of course, because of the fracture. Fractures? His right arm was certainly distorted, and his left was still swelling around the wrist. His watch was painfully tight, the flesh bulging each side of the broad metal strap. He tried to undo it with his teeth, but it was too firm and, besides, it hurt too much to prod about with it unnecessarily.

Please, God, don't let me have two broken arms,

he thought in despair. His mind ran through a list of things he couldn't do with two broken arms—and there were a lot in there that were very personal!

God again, teaching him compassion for his patients? Giving him a closer understanding of their needs and suffering?

Or just fate playing a nasty practical joke?

Where was Lucie Compton? Richard had waxed so lyrical about her after he'd interviewed her that Will had had great hopes—but if her medical skills were as good as her timekeeping, it didn't bode well for her patients. And he, he realised, was going to be her first one.

Hell.

Bruno was barking in the house, shut inside because Will had just been on his way out when he'd checked the cottage and found the leak. However, the dog had been quiet until now apart from the odd bark, and now he was letting loose with a volley. Someone coming?

Odd. Surely not Lucie? Will couldn't hear a car, but there was something. Footsteps. Fast, cross little footsteps.

A woman came into view, small, bedraggled and evidently as mad as a wet hen. She marched up to him, fixed him with a glare and said crisply, 'A bit rough in places?'

What? He opened his mouth to speak, but she rattled on, clearly divesting herself of some pent-up rage.

'I could have you up under the Trades Descriptions Act!' she stormed. 'A bit rough! Do you know I've grounded my car and probably trashed it on your damn drive?'

Oh, hell. It *was* Lucie Compton, finally. And now he'd get to test her medical skills, if he could just get a word in—

'I expect the sump's broken, knowing my luck,' she ranted on, 'and I'll have to get the engine replaced! And I'm wringing wet and frozen, and my mobile phone doesn't work out here in this God-forsaken bit of wilderness, and all you can do is sit there and smirk!'

She lifted her foot, and for a sickening moment he thought she was going to kick him, but she stamped it crossly and spun on her heel, walking away and then wheeling round and striding back.

'Well, for goodness' sake, aren't you going to say anything? Apologise or something? I mean, the very least you could do is get off your idle backside and let me in! I'm soaked to the skin, I'm freezing to death and you don't give a damn.'

God, she was beautiful, with her hair a wild tangle of damp curls and steam coming out of her ears! Her eyes were spitting green sparks, and her mouth when she finally paused for breath was soft and lush and too wide for conventional beauty, but he could imagine it trailing over his poor wounded body and kissing it better. He stifled a groan and met her furious eyes.

'You're late. Help me up,' he said gruffly, and she stopped in her tracks and her wide, soft, pretty mouth fell open in surprise.

'Excuse me?'

'The ladder slipped. I think my arms are broken. Could you, please, help me up?'

Her jaw flapped for a moment, and her eyes widened, tracking over him and filling with horror.

'Well, why on earth didn't you *say* so, instead of just sitting there?'

'I would have done, but you made it well nigh impossible to get a word in edgeways,' he said drily. To his satisfaction she coloured, the anger going out of her like air out of a punctured balloon.

'Sorry,' she conceded gruffly. 'Um...how do you suggest we do this? What have you broken?'

'Right radius and ulna, and maybe something in my left wrist. Oh, and I'm a bit concussed and my legs hurt like hell, but they move, at least. Otherwise I'm just peachy.'

'Right. Um.'

She crouched down and bent over him, the damp tendrils of her wildly curling hair teasing his face. 'May I see?'

He lowered his legs, wincing as he did so, and revealed his forearms. 'Don't touch anything,' he warned through gritted teeth, and she nodded. Thank God she only looked, and didn't feel the need to prod him.

'OK. You need a couple of slings before I try and move you. Have you got any in the house?'

'Yes, but until I get up you can't get in. The keys are in my pocket.'

'Oh.' She glanced down at his jeans, snug around his hips, and she coloured slightly. 'Um—are you sure? Which pocket?'

'The right.'

'You could shift onto your left hip and I could see if I could wriggle my hand in...'

He shifted, swallowing hard and hoping for a good hefty jolt of pain to take his mind off those slender little fingers. They wormed and wriggled their way in, while she blushed and apologised. She gave a little grunt of effort and her breath puffed soft and minty-fresh over his face. He closed his eyes and groaned, and wondered how long it would be before he embarrassed himself with her prodding and probing about so damn close—

'Got them!' she said victoriously, brandishing them in front of his nose.

He sighed with relief. 'Mind the dog. He's all right, but he'll come and jump all over me, and I don't need it just now.'

'I'll keep him in,' she promised. 'Where are the slings?'

'Kitchen. Cupboard on the left of the sink. The dog's called Bruno.' He watched her go, and wondered how, in the midst of so much pain, he could be so aware of her cute little bottom in those tight, unbelievably sexy jeans…

Lucie let herself in and greeted the dog, a huge hairy black thing with doleful eyes and jaws that could have sheared a man's thigh, and hoped the eyes would win.

'Good doggie, nice Bruno. Sit.'

To her amazement he sat, his tail wiggling furiously, and she reached out a tentative hand and patted him. 'Good boy,' she said, a little more confidently, and he barked again, standing up and going to the door to scratch hopefully at it.

'Sorry, babes, you've got to stay inside,' she told him, and looked around. Sink. Good. Cupboard on left—and slings. Excellent. She squirmed past the dog, shut the door and ran back down the steps and over to the barn.

His eyes were shut, and she could see, now she

was less angry, that his face was grey and drawn. She wondered how long he'd been there, and how on earth she'd get him out.

'Dr Ryan?'

'Will,' he mumbled, opening his eyes. 'Lucie, take my watch off, can you? It hurts like hell.'

She carefully unclipped the metal strap, but she couldn't slide it over his hand. The face was cracked, and it had stopped about three hours ago. Had he been there that long? Probably.

'Let's get a support on that right arm first,' she said, and carefully lifted his hand as he shifted his elbow away from his body.

She was as gentle as possible, but he still bit back a groan and braced himself against the barn. She fixed the sling, then put the left arm, which seemed less painful, in a lower sling so it wouldn't interfere with the right.

'OK. Now I need to get you up and out to hospital. Any ideas?'

His eyes flickered open. 'Teleporting?'

Humour, even in all that pain. She felt a flicker of admiration. 'Sorry, not an option. Do you have a car?'

'Yes. It's round the corner in the barn. The keys are with the door keys. Lock the back door again and get the car out and bring it round.'

'What about insurance?' she asked, being practical for once in her life.

'You're covered if you're over twenty-five.' He gave her a sceptical look.

'Well, of course I am!' she said in disgust, and stomped off. 'Idiot. He knows quite well how old I am!' She locked the back door, ignoring Bruno's pleas, and went round the corner.

Oh, lord, it was a massive great Volvo estate! Miles long, and hugely wide. Terrific. She'd never driven anything this big before, and she was going to have to do it smoothly and carefully. With an audience.

Marvellous. She could hardly wait.

She got in, stared at the gear lever and got out again, stomping back round the corner to Will.

'It's automatic,' she said accusingly.

'Yes—that makes it easier.'

'Fiddlesticks.'

'Trust me, I'm a doctor. D is drive, P is park, R is reverse, N is neutral. Leave it in Park, start the engine, put your foot on the brake and put it into Drive. You have to hold down the button on top while you move the lever.'

'Hmm.'

She went back, started it, put it in drive and took her foot cautiously off the brake and screamed when it moved. She hit the brakes, her left foot flailing uselessly, looking for a task. Idiot, she told herself, and eased her foot off the brake again. It rolled gently forwards, and she tried the accelerator, cautiously. OK.

She nosed out of the barn, totally unsure how far she was from anything, and cursed herself for never having driven anything bigger than a supermini. She crept round the end of the barn, stopped as close to Will as she could get and looked at the gear lever in puzzlement.

'Put it in Park,' he told her. 'And put the handbrake on,' he added as an afterthought, as if he didn't quite trust her.

She was about to make a smart-alec retort when she took her foot off the footbrake and the car rolled forwards a fraction.

She gave another little yelp and slammed her foot back down, and he shot her a pitying look.

'It moved!' she said defensively.

'It's fine. It's just taking up the slack. You could have reversed it in so the door was closer.'

'No, I couldn't,' Lucie said tightly, realising with dismay that she was going to have to reverse around the barn to get back to the track. Oh, blast. She got out of the car and slammed the door, and he winced.

'Maybe this wasn't such a good idea,' he muttered.

'You don't have a choice,' she reminded him.

'We could have called an ambulance.'

'We might have to yet. My car's in the way.'

'I've got a tow-rope. We can pull it out.'

'We?' She eyed him up and down, and snorted. 'I don't think so.'

'We'll worry about it later. Just get me in the damn car,' Will said through gritted teeth, and she stood in front of him and grasped him by the shoulders, pulling him forwards and upwards as he got his legs under him and straightened with a groan.

'OK?'

He gave her a dirty look. 'Wonderful. Open the car door.'

She cocked an eyebrow at him. 'Please?'

'Please.'

'Better.'

'Don't push it,' he growled, and she gave up. She stomped round the bonnet, yanked open the front passenger door and came back for him, but he was already on his way, stubborn and self-reliant. Fine. Let him struggle.

Then Will wavered, and she had a sudden vision of him toppling over on those broken arms. Not a good idea, and she needed this post if she was going to finish her training. Stifling her urge to leave him to it, she put her arm around his waist to steady him and helped him round the car, then opened the door and watched as he eased himself in. His jaw was working furiously, his eyes were screwed shut and once he was in he dropped his head back against the headrest and let out a shaky sigh.

'I think we'll pass on the seat belt,' he said through gritted teeth, and she shut the door firmly on him.

Lucie crossed round to the driver's side, wondering how, under these circumstances, she could have been so conscious of the hard, lean feel of his body. Even through the thickness of the soft sweater he was wearing she'd been aware of every rib, every muscle, every breath.

She had a feeling he was, too, and her compassion returned, forcing out her bizarre and untimely thoughts and replacing them with a more appropriate concern for his health. She slid behind the wheel, looked over her shoulder and wondered how on earth she was going to reverse this thing the size of an oil tanker back around the barn…

How could she be so stupid? Will asked himself. How could a woman with apparently enough brain to train and qualify as a doctor be so stupid that she couldn't manage to drive a perfectly normal car?

She panicked, she overreacted, she allowed sometimes too much room, sometimes nothing like enough, and her judgement on the bumpy drive left a great deal to be desired.

No wonder she'd got her car stuck.

'Are you trying to do it again, you idiot woman?' he snapped as she jolted down yet another pothole.

'Don't call me names just because your drive's so awful! There should be a law against it.'

There should be a law against her smart mouth, but he didn't suppose he'd get it past all the women MPs. 'Drive on the centre and the side,' he told her through gritted teeth, but there were places where you had to pick your way and, sure as eggs, she'd pick the wrong one.

And every jolt was agonising. He would have driven himself, except, of course, he couldn't even hold the steering-wheel, never mind turn it. Damn.

They lurched through another pothole and he felt cold sweat spring out on his brow. He needed to lie down. He needed pain relief. He needed oblivion.

He didn't need to be giving some delinquent female driving lessons!

'There's my car,' she announced defiantly, and he cracked his eyes open and sighed with relief.

'You can drive round it. Head for the left—the ground's firm there.'

Well, more or less. They got through it with a bit of lurching and wheel-spinning, and then the track improved. Just another few minutes, he told himself. Just a little longer…

'Yes, it's a lovely clean fracture through the radius and ulna. Classic Colles'. We'll reduce it here, if you like. As for the other one, it's just a nasty sprain, you'll be glad to know.'

He was. He was hugely glad to know that he wasn't going to be dependent on anyone for help with his basic functions. It would probably hurt like hell to use it, but at least if it wasn't plastered, he'd have some rotation in the hand, and that would make all the difference.

Will didn't enjoy having the fracture reduced. They bandaged his hand to compress it and drive the blood out of it, which hurt, then stopped the blood supply to his arm and filled the vessels with local anaesthetic.

That bit was fine. Then the doctor grasped his hand and pulled, and the bones slid back into place with an audible crunch.

To his utter disgust, he threw up, and all he could think was thank God Lucie wasn't there watching him with her wide green eyes and sassy mouth. Just for good measure, he retched again, then sagged back against the bed.

'Finished?' the nurse asked him in a kind voice, and he nodded weakly.

The doctor shot him a thoughtful look. 'I think you've got a touch of concussion. Perhaps we need to keep you in overnight.'

'No,' he said firmly, ignoring the pounding in his head and the tingling sensation in his cheek. What concussion? 'I'm fine. I want to go home.'

'Stubborn sod, aren't you?' the doctor said cheerfully, and stood back to survey his handiwork. 'That looks fine. We'll let the anaesthetic out now and see how it feels when it comes round. Oh, and you'll need another X-ray after we put a back-slab on—an open cast, just in case it swells overnight. You'll need to come back tomorrow for a check-up and have a proper cast on if all's well. OK?'

Will nodded.

'I still think you should stay overnight, but so long as you'll have someone with you, that'll have to do. You know what to look out for.'

He did. He'd dished out advice on head injuries for years, but he'd never had to take it. He wasn't thinking too clearly now, and his hand was beginning to tingle as they let the blood back through it.

At least the other one felt safer now, strapped up and supported from his fingers to his elbow in tight Tubigrip with a hole cut for the thumb.

MICE, he was reminded. Mobilisation, ice, compression, elevation. It used to be RICE, but they'd changed the rules and got rid of the resting in favour of mobilisation. That was good, because without his right arm, the left was going to be mobilised a heck of a lot in the next few weeks!

'I'll write you up for some painkillers,' the doctor said. 'You can take up to eight a day, no more than two at a time and no closer together than four hours.'

He had no intention of taking them, except as a last resort, but he accepted them anyway—not that it was exactly difficult to get a prescription. He'd pick one up on Monday morning when he went to work, he thought, and then it hit him.

How on earth was he going to work with one arm in a cast and the other—the wrong one—in a support? Brilliant. And Lucie was just starting a six-month stint as a trainee, and he was the only member of the practice qualified to train her.

He sighed. Well, she'd just have to cover his patients, and he'd supervise her and tell her what to do and she could drive him around—always assuming he could stand it! She'd be staying at the cottage anyway, he thought, and then remembered the cottage bedroom—the one without a bed, with a stinking, soaked carpet that needed replacing.

He let his breath out on an irritated sigh. She'd have to stay in the house—which might be as well for a day or two, but in the long term would drive him utterly frantic. Still, it wouldn't need to be long term. He could order a bed and a carpet over the phone, and have them installed and move her in there within a couple of days.

He would need to. He guarded his privacy jealously, and he wasn't sharing his house with anyone any longer than was absolutely necessary.

Most particularly not a pretty, sassy little thing with attitude. He'd lose his mind!

Lucie was bored. She'd read all the leaflets, studied all the posters, walked up and down all the corridors, tried out the drinks machine and read half the magazines.

How long could it take, she thought, to do a couple of X-rays and slap on a cast?

A nurse appeared. 'Dr Compton?'

Finally! She bounced to her feet and crossed the room. 'How is he?'

The nurse smiled understandingly. 'Bit grouchy. Men don't like losing their independence. He's ready to go home now.'

Lucie followed her to one of the treatment rooms, and there was Will sitting in the wheelchair, looking like something the cat had dragged in. He shot her a conciliatory look. 'Sorry you've had such a long wait.'

'That's OK. I know more than I ever wanted to know about how to sail the Atlantic, adjust grandfather clocks and make mango chutney. Do you want a wheelchair ride to the car, or shall I bring it to the door?'

'Both,' the nurse said.

'I'll walk,' said Will.

Lucie looked from one to the other, nodded and went out, jingling the car keys in her hand and humming softly, a smile playing around her lips. Stubborn, difficult man. It was going to be an interesting six months.

CHAPTER TWO

'WHAT do you mean, *uninhabitable*?'

Will sighed and shifted his right arm, swore softly and dropped his head back against the wall behind his chair. Lucie had got the distinct impression he'd been about to ram his hand through his hair in irritation. 'There was a missing roof tile. That's what I was doing.'

'You said you were rescuing the cat,' she accused, and he sighed again, even more shortly.

'I was—she'd gone up there because I'd been up there, fixing the roof. Because it was leaking. So the bed was wet. The carpet's ruined. The room is trashed, basically, until I can get a new carpet and bed next week and get the ceiling repainted.'

So not too long to wait, then. Just a few days of each other's company. It might be just as well, the state he was in. Lucie cocked her head on one side and studied Will. He looked awful. She wondered when he was going to relent and have a painkiller. Never, probably.

Stubborn as a mule.

He opened his eyes and looked at her, then looked at the door and dragged in a deep breath. Then he got very slowly and carefully to his feet.

'Can I get you something?'

'I need the loo.'

She went to stand up, and he fixed her with a glare that would have frozen the Atlantic. 'Don't even think about it,' he said tautly, and, suppressing a smile, she fell back in the chair and waited patiently for him to return.

Buttons, Will decided, were the spawn of the devil. Desperation got them undone. Nothing seemed sufficiently urgent to induce him to hurt that much just to do them up. Lord knows why he'd bought button-fly jeans. He must have been mad. So now what? Flies undone, or change into something more sensible, like tracksuit bottoms?

But they were upstairs, and he was down here, and it was all too much like hard work. His head was spinning, and he felt sick again. Damn. He tried to turn the tap on, but the washer needed changing and he always had to turn it off hard to stop it dripping. The other tap might be better.

Apparently not. It wouldn't budge for the feeble urging of his left hand, and his right was totally out of action.

He leant his head against the wall and winced as he encountered a bruise. If he'd been three, he would have thrown himself down on the floor and wailed, but he wasn't. He was thirty-three, and stubborn and proud, and he wasn't giving Lucie the privilege of seeing him this far down.

'Will? Are you OK?'

'Fine,' he lied through clenched teeth.

'I thought you might want these jogging bottoms—I found them on the chair in your bedroom. They'll be more comfortable to slouch around in, I should think.'

He opened the door—thank the Lord he had levers, not knobs—and took them from her. The damn woman must be psychic. He avoided her eyes. He didn't want to see mockery or, worse still, pity in them. He pushed the door shut with his hip.

Her voice came muffled through the wood. 'Thank you. My pleasure, any time. You're too good to me, Lucie. No, no, not at all.'

'Thank you,' he bit out tightly, and looked at the trousers, then at his feet. All he had to do now was get his shoes off and swap the trousers without falling over.

Will looked awful. Grey and drawn and sick. He'd been ages just changing into the jogging bottoms, and now he was slumped in a chair in his cheerless little sitting room while she struggled to light the fire.

Finally it caught, and Lucie put a log on the kindling and prodded it. It spat at her out of gratitude, so she put another log on to keep it company and put the spark guard in front.

Bruno seemed to approve. He gave a deep grunting sigh as he collapsed in front of it, and proceeded to sleep. It was what Will needed to do, of course, but he was fighting it.

'Why don't you go to bed?' she suggested after an hour of watching him wrestle with his eyelids.

'I need to stay awake—concussion,' he told her in a patronising tone that made her grind her teeth.

'No, you need to be monitored so you don't go into a coma without anyone noticing. I can do that—I am almost qualified to tell if a person's alive or dead, you know.'

He gave her a baleful look and shut his eyes again. 'I'm fine.'

Like hell he was fine, but who was she to argue?

Taking the suitcase with her overnight things, which they'd retrieved from her car, she went upstairs, found a bedroom next to his that was obviously a guest room and made the bed with sheets from the airing cupboard in the bathroom.

Once she'd done that, she went into his room, changed his sheets and turned back the bed. He'd need to sleep, whether he liked it or not, and she'd monitor him, again whether he liked it or not.

She went downstairs and stopped in front of him, studying him. He had dozed off, his head resting awkwardly against the wall, and for a moment she contemplated leaving him.

His eyes were shut, the lashes dark against his ashen cheeks, and his brows arched proudly above them. Most people looked younger and even innocent in sleep. Not Will. He looked hard and craggy and implacable. Tough. Indestructible.

Sexy.

Good grief. *Sexy?* She looked again. Well, maybe. He was probably quite good-looking, really, she conceded absently. Tousled mid-brown hair flopped in disorder over a broad, intelligent brow. Beneath it his nose was lean and aristocratic, despite the kink in it that gave away an old injury. Below the sculpted, full lips were a strong jaw and stubborn chin—no surprise there.

Sexy? Maybe. Certainly interesting in a strictly academic, architectural sense. And he did have beautiful, striking pale grey eyes brought into sharp relief by a darker rim. They weren't comfortable eyes. Too piercing. She wondered if they ever softened, if he ever softened.

Probably not.

They flickered slightly, but didn't open. He was awake now, though. She could tell. 'Will?' she said softly.

He opened them, spearing her with a surprisingly alert gaze. 'What?'

'Your bed's ready. Do you want anything to eat before you go to sleep?'

He sighed heavily. 'No. I feel sick still.'

'Water? You ought to drink plenty to help your kidneys deal with all the rubbish in your bloodstream after your fracture.'

He nodded. 'I know. I'll get some water in a minute.'

'How about painkillers?'

'Don't need them,' he said, a little too quickly.

'I'll get you some water, then I think you should go and lie down. You'll be much more comfortable.'

'Did anyone ever tell you just how damn bossy you are?' he growled.

'Mm-hmm. Lots of times,' she said cheerfully. 'Where does the dog sleep?'

'In here, now you've lit the fire, I should think. Anywhere. Usually outside my bedroom door.'

She went upstairs with the water and his painkillers, and came back for him, only to find him halfway up the stairs with that look on his face that brooked no interference.

She stood back and prayed he didn't fall backwards onto his stubborn behind, and once he was up she followed him to his room.

'I can manage,' he said, and she looked at him.

'Are there buttons on your shirt?'

He gave a short sigh of irritation. 'Yes.'

'Will, just for tonight, why don't you let me help you?' she suggested softly.

The fight went out of Will and he sat on the bed, looking at it in confusion. 'You changed the sheets.' His voice held astonishment and—heavens, gratitude? Surely not!

'I always think fresh sheets make you feel much better,' she said matter-of-factly. 'Right, let's get this sweater off and see if your shirt will come over the cast.'

It did, leaving him naked to the waist and utterly fascinating to her. His body was lean and muscled, healthy—and striped with purpling bruises from the rungs of the ladder. She touched his ribs with a gentle finger.

'You need arnica,' she told him, and he rolled his eyes.

'Not witchcraft,' he groaned.

She smiled. 'Midwives use it. You should open your mind.'

He humphed.

'Pyjamas?'

He shook his head slightly. 'No. I can manage now.'

'Socks?'

He looked at his feet, and his shoulders drooped. 'I can sleep in them.'

'Do you usually?'

'Of course not.'

'Fine.' Lucie crouched down and pulled off his socks.

Nice feet. Strong, straight toes, good firm arches, a scatter of dark hair over the instep.

'Now I really can manage,' he repeated, and she

stood up, putting the shirt and socks out of range so she didn't trip over them in the night.

'Water on the side. Can you hold the glass?'

'I'm sure I'll find a way,' he said drily.

'No doubt. OK, I'll see you later. I'm next door. Shout if you want anything.'

She got ready for bed and lay down, and the silence and darkness was astonishing. She looked out of the bedroom window, and could see nothing. No lights, no sign of any other habitation. Something scuttled in the roof over her head, and she ducked and ran back to bed. Her skin crawled with fear until she realised it was in the roof space and not in the room with her.

'It's probably a tiny little mouse,' she told herself, ignoring the vivid imagination that had always been her worse enemy as well as her greatest friend. That imagination was turning the mouse into a rat of terrifying proportions, and she had to force herself to relax. She buried her head under the pillow and then remembered she was supposed to be listening out for Will.

Damn. She poked her head out and listened.

Nothing. Well, nothing human. There was a snort right outside her window, and fear raced over her skin again. What on *earth* was that? She bit her lip, considering creeping into Will's room and sliding into bed next to him for safety, then dismissed it as ridiculous.

Whatever was out there was *out there*, not in here with her. She'd be fine. Fine. Fine.

She chanted it like a mantra, and eventually she drifted off into a light, uneasy doze…

* * *

He'd thought he'd be all right. He'd really thought the pain wouldn't keep him awake, but the hospital's painkiller had worn off well and truly, and his arm was giving him hell. Well, both of them, really, but especially the right.

Will sat up, swinging his legs over the side of the bed and waiting a moment for the world to steady. He didn't know where Lucie had put his painkillers, but he had a bottle in his medical bag downstairs that he kept for emergencies—other people's, not his, but they'd do.

He went down to the kitchen, creeping past Lucie's open door, and struggled with the combination lock on his bag. Finally he broke into it, pulled out the bottle and stared at it in disbelief.

A safety cap! Marvellous. He didn't know if he could turn it, never mind press and turn simultaneously. He tried holding the bottle in his right hand, but his fingers wouldn't co-operate. He held in it his left, and pressed with the cast to release the safety catch while he turned the bottle.

The cap slipped, of course, and was no further off. However, he still had teeth. He held the bottle to his mouth, clamped the cap in his back teeth and pushed and twisted.

Pain shot through his wrist, and with a gasp he dropped the bottle on the floor.

Damn. He'd never get into the blasted thing.

Bruno came to investigate, giving him a great, wet kiss as he bent to pick up the bottle. 'Hello, you vile hound,' he said affectionately, and could have buried his face in the dog's thick, black ruff and howled with despair.

Then he spotted the hammer on the window sill.

* * *

What on earth was Will doing? Lucie tiptoed to the top of the stairs and peered down. She could see his feet in the kitchen, and hear the occasional thump and groan. Then there was an almighty crash, and she ran downstairs and found him slumped over the sink.

'Will?'

He straightened slowly and turned, glaring at her. 'I can't get the bloody lid off,' he bit out through clenched teeth.

'And, of course, it's beyond you to ask for help.'

'I didn't want to wake you.'

'And you think all this crashing around right under my bedroom wouldn't have woken me, even assuming I'd been to sleep? Hell, it's too damn quiet round here to sleep, anyway! I can hear every mouse skittering in the roof, and birds shuffling in their nests, and some—some *thing* snorted outside my window. I nearly died of fright.'

'That would be Henry.'

'Henry?'

'A horse. He lives here.'

A horse? Of course. How obvious. She felt silly. She got back to basics. 'Where's the bottle?'

'Here.' He jerked his head at the worktop, and she picked the bottle up and studied it.

'These aren't the ones.'

'They'll do. I didn't know where the others were.'

'Beside your bed. I put two out.'

He closed his eyes and sighed harshly. 'Right. Fine. Thanks.'

'How's the nausea?'

'Gorgeous. I don't even know if I'll keep them down.'

'Yes, you will,' she said in her best comforting voice. 'Come on, let's get you back upstairs and into bed before you fall over. What was the crash, by the way?'

'The hammer.'

'*Hammer?*' she said in disbelief. 'What, did you think you'd tackle a few outstanding DIY jobs or something?'

He snorted in disgust. 'I was trying to break the bottle. I couldn't even hold the damn thing. It fell in the sink.'

Compassion filled her soft heart. 'Come on,' she said gently, putting an arm around his waist and steering him towards the stairs. 'Bedtime. I'll give you your painkillers and you can get to sleep.'

This time Bruno followed them, and with just the tiniest bit of encouragement he curled up across the foot of her bed and crushed her feet. She didn't care. She felt safe with him there, and she knew he'd hear every move that Will made. Finally able to relax, she went to sleep at last.

Will slept for most of the next day. Lucie took advantage of it to go and rescue her car. The puddles had more or less drained away, and she found some old bricks and put them in the back of Will's Volvo, then drove carefully—on the middle and the side—up to her car. She jacked it up, put bricks under the wheels and leading out of the puddle, then let the jack down and drove out.

No engine damage, or not obviously, and she'd done it herself. She felt disgustingly proud of her achievement, and couldn't wait to see Will's face. Leaving the bricks *in situ* to fill up the pothole a little, she headed back in her car, parked it in the yard beside the cottage and walked back for Will's.

By the time she drove back into the yard the second time, she was hot and sticky and Will was up.

'Where the hell have you been?' he asked crossly as she went into the kitchen.

'Well, pardon me for breathing! I fetched my car.'

He cobbled his eyebrows together. 'You did?'

'Yup. I found some old bricks at the side of the barn—'

'Bricks?'

'Yes—you know, rectangular red things that they build houses out of? Except these are dirty yellow and grey.'

'I know what you're talking about,' he snarled. 'I just wonder if you do! They were floor bricks—carefully cleaned and ready to go down in the kitchen here, once I had a minute. How many did you take?'

She shrugged, feeling a twinge of guilt. 'About forty or so?'

'*Forty!*' He rolled his eyes and gave an exasperated sigh.

Whoops.

'They'll clean up again,' she suggested. 'They only need a wash.'

'Good. You might go and fetch them and do it—and don't put them all covered in mud into the back of my car!'

'Well, what on earth am I supposed to do?' she ranted, finally losing her grip on her temper. 'Lick them clean?'

'At least it would be something useful to do with your tongue,' he shot back, and stalked out of the kitchen, the dog slinking anxiously at his heels.

Lucie thought she was going to scream. At the very least she was going to throw something! She stormed out of the door before she hurled a pan through the window, grabbed a pile of newspapers from the lobby—presumably he wouldn't mind her using them—and headed off in her car to retrieve his precious floor bricks.

How was she supposed to know they were so special? Darn the man, he didn't have to be quite so evil about it! Something useful to do with her tongue, indeed!

Will phoned Richard, his senior partner, and told him about his arms.

'Lord! Are you all right?' he asked, his voice full of concern. 'Let me come round—'

'Richard, I'm fine. I've got Lucie here, don't forget.'

'Lucie?'

'Compton—our new registrar?'

'Ah, yes. Lucie.' Something shifted in his voice. 'How is she? Dear girl.'

Will rolled his eyes. 'She's in fine form. She's a tyrant. My house isn't my own.'

'Excellent. I'm sure she's doing a grand job. Just don't alienate her—she can do your locum work until you recover. You can train her—you *are* still well enough to do that, aren't you?'

'Barely,' he admitted grudgingly. 'I can't write—I can't hold anything in my hand. I've got to go back to the hospital for a check-up and a cast—they've only put a back-slab on.'

'Want me to come and take you?'

He was tempted, but for some perverse reason he

wanted Lucie to do it. To torture him even more by exposure to her endless cheer and mindless chatter? Or was it something to do with the firm press of those taut little buttocks in her jeans, and the pert tilt of her breasts beneath that silky soft sweater?

He dragged his mind back into order. 'I'll be fine. I'll bribe Lucie with a take-away,' he told Richard, and went and watched her from the bedroom window.

He could see her in the distance, struggling with the bricks, hauling them out of the puddles and plopping them into the car. Hers, thankfully, not his. She was going to be furious, of course, and he could have been a bit kinder about it, but his arm hurt and he was frustrated by the pain and the disability.

She came back an hour later, muddy and dishevelled, and hosed the bricks off on the yard. She looked even madder than she had yesterday, and he lurked quietly out of the way, his conscience pricking. Then Amanda came down to ride her horse, and introduced herself to Lucie, and moments later was heading for the kitchen at a lope.

Damn. Lucie must have told her about his accident. Amanda had been fussing round him already, and would, no doubt, seize this opportunity to ingratiate herself with him. She knocked on the door and came in, her eyes anxiously scanning him for signs of damage.

'Are you all right? You poor love! Fancy falling off the ladder! Anything I can do for you?'

He shook his head. 'No, really, I'm fine. Lucie's looking after me.'

Something that could have been jealousy flashed in her eyes. 'There's no need for that—you don't want strangers doing those sorts of things for you. I could help—'

'No, really,' Will cut in quickly. The very thought of Amanda 'helping' him chilled his blood, and he didn't dare to hazard a guess at what 'those sorts of things' might be. He suppressed a shudder. 'I'll be fine. My left hand's good—see?' He held it up and waggled it, stifling a moan of pain, and grinned convincingly. He hoped.

'Oh. Well, OK, then, but if there's anything I can do, you will ask, won't you?'

'Of course—and thank you.'

She paused at the door. 'Is she staying in the cottage?'

A hellion in him rose to the surface of the scummy pond that was his integrity. 'Lucie?' he said innocently. 'Ah—no. She's staying here—with me.' He winked, just for good measure, and Amanda coloured and backed away.

'Um. Right. OK. Well, take care.'

He felt guilty. She was a nice enough girl, but she was so—well, wholesome, really. Earnest and energetic and frightfully jolly.

And he was a rat.

He sighed. He was thirsty, and the orange juice in the carton was finished. He contemplated the scissors, and got another carton out of the fridge, wincing and juggling it onto the cast to support the weight. He dropped it on the worktop, picked the scissors up in his left hand and proceeded to mash the corner of the carton, not very effectively.

Of course, a decent brand of orange juice would have a pull tab, but that would probably have been

beyond him, too, he wa
realise.

He managed to chew a sn
scissors, then squeezed it out o
he ended up with juice soaking d
slab and drenching the Tubigrip o
There was damn all in the glass, of

Disgusted, he balanced the carton cast, tipped it to his mouth and drank it throu the mangled hole.

And of course that was how Lucie found him moments later.

She cocked a brow at him, squeezed past and washed her hands and arms in the sink. 'Couldn't you wait?'

'No. I was thirsty. Want some?'

She gave him a withering look, took a glass out of the cupboard and filled it with water, then drained it in a couple of swallows. How did women manage to find their way around kitchens so damned fast?

'Do you want to drink that out of the carton leaking all over your shirt, or would you rather I put some in a glass for you?'

One day, he thought, his pride was going to choke him. He hesitated, then gave up. 'Would you mind?' he said meekly.

She shot him a suspicious look and relieved him of the carton, trimming the opening straight and pouring it neatly into a fresh glass. 'Don't you have to go for a check-up today?' she asked as he drank.

'Mmm.'

'So shouldn't we go?'

'Probably. I've got juice all over these, I could do with some fresh supports.'

...ure they'll oblige.'

...he helped him into his sweater, then led the way to her car. He eyed it in dismay.

'Your car? Really?'

She paused in the act of getting in, one hand on the roof, the other on the top of the door. 'Really,' she vowed, refusing to relent. Yesterday had been quite enough. 'You can move the seat back,' she conceded.

She leant across and opened the door, pushing it ajar for him. He folded himself into the seat with much grunting, and slid it back when she lifted the adjustment lever.

'Are you in?'

'Just about,' he muttered ungraciously, and she leant across him to pull the door shut.

Hard, muscled thighs tensed under her weight as she sprawled over him, and she regretted not getting out and going round to close it. She hoisted herself upright, conscious of the heat in her cheeks and the gimlet gaze of Amanda watching them from beside the barn, and fastened his seat belt.

'That woman's got the hots for you,' she said candidly, watching Amanda in the rear-view mirror as they pulled away and hoping Will didn't misconstrue her remark as jealousy.

Apparently not. He rolled his eyes and groaned. 'Tell me about it,' he muttered. 'I'm afraid I rather exaggerated our—er—relationship. She was offering to help me in all sorts of hideously personal ways, so I'm afraid I used you as a way out. No doubt she'll hate you.'

Lucie spluttered with laughter, and Will's lips twitched. Not a smile—quite—but almost.

Maybe working with him wouldn't be so bad after all…

'Right, you met Richard at your interview, and this is Kathy, and Simon's about somewhere, and then there are all the receptionists, the practice manager, the practice and community nurses, the midwives…'

Lucie smiled and nodded and hoped she could remember a tenth of what he was telling her.

It all made sense, of course, and in many ways it was just like her city-centre practice had been, but in other ways it couldn't have been more different.

Take the setting, for example. Her London practice had been in a converted Victorian house, with a rabbit warren of rooms and corridors and odd little corners. This was modern, purpose built and astonishingly unprovincial.

All the equipment and methods in both were right up to date, of course, as they had to be in a training practice, but of the two environments, she had to say this was lighter and more spacious. Whether that was better or not she wasn't sure yet.

She had a pang of nostalgia for the untidy pile of anomalies she'd left behind, and a moment of fear that it wouldn't work out. She would have stayed in the other practice, given a choice, but she hadn't been. The trainer had had a heart attack and had had to take early retirement, and that had left nobody in the practice to take over.

It was only by luck that this vacancy had come up when it had.

She just hoped it was *good* luck.

Will had finished the introductions, and they went into his consulting room and settled down to start her first surgery. 'I'm going to sit in for a few days, make sure you've got all the referrals and so on at your fingertips and that you're up to speed on the way we do things. Then, if we're both happy, I'll leave you to it,' he said.

Great. An audience. And she'd thought driving the car had been bad!

Her first patient was a girl of fifteen, whose mother had brought her in 'because there's nothing wrong with her and I want you to tell her so, Doctor.'

Lucie and Will exchanged glances, and Lucie smiled at the girl. 'Let's see, you're Clare, aren't you?'

'Yes.' She coughed convulsively, and Lucie frowned. She'd already noticed that the teenager had been short of breath when they'd come in, and, unlike her other practice, there were no stairs here to blame!

'Tell me what seems to be wrong,' she coaxed, but the mother butted in again.

'She should have gone back to school today, but she's been flopping about and coughing for the last week, and she's got exams coming up—she's doing her GCSEs and she can't afford to have time off!'

'So what's the matter, Clare?' Lucie asked again. 'Tell me in what way you aren't feeling quite right.'

'My cough,' she began.

'She's not eating. She's starving herself to death—I think she's got anorexia or something. I think the cough is just a big put-on, but if you give her antibiotics she won't have any excuse, she won't be able to swing the lead. I've given her a good talking-to about this eating business. Dr Ryan, you tell her.'

Will shook his head and smiled. 'Dr Compton is

quite capable of making a diagnosis, Mrs Reid. We'll let her see what she comes up with first, shall we?'

Lucie felt like a bug under a microscope. Will had thrown his support behind her, but almost in the form of a challenge, and now she had to find something wrong. She was just warming up to her 'we can't give out antibiotics like sweets' talk, when Clare coughed again.

Listen to her chest, her common sense advised, and, to her huge relief, there was a crackle. Her face broke into a broad smile. 'There's your answer—she's got a chest infection. No anorexia, no skiving, just a genuine sick girl who needs antibiotics.'

'Well, that was easy. I thought you didn't dish them out these days?' Mrs Reid said sceptically, looking to Will for reassurance.

'Only when necessary,' Lucie confirmed, 'and with all those crackles in her chest, trust me, it's necessary. It sounds like someone eating a packet of crisps in there.'

Clare giggled, clearly relieved to have been taken seriously, and Lucie smiled at her. 'You'll soon feel better. You need to rest, drink lots and get back to school as soon as you feel right. When do you do your exams, is it this year or next?'

'Next year, the real thing, but we've got end-of-year ones coming up after half-term, and Dad'll kill me if I don't do well.' She pulled a face. 'He's a teacher.'

Lucie laughed. 'I know the feeling. My father's a teacher, too. He used to look at me over his half-glasses and say, "You don't seem to be doing very much homework these days." It drove me nuts—especially as I was working my socks off!'

'I bet he's pleased with you now, though,' Clare said thoughtfully. 'I want to be a doctor, too, but I don't know if I'm clever enough.'

'You know, there are lots of things you can do apart from medicine in the medical field. Wait and see how it pans out. Your grades might be good enough, and if not, there are lots of other options.'

Will cleared his throat quietly in the background, and Lucie looked at him. He was staring pointedly at the clock on the wall, and she gulped guiltily and brought up the girl's details on the computer, printed off her prescription and sent her and her over-anxious mother away.

Then she sat back and waited for the lecture.

He said nothing.

She looked at him. 'Aren't you going to criticise me?'

He smiled smugly and shook his head. 'Oh, yes—but later. I think your next patient has had to wait quite long enough, don't you?'

She stifled the urge to hit him.

CHAPTER THREE

IT WAS lunchtime. Apart from Clare, her first case, she had seen another fifteen patients that morning—and overrun surgery by an hour.

Now they were going on visits and, because she didn't know the way, Will was having to direct her.

Which meant, of course, that his mouth was busy with 'Turn left, go up there, it's on the right,' instead of 'Why didn't you do such and such?'. That was a huge relief to Lucie, who was coping—just—with his presence, without the added burden of her sins being heaped upon her head.

Actually she thought the surgery had gone quite well, but several times she'd caught Will rolling his eyes in the background or flicking glances at the clock. Had he been able to write, she knew he would have been making copious notes on her abysmal performance.

Tough. Anyway, it wasn't abysmal. Just a tad slow. She told herself it was because she was being thorough.

'Go along that road there to the end,' he instructed. 'It's the white house near the corner.'

There were two white houses near the corner. Of course she pulled up outside the wrong one, and couldn't resist the smirk of satisfaction when he objected.

He heaved a sigh, went to stab his hand through his hair and clonked his head with the cast.

'You should have a sling on,' she reminded him.

'I don't like slings. They mess my neck up.'

'Your hand will swell.'

'That's fine, there's room, it's still got the back-slab on.'

'Only because you won't wear a sling!'

Will turned to her, his eyes flying sparks. 'Lucie, it's my arm. If I don't want to wear a sling, I won't wear a sling. I most particularly won't wear two slings. And I won't be nagged by a junior doctor that I'm training!'

'I am not a junior doctor,' she bit out through clenched teeth. 'I am a registrar. I am not a complete incompetent, whatever you might think, and how you got the job of trainer I can't imagine. You're patronising, unfairly critical and judgmental.'

'I haven't said a word—'

'Yet! No doubt it's coming.'

He sat back and studied her curiously. 'So what did you think you did wrong this morning?' he asked with studied calm.

'Apart from breathe?' Lucie muttered under her breath. 'Overran the surgery time.'

'What else?'

'Nothing,' she said defensively.

'I would have got a sputum sample from Clare to make sure she'd got the right antibiotic.'

Oh, would he? Damn. He was right, and she would have done if he hadn't put her off by clearing his throat pointedly and looking at the clock. She wondered if Clare had taken the first dose yet, or if she should ring—

'I've rung and ordered it. They'll pick the pot up before she takes the first dose,' Will added, as if he'd read her mind. 'They live very close to the surgery. What else?'

She stuffed her irritation into a mental pending tray to deal with later and scanned through her morning list. 'That man with indigestion-like pain—'

'Mr Gregory.'

'Yes. He's obese.'

'Actually, technically he's just overweight. His body mass index is 29.4. He's working on getting it down, but he's aiming for a 10 kg weight loss. That's probably why he's got indigestion. Faddy diets and varied eating habits can cause that.'

'It would have been helpful to know that before the consultation. I was wondering about the choice between angina and *Helicobacter pylori*, and it's probably just too much cucumber!'

A flicker of guilt came and went in his eyes. 'Sorry. It's the painkillers. I'm not really concentrating. You're right.'

Lucie's jaw nearly dropped. An apology? Good grief, wonders will never cease, she thought.

'Since you're on a roll, I don't suppose you want to apologise for that remark about licking the bricks, do you?' she challenged, pushing her luck.

He smiled. It was a dangerous, predatory smile. 'Not really,' he said, and opened the car door with a wince. 'Let's get on or we'll be late.'

'So, are you going to tell me about this patient, or let me go in blind?' she asked his retreating form.

He sat back, letting the door fall shut and looking at her over his shoulder. 'He's fifty-five or so, he's had a heart attack, he's been under a cardiologist but cancelled his follow-up appointment on a flimsy pretext. I reckon he's in line for bypass surgery but he won't stick to a diet or exercise programme and he keeps getting chest pain. This is just a routine check-up. I suggest you take routine obs while I talk.'

'I thought I was taking on your patients?' she objected, but he shook his head.

'Not this one. His wife's too nice—she doesn't deserve all this worry. She needs moral support.'

'And I can't give it?'

'Not like I can. I've known her for years,' he pointed out fairly.

'Not that many, Old Father Time. How old are you?'

He shot her a grin. 'I've been here six years. We've gone through the menopause together, Pam and I. I know her well, trust me.'

She gave a quiet and not very ladylike snort as he got out of the car. Retrieving her bag from the back, she locked the car and followed him across the road.

A woman was standing in the front garden of the other white house, stripping off bright yellow rubber gloves, and he bent and kissed her cheek. 'Hello, Pam,' he said gently. 'How are things?'

She rolled her eyes despairingly, then shot him a keen look. 'Never mind me—is that a cast on your arm? *And* a bandage on the other one—what on earth have you been up to?'

He told her the story, played down the drama and played up the farce, and introduced Lucie as the cavalry. 'Very timely arrival, although, of course, if she hadn't been coming I wouldn't have been mending the roof of the cottage and I wouldn't have been up the ladder, so in a way it's her fault.'

'That's right, blame me,' Lucie said, rolling her

eyes and laughing. 'Although as I remember it, you were rescuing the cat, actually.'

'She's doing all the physical stuff for me, I'm doing the talking,' Will explained, cutting her off with a grin. 'She's our new trainee registrar.'

'Are you? Poor you,' Pam said comfortingly. 'He can be a bit of a slave-driver, I gather. His last one left in a hurry.'

'His last one was useless,' Will pointed out fast. 'Don't slag me off, Pam, she already thinks I've got a broomstick stashed in the barn.'

'Yes—a Swedish one,' Lucie chipped in. 'Estate version.'

He laughed, not unkindly. 'It's a lovely car.'

'It's too big.'

'We're using it tomorrow. That thing of yours gives me backache and cramp.'

'Poor baby.'

Pam eyed them with curiosity. 'I think you'll survive, Lucie,' she said consideringly, and smiled at her. 'Welcome to Bredford.'

'Thank you.' She returned the smile, comforted that at least someone was going to be on her side, and followed them in.

Their patient was sitting in an upright chair, a folded newspaper on the floor at his side and a cup of what looked like very strong coffee on the table next to him.

'Hello, Dick,' Will said easily, perching on the sofa near their patient's chair. 'I won't shake hands, I've mashed myself. This is Lucie Compton, my new registrar.'

Lucie shook hands with him, noticing the pallor of his skin except for the high flush over his nose and cheekbones, and wondered just how bad his heart condition was.

'Lucie, why don't you run the ruler over him while we chat, to save time?' Will suggested, and she opened her bag and took out her stethoscope, listening to the patient's chest first to hear his heart.

It was a little irregular, but without an ECG it was difficult to tell what was wrong about it. His chest was clear, at least. She took his pulse and respiration, while Will propped his arms on his knees and smiled at Dick encouragingly. 'So, tell me, how are you doing?'

'Oh, not so bad.'

'He's been getting chest pain.'

Will looked from Dick to Pam and back again. 'On exertion, or at rest?'

'At night. At least, that's when I know about it,' Pam confirmed.

Will nodded. 'And how about the daytime, Dick? Anything then?'

The man shrugged. 'Off and on.'

'Are you taking the pills?'

'Yes.'

'No.'

Will's eyes flicked to Pam again. 'He's not?'

She shook her head. 'Not always. Not unless I nag him.'

'Which she does all the time, of course,' Dick put in with a rueful, indulgent smile. 'Oh, I don't know, Will, I just feel there's no point. I'm a great believer in Fate. If my number's up, it's up. I'm not going to bugger up the rest of my life taking pills and watching what I eat and drink. It's like the old joke about giving up drinking, women and red meat. It doesn't make you live longer, it just feels that way!'

Will chuckled obediently, and glanced at Pam again. 'I wouldn't suggest you give up women—at least, not this one. She's a star. But the food and drink are real issues, Dick. The next step down the line for you could be bypass surgery, and you really owe it to yourself to be as fit as possible for it.'

'Oh, I know. You're going to tell me to lay off the booze, cut my fat intake and get off my backside and walk two miles a day, aren't you?'

'Something like that. Sounds as if you've heard it before somewhere. And while we're at it, I'll throw in caffeine. Decaff tea and coffee, please.'

Lucie bent down to her bag to remove the blood-pressure cuff, and hid a smile. Dick curled his lip. 'Decaff? Filthy stuff.'

'Rubbish. You can't tell the difference.'

'I can.'

'So drink fruit teas or orange juice.'

Will was treated to another withering look. 'Fruit teas,' Dick said disgustedly.

'Unlaced.'

He shook his head slowly. 'You're a hard man.'

'I'm trying to keep you alive. No point in dying on the waiting list, Dick—always assuming you ever get on it. Have you made another appointment yet?'

Something flickered in Dick's eyes—something that could have been fear.

'Not yet. Keep forgetting.'

Lucie slipped the blood-pressure cuff off his arm and chipped in.

'A patient at my last practice had a by-pass op. He felt like you—what was the point? If it was going to get him, there was no point in worrying. He felt so much better after the op, he realised it had been worth worrying about. I had a letter from him the other day. He's taken early retirement, moved to the country and started playing golf, and he feels great. He's lost two stone, he's fitter than he's been for years and he says there's a twinkle in his wife's eye that's been missing for ages.'

Dick moistened his lips and cleared his throat. 'He feels better?'

'Yes. He felt better straight away. His chest was a bit sore for a while, of course, but he said the hospital were excellent and it was more than worth it. He sent me a photo—he looks terrific. Why don't you give it the benefit of the doubt and find out more?'

He looked thoughtful, and Lucie put the rest of her equipment away and straightened up. 'That all seems OK,' she said to Will. 'Anything else you want me to check?'

He shook his head and stood up. 'Listen to us, Dick. We aren't all telling you the same thing by coincidence, you know. Give it a whirl.'

Dick nodded grudgingly, and Will looked at Pam. 'Your garden's looking good. You must show me round it on the way out—I want to see your osteospermums. I can't believe you overwinter them outside. Mine all die without fail.'

Gardening already, for heaven's sake! Lucie cleared her throat, and glanced pointedly at her watch. Will ignored her.

'I've got some cuttings I've done for you—come down to the greenhouse and I'll give them to you,' Pam was saying.

'You're a marvel.'

Lucie sighed. 'I'll wait here,' she said, and sat down again with Dick. Maybe she could spend the time usefully after all…

For a moment he didn't speak, then he looked at her searchingly. 'Now tell me the truth. How much will it hurt after the op?'

Right for the jugular. 'A lot,' she said honestly, 'but less than another heart attack. The breastbone is the worst bit, and the leg can be quite sore for a few days, apparently, but they give you pain relief intravenously, and you have control over that. If it hurts, you can give yourself a shot, and it really does make it bearable. Everyone who's had it says it's worth it.'

He nodded, and licked his lips nervously. 'I'm scared,' he confessed. 'I can't tell Pam—seems so silly, really, to be afraid of pain, but I've never been good with it. Pam wants me to have it done privately to cut the waiting time, but I don't want to, even though we've got private health insurance as part of my work package. I suppose there's a bit of me that would rather wait longer and maybe die, so I don't have to deal with it. Does that seem strange to you?'

Lucie shook her head and smiled. 'No. Quite normal. Most people aren't afraid of being dead. They're afraid of suffering. I think you're actually very ordinary like that. Nobody likes pain. The thing is, if you have another heart attack, there's no guarantee it will kill you, but it will make you less well for the operation and it will, of course, be very painful in itself. I think at the very least you should see a cardiologist and discuss it.'

'I just—it scares me.'

'I take it you've had an angiogram and aren't suitable for balloon angioplasty?' she said as an afterthought.

He shook his head. 'No. They were talking about it, but I didn't know what it was.'

'So ask.'

'Everyone's always busy.'

Lucie smiled. 'That's life for you. An angiogram is a diagnostic image of the heart with radio-opaque dye injected into the coronary arteries, so they can see just where the arteries are clogging.'

'Oh, I had that. I never got the results, though. I thought you meant the other thing. The pasty thing.'

'Plasty. Angioplasty. If you're a suitable candidate, there's always the possibility that you won't have to have bypass surgery. Lots of people have balloon angioplasty instead. That's where they stick a little inflatable catheter in through a nick in the groin, track it with X-rays until it's in the right place and inflate it. It stretches the arteries and relieves the narrow point, if it's just one small constriction. And, of course, until you get the results of the angiogram, you won't know.'

Dick nodded. 'You're right, of course. I'll go back. I will. Thanks.'

'My pleasure. Have you got a computer? If you have, you could find out more about it on the internet. It's brilliant for things like that.' Lucie stood up. 'You will keep the appointment this time, won't you? It can't hurt to find out, and even if you ended up with surgery, you could have a whole new life ahead of you. Think of all the years you've worked, just to throw it all away before you retire.' She glanced at her watch again. 'I must go—we've got lots of other visits to do yet and I'm already running behind. It's only my first day.'

'And Will with broken arms, eh? Still, he's got such a nice, even temper. Anyone else might be really grumpy.'

Lucie nearly choked, swallowing the retort. Instead she smiled at Dick, exorted him to give the consultant a chance and reached the door just as Will and Pam came in.

'Right, are you all done?' Will asked. He had plant pots balanced on his cast, and Lucie rolled her eyes.

'Scrounging off the patients?' she teased as they went out to the car.

'Absolutely. Cheers, Pam. Thanks. Cheerio, Dick. Mind how you go.'

Lucie stuck her keys in the door of the car and paused. 'It would never happen in the city,' she remarked over the roof in a quiet voice.

'It's a cover. She wanted to talk to me about him. He won't go back to the consultant.'

'Yes, he will,' Lucie said smugly. 'I just talked him into it—at least, I think I did. The only reason he wouldn't do it is because he's afraid of the pain. He's hoping he'll die before he gets to the front of the waiting list. I told him it was possible he'd be suitable for balloon angioplasty, and even if he wasn't, how about his retirement?'

Will stared at her over the top of the car. 'And you've talked him round?'

'Yup.'

Respect dawned in his eyes. 'Good girl, well done,' he said softly. 'It's a shame he can't afford to go privately and get it over with, now he's psyched up. Not that it should be necessary, but I don't want to start on the politics of funding.'

'Pointless, really,' Lucie said with a cheeky grin. 'We'd probably be in agreement, and that would never do, would it? Anyway, he's got private health insurance through his work.'

She opened the car, slid behind the wheel and pushed his door open. He tried to pass the plants to her, but, of course, he dropped one on the seat, and it splattered wet black compost all over her upholstery.

'"Don't you dare put those bricks in my car like that,"' she mimicked, and he groaned and met her eyes, his own apologetic.

'I'm sorry.'

'Don't fret, I don't have to sit on it. Just brush it off for now—you can lick it clean later.'

Shooting her a foul look, he used his sprained wrist to flick the little bits of black aside, leaving dirty streaks on his bandage and the seat.

She stifled a smile. 'On second thoughts, using your car in future might be a good idea, if you're going to take up horticulture as a sideline,' she said sweetly. 'Mind you don't stand on them.'

He clenched his jaw and got into the car, tucking his arm into the seat belt and pulling it through with care and much wincing. She let him struggle for a moment, then took the buckle and clipped it in.

Her hand brushed his thigh, and it tensed again as it had before. She stifled another smile. Interesting.

'When are you going to go back to the hospital? You ought to go to the fracture clinic.'

'I'll go tomorrow,' he said. 'Right, where to next?'

* * *

Lucie was right, of course, he did need a sling on it, but now his pride was going to get in the way and so he surreptitiously propped his right arm up on anything that was handy, just to take the pressure off it.

It was pounding and, of course, with only a back-slab it was marginally unstable, too, and grated nicely every now and again if he was a bit rash. He really should get it seen to, he thought with a sigh.

The day seemed to drag interminably, and Lucie didn't need to be watched every second. She was more than capable of running his afternoon clinic on her own, and in the end he left her to it and called a patient who ran a minicab.

He was an ex-London cabbie, and always good value, and he entertained Will all the way to the hospital. He took himself off for a cup of tea while Will saw the fracture clinic staff and got a lecture about the swelling and resting it in a sling. Then the cabbie took him home, after Will had bribed the man to go down his track.

'Blimey, gov, it's a miracle nobody's got stuck on this,' he said in a broad Cockney accent.

'Mmm,' Will agreed noncommitally, saying nothing about Lucie. He gave the man a hefty tip, crawled into the house and greeted Bruno with guarded enthusiasm.

'Hello, mate. Good dog, get off. Ouch!' He raised his arms out of reach, kneed the dog out of the way and sat down at the table with his arms in front of him, safe. Now all he needed was some pills, and they, of course, were in his pocket. Could he get them out?

He struggled, but came up with them, and even

managed to open the lid. Amazing. He took two, thought about another and put the lid back on. He'd have more later. In the meantime, he was going to stretch out on the sofa with the dog at his feet and have forty winks…

'Hello, Lucie. How are you doing?'

She looked up from her paperwork and smiled at Richard Brayne, the senior partner. 'Oh, hi, there. I'm fine. I don't know where Will is—have you seen him?'

'Gone to the fracture clinic and then home, he said.' Richard settled himself beside her and pushed a mug of tea across the table to her. 'You must be doing well if he'll leave you alone all ready.'

'Or he feels like death warmed up, which is more likely,' Lucie said drily, harbouring no illusions about her brilliance or Will's understanding of it. 'I suppose he wants me to cover his evening surgery—is he on call tonight, by any chance, just to add to the joys?'

Richard shook his head and grinned. 'No. You get lucky. We have night cover—a co-operative. You don't have to do any nights. Will doesn't—he has too much to do on the farm.'

Lucie tipped her head and looked searchingly at Richard, puzzled. 'On the farm?' she asked. 'Such as what?'

'Oh, I don't know, fencing the fields, mending the barn, doing up the house, getting the cottage ready for guests. He's always busy. Just at the moment he's redoing the ground floor of the house, I think—or he was.'

Lucie was relieved. She had wondered, for a moment there, if he had masses of stock all starving to death without him—stock she was about to have to look after. She didn't mind the dog or the cat, and she'd get used to the snorting horse given time, but anything more agricultural was beyond her.

It was a pity, she thought on her way back there later that evening, that Will didn't spend some of that time being busy doing the drive. She picked her way along it with caution, and went in to find him sprawled full length on the sofa.

Bruno had greeted her rapturously, whining and wagging and pushing his great face into her hand, and she'd patted him and done the 'good dog' thing, and had then looked for Will.

And there he was, spark out, looking curiously vulnerable this time. There was a sling round his neck but the arm was out of it, propped beside him on a pillow with a cool pack over the gap in the back of the plaster. He'd obviously been ticked off at the fracture clinic, she thought with wry amusement, and was now doing as he was told.

Or perhaps the pain had finally penetrated his common sense. Whatever, he was now doing what he should have been doing ever since he'd hurt himself.

Finally, she thought, and then wondered what was for supper.

Whatever she cooked, she realised. She went into the kitchen, followed by the clearly hopeful dog, and fed him first. The cat materialised at the sound of Bruno's bowl clunking round the floor, and she fed her, too.

'OK, guys, what about us?' she asked, and Bruno cocked his head on one side for a moment, before going back to his optimistic licking.

She found some steak mince in the freezer, and onions and tinned tomatoes and some ready-made Bolognese sauce, and in the cupboard next to the sink, under the first-aid kit, she found a bag of pasta shells.

Easy—and he could eat it without difficulty. She threw it together, dished up and went and woke him.

'Supper's ready,' she announced, and he propped himself up groggily on his left elbow and peered at her out of dazed eyes.

'Supper?'

'Spag Bol. Well, pasta shells, anyway.'

'Oh, God.' He pulled a face and flopped back down on the cushions. 'Right at the moment, I can't think of anything I want less.'

She stared at him in amazement, then flipped. 'Fine,' she said tightly. 'I'm sure it'll find a more appreciative audience.'

And she stalked into the kitchen, seized his plate and scraped it into the dog's bowl, just as Will came through the doorway.

'What the hell are you doing?' he asked, stunned.

She banged the bowl down defiantly. 'You said you didn't want it.'

'No, I said I couldn't think of anything I wanted less than food. That didn't mean I wouldn't have eaten it! Hells teeth, woman!'

He stared with evident dismay at the dog, who had swallowed the plateful almost whole and was busy doing the dish-licking thing again.

Throwing her one last disbelieving look, he let his breath out on a sharp sigh, turned on his heel and went back into the sitting room, banging the door behind him.

Whoops. OK. So she'd overreacted. Hardly the first time, but he just seemed to set her off. She looked at her own food with regret. She could give it to him…

Or she could eat it, and he could contemplate the wisdom of thinking before he spoke. She was sure he managed it with his patients, so why not her?

No. She was eating it. All of it. Every bite.

It nearly choked her.

Will was starving. Only pride prevented him from going into the kitchen and making himself something to eat—pride and the fact that Lucie was in there with the radio on, singing along to some ghastly noise and chattering to the dog, who was her devoted slave.

'Fickle beast,' he mumbled, flicking through the television channels with the remote control in his reluctant left hand. He found a wildlife programme, and settled down to watch it, disturbed only by the noise from the kitchen.

After five minutes, it had driven him crazy. He stood up, walked over to the door and yanked it open, just stifling the little yelp of pain in time. 'Do you suppose you could turn that bloody awful racket down?' he snarled, and kicked the door shut again, retreating to the sofa to nurse his throbbing wrist.

'Sor-ry,' she carolled through the door, and then started humming and singing, which was worse, because she had a throaty, sexy voice that did unforgivable things to his libido.

He turned the TV up in self-defence, and forced himself to concentrate on the mating habits of some obscure Australian spider. Riveting it wasn't, and finally he went upstairs to bed, propped himself up and read a book until he'd heard Lucie settle for the night.

Then, like a fugitive in his own home, he crept down to the kitchen, raided the bread bin and managed painfully and raggedly to hack the end off the loaf.

He found a chunk of cheese in the fridge, looked in despair at the tub of olive-oil spread and realised that the effort was more than he could be bothered to make. He wrapped the cheese in the wavering doorstep of dry bread, bit the end off and poured a glass of milk. It would have to do. Anything else was beyond him.

He carried the rustic little snack up to bed, wondering as he went where Bruno was, and then saw him through the crack in Lucie's door, curled up across the foot of her bed, one eye open and tail waving gently in apology at his defection.

Lucie was scrunched up at the top, forced out by the dog, and he smiled nastily. Good. Serve her right. If there was any justice Bruno would be sick on her floor and she'd have to clear it up—and lying like that she'd almost inevitably wake up with a crick in her neck.

He sighed and shook his head. Lord, she really brought out the worst in him, but she was so disruptive! He was used to silence, broken only by the sounds of nature or by the television or radio if he chose to have them on, which he often didn't.

It wasn't her fault she was here, of course. The sooner he got the bed ordered, the sooner he could have his peace and quiet back. He vowed to do it the next day.

First thing in the morning…

CHAPTER FOUR

'WHAT do you mean, you can't do it till next week?'

'Sorry, sir, all our carpet-fitters are busy. It's because of the spring, you see.'

Will didn't. All he saw was the next week stretching ahead of him, fighting with Lucie for his personal space.

'But surely you can manage one small room.'

'That's what they all say, sir,' the salesman told him cheerfully. 'Next Wednesday's the earliest we can possibly get to you.'

'But I have to have it!' He heard the rising, frenzied tone and cleared his throat, dropping his voice an octave and striving for authority. 'I really have to have it,' he insisted, and then added coaxingly, 'Can't you manage this Friday? Perhaps for an incentive payment?'

'Not even if you double it, sir,' the man said implacably. 'If you really are in such a hurry, I suggest you buy a piece off the roll and fit it yourself.'

'I might just do that,' he lied. 'Elsewhere.' If he had arms. Hah. He would have hung up with a flourish, but remembered just in time that it would hurt too much. Instead, he replaced the receiver with exaggerated care and swore, just as Lucie came back into the consulting room bearing two cups of coffee and a pile of patient envelopes.

'No joy?' she said sweetly, plonking the mug down in front of him, and if he'd had two hands, he would have strangled her while she was in range. Instead, he withdrew into dignity.

'There are other firms,' he said tautly. 'I shall keep trying. Are those this morning's notes?'

'No, tomorrow's. I thought we could get ahead.'

'Don't get sarky,' he growled, and her lips twitched. Aggravating woman. He dragged his eyes off her lips and tried to stop fantasising about them. He had to concentrate…

Will seemed to be getting a little better, Lucie thought as the day wore on, if his temper was anything to go by. He was crabbier than ever, possibly from pain, but more likely because now he was over the initial shock of his fall, the enforced inactivity was starting to get to him. By all accounts he was usually a busy person, and just now he was having to put up and shut up. It clearly didn't sit well on him.

Nor did not being able to drive, and her refusal to drive his car instead of hers. 'I hate it,' she'd insisted. 'We take mine or we don't go—or you can pay for a taxi.'

It hadn't really been fair, and in truth there was nothing at all wrong with the bigger car. It was easy to drive, but she was used to hers, and anyway, it was the principle.

So he'd folded himself up and threaded himself through the door like a camel through the eye of the needle, and sat in grim-lipped silence most of the time they were out.

And then, after their last call, he climbed out of the car and winced, and she noticed he was limping.

Oh, blast. Guilt washed over her, and she hurried after him.

'Are you OK?' she asked with genuine concern, and he shot her a look like a shard of ice.

'Just peachy. How the hell do you think I am?'

She shrugged. 'Just asking.'

'Well, don't bother,' he snapped. 'Everything hurts like the devil.'

'Did you take your painkillers earlier?' she asked, and got another murderous look for her pains.

No, then. She made him a drink, and they talked through her calls until it was time for her afternoon clinic, and then, because it was a shared antenatal with the midwife and she had plenty of supervision, he took himself off to an empty consulting room.

'To sort this darned carpet out,' he said with determination, and she pitied the salesmen he was about to browbeat into submission.

She enjoyed the antenatal clinic. She'd always liked maternity, mainly because it was the one branch of medicine where everyone, by and large, was well. She felt her first set of triplets, and listened to their heartbeats, and discussed the management of the delivery with the midwife and the mother, Angela Brown.

It had been planned that she would have a hospital delivery by Caesarean section, and was being seen alternately at the hospital and the GP clinic. As the time went on, she would transfer entirely to the hospital, and although she was happy to do that for the sake of the babies, she expressed regret that it couldn't be a more normal birth.

'Are you looking forward to it?' Lucie asked,

wondering how she'd cope with three at once. Apparently she wasn't the only one wondering.

'Actually, I'm dreading it,' the patient confessed. 'I don't know how I'll manage. My mother's said she'll help, and my husband's going to take some time off, but it's going to be hell at first, and we're only in a small house. This wasn't exactly planned, and I was going back to work afterwards, but there's no way I can afford to pay child care for three!'

Good grief, Lucie thought. Accidental triplets on a tight budget? Rather her than me.

They finished their clinic, and she found Will in the office, hunched over a cup of tea. He looked up at her as she approached, and his lip moved a fraction. A smile? Perhaps his face muscles were on a tight budget, like Mrs Brown, she thought, and stifled a chuckle.

'Got your carpet sorted?' she asked, and a frown replaced the sorry excuse for a smile.

'More or less. I've had to pay more, but it comes on Monday. I thought it was worth it.'

She ignored the implied insult. 'So we'll be stuck with each other over the weekend,' she said breezily. 'I dare say we'll survive.'

He muttered something inaudible, and she felt another flicker of irritation and hurt. How silly of her. It wasn't personal, he just liked his space, she told herself. 'How about the bed?'

'From the same place. It'll come later in the day. I've arranged to leave them a key. Security's not a problem—nobody ever goes down my track except for the occasional dog walker who's got mislaid on the footpath from the ferry.'

She settled her chin on her hands and looked

across the table at him, wishing he wasn't quite so prickly with her. 'Tell me about this ferry,' she said, trying to bridge the gulf between them. 'When does it run? I've looked and looked, but I can't see anything.'

'You won't. It doesn't exist. It's just the name of the little jut of land. It used to be a chain ferry that crossed the mouth of the river, but they built a bridge further up. The only thing left is the name.'

'Oh.' And that was the end of that attempt at conversation. She switched to Mrs Brown and her triplets. 'I saw your triplet lady,' she told him. 'She's worried about how she'll cope.'

'She needs to,' he told her bluntly. 'Her husband's quite demanding, and I can't see him tolerating slipping standards. He didn't want her to have one—pressed for a termination before they even discovered it was three.'

Lucie was shocked. 'She didn't tell me that,' she murmured slowly. 'How sad. I wonder if they'll survive?'

'The triplets, or the Browns?'

'I meant the Browns, but all of them, really. The babies seem quite small.'

'Triplets often are, especially at term, and who knows what'll happen to them all? In their financial situation three babies is the last thing they need. Sometimes I'm glad I'm a GP, not a social worker.' He leant back, easing the kinks out of his shoulders and wincing. 'Right, what's next? No surgery tonight—no more calls to make. Do you have paperwork to deal with, or can we go?'

She blinked. 'No surgery?'

'Nope. Not on Tuesdays. Not for me, anyway.'

'Oh. Well, we can go, then. I'm all up to date. How about you? Are you supposed to go back to the fracture clinic?'

He held up his arm, and for the first time she saw the brand-new lightweight cast. 'Oh! You've been!'

'Ten out of ten,' he drawled sarcastically. 'Took you long enough to notice. I went while you were doing the antenatals.'

'That was very quick.'

'I charmed the plaster nurse,' he said, deadpan, and she wondered how on earth he'd done that. There was precious little sign of his charm being exercised around her. She pushed back her chair and stood up. 'Shall we go, then?'

'Sounds like a fine idea.'

He winced again as he threaded himself back into the car, and hit his head on the doorframe as he sat down. She ignored the muttered oath, and let him struggle with the seat belt for a moment before helping him with the clip.

'You really are rather big for this car, aren't you?' she conceded.

'Oh, the penny's dropped,' he said with thinly veiled sarcasm. 'Of course, a less obstructive person...'

He let the rest of the sentence hang, and she snapped her mouth shut and declined to comment. She was damned if she was going to tell him *now* that she'd decided to take his car in future. Let him stew on it for the night.

Talking of which...

'Should we call into a supermarket on the way and pick up some food? There's not a lot in your fridge.'

'Good idea. We can buy some ready meals so you don't have to cook.'

She shot him a sideways glance. Was that guilt after his reaction to her spaghetti dish last night, or a dig at her choice of menu? Whatever, if he chose the food, he couldn't complain that it was the last thing he wanted.

Besides, she didn't like cooking anyway—not your everyday meat and two veg stuff. She liked tinkering about with fancy ingredients and playing with dinner party menus, but that was all. Anything else was just basic nutrition to keep body and soul together, and it bored her senseless. She didn't normally succumb, but she had to admit that just for today an instant meal sounded fine.

Convenience foods, Will decided, were not all they were cracked up to be. He pushed the soggy pasta twirls round in the over-seasoned sauce and sighed. It didn't smell anything like as good as the Bolognese she'd made last night—the Bolognese she'd fed to the dog.

Still, Bruno didn't complain when he put the cardboard dish on the floor and let the dog finish it. Twice running, Will thought. The dog would be huge.

'Don't you like it?' Lucie asked, and his stomach growled.

'I'm not really hungry,' he lied. 'I'll make myself something later.'

She gave him a searching look. 'Do you want me to make you something? A bacon sandwich?'

His stomach growled even more enthusiastically, and he gave a wry, bitter little smile. 'Why would you do that?'

She stood up, dumped her plate on the floor in front of the bemused but receptive dog and headed for the fridge. 'Because I want one and it would seem churlish not to make yours? Because I don't like instant food any more than I imagine you do? Because I need you alive if I'm to finish my training? Take your pick.'

How about, Because I'm sorry I gave your dinner to the dog? Will wanted to suggest, but he thought he'd quit while he was winning. 'A bacon sandwich sounds fine,' he muttered, and then sighed inwardly. Did that sound a bit grudging? Oh, hell. He wasn't used to being dependent, and he didn't like it. 'Please,' he added, too late to be spontaneous, and caught her stifled smile out of the corner of his eye.

'While you do that I think I'll go and change,' he said, and went upstairs and struggled one-handed out of the trousers he'd been wearing for work. They had a hook fastening that was possible even with his reluctant arms, and a little easy-running nylon zip, but the belt was more of a problem. He shut the end in the door, tugged gently until the buckle was free and then slid the end out.

He was getting resourceful, he thought as he squirmed and shuffled his way into his jogging bottoms. Learning to adapt. One thing that was almost impossible, though, was washing. He'd managed so far—more or less—by removing the support on his left wrist and using his left hand, but it wasn't satisfactory and it hurt like hell. And it relied on Lucie to put the support back on.

He thought of the bath longingly. What he wanted more than anything in the world was a long, hot soak, but he didn't think he could manage without help, and he was damned if he was asking Lucie Compton to supervise his ablutions!

Perhaps he should ask Amanda, he thought with a wry twist of humour, and shuddered. The thought was terrifying. She'd probably rub him down with a dandy brush, to get his circulation going.

A wonderful smell of frying bacon drifted up the stairs, and he arrived back in the kitchen just as she set two plates down on the table. 'There you are,' she said cheerfully. 'Wrap yourself around that.'

He did, wondering idly where his five portions of fruit and veg were coming from that day, but there was no point in worrying. He'd eat an apple later. He'd rather have an orange, but he couldn't work out how to peel it.

'Um—about washing,' Lucie said, and he nodded his head towards the washing machine.

'Help yourself. Powder's in the cupboard.'

'Not clothes—you,' she corrected, and he felt a skittering moment of panic and anticipation.

'Me?' Will croaked, almost choking on a bite of sandwich.

'Well, you must be in need of a good long soak, I would have thought. Do you want me to wrap your cast up in plastic bags and run you a bath?'

Was she a mind-reader, or did he smell worse than he realised?

He sniffed experimentally. 'Is it that bad?' he asked, groping for a light note and managing instead to sound defensive.

Lucie gave a pitying smile. 'I just thought, by now, you must be feeling pretty dreadful. Of course,' she added lightly, 'there's always Amanda—perhaps you'd like me to give her a call and ask her to come over? I'm sure she'd be more than willing...'

'That won't be necessary,' he growled, not quite knowing how to take her teasing. 'I think I can manage—and before you offer, I don't need my back washed.'

Her lips twitched. 'I'm sure I'll live. Still, you can always yell if you get stuck. I don't suppose you've got anything that everybody else hasn't got.'

Except a body that even in adversity seemed hell bent on betraying his baser feelings! He focused on his sandwich. 'Thanks. Maybe later,' he said, knowing full well that he was going to take her up on it. He just hoped he didn't get stuck, because the consequences didn't bear thinking about!

Lucie's imagination was running riot. He'd been ages, and she was hovering in her bedroom, listening to every splash and groan. The door wasn't locked, of course. Not even Will Ryan was that bent on self-destruction.

'Are you OK?' she called.

'Fine,' he yelled, then added a belated, 'thanks.'

She shook her head and smiled. He really, really hated this. He was so stubborn and fiercely proud, and it was all so unnecessary. She was quite happy to help—if he only could bring himself to be at least civil about it!

While she waited, she thought it might be interesting to have a look at the rest of the house. So far she'd only seen the rooms they were using, and there were some intriguing doors...

'Can I look round the house?' she asked, pausing outside the bathroom, and there was a splash and a stream of something not quite audible. She decided she should be probably grateful for that.

'Sure,' he said shortly. 'Be careful upstairs, there's no light. There's a torch just inside the door. Mind the holes.'

Holes? Her curiosity well aroused, she opened the door and went through, flicking on the torch. Its powerful beam pierced the gloom, slicing through the dusty air and highlighting the cobwebs. She suppressed a shudder and looked around. It was all but derelict, or it had been. The roof was obviously repaired now—she could see that through the gaps where the ceiling had fallen down.

Beneath the holes in the ceiling were areas of rotten boards, some taken up, others just gaping and twisted. Some showed evidence of recent repair, to her comfort. She looked at the untouched parts, and rolled her eyes.

'Mind the holes' didn't even begin to scratch the surface! It was on a par with 'a bit rough in places', and typical of Will's under-estimation of the awfulness of a situation. She had visions of him telling a dying patient he'd feel 'a little bit dicky for a day or two'.

Mind the holes, indeed. She picked her way carefully down the long room, sticking to the patched bits, and peered out of the windows towards the distant river, eerily silvered with moonlight.

It would be a beautiful view in daylight, and the windows were positioned to take full advantage. She could see it would be a lovely room once it was repaired. Rooms, in fact. It would easily make two.

She glanced round again. No wonder he was frustrated with inactivity, if this was waiting for him! She wondered if he'd done the work himself in the rest of the house, or if he'd had the builders in.

Poor builders, she thought pityingly, and went downstairs. Beyond the hall was the room below the one she'd just investigated, and she opened the door cautiously.

It was a mess. Well, to be exact it was a paint and tool and timber store, and was obviously where he kept everything for the work in progress. Again, it was a lovely room, with a huge inglenook fireplace on one wall and windows on three sides, and at least this one had a light that worked, after a fashion—if you counted a dangling bulb on the end of a bit of flex.

It was heavily timbered, and there was a smell of preservative in the air when she sniffed. Preservative and mice. Lovely.

She shuddered and backed quickly out, bumping into the dog and making herself jump.

'You scared me half to death, you stupid mutt!' she told him with a nervous laugh, conveniently ignoring the fact that it had been her fault in the first place. Conscious of the time, she went back upstairs and listened at the bathroom door, Bruno at her heels.

She could hear nothing. She knocked lightly. 'Will? Are you OK?'

Absolute silence.

'Will?'

Oh, lord, what if he'd slipped and drowned while she'd been downstairs out of earshot? She called his name again, then, when he still didn't reply, she pressed the lever down and inched the door open, her heart in her mouth.

Please, God, don't let him be dead, she prayed

silently, and, pushing the door open, she took a step in.

He was asleep, his plastic-wrapped arm propped up on the side of the bath, his head lolling back against the end of the tub, his lashes dark against his pale cheeks. He was out for the count. Unable to help herself, she let her eyes wander over him—purely professionally, of course, to see how his bruises were progressing.

The water was soapy, but not that soapy. Not so cloudy that she couldn't see every inch of his beautifully made body. Where his chest and knees protruded from the water, wiry curls clung enticingly to the damp, sleek skin, emphasising his maleness.

Not that it needed emphasising, not with the water as clear as it was and none too deep, either. Oh, lord.

She backed away, retreating to safety, and took a long, steadying breath before rapping sharply on the door. 'Will?' she called. 'You all right?'

There was a grunt and a splash, and another oath. His language was taking a battering, she thought with a smile.

'Yes, fine,' he said groggily. 'I'll be out in a minute.'

She hovered, listening to grunts and clonks and the odd cuss, until she heard the creak of a board and a sigh of relief that signalled his safe retreat from the bath.

Heaving a sigh of her own, she retreated with Bruno to the safety of the kitchen, turned on the radio and tried not to think about Will and his delectable naked body while she cleared up after their supper. It didn't work, of course, because she just managed to hit the love-songs happy hour, or that's what it sounded like.

One husky, softly crooned love song after another, all her old favourites, and, of course, she knew the words, so she sang along, misty-eyed and wistful, and for some reason an image of Will kept superimposing itself on her mental pictures, just to add to the delicious torture.

She wiped down the worktop, humming absently, her mind full of him. He'd looked so—oh, so male, so virile, so incredibly *potent.* A powerful aphrodisiac. The image was so clear she could have reached out and touched him, felt the smooth silk of his skin, the slight roughness of the hair, the taut, corded muscles beneath—

'Oh, hell,' she groaned, throwing the packet of bacon back into the fridge and trying to put him out of her mind. Not easy. She found herself singing again, the words she knew so well coming naturally to her lips.

Swaying gently to the music, she turned to clear the table, and there he was, standing in the doorway watching her, his face inscrutable.

The song died on her lips. Colour streaming up her cheeks, she turned hastily away, dumping the mugs and plates into the sink and busying herself with the kettle. Lord, she must have looked such a fool! 'Cup of tea?' she suggested briskly, and, stabbing the 'off' button on the radio she killed the slow, sexy song. In the shocking silence that followed she heard him coming towards her, his bare feet padding softly on the floor.

His voice was deep and husky, right behind her, and made all the little hairs on the nape of her neck stand to attention. 'Please. Could you put this on for me first and take off the plastic bag?'

Reluctantly she turned back to him, avoiding his eyes. Careful not to touch his fingers, she took the support bandage from him and gathered it up to slide it over his left arm. It was still swollen, but less so, the skin discoloured where the bruising had come out. She had an insane urge to kiss it better, and stifled it. She felt enough of an idiot without adding insult to injury.

'How is it?' she asked, easing the support over his fingers and trying still not to touch him.

'Still sore—ouch!'

'Sorry. It would be easier with one of those sleeve things to gather it on.'

'It's fine. Just pull it up. It doesn't hurt that much. I'm just a wimp.'

She gave a soft snort of laughter and eased the bandage into place, smoothing it down with hands that wanted to linger. His arm trembled under her fingertips, and she released it, glad to break the contact that was doing her no good at all.

'Want to do this yourself, or do you want me to do it?' she asked, indicating the shopping bags stuck over the cast to protect it from the water.

'Could you? I tried but I couldn't get the end of the tape.'

'Sure.' She found the end, managed to lift it with her nail and started to peel it off, but he yelped and yanked his arm away.

'Hell, woman! Mind the hairs!' he protested, and she gave him a syrupy smile and took his arm back in an iron grip.

'Now you know how it feels to have your legs

waxed,' she said unsympathetically, and eased off another inch, holding down the hairs with one hand and peeling with the other.

He bore it in grim-lipped silence, and when the bags were off and consigned to the bin, he massaged his sore skin gingerly and gave her a baleful look. 'Next time,' he said clearly, 'we'll use elastic bands.'

She had to turn away to hide the smile. 'How about that cup of tea now?' she said, feeling sorry for him despite herself.

He sighed. 'What I feel like is a damn great Scotch, but I suppose you're going to veto that on medical grounds?'

She arched a brow in surprise. 'Me, with the right of veto? I hardly think so. Since when was I your mother?'

He snorted. 'Doesn't stop you having an opinion on everything else,' he told her bluntly, and she felt a wash of guilty colour sweep her cheeks.

'It's entirely up to you what you do to your body,' she said virtuously. 'Don't hold back on my account.'

'I won't,' he retorted, reaching past her for a glass. He was just lowering it to the worktop when he caught his elbow on the bread crock and the glass slipped from his fingers, shattering on the hard floor.

Bruno rushed forwards to investigate, and as one they turned and yelled, '*No!*' at the poor dog. He stopped in his tracks, and Lucie looked down at Will's bare feet covered in sparkling slivers of glass.

'I should stand right there if I were you,' she told him.

'You don't say,' he murmured drily, and she shot him a look before fetching the dustpan and brush.

She swept carefully around his feet and then went over the whole floor before mopping it to pick up the last tiny shards.

'Right, you can move,' she told him, and with a sigh he sat down at the table and gave a resigned, wry smile.

'I'll settle for tea,' he said, picking a sliver of glass off his foot with his uncooperative right hand. 'God obviously didn't want me to have that Scotch.'

'Apparently not,' Lucie said, returning his smile. She made the tea, put the mugs on the table and they sat together in what could almost have been called companionable silence.

A truce? Wonders will never cease, Lucie thought, but her luck was about to run out. The phone rang, shattering the stillness, and Will answered it.

'For you,' he said, holding out the phone to her.

She took it, puzzled. Who on earth could it be?

'Hello?'

'Lucie? It's me.'

It took her a moment, she was so far away from the reality of London. 'Fergus?' she said, puzzled. 'Hi. How are you?'

Behind her she heard a chair scrape, and Will retreated to the sitting room, the dog following, nails clattering on the bare floor.

The room seemed suddenly empty, and she had to force herself to concentrate on Fergus. He was missing her. He said so, over and over again. He missed her company. He missed her smile. He missed sitting in her flat watching TV. He even missed her temper, he said.

'Do you miss me?' he asked her, and she was shocked to realise that, no, she didn't, not at all. She hadn't given him so much as a passing thought. She made some noncommital reply, and it seemed to satisfy him, probably because his ego was so undentable that he couldn't imagine she wasn't desolate.

'I thought I'd pop down and see you this weekend,' he told her.

'Ah, no. Um. I'm coming to town. I'll see you—I'll ring you from the flat.'

'We'll do lunch.'

'Lovely. I have to go, my tea's getting cold,' she said, and hung up after the briefest of farewells. It was only as she cradled the phone that she realised how cavalier it had sounded.

Poor Fergus. Still, he just wouldn't take the hint.

Her eyes strayed to the sitting-room door, open just a crack. Had Will heard her conversation? And if so, what had he made of it?

And what, in any case, did it matter?

Lucie wasn't sure. She knew one thing, though—it did matter. For some reason that wasn't really clear to her she wanted Will to have a good opinion of her, and it was nothing to do with her professional role and everything to do with a man with a body to die for and the temper of a crotchety rattlesnake.

Oh, dear. She was in big trouble…

CHAPTER FIVE

WILL was annoyed.

Lucie was going back to London for the weekend, and seeing Fergus, whoever the hell Fergus was. It was none of his business, of course, and he kept telling himself that, but it didn't stop it annoying the life out of him all week.

He had a phone call from Pam, to say that Dick had seen the cardiologist and was booked in for angioplasty. The angiogram had shown that he was a suitable candidate, and didn't need the more extensive intervention of open-heart surgery and a bypass operation.

On a professional level Will was pleased for them. On a personal level he was irritated that after all the time he'd spent cajoling Dick, it had been Lucie who'd talked him into taking this final step.

He told himself he was being a child, but she was getting to him. Getting to him in ways he didn't want to think about. Ways that kept him awake at night and then, when he finally slept, coloured his dreams so that even the memory of them made his blood pressure soar.

Crazy, because she drove him mad, but there was just something about her that made him restless and edgy, and made him long for things he couldn't have.

Like her, for instance.

Damn.

He forced himself to concentrate. She was in the

middle of surgery, and he was sitting in, keeping an eye on the time and watching her wheedle and cajole and sympathise and generally make everyone feel better.

Except young Clare Reid, who had come in on Monday with a cough and a disbelieving mother, and was back today with much worse symptoms and a mother who now was berating herself for not listening.

'I knew there was something wrong,' Mrs Reid was saying. 'I can't believe I didn't pay more attention. Whatever is wrong with her?'

Lucie checked through the notes, but the results weren't back. 'I'll check with the lab,' she promised. 'I'll call you back later today, because, I quite agree, it isn't right that she should be feeling so rough.'

Clare coughed again, and Lucie frowned and looked at Will.

'Sounds like whooping cough,' she said thoughtfully, and he frowned. Whooping cough? Although she could have a point…

'Let me ring the lab. If you two could wait outside while Dr Compton sees her next patient, I'll see what I can find out for you, and then we can have you back in and let you know if there's anything to report, OK?'

They nodded, and he went through to another room to make the call.

'Oh, yes, we were just sending that out to you. It's not whooping cough, but it's a related virus. Unfortunately it's not proved susceptible to any of the antivirals. Sorry. Oh, and by the way, it's not notifiable.'

He thanked them and went back to Lucie, and after

she'd finished with her patient, he told her the result.

'So what can we do for her? An anti-viral?'

He shook his head. 'Apparently not. Anyway, I should imagine she's past the acute stage of the illness. Any treatment now will be palliative. I would send her to a good pharmacist for advice on cough remedies, and tell her to sit in a hot, steamy bath and hang wet towels on her radiator at night and sniff Olbas oil.'

'Gorgeous. I wonder if she was still infectious on Monday?' Lucie said drily, and he grinned despite himself.

'Maybe. If so, knowing how my luck's running at the moment, I'll get it. All I need now is a good dose of mumps or chickenpox and my happiness will be complete.'

Lucie chuckled, and he looked at her and thought how incredibly sexy she was with that wide smile and her eyes crinkling with humour. It was just such a hell of a shame they weren't like this with each other all the time, but they weren't. For some reason he couldn't fathom, they seemed to rub each other up the wrong way the entire time.

He stifled a sigh. Probably just as well, really. He didn't need any more complications in his life, particularly not complications that he had to work with, and, like it or not, he and Lucie were stuck with each other for almost six more months.

And, he reminded himself, she was about to go back to London for the weekend to Fergus. Good. He'd have the house to himself again.

Bliss.

* * *

The flat seemed incredibly noisy. Lucie packed up the remainder of her things, and put what she didn't want with her into a cupboard in her room.

Her flatmate's partner was moving in—well, had moved in, more or less, some time ago, and was officially taking over her portion of the rent now, which was a relief. It also meant she could come back and stay for a while until she found another place, and she'd have a bolt-hole if necessary.

And it might well be necessary if Will Ryan was as grumpy for the next six months as he'd been for the last week. She sighed and threw the last few things into a case, clipped it shut and stood it by the wall. She didn't want to put it in her car until she left. Security wasn't London's strong point, and there was no point tempting fate.

She rang Fergus to arrange to meet for lunch, and he was round within minutes. Not quite what she'd had in mind, but he'd insisted on escorting her to their venue.

He spoiled her. He was rich enough to do it, but still, he spoiled her and took her to one of those exclusive places where you had to book weeks in advance. A man of power and influence, she thought with humour, but it didn't influence her at all. All the pomp and ceremony and discreet yet ostentatious service just got on her nerves, and she found herself thinking of eating bacon sandwiches in the kitchen with Will.

Not a good start to their lunch. Lucie forced herself to concentrate on Fergus, and realised that he was talking about himself as usual.

Finally, as they pushed aside the remains of their dark chocolate baskets with summer fruits in Kirch, topped with a delicate trail of cream and chocolate sauce in a puddle of raspberry coulis garnished with a sprig of mint, Fergus asked about her.

'So, how's life in the boonies?' he said, sitting back with an indulgent smile. 'I've missed you, you know.'

'You said—and it's fine,' she lied. 'There's a horse that grazes outside my bedroom window, and a dog called Bruno and a cat called Minnie—and my trainer's fallen off a ladder and broken his arm, so at the moment I'm helping him out a bit in the evenings and doing all the driving to work and back.'

'Poor old boy,' Fergus said kindly, and Lucie thought of Will, dark and irritable and pacing round like a wounded grizzly, and stifled a smile. Poor old boy? Not in this lifetime! Still, she didn't bother to correct Fergus. If he realised that Will was only thirty-three, he'd be down there like a shot, getting possessive and territorial, and Lucie would be forced to kill him.

And that would stuff up her Hippocratic oath and probably interfere more than a little with the progress of her career.

Oh, well. She'd have to keep them apart, which was no hardship. She couldn't see Fergus on Will's farm, picking his way through the puddles and pushing the dog aside when he was muddy and bouncy and over-enthusiastic—and for some reason she didn't care to analyse, she didn't want Fergus there anyway.

'So, how are the patients? Do they all chew straw and say, ''Ooh, aa-rr''?' Fergus asked her with a patronising smile.

She thought of Pam and Dick, lovely people—

people she'd been able to help by her presence there. 'Only half of them. The others are mostly inarticulate.'

He laughed as if she'd told the funniest joke in the world, and she sighed. She really couldn't be bothered with this.

'Fergus, it's been a lovely lunch,' she began, but he wasn't one to pick up subtle hints.

'And it's not over,' he announced proudly. 'I thought we could go back to my flat for coffee, and then I thought we could take a stroll through St James's Park, and then tonight I thought we could take in a show—there's that new one that's just opened with rave reviews. I'm sure I can get tickets.'

She was sure he could, too, but she wasn't interested.

'Fergus, I don't really have time,' she told him. 'I have to get back to Suffolk tonight—I'm on duty tomorrow.'

She waited for the lightning bolt to strike her down, but it didn't come. It should. She was starting to tell so many lies. She ought to just say, Look, Fergus, you're a nice man but not for me.

Actually, she had said it! She'd said it over and over again. Most recently last weekend, just before she'd left for Suffolk.

Blast.

'Perhaps next weekend,' he coaxed, and she sighed.

'I can't.'

'Then I'll come to you. I'll fit in round you. I'll buy some wellies and take a stroll while you're busy, and we can find a restaurant and eat out in the evening. I assume they do *have* restaurants?'

'I'm sure we can find a fish-and-chip shop,' she said drily, and he recoiled. Oh, lord, how had she ever let him talk her into this?

She realised with a sense of shock that she was feeling defensive about his attitude—an attitude she'd shared until this last week. How strange.

'I really have to go—I've still got a lot of clearing up to do at the flat before I leave,' she told him, adding another lie to the heap that teetered on the funeral pyre of her conscience.

'Wait for me. I'll pay the bill and take you back.'

'No, don't,' she said, hastily pushing him back into his chair. 'You stay and have coffee, and I'll get on. I've got some shopping to do on the way back.'

She stooped and kissed his cheek, thanked him again and made her escape into the fresh air, or what passed for it in London. She inhaled deeply. It was familiar and comforting, but somehow strange.

She went back to her flat, made coffee and waited till she thought she'd given her glass of wine time to clear her system, then left a note for her flatmate, threw her stuff into the car and headed back to Suffolk and Will.

The house seemed empty. At first Will revelled in the silence, listening to the songs of the birds and the gentle snort of Henry outside the window. Then, after he'd struggled to wash and dress, he went down to the kitchen and looked around for something easy to eat.

Cereal, he thought, and sat at the table with nothing to break the silence but the crunching of cornflakes and the sigh of the dog. No Lucie humming as she pottered, or chattering brightly about nothing in particular.

It was good, he told himself, but a sliver of loneliness sneaked in and made him restless. He went over to the cottage and let himself in, opening the windows and letting the air circulate. He'd had the old bed and carpet collected and taken away during the week, but the room still smelled musty, and today a man was coming to paint the ceiling.

His incapacity infuriated him. He was perfectly capable of doing all the things he'd just had to pay good money to have done, and much worse than that was having to rely on Lucie for his transport.

He went into the sitting room and looked around. She'd brought some of her things in here last weekend and stacked them in an untidy heap on one side, and he had a burning urge to know what she considered essential. A jumper spilled out of a carrier bag, a belt hung out of the side of a suitcase. And there, in a bag at the back, was a dog-eared teddy bear.

He found himself smiling, and frowned. It wasn't funny. She was hopelessly disorganised, and he had to turn her into a GP. What chance was there? She had to be highly ordered and disciplined to work in a modern practice with all the rules and regulations that applied.

Her cheerful disregard for convention might be all very well in a musician or an artist, but in a doctor it was a recipe for disaster.

Still frowning, he went back to the bedroom and sniffed. Not too bad. The clouds looked a bit threatening, so he closed the windows again, except for the little fanlight, and crossed the yard to his house. Amanda drew up just before he gained the safety of the back door, and bounded out of the car, waving cheerfully.

'Hi! How are you?' she asked, bearing down on him.

He sighed inwardly. 'Better, thanks. My left hand's almost back to normal,' he told her, waggling it rather further than it wanted to go and smiling to cover the wince. 'See? All but fixed.'

'Anything I can do? Shopping, cooking—washing?'

He thought of his back in the bath and nearly choked. 'No, no, it's fine,' he said hastily. 'I've got everything I need, and Lucie did my washing before she went away.'

Amanda's face brightened. 'She's gone?'

'Only for the weekend,' he corrected quickly. 'Just to sort out her flat.'

Her face fell again. 'Oh, well. If there's anything I can do, just holler.'

'I will. Thanks.' He retreated inside, closing the door with indecent haste, and sank down at the kitchen table. 'She's getting worse, Bruno,' he told the dog in an undertone. 'What are we going to do?'

Bruno wagged his tail, looking hopeful. 'Come on, then,' he said, relenting, and with a lot of wiggling and shoving and swearing he managed to get his boots on. They headed off down the track to the woods, turned left and followed the little path down through the edge of the wood amongst the bluebells.

It was beautiful, peaceful and still and restoring. He felt the tranquillity easing back into him, and, tucking his right hand into the pocket of his jacket, he strolled along, breathing in the cool, fresh air and listening to the sounds of the countryside while

Bruno fossicked in the undergrowth and chased interesting smells and the odd rabbit.

They reached the edge of the river and he sat down on a stone, ignoring the creeping damp and absorbing the glorious views. The sun was high now, and its warmth caressed his face and seeped through his jacket, driving out the chill.

Bliss. What more could a man possibly want?

Someone to share it with?

'Bruno!' he called, standing abruptly and heading back. He had someone to share it with—someone loyal and devoted and emotionally undemanding.

Well, perhaps not loyal. The mutt had spent the week on Lucie's bed, proving his fickle nature. Just because she was feeding him whole suppers, of course. He'd be her friend for life because of that.

He wondered what Lucie was doing now and who'd slept with her last night.

Fergus?

A writhing knot of something that surely wasn't jealousy wrapped itself around his gut and squeezed. Ridiculous. It was entirely her own business who she slept with!

He went back to the house, hooked his boots off and stomped upstairs. He really ought to be getting on with this room, he thought, and opened the door.

Frustration hit him like a fist in the chest. It would be weeks—months, probably—before he could get back to work in here.

Slamming the door, he went back downstairs and over to the cottage. Pete had arrived and set up his dustsheets, and was priming the ceiling so the damp mark didn't bleed through the new paint.

'Come and have a coffee while that dries,' he suggested, and Pete nodded.

'Will do, mate. Give us a few more minutes.'

'OK.'

Will went back to the kitchen and stared morosely at the washing-up in the sink. Lucie had bought him some huge rubber gloves that he could just about get on over the cast and support bandage, but putting them on was an act that required more patience than he would find in his lifetime, and he gave up. The washing up could wait. She'd be back tomorrow.

Late, probably, and overtired from her activities with Fergus.

'Fergus.' He spat the name, realising he was beginning to hate the man without any justification. Irrational, stupid behavior, he told himself, but the thought of someone—anyone—touching Lucie intimately made him want to kill.

Which was totally ridiculous, because there was no way he wanted her.

Was there?

It had been a lovely day, Lucie realised in surprise. Odd, how insulated from the weather she'd been in London. Much less aware.

Now, driving back down the once-unnerving track towards the house, she wound down the window and breathed in deeply. Something was flowering, and the heady scent wafted through the window. It was gorgeous. Humming to herself, she turned into the farmyard and saw a man in white overalls sitting on the steps by the back door, drinking tea.

Not Will. Her eyes scanned the yard, irrationally disappointed to find him missing, and then he came out of the back door armed with a biscuit tin, and she felt an involuntary smile curve the corners of her mouth.

He lifted one hand in a wave, and she pulled up outside the cottage and got out, strolling over. No London strut, no rush, no hurry, just an amble in the evening sun.

'Hi.'

'You're back early,' Will said, sounding almost accusing. 'I wasn't expecting you till tomorrow.'

Damn. He'd probably planned a quiet evening with a woman, she thought, and felt a soft tide of colour invade her cheeks. 'I'll keep out of the way,' she promised. 'If that's all right. Clearing up the flat didn't take as long as I thought.'

And for some reason she couldn't get away from Fergus quick enough.

'It's fine,' Will said shortly, leaving her with the distinct impression that it was far from fine and it was only good manners that prevented him from telling her where to go.

'Is it all right to put my things straight into the cottage?' she asked, and the man in the white overalls tipped back his baseball cap with one finger and shot her a searching look.

'Mind the bedroom—ceiling's wet and the air might be a bit damp for an hour or two.'

'I'll use the sitting room,' she promised, and since there was no offer of a cup of tea forthcoming, she took herself off and unloaded her car while they sat on the steps and watched her struggle.

Not that Will could do anything, but he could at least have put the kettle on, she thought.

And to think she'd been looking forward to coming back!

By Monday morning Lucie was ready to kill Will. He'd been remote and surly all weekend, and she'd got the distinct impression he was cross with her—but why? He'd said—so firmly that she'd dropped the subject like a hot brick—that she wasn't interfering with his plans.

Perhaps he was just in pain. He'd probably decided he didn't need pills any more, and she was the one to catch the flak. Well, damn him.

By the time they were ready for work he was as crotchety as a bear with a sore head, and when he went outside and sat firmly in the passenger seat of the Volvo, she couldn't be bothered to argue. She got the distinct impression he was spoiling for a fight, and she was damned if she was going to give him one!

Instead she smiled meekly, slid behind the wheel and drove up the track as if she were carrying a nuclear warhead in the back. He shot her a suspicious look, folded his arms across his chest and winced as he bent his left wrist.

Out of the corner of her eye she saw him shuffling his arms uncomfortably, and had to suppress her sympathy. He was being crabby and ungracious, and she had no intention of feeling sorry for him!

Her surgery got off to a flying start with the return of Mr Gregory, her overweight patient who was trying to lose weight and was suffering from indigestion. His pain was worse, and Lucie decided to take the bull by the horns.

'Have you had an ECG recently?' she asked, taking his blood pressure.

'No. Can't say I've ever had one,' he told her.

'Right. Just to eliminate it from our enquiries, then, I'd like you to see the nurse and have an ECG done, and we'll also get her to take some bloods to test for *Helicobacter pylori*.'

'Is that the gastric ulcer bug? A friend of mine had that not so long ago.'

'Really?' Lucie said, thoughtful. 'Is it possible you picked it up in the same place?'

'Maybe. We teach in the same school, and we went on a school trip together. The food was pretty rough.'

'I think it's hygiene rather than quality that matters, but it's possible it came from there. It can give painful symptoms. And while we wait for the results of that we can give you a drug to suppress the symptoms so you don't feel so bad. OK? So if you go and see the nurse, she can get it all under way, and I'll give you a prescription now for the thing to reduce your stomach acid. You should be much more comfortable.'

'So you don't think it's my heart, then?'

She shook her head. 'No, I don't, but I have to be sure. I can't just hope, I have to know, and so do you.'

He stood up. 'Thanks, Doc. When do I see you again?'

She looked at Will. 'How soon do the results come back?'

'Leave it a week,' he advised. 'They should be back then.'

'Next Monday, then,' Lucie suggested, and Mr Gregory nodded.

'Will do. Thanks again.'

She waited, after the door closed, for Will to comment, but he didn't. To her surprise, when she turned round he was slowly writing a comment on a piece of paper. Later, then, she thought, and sighed. Oh, well.

The carpet was down, the bed was in and Lucie was moving out.

Will gave her the bedding out of the little airing cupboard in the cottage, and watched her make the bed. It was a mistake. She ran a slender, capable hand over the sheet, smoothing it flat, and he imagined feeling its texture on his skin.

She plumped the pillows, dropped them in place, straightened and smiled at him, and he felt the heat balloon inside him.

'I'd help you with the quilt but I'm not sure I can be much use,' he said gruffly, and she shrugged and smiled again.

'It's not a problem. I can cope. Shall we christen the kettle?'

And he realised that he would get his kitchen back to himself now. No more cosy chats over tea, no more bickering over the menu or skiving off the washing-up.

No more radio. That was a plus.

No more Lucie singing along to it with that slightly husky voice. That had to be a plus—didn't it?

He went and put the kettle on, as much to distance himself from Lucie and the bed as anything. There wasn't any milk, and there were no teabags or coffee granules, so he went over to his house and brought a selection of bits and pieces to start her off.

By the time the kettle boiled, she was in the kitchen looking hopeful, and he took two mugs down awkwardly with his left hand and looked at her.

'Tea or coffee?'

'Is there a choice?'

'I've even brought you over some hot chocolate.'

Her smile seemed to light up the room, and it touched his heart. 'Oh, thanks. I ought to go shopping. I could do that now, actually, when we've had our tea. You could probably do with some stocking up, as well, couldn't you?'

'Probably. So did you want tea, or was that a figure of speech?'

'Tea. I'll make it, you sit down.'

So he sank gratefully into one of the comfy armchairs and waited, and a moment later she came round the corner from the kitchen area with two mugs and curled herself up in the other chair opposite him, her feet tucked up under her bottom and her nose buried in the mug.

It was so ridiculously homely and cosy that he nearly laughed, but it would have been a cynical, bitter laugh and she didn't deserve it. He wasn't sure why he felt like that, anyway. Frustration? Probably.

And now he was going to have to endure the joys of the supermarket with her. Wonderful. He scowled into his tea.

'Is it all right?' Lucie asked, and he looked up.

'What?'

'The tea. Is it all right? You gave it such a look.'

He laughed self-consciously. 'It's fine. Sorry. I was thinking about something else.'

'Lord, I hope it wasn't me,' she said with her husky chuckle.

'No,' he denied, and realised it was probably true. It wasn't so much Lucie as what she represented that was making him edgy and restless. He drank the tea too hot, and unfolded himself from the chair.

'I'll get ready for the supermarket.'

'Oh, you don't have to go!' she exclaimed. 'You look tired. Why don't you give me a list and stay here and have a rest? I'll get your shopping. You can owe me.'

And then, perversely, he felt disappointed.

Lucie screwed up her eyebrows and peered at his list. What on earth did that say? She should have asked him to translate. She had the distinct feeling that his writing was awful when he had a functioning arm. Now it was atrocious.

Liver? She shuddered gently, but it was on his list. OK, liver, then. She looked in the chiller cabinet, fished out what looked as if it might be the right sort and volume, and dropped it in the trolley. Gross.

She moved on, shaking her head over his list on several more occasions, and finally she reached the end. Oh, well, what she didn't have she—or he—could manage without for another day or two. She was tired, and she wanted to get settled into the cottage.

She was looking forward to being herself, to relaxing and not having to worry about disturbing Will, or doing any of the thousands of things that seemed to make him scowl.

* * *

'Liver?'

'It was on your list.'

'Was it, hell. Show me.'

She pulled the list out of her pocket and thrust it under his nose. 'See? Liver.'

'Limes,' he corrected with a short sigh. 'It says limes.'

She looked at him as if he'd grown two heads. 'Limes? Why on earth would you want limes?'

'To squeeze over grilled chicken breasts, with salad. I just fancied some. I *hate* liver.'

A smile lit up her face. 'Hey, we agree on something,' she said cheerfully. 'Never mind, I'm sure Bruno likes liver.'

Will gave the dog a disgusted look. 'I'm sure he does. Are you certain you two aren't in league?'

She took out the rest of his shopping while he watched and commented, and then handed him the bill. 'Charge the dog for the liver,' she advised, and then headed for the door. 'I'm just going to put my shopping away, and I'll be back for my overnight things.'

He nodded and watched her go, and then found himself standing at the window, watching her across the yard. The curtains in the cottage were open, and he could see her moving around, putting her shopping away in the cupboards and the fridge.

Liver, he thought disgustedly, and caught the dog's eye. 'Definitely in cahoots,' he growled, and Bruno wagged his tail cheerfully.

'You're going to have to sleep with me tonight, sport, and don't get any ideas about lying on the bed, either. She's spoiled you.'

The dog woofed softly, and Will relented and

scratched his ears. 'You're a good boy, really,' he murmured, and the dog collapsed on the floor at his feet, quite content. He went back to watching Lucie, and a few moments later he saw her crossing the yard.

She came in with a smile, and ran upstairs, returning a few minutes later with an armful of clothes and her washbag. 'I can get the rest tomorrow. I want to unpack some things tonight.'

He nodded, and then there was an awkward pause.

'Thank you for putting up with me until the cottage was done,' she said softly, and he felt churlish for his resentment.

'It's been a pleasure,' he said, and she laughed.

'Liar.'

He looked down at his hands. 'No, really. You've been very kind while I've been out of action. You've done all sorts of things for me. I'm sorry I haven't been more grateful. I just—I'm usually pretty self-sufficient and it comes a bit hard having to rely on someone else.'

He looked up again, and their eyes locked. 'I'll help you over there—you've got your hands rather full to open the doors.'

'Oh—thanks.'

At the door of the cottage he paused, curiously unwilling to go in. 'I'll leave you to it,' he said gruffly, and she went up on tiptoe and kissed his cheek.

'Thanks,' she murmured.

'Any time,' he said, and then something shifted, tilting the world on its axis. For a moment neither of them moved, and then as if in slow motion he lowered his head and kissed her lips.

For a second they both froze, and then she melted, her mouth soft and yielding, and he could taste her. Heat shot through him, shocking him, and he drew away.

'Goodnight, Lucie,' he said, his voice husky with the desire that was ripping through him, and he backed away, turning on his heel and striding away from her, towards his house and sanity.

He didn't look back.

CHAPTER SIX

LUCIE watched Will go, striding away from her as if she might give him some terrible disease. And yet his kiss had been so tender, so gentle and coaxing—so unlike him.

At first. Then it had taken off, and she'd wanted to hold him, but her arms had still been clutching the clothes in front of her, so that the only point of contact had been their fevered mouths.

The heat had threatened to consume her, but it had been over in seconds, so brief that now she could hardly believe it had happened, and Will had pulled away, his face stunned.

That he hadn't meant the kiss to happen was obvious. What was less obvious to Lucie was why it had been such a beautiful and tender kiss. A cherishing kiss. A needy kiss. Lord, so needy…

Lucie swallowed hard, turned and pushed the door shut behind her, heading for the bedroom. The clothes had to be hung up, her wash things put away in the bathroom, and she could do with sorting out some of her other clothes that had been in a suitcase all week.

Nevertheless, she sank down on the edge of the newly made bed, the clothes still in her arms, and relived the touch of Will's mouth on hers. She could still feel the imprint of his lips, the soft velvet texture so at odds with the slight rasp of his chin.

He'd angled his mouth over hers, taking advantage

of her willing response to deepen the kiss, and it had grown a little wild then, suddenly. Until he'd pulled away.

Perhaps it was just as well she'd moved out of the house and wasn't going to be exposed to him crossing the landing to the bathroom in nothing more than a pair of jogging bottoms hanging loosely on his hips!

Too much sex appeal for comfort, Lucie thought, and for some reason she had an image of Fergus—bland, mild-mannered, successful and totally without that edge that made Will so very tempting. Fergus was safe—and Lucie realised with some astonishment that she didn't want to be safe. She was sick of being safe. She'd been safe too long, and now she wanted more.

She wanted Will.

It was equally clear to her, however, that Will didn't want her—or, rather, that he didn't *want* to want her. Because he did want her, that much she was utterly sure of.

A thread of excitement wove itself along her veins, and she stood up, humming softly to herself, and put her clothes away, then started on her boxes. She pottered for ages, quietly working through the strange collection of things she'd acquired over the years, and thinking of Will.

Finally the room was clear and she could find a chair to sit in, so she made a hot drink and curled up in the chair with the TV on and watched the late news. She could see Will's house through the window, and after a while she heard him calling Bruno, then the kitchen light went off and a few moments later the bedroom light went on.

She wondered how he was coping, and if there was anything he couldn't manage to do for himself. She should have offered to help him still, but she'd got the distinct impression he'd wanted her out as quickly as possible.

No wonder, if all that heat was steaming gently under his collar the entire time! She turned off the television and got ready for bed, enjoying the privacy of a house of her own for the very first time.

Well, sort of enjoying it. It seemed terribly quiet, with not even so much as a passing car to break the silence, and every creak seemed curiously sinister. She wondered what Will was thinking, and if he, too, was remembering their kiss.

She climbed into bed and picked up her diary off the bedside table. She had more than a week's worth to write up, and with all that had happened she was going to be up all night doing it. What on earth had possessed her to pack it?

She wrote furiously, and finally arrived at today's entry. She wrote, 'He kissed me. Don't think he meant to. Don't think he means to do it again—we'll have to see about that! I have a feeling he needs rescuing from himself. It can be my next challenge—RESCUING DR RYAN.'

With a smile on her lips, she put the diary down, turned out the light and snuggled under the quilt, falling asleep almost instantly.

Will had hardly slept a wink. Bruno had insisted on lying across his feet, so he'd woken with two more compromised limbs and a deep and abiding hatred of things canine.

He washed and dressed with difficulty, fed the dog

and cat and pulled on a coat, shoving his feet into his boots. 'Come on, pest,' he said to Bruno, who was still fruitlessly chasing his empty bowl around the floor. 'Let's go and see the river—*if* I can walk that far.'

Bruno, blissfully unaware of his master's sarcasm, shot out of the back door and ran over to the cottage, then sat whining by the door. Will sighed.

'Get in the queue,' he muttered, and turned towards the track. 'Come on, dog. We don't have women in our lives—remember?'

After a last, lingering look at the door, Bruno turned and trotted obediently at his side all the way down to the river and back, cheerfully retrieving dead goodness-knows-whats and presenting them to Will. And gradually the dawning of a beautiful day drove out the blues and restored the peace in his soul, and he wandered back to the house with Bruno in tow. The dog had brought home a souvenir, a festering bit of rabbit leg dangling from his jaws, and he offered it to Will with a grin.

'You're revolting,' he said disparagingly, just as they turned the corner and found Lucie poised at the back door of his house. She looked at the dog and her eyes widened.

'Yuck, Bruno, that's foul! You horrid dog!'

'He's just being a dog. They are foul. Have you got a problem with the cottage?'

She shook her head. 'No. I just thought I ought to pop over and see if there was anything you needed help with—you know, with your arms and everything.'

A genuine offer? Or any feeble excuse to interfere in his life?

How could he tell? He couldn't, so he played safe.

'I'm fine,' he said, possibly a bit shortly, and after a second's startled hesitation she ran down the steps to the yard and gave him a fleeting little smile.

'That's OK, then. Shout if you need anything. I'll be ready to go in twenty minutes.'

And she was gone, all but running round the corner and leaving him nursing a massive guilt trip and a whole truckload of resentment as a result.

Hell. Life had been much simpler before he'd met her!

The rest of the week passed. That was all Lucie could say. The days were sometimes easy, sometimes difficult. The evenings were long and lonely, and the nights—she didn't want to think about the nights. Suffice it to say Will featured extensively in her dreams, and she began to wonder if she'd bitten off more than she could chew with her challenge to rescue him. Certainly she didn't seem to be making any progress.

Nor did her first patient on Friday morning. Mr Gregory's stomach was still proving a problem, pending the result of his blood test, but at least the ECG had proved normal, as she'd expected.

'I think I ought to start him on the treatment,' Lucie said to Will thoughtfully, just before Mr Gregory came in. 'If he's back because it's worse, I have to do something.'

'The treatment's very expensive, and might mask other symptoms,' he warned.

'So what would you do?'

He leant back in his chair, steepled his fingers and pressed them against his lips, peering at her thoughtfully. 'I don't know. Encourage him to wait and give the palliative treatment which was all we had until a short while ago.'

'I've done that. He's coming back. There must be a reason.'

Will shrugged. 'Reassure him. I think he's worried. We'll see.'

Will was right, of course. He was just worried and wanted reassurance that it wasn't, in fact, his heart. Finally satisfied that he was in no danger, Mr Gregory left, and Lucie finished her surgery without any further complications. She was just about to leave on her calls when the receptionist took a call from an anxious mother whose seventeen-year-old daughter was vomiting and looking very peaky.

'We'll call in—we have to go that way,' Will told the receptionist. 'I doubt if it's anything urgent—probably a hangover.'

'Sceptic,' Lucie said with a chuckle, and his mouth cracked into a fleeting smile.

'Absolutely. That's the modern youth for you. No restraint and no stamina.'

Lucie shook her head, stifling the smile. 'Such a sweeping generalisation. I bet you were really wild at university.'

A wry grin tilted his lips. 'I had my moments, I confess—although nothing like they get up to these days.'

'Ah, poor old man,' she teased, and he snorted.

'Can we get on, please? We've got another call to fit in now and, hangover or not, it'll take time.' He scooped up the notes in his right hand, and Lucie noticed that it seemed to be co-operating fairly well.

He'd been using it much more in the last few days, and it was obviously less painful.

Not good enough, though, that he could drive yet, and she could tell that was frustrating him. Will went out to the car park, went round to the driver's side, swore colourfully under his breath and went round to the passenger side instead.

'When can you drive?' she asked him, and he glowered at her over the roof of the car.

'Not until the cast is off. I always advise my patients not to drive until they've had the cast off and their arms are functioning normally without undue pain. It's for insurance reasons, really.'

'So I suppose you ought to take your own advice.'

He snorted. 'Very probably.'

'Mmm,' she agreed, sucking in her cheeks and ducking behind the wheel before he could see the smile that was sure to show in her eyes.

He appeared beside her, shooting her an unreadable look. 'In the meantime,' he continued, 'you're stuck with me, and vice versa, so we might as well both make the best of it.'

He then proceeded to spend the entire journey telling her she was in the wrong lane or had missed a turning.

'For God's sake, didn't you see that cyclist?' he yelled as they neared their destination, and she glowered at him and turned on the radio. Anything was preferable to listening to him ranting!

'Do we have to have that on?'

She pulled over, switched off the engine and turned to face him. 'Will, I am an adult,' she said with exaggerated patience. 'I have a current, valid, clean driving licence. I do not need you giving me a hard time just because you want to be able to drive and can't! I've been driving for ten years and I've never had an accident or been pulled up by the police.'

'That's a miracle!'

'And I don't need you telling me how to do everything all the time!' she finished. 'Now, either we're going to do this in my car, or you're going to shut up, because frankly I've had enough!'

He turned away, letting out a short, harsh sigh and glaring hard enough to melt the glass. 'I'm sorry,' he said gruffly, and she nearly choked. An apology? From Will?

'Thank you,' she replied, struggling for a humble tone. 'Now, where do you want me to go from here—apart from hell?'

He turned and met her eyes, and gave a rueful grin. 'It's not personal,' he confessed. 'I just can't delegate—and I hate being driven. The only accident I've ever been in, someone else was driving. I find it hard not being in control.'

'That's because you're a control freak,' Lucie told him drily. 'If it's any help, I passed first time and I've taken my advanced driving test as well.'

'And passed?' he asked her, picking up on her careful phrasing.

She grinned. 'Not exactly—but I didn't fail drastically.'

He gave a soft snort and shook his head, but the tension was gone, and at least the atmosphere in the car was restored.

'So, where to, boss?' she asked again, and he directed her, and for the rest of the journey he kept his mouth firmly shut.

They arrived at the house of the girl with the 'hangover', and her mother opened the door.

'Mrs Webb? I'm Dr Lucie Compton, and I'm covering for Dr Ryan at the moment. I've come to see Harriet.'

'Oh, I am glad you're here. She's looking awful. Come on up.' She led them to a bedroom where a thin, pale girl lay under a quilt, looking extremely unwell. Her skin was waxy, her eyes were sunken and she looked exhausted. It was certainly more than a simple hangover.

'This is Harriet,' her mother said. 'Harriet, darling, it's the doctor.'

Lucie smiled at her gently and crouched down beside the bed. 'Hello, I'm Lucie Compton, and this is Dr Ryan,' she told the girl. 'I'm covering his patients at the moment. Can you tell me how you're feeling?'

'Sick,' Harriet said weakly. 'So sick. I never feel very hungry, but just now I feel really ill if I eat.'

'Are you being sick?' Lucie asked her.

She nodded. 'A bit. Not enough. I feel I want to do more, but all I can do is retch.'

'Any diarrhoea, or constipation? Any other tummy problems?'

Harriet shook her head. 'Not really.'

'Mind if I have a look at your tummy?' Lucie asked, and at a nod from Harriet she peeled back the quilt.

In contrast to her thin face and arms, her abdomen seemed bloated, and Lucie lifted her nightshirt out of the way and examined the skin. There was no sign of abnormal colouration, no hot spots or rashes, but there was a definite mass in the midline, consistent with an aortic aneurysm or an intestinal obstruction.

'Are you bringing up any blood?' Lucie asked, feeling round the margins of the mass.

'A little—sort of streaks of it.'

'Red, or brown?'

'Oh—I don't know. Maybe both. Brown gritty bits sometimes.'

Lucie shot a look over her shoulder at Will. 'How good are your hands? I'd like a second opinion.'

'I'm sure I can manage,' he murmured, and, bending over Harriet, he worked his way over the mass, his fingers probing gently. A fleeting frown crossed his brow, and he quirked an eyebrow at Lucie.

'It feels like a mass in the stomach,' he said, confirming her fears, and Lucie nodded.

She scanned Harriet's hair, and, yes, it seemed thin and wispy.

'Harriet, have you ever eaten your hair?' she asked gently.

'Oh, no!' her mother said. 'She used to, when she was tiny, so she always had it short. Right up until two years ago, but we thought she'd outgrown it.'

'I have!' Harriet protested feebly. 'I don't do it any more, I swear!'

'You might be doing it in your sleep,' Will suggested. 'It happens, especially during times of stress, and I imagine you're doing the first year of your A-levels?'

Harriet nodded. 'Yes—and I have been worried. Do you think I've got a hairball or something?'

'Very possibly,' Lucie confirmed. 'I think you need to go to hospital for investigation, and if we're right, you'll have to have it removed. They'll know the best way of doing it. I'll contact the hospital now and get you admitted. Is that all right, Mrs Webb?'

Mrs Webb was sitting down on the end of the bed, looking shocked. 'A hairball?'

'The correct term is a trichobezoar,' Will explained. 'It's very rare, but the fact that she used to eat her hair points to it being highly likely in the light of her other symptoms. We do need to get it checked out as a matter of urgency, though.'

'So should I take her in now?'

Will shook his head. 'I would suggest we call an ambulance and admit her direct to the surgical team on take, and they can decide what they want to do. If you take her in yourself, you'll have to queue through Accident and Emergency, which isn't a good idea with Harriet feeling so unwell.'

'Mum,' Harriet said feebly, and Mrs Webb moved up the bed and put her arms round her distressed daughter.

'It's all right, darling. It'll be all right.'

'I thought I'd stopped!' she wept, and then started to retch again.

Will looked at Lucie. 'I think we need to mobilise the ambulance,' he said in an undertone. 'She's very weak, and I don't like the feel of that mass. It's utterly rigid and very large. I think her stomach's within an inch of rupture.'

'Me, too. Can I leave it to you to talk to them? You know who to refer to.'

He nodded. 'Mrs Webb, may I use your phone, please?' he asked, and she looked up.

'Oh. Yes, of course. There's one in the front bedroom, by the bed.'

He went out, and Lucie stayed with them, telling them more about the tests that might be performed and getting a little more history. She made some notes for the receiving surgical team, and by the time the ambulance arrived Harriet's bag was packed and Mrs Webb had contacted her husband and explained what was going on.

They all left together, Harriet and her mother in the ambulance, Lucie and Will to their next case, and as soon as they were out of earshot Lucie let out her breath in a rush.

'Wow. I've never seen anything like it,' she confessed.

'Nor have I. It's very rare, but there was a tragic case not all that long ago. I think it's all part and parcel of the pressure we put kids under. Look at Clare Reid, worrying because her father will be cross if she's sick and doesn't do well in her end-of-year exams. But this, I have to say, is much more serious. I wonder if she's got psychiatric history. Let me look in the notes.'

He fumbled through them as Lucie drove, checking through the early correspondence, and then stabbed the paper with a triumphant finger. 'Yup. Here it is. Trichotillomania—hair pulling and eating. Age five. Psychiatric referral, discharged six months later—presumably after she was ''cured'' with a haircut. Poor kid.'

'Do you think she'll make it?' Lucie asked, dwelling on the terrified mother's face. She, too, had probably seen the news a couple of years ago about the teenager who had died with the condition. It must have struck fear into her heart, and rightly so, given her daughter's history.

'I hope so,' Will said heavily. 'She looks pretty grim, though, and she's obviously lost quite a bit of blood over recent weeks. She's as white as a sheet.

Still, hopefully we were called in time and they'll be able to do something if the inside of her stomach isn't too raw and vulnerable to haemorrhage.'

If.

Their next few calls were much more routine—a case of tonsillitis which could easily have been brought to the surgery, a fall in an elderly lady which had resulted in stiffness and soreness, not surprisingly, a baby with diarrhoea and vomiting who was getting dehydrated but had actually started keeping some boiled water down by the time they arrived. Lucie gave the mother some sachets of electrolyte replacement, and instructions that if the baby didn't pick up by four, they were to be called out again and the baby might have to be admitted to hospital for rehydration.

Then they went back, dealt with the correspondence and notes from the week, had a meeting about practice policy on drug offenders and then while Lucie did the evening surgery, Will called the hospital about Harriet Webb.

He popped his head round the door between patients. 'Harriet's all right—they've removed a massive hairball but they think her stomach will heal. Amazingly it didn't look too bad. She's had a blood transfusion and she's holding well.'

Lucie felt her shoulders drop a few inches, and laughed. 'Excellent. I really wasn't sure she'd make it.'

'Nor was I. How many more have you got?'

'Three—I won't be long.'

'Take your time. I'll have a cup of tea—do you want one?'

'I'll wait,' she said with a shake of her head. 'I'd rather get home.'

He nodded and left her to it, and half an hour later they were on their way.

'Any plans for the weekend?' Will asked her, and she had a sudden chill. Fergus had said he'd come down, but he hadn't contacted her, thank God. Maybe he'd taken the hint from her abrupt departure after lunch on Saturday.

'Not really,' she said evasively. 'How about you?'

He shrugged. 'What can I do? Sit about and fret because I can't get on? Walk the dog till his legs fall off? You tell me.'

'What would you normally have been doing?' she asked.

His laugh was short and wry. 'The house? In case you haven't noticed it's barely habitable. I've done the roof and the dampproofing and started with the kitchen and breakfast room and two bedrooms and some basic plumbing, but nothing's finished, and the rest of it is crying out for some progress. The only rooms that are virtually done are the two bedrooms, and they just need decorating.'

'Why on earth,' she asked, negotiating the track carefully, 'did you take on something so challenging?'

'Because I like a challenge? Because I wanted to live here and it was falling down, so there wasn't a lot of choice. The barn had planning permission for conversion to guest accommodation, so I lived in a caravan and did that first, then lived there while I made the house weathertight and sound and installed the basics.'

'So why don't you still live in the cottage? Or let it?'

'Well, I am letting it. I'm letting it to trainees at the moment.'

'But not for as much as you'd get for holiday lets.'

'No, but it's less hassle, and I'm too busy at the weekends to deal with change-overs and guests and their trivial problems and queries. That's the plan, in the end, but not until I've got the house knocked into shape—and with my arms out of action, DIY's taken a definite back seat.'

Lucie chuckled. 'You amaze me. I would have thought you'd have a go anyway.'

He looked rueful. 'I have to confess I did have a go, during the week. I thought I might be able to tackle some of the simple things upstairs, but I couldn't even hold the electric screwdriver with my right hand, and my left—well, let's just say I'm not ambidextrous. Anyway, it still hurts, so what the hell. I gave up.'

And it didn't agree with him, Lucie realised, because he wasn't a quitter.

And nor, she realised with a sinking heart, was Fergus.

They pulled up on the drive beside his car, and Will arched a brow at her. 'Have you got a visitor?'

'Apparently,' she said tightly, and got out of the car at the same time as Fergus emerged from his, a wide smile on his face.

'Lucie, darling! I thought you'd never get here! The dog's been barking its head off—I stayed in the car just in case it got out.'

'You should have rung,' she told him, unable to

be more welcoming, and dredged up a smile. 'I'm sorry we're late. I had evening surgery.'

She offered a cheek for his kiss, and turned to Will, who was coming round the front of the car with a look in his eye that she didn't want to analyse. 'Will, meet Fergus Daly, a friend of mine from London,' she said smoothly. 'Fergus, this is Will Ryan, my trainer.'

'I won't shake hands,' Will said a little curtly, holding up his cast, and looked at Lucie. 'You're obviously busy. If I can have the keys, I'll leave you to it.'

She dropped them in his outstretched hand, and he turned on his heel and strode away, leaving Fergus staring after him.

'What an odd fellow. Not very welcoming.'

Nor was Lucie, but Fergus hadn't noticed—or wasn't acknowledging it. 'So, is this your little *pied-à-terre*?'

She nodded, unlocking the door and pushing it open. 'Come in. I haven't done anything today, it's a bit of a mess. Tea?'

'Nothing stronger?' he said hopefully.

'No, nothing stronger. You're driving.'

'Am I? Where are we going?'

She gave a short sigh. 'To your hotel?'

He reached for her, his hands cupping her shoulders, drawing her towards him. 'I had rather hoped I might be allowed to stay with you,' he murmured, and bent to kiss her.

She turned her head and moved out of his reach. 'I think not, Fergus. I told you that before I left London, and nothing's changed. It was no then, and it's no now.'

'But I miss you, Lucie.'

'I know you miss me—or you think you do—but I don't miss you, Fergus. I'm sorry, but that's the way it is.'

He stood dumbstruck, staring at her with astonished eyes. 'Lucie?'

'Oh, Fergus, come on, it's not as if it's the first time you've heard me say it! We're friends—nothing more. If you can't accept that, then I don't know how else to tell you to make you understand. There is nothing between us—nothing!'

'Oh.' He suddenly seemed to find the carpet absolutely fascinating, and she felt a pang of guilt.

'Fergus, I'm sorry.'

'I was really looking forward to this weekend,' he murmured.

'Only because you've failed to listen to me for weeks now. If you'd been paying attention, you would have realised it was a waste of time.' She moved closer, putting her hand on his arm. 'Have a cup of tea before you go.'

He pulled his arm away and looked up, his eyes suspiciously moist. 'I won't, thank you. I'll get out of your way.' He moved to the door, then paused, looking back at her. 'It's Will, isn't it?'

She sighed. 'No, it's not Will. This was over before I left London, Fergus. Will has nothing to do with it.'

'He may not have been then, but he is now,' he said with unusual perception. 'I hope you find what you're looking for, Lucie. You deserve to, you're a lovely girl.'

The door closed gently behind him, and Lucie sat down and swallowed hard. Poor Fergus. It wasn't his fault he was too safe and too boring. Perhaps it was a failing in her, that she wanted danger and excitement in her relationships?

She looked across at the house, and saw Will standing at the window, watching Fergus drive away, and she wondered what he was thinking.

Then he turned his head and looked towards her, and she felt her heart kick beneath her ribs. Failing or not, it was the way she was, and perhaps this weekend would give her an opportunity to get closer to him. After all, she couldn't rescue him from himself long distance, could she?

A tremor of excitement shivered through her, and she stood up and went into the kitchen area, clearing up her breakfast things and tidying, while her mind plotted her next move.

CHAPTER SEVEN

FERGUS was going off—probably to fetch a take-away or a bottle of fine wine and some candles to romance Lucie. Will was surprised he hadn't brought a hamper with him from Fortnum's. He looked and sounded the type.

The car went up the track away from the house, weaving painstakingly between the potholes, and disappeared from view around the corner of the track. It would probably ground and he'd be back, whimpering about his flashy car that was so tragically unsuited to the rigours of country driving.

He turned away in disgust, and looked at the cottage. Was that Lucie, sitting in the chair on the far side? He couldn't really see, but then she moved, standing up and going into the kitchen, and he wondered what she was doing. Preparing a meal? Setting the scene for the nice romantic dinner Fergus had gone to fetch?

He felt something he didn't really understand and didn't want to analyse, but it burned like a vindaloo. Damn Fergus, with his slick car and polished brogues and slimy manoeuvres. Will didn't know what Fergus had gone to fetch, but he didn't want to hang around and watch the romantic little scene take place.

He called Bruno, put his boots on and stomped down to the river, staying there until it was too cold and too dark for common sense, and then almost had to feel his way back to the house.

There was no sign of Fergus's car, and he thought they'd probably gone out—although he hadn't heard a car. Still, that ostentatious, sexy car wouldn't make a great deal of noise. The engine was the sort that purred rather than growled, and he would certainly take it slowly on the track.

Maybe he *had* grounded it, Will thought, and realised he was gloating. Dammit, that woman was certainly bringing out the worst in him!

He went into the kitchen and put on the kettle, debated lighting the fire and decided he couldn't be bothered. He made some toast, fried a couple of slices of bacon, hacked up a tomato and slapped them together in a sandwich, washing it down with a cup of tea.

He wondered what Lucie and Fergus had had for dinner.

Smoked salmon? Lobster?

Not bacon sandwiches, that was for sure!

There was a knock at the door, and he opened it to find Lucie there, alone.

'Lucie?' he murmured. 'I thought you were out with Fergus.'

She shook her head. 'He's gone,' she said, and he wasn't sure, but he thought she sounded forlorn. Obviously a flying visit that had left her wanting more. Damn.

She looked at the remains of his sandwich clamped in his left hand, then up at his face.

'Is that a bacon sandwich?' she said wistfully, and he gave a crooked smile and opened the door, irrationally pleased to see her and disgustingly glad that Fergus had gone, for whatever reason.

'Want one?'

'I'd kill for one.'

'No need. Just sit patiently at the table and I'll make you one.'

'I'll help.'

So he ended up bumping into her and having her squeeze past him and generally giving his hormones a hard time. She smelt wonderful. He wasn't sure what it was—it might have been shampoo, her hair was still wet from the bath. The thought sent his blood pressure sky-rocketing, and he flipped the bacon onto the toast with an awkward wrist and pushed the plate towards her.

'Here—I'll let you do the tomato, I have to hack it.'

'Forget the tomato, just give me the bacon,' she said with a grin. Picking up the plate, she sat down at the table, one foot hitched up under her bottom, and bit into the sandwich.

Her eyes closed and she groaned with ecstasy, and he had to stifle his own groan of frustration. What *was* it about her?

'This is bliss,' she said with her mouth full. 'I'm starving.'

'Why didn't you eat?'

She shrugged. 'Nothing I fancied in the fridge, and—I don't know, I just didn't feel like it.'

'So you thought you'd come and raid my bacon,' he said, trying hard not to pry and just barely resisting the urge to ask why she hadn't eaten with Fergus.

She laughed self-consciously. 'Actually, I thought I'd see if you were all right. You seemed to be gone for such a long time, and when it got dark I was worried about you.'

'I went down to the river,' he said, a little gruffly

because he was touched at her concern. 'You don't need to worry about me, Lucie, I'm not a kid, you know.'

'I know, but with your arms and everything…'

'Everything?' He smiled. 'You mean my mental disability?'

She grinned. 'You *did* have a head injury.'

He couldn't stop the smile. 'You're crazy,' he said softly, leaning back in the chair and studying her. Her hair was drying in damp tendrils around her face, like a wispy halo, and her mouth was wide and slightly parted and unbelievably sexy. He ached to feel it again under his lips.

'Fancy a coffee?' she suggested. 'It's freezing in here, and I've got the heating on. And Fergus brought me chocolates.'

He'd pass on the chocolates, but only because they'd choke him. Coffee with Lucie in a warm room, though, was too tempting to refuse. He stood up and dumped the plates in the sink. 'Sounds good. What are we waiting for?'

He left Bruno behind, drying off after his frolic in the river, and followed her over to the cottage. She put the kettle on as they went in, then held up a bottle about a third full of something amber and interesting.

'Fancy a malt whisky?' she suggested, and he raised a brow.

'Secret vice?'

She shook her head and smiled. 'My father likes it. He used to pop up to see me from time to time when he was in London on business, and he kept a bottle in my flat. So, do you want some?'

Now he knew it didn't belong to Fergus? 'Just a small one.'

She slopped a hefty measure into a tumbler and handed it to him, and he sat down in one of the wonderfully comfortable armchairs and nursed it while she made the coffee.

It was bliss to sit there with her—not fighting, for once, because he was tired after his walk by the river and the long week and the pain in his arm, and fighting with her would have been too much like hard work.

So he sat, and he sipped his whisky and coffee alternately, and Lucie put some music on softly in the background and curled up opposite him in the other chair, and a great lump of regret formed in his throat that they could never have any more than this.

He sighed softly to himself. What was it about him that made him unable to live with anyone? Every time he'd tried, he'd ended up bitter and resentful. He was just too intolerant, that was the trouble—or maybe nobody had ever been special enough to make the effort for.

Lucie could be special enough, he thought, but they bickered constantly and the irritation he felt was clearly mutual, even if his was largely fueled by sexual frustration.

And anyway, she belonged to Fergus.

'Want a chocolate?' she asked, holding out a box of beautiful hand-made confectionery that must have cost the absent Fergus a small fortune.

He resisted, but Lucie didn't. She tucked in with relish, and he had to watch her sucking and nibbling and fiddling with them—because, of course, being Lucie she couldn't just put one in her mouth and eat it. Oh, no. She had to bite the chocolate off the outside of the hard ones, and curl her tongue inside the soft fondant ones, and generally get totally absorbed in the structure of every single chocolate.

And every bite drove him crazy.

He tried closing his eyes, but that was no better. He imagined her mouth moving over his body, nipping and licking and tormenting the life out of him, and watching her eat the chocolates was probably safer, so he opened them again and found her looking at him, a curious expression on her face.

'What?' he said softly.

'You look as if you're in pain. Is your arm hurting?'

He almost stifled the snort of laughter, but not quite. 'Let's just say I've been more comfortable,' he prevaricated, and crossed one ankle over the other knee to disguise his embarrassment.

She got up to change the CD, and his eyes faithfully tracked the soft curve of her bottom as she bent over the music system. Beautiful. Just lush enough to make the fit of his jeans impossibly tight. Damn. He looked away, into the depths of his malt whisky, and as the slow, sexy music curled round them, he drained the Scotch, stood up and put the glass down with a little smack on the table.

'I have to go.'

'Really?'

She looked wistful, and it occurred to him that she was probably lonely and missing Fergus. He didn't know why the man had left so soon—perhaps it had only ever been meant as a flying visit. Although, thinking about it, she hadn't seemed overjoyed to see him.

'Really,' he said gently. Whatever she was feeling

about Fergus, he didn't want to be used as a substitute.

Liar, his body screamed, but he ignored it until he got to the door, and then he turned to thank her for the coffee and bumped into her, and his hands flew up to cup her shoulders and steady her, and instead of steadying her they drew her closer, just as his head lowered of its own accord and his lips found hers.

She tasted of chocolate and coffee, and her mouth yielded with a tiny sound of surrender that nearly blew his control. Her back was to the bedroom door, and beyond it the bed was only a pace or two away. The knowledge tortured him.

He let go of her shoulders, meaning to ease back, but his arms slid round her of their own volition, drawing her closer, cupping her soft, lush bottom and lifting her into the cradle of his hips.

She gasped softly, and he plundered her mouth, need clawing at him. He wanted her—wanted to hold her and touch her and bury himself deep inside her.

He wanted things he had no business wanting, and she belonged to Fergus.

With a deep groan he released her, stepping back and fumbling behind him for the doorhandle. 'Lucie, I...' He trailed off, lost for words, and she put a finger over his lips.

'Shh. Don't say anything.'

He took her hand, lifting it slightly and pressing a lingering kiss into the palm. 'I have to go.'

'I know. I'll see you tomorrow.'

She came up on tiptoe and kissed his cheek, her soft breasts bumping into his chest and tormenting him again. He pulled the door open and backed through it, almost falling over the cat.

'Damn, she's sneaked in,' he said, but Lucie laughed, a low, sexy little laugh that tortured him.

'She always sneaks in. I don't mind. She comes through the bedroom window most nights and sleeps on the bed.'

Lucky cat, he thought enviously, and dredged up a crooked, rather tragic smile. 'See you tomorrow.'

He turned and strode back to his house, refusing to allow himself to look back over his shoulder, and let himself in. Bruno greeted him with a thump of his tail, and he patted the dog absently and went upstairs to bed.

There was no way he would sleep, but his body was tired and he needed to rest.

Correction. He needed Lucie, and he wasn't about to get her.

Not now, not ever.

Lucie went to bed, her lips still tingling from his kiss. Poor Fergus. He was right. Will hadn't been an issue before she'd left London, but he certainly was now, and even if Fergus had been in with a chance before, that would have changed.

Especially after Will's kiss.

Fergus had kissed her before, of course, but only fairly briefly, because it had been all she'd allowed. She would have given Will anything he'd asked for.

Anything.

She reached for her diary, and wrote, 'Progress. We kissed again. He still seemed to regret it, but I don't. Oh, no! Wish he could have stayed the night.'

She put the diary down and switched off the light, then curled up on her side and relived the kiss. It brought an ache that wouldn't go away, an ache that was more than just physical and gave her a lump in her throat, because some time in the course of that kiss, she'd realised that she loved him.

How could she possibly have fallen in love with someone so grumpy and touchy and difficult?

Because that isn't the real him? her alter ego suggested. Because the real him is gentle and tender and loving, and crying out for a partner to share life's trials?

Crying out for peace and quiet and solitude, more like, she corrected herself. She didn't think for a moment that Will was looking for a partner. A more solitary person she didn't think she'd ever met, and even now, wanting her as he very obviously did, he still resented it.

Why?

Maybe Richard would know, but it seemed a little unfair to ask his senior partner to tell her about Will's personal life. She wouldn't want it done to her.

So, then, she'd have to ask him directly.

Or not!

Will rapped on Lucie's door at ten-thirty, just as she finished clearing up after her breakfast. She wiped her hands on her jeans and opened the door, greeting him with a smile that probably said far too much. She'd never been good at keeping her feelings secret.

'Hi, come in,' she said cheerfully. 'Coffee?'

'I get a definite feeling of *déjà vu*,' he murmured, and she swallowed hard. Heavens, he looked sexy today! He was wearing jeans, the same snug-fitting jeans he'd been wearing when he'd fallen, if she remembered correctly, so his fingers must be better with buttons now.

'Is that a yes or a no?' she asked, going to put the kettle on anyway.

'Make it a yes,' he said, following her. 'I've been thinking—about your training.'

Her heart sank. Oh, no, she thought, he's going to say he can't go on doing it because of our personal involvement and I'm going to have to go away.

'The patients are all being too obliging,' he continued. 'Apart from Harriet with her hairball and Mr Gregory with his gastric problems, they're all too cut and dried, and none of them are being awkward. You aren't getting enough experience with the awkward ones.'

She laughed and turned to face him, astonished. 'So what are you asking me to do? Argue with them? Tell them they're boring?'

'Role play,' he said, and her jaw dropped.

'Role play?' she parroted weakly. Of all the things she'd hated about her entire education, role play was top of the list. Oh, she was good at it—but she couldn't seem to take it seriously, and she always wanted to add something trivial to mess it up.

She'd been in constant trouble with the drama teacher at school, and her clinical medicine tutors had thrown up their hands in despair at her attitude.

And now Will, who already thought she was a silly, flighty little piece, wanted her to do role-play exercises *with him*?

'I can't do it,' she said firmly.

'Yes, you can,' he told her, just as firmly. 'You just have to try. You'll feel self-conscious for a while, but then you'll get used to it.'

Self-conscious? Not a chance! She'd probably just shock him so badly she'd fail this part of her training.

Still, he had that implacable look on his face, and she had a feeling he intended to win this argument.

'When?' she said, resigning herself to disaster.

'Now?'

'Now!' She nearly dropped the coffee. 'Now, as in *now*?'

He shrugged. 'Are you busy? We can always do it another time.'

'But it's your weekend,' she said feebly, hunting for excuses.

He raised his hands, one in a cast, the other still swollen and in a support. 'And there's so much else I can do.'

You could make love to me, she thought, and for a moment she wondered if she'd said it out loud. Apparently not, because he calmly took the coffee she passed him and set it down without incident on the table beside him.

'I don't bite,' he said softly, and she stifled a laugh.

'OK,' she agreed, giving in. It might be a bit of fun, and if she didn't overdo it, maybe he wouldn't get too mad with her.

He knocked on the door, and she opened it and drew him in. 'Hello, there,' she said brightly. 'I'm Dr Compton—come in and sit down. What can I do for you?'

Wouldn't you like to know? Will thought, and limped over to the chair. 'I'm having trouble with my bowels, Doctor,' he said, and met her eyes.

They were sparkling with mischief, and he sighed inwardly. She'd make a lousy poker player. 'What sort of trouble?' she asked.

'Oh, you know—either I go or I don't.'

Her lips twitched. 'How long's it been going on?' she said. 'Is it a recent problem, or have you always been like this, or does it come and go?'

'Oh, comes and goes,' he ad libbed. 'Well, it has done recently. Never used to. I used to have it all the time.'

'And what exactly is the trouble?' she probed.

'Well, as I say, either I go, or—I don't.'

'Have you changed your diet?'

'Well, not really. Stopped eating vegetables after my Katie died.'

'Oh, I see. So your wife died recently?'

'Oh, no, not my wife. Katie was the dog.'

Her mouth twitched, and Will had to admit he was having trouble keeping a straight face. However, she carried on. 'So, are you still eating less vegetables?'

'I get meals on wheels. I don't like soggy sprouts. Every day it's soggy sprouts—either that or cabbage, or those awful tinned carrots. You ever had those tinned carrots, Doctor?'

'Not that I recall. So, you're probably not eating enough vegetables. How about fruit?'

'I like tinned peaches,' he said, wondering how long he could keep her going. 'Strawberries, though—they're my favourite, although they usually give me the trouble.'

'You mean, you go?'

'Oh, yes. Well, of course, it depends how many I have. If I have too many, then I do, but if I don't have too many, I—'

'Don't,' she said with him, meeting his eyes in a direct challenge. 'I see. So how about apples, pears, that sort of thing? Breakfast cereal?'

'You're talking about roughage, aren't you, Doctor? Never had no shortage of that in the war. I remember—'

'And you were all probably a lot healthier for it,' she said, cutting him off neatly before he had time to ramble. 'Still, we need to worry about what would help you now, and see what we can do to make things more regular.'

'Oh, yes, regular, that's what I'd like to be,' he said fervently, stifling the smile. Her eyes twinkled. He should have been warned, but he wasn't, and her next remark shocked him.

'I think I need to examine you,' she said blandly. 'If you could slip your trousers down and lie on the couch.' She pointed at the settee, and he raised an eyebrow. 'Please?' she added.

'Is this really necessary?' he asked in his usual voice.

She propped her hands her hips and looked at him with that sassy little smile, all innocent and wicked at once. 'Of course. How will you know if I've been sufficiently thorough if I don't do everything I would normally do?'

'Hmm,' he muttered under his breath. 'We'll imagine the trousers,' he said firmly, and lay down, his legs dangling over the end.

'I'll just undo them,' she said, and before he could protest the button fly was popping open and her little hands were in there, prodding and poking about at his innards and getting perilously close to finding out just how much he was getting out of this whole bit of nonsense.

She tugged up his shirt and peered at the skin of

his abdomen. 'Nice neat scar—is that appendix or a hernia repair?' she asked innocently.

'Appendix,' he said in a strangled voice.

'And have you had trouble ever since it was removed?'

Damn, how did she keep it going? 'Well, off and on. Like I said, sometimes I go, and—'

'Sometimes you don't. Yes. I remember.' She pressed down in the centre of his abdomen and released sharply, and he obligingly grunted, feigning rebound tenderness.

'Oh, dear, was that a bit sore?' she asked sympathetically.

'It was.'

Mischief danced in her eyes. 'What about if I do it here, further down?'

He caught her wrists, just in the nick of time. 'I think we get the picture,' he said, swinging his legs off the settee and struggling to fasten his jeans.

'Here, let me,' she said, and then those little fingers were in there again, brushing against his abdomen and driving him crazy. He sucked in his breath to get out of her way, but she was done, and he tugged the rest of the shirt out of the waistband and let it provide a little modesty.

Had she noticed? Goodness knows, but he wasn't taking any chances. He sat back down in his chair and crossed his leg over his other knee. He seemed to spend a lot of time in this position, he thought, and sighed.

Perhaps role play wasn't such a good idea after all.

* * *

Lucie was enjoying herself. They swapped roles, they touched on difficult and serious issues, and other more trivial and silly ones, and she did learn a lot from him.

She also learned a lot about him. She learned that he had a sense of humour—a wonderful sense of humour, every bit as wicked as her own—and that he cared deeply about his patients, and that he was a stickler for exactitude and wouldn't tolerate inconsistencies.

If she was vague he chivvied her up, making her be more specific, and although she threw in the odd bit of nonsense to liven the proceedings, in fact it was astonishingly easy to get into the roles with him and she found herself doing it seriously.

She also learned that she could turn him on just by stroking her fingers over the tender skin of his abdomen, so that his body betrayed his true reactions despite the fact that he stayed in role.

And she learned that as far as he was concerned, that was a no-go area and she wasn't to be allowed to tease him into breaking out of role.

Finally, at about lunchtime, he sat back and blew out his breath in a long stream. 'Well?'

'Thank you,' she said, genuinely meaning it. 'That was very useful. How did I do?'

'When you were being serious? Fine. Very good, mostly. The rest is just experience, but I think you've got what it takes. I think you'll do, Lucie Compton. If you were my GP, I'd be confident I was being looked after properly.'

Her cheeks coloured softly, and she let out a soft laugh. 'Well—thanks, Dr Ryan.'

'My pleasure. I think we deserve lunch. How about going to the pub?'

She wrinkled her nose. 'Typical. I'm driving, of course.'

He grinned. 'That's right, but fair's fair. As you so rightly pointed out, I just gave up my Saturday morning for you, so I deserve a drink more than you.'

There was no answer to that.

CHAPTER EIGHT

WITH her confidence bolstered by Will's praise, Lucie found working with him easier after that, although he continued to make notes and criticise and nit-pick.

Still, his comments were all fair and helpful and, although it annoyed her, she could see the point.

A fortnight after their role-play session, Harriet Webb came to see her for a check-up. She'd been discharged from hospital a week earlier, and before they arranged to go on holiday at the end of May, her mother wanted to be sure she would be well enough. Lucie had to admit Harriet looked considerably better than she had when they'd first seen her.

Her hair was cut short, as well—spiky and fun and a very pretty style that was too short to pull out in her sleep.

'Are you finding it easier to eat now?' Lucie asked her, and Harriet laughed.

'I'm starving. I've never been so hungry in my life. I think it's having room to really eat—I've probably never had that before. They said the hairball has probably been forming all my life. It was amazing—they showed it to me, and it was just the shape of my stomach and so huge! All my clothes are loose now, and my waist is so much smaller. They're putting it in their museum at the hospital, for the nurse training department, so I'll be famous. How cool is that?'

Lucie chuckled. 'Ultra-cool. You look good. I like the hair.'

She patted it experimentally. 'I'm still getting used to it. I used to fiddle with it all the time. It's like having my hands cut off! Still, I don't want another of those things, no way!' She shuddered.

'Are you seeing anyone about why you might have done it?' Lucie asked cautiously, and Harriet pulled a face.

'You mean the therapist? She's useless.'

'Give her a chance,' Lucie urged. 'She might be able to help you find out why you did it, and I know it might not be what you want to do, rummaging around inside all your personal thoughts and feelings, but if it stops it happening again and helps you move forward, that has to be good, doesn't it?'

Harriet nodded. 'I s'pose. It's just all a bit—I don't know. She keeps going back to when I was little and my sister died, and it—you know. It's difficult to talk about. I don't like to remember.'

'I'm sure,' Lucie said with sympathy.

Mrs Webb was sitting quietly in the background, and she met Lucie's eyes and shrugged helplessly. 'She seemed all right at the time, although it was awful, but that's when the hair thing started. Maybe this girl can get to the bottom of her problems. We're hopeful.'

'Well, as far as I'm concerned she's in excellent physical shape now and I can't see any reason why you shouldn't go on holiday. I expect it will do you all good. Are you going anywhere nice?'

'Only France,' Mrs Webb said. 'We go most years, but we thought we'd go earlier this year, to give Harriet a treat.'

'Well, I hope you have a lovely time,' Lucie said with a smile as they left.

'Make a note of that,' Will said from behind her.

'Of the sister?'

'Yes. Sounds as if Harriet was involved in some way in her death—maybe she found her, or feels it was her fault. Whatever, it could be relevant. Just jot it down.'

'I have.' She turned to face him. 'She's looking better, isn't she? Funny hangover, that.'

Will smiled slightly, letting her score the point. 'Who's next?' he asked.

'Mr Gregory. He's had the course of treatment for his *H. pylori*—this is a follow-up. Hopefully he's better.'

He was. He felt better than he had for months, he said, and although the treatment had been awful, it had done the trick and he felt much more like his old self.

'So, how's the diet going now?' Lucie asked. 'Dr Ryan tells me you're trying to cut down and lose a few kilos.'

'Oh, well, I gave all that up when this got out of hand, but I suppose I could start again. Maybe I need a bit less dressing on the salad. That seemed to set me off.'

'You don't have to eat salad just because you're on a diet,' Lucie reminded him. 'You can have normal meals, but cooked with much less fat, and with low-fat gravy and sauces and loads of veg. It doesn't have to be cold and raw to be less fattening!'

He chuckled. 'I know. Somehow it feels more like a diet, though, if it's cold. Still, I'll persevere.'

'Why don't we weigh you now, since you're here,

and we can check you again in a few weeks? Slip off your jacket and shoes, that's right.'

She weighed him, jotted it down on his notes and smiled. 'Well, I'm glad the treatment worked.'

'So am I. I'll go and have some hot tomatoes.'

He went out chuckling, and Will rolled his eyes. 'The nurse can weigh him.'

'He was in here.'

'And your next patient should have been. You're running behind now.'

She turned to face him again. 'Are you sure you aren't well enough to go and do something useful, like run a surgery?'

'With only one hand? Hardly. I've told you, I'm hopeless with my left hand. How could I do internals?'

'You couldn't. You'd have to ask for help.'

'And if there was nobody about? Don't worry, Lucie, I've thought about it. This is working.'

Not for me, she wanted to say, but that wasn't fair. They only crossed swords a few times a day now, instead of a few times an hour.

Progress?

The phone rang, and she picked it up. 'Dr Compton.'

'Doctor, I've got Mrs Brown on the line. She's expecting triplets? She says she's got cramp in her stomach and she's a bit worried. Could you go?'

She covered the receiver and repeated the message to Will. 'I'll talk to her,' he said, and took the phone.

After a brief exchange, he said, 'All right, hang on, we'll come now. You stay where you are.'

'I have a surgery.'

'The patients can either wait or switch to Richard,'

he said firmly. 'Angela Brown is about to lose her triplets, unless I'm very much mistaken, and I want to see her now. She can't wait. They can.' He nodded towards the waiting room.

'OK. I'll get my bag.'

'Come on, Lucie, move. She's in distress.'

They moved. They got there within ten minutes, to find that Angela had started to bleed.

It was only a little trickle, but her blood pressure was low and it was likely that she was haemorrhaging.

'I think you need the obstetric flying squad,' he told her gently. 'I'm sorry, but you need to be in hospital now, and you need a qualified obstetric team with you.'

'What about the babies?' she asked worriedly.

'I don't know about the babies. At the moment I'm worried about you. Lucie, can you call?' He told her the number, and she rang, relayed his instructions and asked for immediate assistance while he checked Angela's blood pressure again and listened to the babies through the foetal stethoscope.

'She needs a line in,' he instructed, and Lucie put an intravenous connector into her hand, ready for the drip, and took some blood for cross-matching, just in case.

'Shouldn't you examine me?' Angela asked them, and Will shook his head.

'No. You don't want to be poked about—it can cause the uterus to contract, and it might settle down. I want you in hospital fast, and I want that specialist team with you, just to be on the safe side. And in the meantime, I want you to lie as still as you can and not worry.'

It seemed to take ages for the obstetric team to arrive, but when it did, they moved smoothly into action and Will and Lucie shut up the house and followed them out.

'I wonder if she'll lose them?' Lucie said thoughtfully. 'She was so worried about having them, and now she's worried about not having them.'

'I don't know. Maybe they'll live, maybe not. Whatever, it'll be hard for her. I have to say my instinct is she'd be better without them, but I doubt if she'd see that in the same way as me.'

Lucie doubted it, too, and was glad she didn't have to make those sorts of choices. Nature would take its course, aided and abetted—or thwarted, depending on how you looked at it—by medical intervention, and Mrs Brown would come out at the end somehow, unless there was a drastic hiccup.

They went back to the surgery to find that Richard had finished her patients for her and everyone was in the office, sipping champagne.

'What are we celebrating?' Will asked, and Gina, one of the receptionists, waved her hand at them.

'Look! He finally did it!'

Will grabbed her flailing hand and peered at the ring, then gave her a hug. 'Congratulations. He took some pinning down.'

'Absolutely. Still, it's all going ahead now, and because I don't trust him not to change his mind, it's on Friday afternoon. Now, I know you can't skive off, all of you, but you can come to a party in the evening, can't you?'

'I'm sure we can all manage that, can't we?' Richard agreed, and fixed Will with a look. 'And since Will's broken his arm and won't be up a ladder, I imagine you'll even get him.'

'And Lucie—if you'd like to,' Gina said with a beaming smile. Lucie guessed that just then she'd have invited all the patients as well if there had been any about, but Lucie agreed, as much as anything because she thought it might be interesting to see Will at a party.

And who knows? she thought. It might even be fun.

'I really, really don't want to go,' Will said with a sigh.

Lucie looked at him across the car. 'You have to, Will. You said you would, and it's her wedding day.'

He sighed again. 'I know. I'm going. I just don't want to.'

'It might be fun,' she said encouragingly, and he shot her a black look.

'That's exactly what I'm afraid of,' he said darkly.

'Oh, pooh. You need to lighten up,' she said with grin. 'You never know, we might get you doing Karaoke by the end of the evening.'

'Hmm. See that pig up there in the sky?'

She chuckled, and opened the door. 'Come on. We have to get ready. We've got to leave in an hour. Do you want me to put your glove on?'

'Please,' he agreed, so she went in with him, waited while he stripped off his shirt and helped him into the long loose glove he'd got off a veterinary friend. A rubber band around the top held it in place, and it covered the entire cast without messing around with tape.

And that, they were both agreed, was a huge improvement.

The only problem was that she had to put it on after he'd taken off his shirt, and so she was treated on an almost daily basis to the delicious sight of Will's muscular and enviable torso, just inches away.

Close enough to touch.

She snapped the elastic band in place, flashed him a grin and all but ran back to her cottage. He could get the glove off, so her time was now her own, and she had to bath, wash her hair and get it into some semblance of order, and put her glad rags on.

The party was in a village hall, and she didn't think it would be dreadfully smart, but it might be quite dressy in a different sort of way, and she sifted through her clothes until she found black trousers and a flirty, floaty top with a camisole under it that dressed the whole thing up.

She put on her make-up, added a bit more jewellery and stood back and looked at herself. Fine. A little brash, but what the hell? She wasn't going out to one of Fergus's posh restaurants, she was going to a wedding party in a village hall, and she intended to have fun.

Lucie didn't know what she was doing to him. She was like a bright little butterfly, flitting about in that gauzy bit of nonsense. Granted, she wore a little top under it, but even so!

And she was in her element, of course. She could talk to anyone, and she did. She talked to everyone, without exception, from the bride's father to the kids in the corner who were throwing peanuts at the guests and giggling.

She threw one at him and it landed in his drink, splashing him. He met her eyes, and she was laughing, her hand over her mouth, looking as guilty as the kids and as full of mischief.

He shook his head in despair and turned back to his conversation with Richard's wife. She, however, seemed quite happy to be distracted by Lucie.

'What a charming girl,' she said, and Will nearly groaned.

'Yes, she is. Well, she can be.'

'And you can be charming, too, of course, if you put your mind to it,' Sylvia said in gentle reprimand.

'Sorry.' He gave her a rueful smile. 'I'm just feeling a bit old.'

'Old?' She laughed. 'You wait until you hit forty-five, if you want to feel old! Did Richard tell you we're going to be grandparents?'

'No, he didn't. Congratulations.'

She pulled a face. 'I'm pleased really, I suppose, but I had hoped they'd wait until they were a bit more secure.'

'What, like you did?'

She laughed and slapped his arm, her hand bouncing harmlessly off the cast. 'You know what I mean.'

'Yes, I do. But there's a danger to that, you know, Sylvia. You can be too measured, too organised, too planned. And then you find that life's gone on without you.'

'Well, this party's certainly going on without you,' she admonished, standing up. 'Come on, you can dance with me.'

'What?'

'Come on, you can't refuse, it's rude.' She pulled him to his feet and dragged him to the dance floor, and he could feel Lucie's eyes on his back all the way across the room.

Sylvia was kind to him and let him shuffle without expecting anything too outrageous.

And then the music changed, and Lucie appeared at their sides.

'I believe this is the ladies' excuse-me,' she said with a smile to Sylvia, and slid neatly into Will's arms before he could protest.

The cast felt awkward against her back, but his fingertips could feel the subtle shift of her spine, and he cradled her right hand in his left against his chest, his thumb idly tracing the back of her fingers. Her breast chafed against the back of his hand, and he could feel the occasional brush of her thighs against his.

It felt good. Too good, really, but he wasn't stopping. It was a genuine reason to hold her, and he was going to make the best of it!

And then the best man commandeered the microphone, and announced that the Karaoke machine was now working and they wanted the bride and groom to kick off.

'I'm out of here,' Will muttered, and Lucie laughed and led him back to their table.

'It'll be a laugh. Just go with the flow.'

So he did, and, in fact, it wasn't as awful as he'd imagined. Lots of the guests had a go, and some of them were quite good, and everyone seemed to enjoy themselves. Then, to his horror and amazement, Lucie was pounced on.

'Come on, you can sing, we've heard you,' the receptionists told her, and Will watched, transfixed, as she was towed, laughing, to the stage and presented with the microphone by the best man.

'So, ladies and gentlemen, here we go. It's Dr Lucie Compton singing Whitney Houston's song from *The Bodyguard*, "And I Will Always Love You". Let's hear it for Lucie!'

The crowd clapped and cheered, and then went quiet for the slow, haunting introduction. Lord, she was wonderful! Will felt his skin shiver, and then as she reached the first repeat of the title, her eyes found his, and he felt a huge lump in his throat.

There was no way she was singing it for him, but he could let himself dream, and then she hit the volume and he went cold all over with the power of her voice.

Lord, she was spectacular! He'd had no idea she was *so* good, and neither, by the look of them, had any of the others. She was really into it now, her voice mellow and yet pure, every note true, every word filled with meaning.

She finished, holding the last note until Will thought she'd die of lack of oxygen, but then she cut it and bowed, laughing, as the guests went wild.

'Encore!' 'Again!' 'More!' they yelled, and she turned to the best man and shrugged.

'OK. What have you got?'

'What can you do?'

She laughed. 'Anything. Try me.'

He did, and she was right. She knew them all, and hardly fluffed a note. Most of the time she didn't even glance at the monitor for the words, and Will was stunned. Finally, though, she surrendered the microphone to thunderous applause, and came back to the table.

'Sorry about that, I got hijacked,' she said with a chuckle, and pointed to his drink. 'Is that just mineral water?'

'Yes.'

'May I?'

He pushed it towards her, and she drained it, then set it down with a grin.

'I enjoyed that. I haven't done it for ages.'

'You were good,' he said gruffly. 'Very good.' Stunning.

She smiled a little shyly. 'Thanks,' she said, as if she really cared what he thought, and he wanted to hug her. Well, he wanted to do more than hug her, but it would be a good start.

'So how come you know them all?' he asked, trying to concentrate on something other than holding her in his arms, and she shrugged.

'I used to sing in a nightclub to earn money when I was at college,' she explained. 'The hours fitted, and the money was good, and I enjoyed it mostly, except for the smoke and the lechers.'

Will was feeling pretty much of a lecher himself just now, but he didn't want to think too much about that.

'I could kill a drink,' Lucie said, and he thought for a moment he was going to have to walk across the room in his state of heightened awareness, but he was saved by the best man descending on them and buying them both drinks to thank Lucie for her contribution to the evening.

The Karaoke had packed up after she'd sung. She was, as they said, a hard act to follow, and so they'd gone back to the disco music and everyone was dancing again.

They had a drink, and this time Will had a whisky. Well, he wasn't driving, and he needed something to act as anaesthetic if he was going to sleep that night!

'Are you ready to go?' he asked her a short while later, and she grinned and stuck her finger under his chin, tickling it.

'Is it past your bedtime, you poor old thing?' she crooned, and he nearly choked.

Way past, he thought, but not in the way she was implying! He glowered at her, and she just laughed and stood up. 'Come on, then, Cinderella, your carriage awaits.'

They said goodbye to their hosts, and twenty minutes later they were pulling up outside the house and she was going to go her way and he was going to have to go his, and he suddenly didn't want the evening to end.

God, however, was on his side. 'Coffee?' she said, and he sent up a silent word of thanks.

'That would be lovely.'

He followed her into the cottage and stood leaning on the old timber-stud wall in the kitchen while she put the kettle on. 'So, did you have fun?' she asked him, turning to face him and standing with one hand on her hip in an unconsciously provocative pose.

His libido leapt to life again. 'Yes, I had fun,' he confessed. 'You were wonderful, Lucie. You've got a beautiful voice.'

'Thanks.'

She met his eyes again, that shy smile playing over her lips, and he suddenly knew he'd die if he didn't kiss her.

He hadn't kissed her for weeks—three weeks, to

be exact, not since Fergus had been down, and it had been far too long.

He held out his arms, and she moved into them without a murmur, pressing her body softly up against him as she turned her face up for his kiss.

A deep groan dragged itself up from the depths of his body, and his mouth found hers and relief poured through him.

Not for long, though. He shifted against her, aching for her, and with a tiny moan she pressed herself harder against him and wrapped her arms around his neck. Her fingers tunnelled through his hair, her body wriggled against him and then finally she lifted her head, undid the top buttons of his shirt and laid her lips against his skin.

Heat exploded in him, and he gave a deep groan. 'Lucie, in the name of God, what are you doing?' he asked in a strangled voice, and she laughed a little unsteadily.

'You need lessons?' she said, and her voice was deep and husky and unbelievably sexy.

'I don't need lessons. I thought I was the trainer.'

'Mmm,' she murmured, nuzzling the base of his throat. 'You are. How am I doing?'

'Just fine,' he croaked, and, putting his fingers under her chin, he tilted her face firmly up to face him. 'Don't tease me, Lucie.'

Her eyes lost their playful look and became intensely serious. 'I'm not teasing,' she vowed. 'I want to make love with you.'

Will closed his eyes and let his breath out in a rush. She wanted to make love with him, and had he thought of this in advance? Was he prepared?

He felt as if he'd won the lottery and lost the ticket.

'We can't,' he said. 'No protection.'

'Yes, we have,' Lucie said, and smiled a smile as old as time.

It had lost nothing of its power over the countless generations. He felt as if his knees were going to buckle, and when she moved away and held out her hand, he took it and followed her through to the bedroom.

She was incredible. She was gentle, teasing, earnest—she was a thousand different women, and he wanted them all. He wanted her, and he could think of nothing else.

It was only afterwards, when he lay spent beside her, his heart pounding and his body exhausted, that he remembered that she belonged to Fergus…

CHAPTER NINE

LUCIE woke to a feeling of utter contentment. She'd never—*never*—been loved like that, and she felt whole as she'd never felt whole in her life before.

She opened her eyes, a smile forming on her lips, but Will was gone. She sat up, throwing off the quilt, not heeding her nakedness. 'Will?'

There was no reply, and the cottage was too quiet. Quiet with the silence of emptiness. She felt ice slide over her and, shivering, she pulled on her dressing-gown and went through to the sitting room. She knew he wasn't in the bathroom, because the door had been open and there was no sign of him.

Nor was he in the sitting room. She felt the kettle, and it was stone cold. When had he left? Just now, or earlier in the night?

She looked across at his house, but it was daylight and there would be no lights on anyway. She went back into the bedroom and felt the other side of the bed but, like the kettle, it was cold. He must have gone back to let the dog out, she realised, and stayed.

He was bound to be up, though, so she showered quickly, threw on her jeans and an old rugby shirt and some thick socks, and went over to the house. The back door was open, as usual, and she went in and found him sitting at the table, staring broodingly into a mug.

'Hi,' she said softly.

Will looked up, and to her surprise his eyes were

unreadable. They certainly hadn't been unreadable last night, but today they were. Distant and remote and expressionless. 'Hi.'

She faltered, suddenly uncertain of her welcome and not knowing why. 'Is something wrong?' she asked with her usual directness, and he shrugged.

'I don't do the morning-after thing very well.'

She stared at him. 'I noticed,' she said wryly, and went over to the kettle. 'Mind if I have a cup of tea?'

'Help yourself. You usually do.'

Oh, lord. All that beautiful intimacy, the tenderness, the whispered endearments—all gone, wiped out with the dawn. She felt sick inside, cold and afraid.

'Have you had breakfast?' she asked, striving for normality, and he shook his head.

'Not yet.'

'Want some toast?'

'If you're making it.'

Well, he wasn't going to make it easy, that was for sure, but she wasn't giving up either.

She cut four slices of bread, stuck them in the toaster and sat down opposite him, so he couldn't avoid looking at her.

He did, though. He stared down into his tea as if his life depended on it, and when she reached out a hand and touched him, he all but recoiled.

'Have I done something wrong?' she asked gently.

He looked up then, his eyes piercing and remote. 'No. Ignore me. I'm always like this.'

'Might explain why you're still single at thirty-three, then,' she said lightly, and went to collect the toast.

They ate in silence, and when he'd finished he

scraped his chair back and stood up. 'I'm taking the dog out.'

'Mind if I come?'

He shrugged. 'Please yourself. You usually do, but I'm going down by the river and your trainers will get ruined.'

'I've got boots. Give me a minute.'

She ran over to the cottage, dug out the wellies that hadn't seen the light of day for years and pulled them on, snagged a jacket off the hook by the door and went back out to find Will standing on the edge of the track, his hands rammed in his pockets, Bruno running in circles round the lawn barking impatiently.

As soon as he saw her, he turned and headed off, not waiting for her to catch up, and feeling sick inside she hurried after him, drawing level just in time to fall behind as the path narrowed.

And he wasn't hanging around for her or making any concessions, of course. Oh, no. That would be out of character. Whoever had made such beautiful love to her last night had been put firmly back in his place and the Will she knew—and loved?—was back with a vengeance.

She struggled down the path after him over the uneven ground, and finally, when she thought she'd die of exhaustion, they arrived at the river. Thank God, she thought, but that wasn't the end of it.

He turned sharply left and carried on along the path, striding out so that she almost had to run to catch up. Well, damn him, she wouldn't run! She slowed down, taking her time to enjoy the walk, looking out over the quiet beauty of the morning light on the water, and she thought she'd never seen anything quite so lovely in her life.

They were near the sea, and gulls were wheeling overhead, their keening cry reminding her of seaside holidays as a child. A wader was standing on one leg, and the water was so still she could see the ripples spreading out in the water around it, perfectly concentric rings interrupted only by the thin stalks of the reeds that broke the surface of the water in places.

It stabbed the mud with its beak, breaking the pattern, and she breathed again and moved on, following Will and wondering how anyone who loved this land as he so obviously did could be so changeable.

Maybe he loved it because it, too, constantly changed, continually affected by external influences.

Or was Will just bad-tempered and grumpy, and was she making too many allowances for him?

Probably, she acknowledged, looking ahead to where he was standing waiting for her, staring out over the river, his body utterly motionless.

Then he turned his head, and she told herself she imagined the pain in his eyes. Over that distance she could hardly make out his features, never mind read an expression!

Lucie hurried towards him, and this time he waited until she reached him.

'It's beautiful,' she said softly, and he nodded.

'I try and come down here every day. It's harder in the winter because it's dark so early, but I still try. Sometimes it freezes, and the birds skid about on the ice at the sides and Bruno tries to chase them. He always falls through, though. It never freezes that hard.'

She smiled, imagining it, and looked up at him.

His eyes tracked over her face, and she reached up and laid her hand on his cheek. 'You haven't kissed me this morning,' she said, and, going up on tiptoe, she brushed his lips with hers.

'Lucie,' he whispered, and then his arms went round her and his mouth found hers again and he kissed with a trembling hesitation that brought tears to her eyes.

Then Will lifted his head and stared out over the river again, and this time she saw the pain quite clearly, for the second it took him to gather his composure around him like a cloak.

'We shouldn't have made love last night,' he said, and his voice sounded rusty, as if he'd left it down by the river at the water's edge for the tide to wash over it and reclaim it.

Her knees threatened to buckle. Why? she wanted to cry, but she couldn't speak. Her throat had closed, clogged with tears, and it was as much as she could do to breathe.

She turned away before he could see the tears in her eyes, and headed back up to the house. She was damned if she'd let him see her cry!

She heard the drumming of hoofbeats, and in the distance she could make out Amanda and Henry, flying along the track that ran along the far side of the field beside her.

She felt a pang of envy. To feel the wind in your face and see the trees rushing past and feel so free—it must be wonderful. She brushed aside the tears and turned her attention back to the path, concentrating on putting one foot in front of the other.

And then she heard the unearthly scream, and the

hideous crash, and, looking up, she saw Henry struggling to his feet, unable to stand properly.

'Oh, my God,' she whispered. 'Oh, Amanda!'

She turned her head to call Will, but he'd seen and heard as well, and he was running up the field towards them, his long legs eating up the ground, Bruno streaking ahead.

She ran after him, her breath tearing in her throat, and adrenaline was surging through her, making her heart pound so hard she thought it would come out of her chest.

Will had reached Amanda now, and he was kneeling down when Lucie ran up, and his face was ashen.

'I think she's dead,' he said, and his voice was hollow and empty.

Lucie dropped to her knees beside him. 'She can't be. Let me feel.'

'She's not breathing, and I can't feel a pulse. I think her neck's broken, but I can't do anything with this bloody stupid hand…'

Lucie slipped her fingers behind the back of Amanda's neck, but she could feel nothing displaced. 'Maybe not. She might just be winded. Run and get my bag, and call an ambulance. You can go faster than me, and I've got hands that work. Take the dog with you.'

He was gone before she'd finished speaking, and she quickly ran her fingers down under Amanda's spine, feeling for any irregularity. If there was one, it was undetectable. So why…?

'Come on, Amanda, you can't do this,' she said. Ripping open her shirt, she laid her head on Amanda's chest. Yes, there was a faint heartbeat, but she wasn't breathing. Her airway, Lucie thought, and, supporting the neck by sliding her hand under it, she lifted Amanda's chin.

Amanda gasped, and as Lucie continued to support her neck, her eyelids fluttered open and she dragged in another breath.

Lucie let hers out in a rush. 'You're all right. Just lie still, you'll be OK.'

'Hurt,' she whispered.

'I know. Lie still, Will's getting the ambulance. Where do you hurt?'

'Everywhere. Legs—back—don't know. Pelvis?'

Lucie nodded. Amanda's legs were lying at a very strange angle, and it was obvious that she was very seriously injured. The first thing she needed was a neck brace, just to be on the safe side.

'You'll be OK,' she told her without any great faith, and prayed for Will to hurry. She wanted to get a line in, so that the ambulance crew could get some fluids into her as soon as possible to counteract the shock, because Lucie could tell that Amanda's blood pressure was going down, and goodness knows what internal injuries she might have sustained.

'Henry,' Amanda whispered a little breathlessly. 'Is he…?'

'He's over there, behind you. He's up.' On three legs, with the fourth dangling at a very strange angle, but Amanda didn't need to know that. 'Do you know what happened?'

'No. He—just seemed to—hit something—in the grass. Don't know what. Is he all right?'

'I don't know anything about horses,' Lucie said with perfect truth. 'Just keep very still, sweetheart. Try not to move.'

Amanda's eyes fluttered shut then, and Lucie had

never felt more alone in her life. Come on, Will, she thought, and then he appeared, her medical bag in his left hand, a bundle of towels and sheets under his right arm.

'Any joy?'

'She's breathing. Her airway was obstructed. I think her tongue had been driven back with the force of the fall. She's just resting.'

He looked down at her, just as Amanda's eyes opened and she looked up at him. 'Will? Look after Henry.'

'I will.'

'Got insurance. Call the vet. Anything...'

'OK. Don't worry about Henry. I've called the vet.'

He shot a glance in the horse's direction, and met Lucie's eyes. So they agreed on that, at least. Henry was in deep trouble. 'They're sending an air ambulance, because of the track. It should be here any minute. It was being scrambled from Wattisham airbase.'

She nodded. 'Good. The sooner the better.'

'I've just got to put out markers.' He ran down the field, opening out the sheets and spreading them in a rough H on the emerging crops. Moments later he was back, and knelt down opposite Lucie. 'Anything I can do? She needs a line in.'

'I know. Can you take over her neck so I can do it?'

'Sure.' His fingers slid around hers, cupping the fragile neck, and she eased her hand away carefully and then busied herself opening her bag and finding what she needed to get an intravenous line in. 'She needs saline.'

'They're bringing plenty of fluids. I told them to expect circulatory collapse.'

'Let's hope they get here soon,' Lucie said, checking Amanda's pulse and finding it weaker. 'Her pressure's dropping. Where the hell are they?'

'God knows, but the horse is going to be spooked by the helicopter.'

She'd got the line into Amanda's hand, and she taped the connector down and looked at Henry doubtfully. 'Can you lead him back to the stable?'

'Are you all right with her?'

'I'll manage. I don't need a terrified horse galloping over me.'

'I don't think he's galloping anywhere,' Will said softly, and she slid her fingers back under his and watched him as he went quietly up to Henry, speaking softly to him and holding out a reassuring hand.

The horse was shivering, clearly in shock himself, and Will led him slowly, hobbling on three legs, up the track and over the field towards the house.

He was back in no time, just as the helicopter came into view over the hill.

'That was quick.'

'I met up with the vet on the track. He's taken him on up,' he yelled, and then his voice was drowned out by the whop-whop-whop of the helicopter, and the grass was flattened all around them and Lucie ducked involuntarily.

Never mind spooking the horse, it didn't do a lot for her, but she was pleased to see it!

Seconds later the paramedic team was there, taking over from her, checking what had been done, getting fluids up and running, giving Amanda gas and air for pain relief and straightening her legs out to splint them, before putting on the spinal boards and lifting her into the ambulance.

Then they were away, and Will and Lucie stood watching the helicopter fade to a dot in the distance. 'I need to ring her mother—they'll have to talk to the vet and make decisions about Henry.'

'What did he hit? She said they hit something on the track.'

They walked back along it, and there, sticking up in the grass, was the end of a steel frame from a piece of redundant farm machinery. It had probably been there for ages, but this wasn't Will's land, and he didn't walk along this track often, he said.

It was just bad luck that Henry had gone so far over to the side, rather than sticking to the centre of the tracks, and it might have cost them both their lives.

Lucie shuddered. To think she'd just been envying them their headlong flight!

They went back to the house and found the vet in the stable with Henry, running his hands over the trembling horse and murmuring soothingly.

'How is he?' Will asked tautly.

'Shattered the cannon-bone of his off fore. It's not a clean break. They might be able to save it, but he'll never work again.'

'She's got insurance.'

The vet straightened up and met their eyes. 'I need to speak to his owners. My instinct is to shoot him now, but sentiment often gets in the way.'

'I'm sure they'd want him saved if possible,' Will said, and the vet nodded.

'I'll call Newmarket. They'll have to come and get

him. They have special transport with slings. He can't travel like this, he'll just fall over.'

He came into the house with them, and after Will had spoken to Amanda's parents and told them that Amanda was on her way to hospital, they confirmed that they wanted Henry saved if possible, and so the vet made several calls to set up the transport arrangements.

It seemed to be hours before Henry was loaded and away, the lorry picking its way infinitely slowly along the uneven track.

'I'm going to have to do something about that track,' Will said heavily, and turned away. 'I'm going to ring the hospital,' he said, and went into the house, leaving the door open as if he expected Lucie to follow. She did, sitting impatiently waiting until he finally got through to the right department. After a short exchange he replaced the receiver.

'She's in Theatre. She's got a pelvic fracture, both lower legs and right femur, and a crack in one of her cervical vertebrae, as well as cerebral contusions. Thank God she had her hat on, or she probably would have died of head injuries, but she'll be in for a long time, I think, judging by the sound of it. Her parents are both there, waiting for her to come round.'

Will glanced at his watch, or where his watch would have been, and swore softly before looking up at the clock. 'The day's nearly gone,' he said, and he sounded exasperated and irritable.

'I need another watch,' he went on. 'I don't suppose you feel like a trip to town, do you? I haven't bothered to get one till now because I couldn't wear it on that wrist, but I think the swelling's down enough now, especially if I get one with an adjustable strap.'

'Sure,' she agreed. She wasn't sure how far she could walk. Her feet were rubbed raw after her long walk in the badly fitting wellies—not to mention running up the field in them with her socks gathered up round her toes. Still, she'd manage. She wanted to be with him, if only so she could try and get their relationship back on an even keel after last night.

She didn't know what had happened to change his attitude, but something had, and if nothing else she wanted at least to go back to how they had been, instead of this icy and terrifying remoteness.

Will felt sick. Lucie was so sweet and open, almost as if Fergus was nothing. How could she be so fickle? He couldn't bear to think about it, so he closed his mind and tried to get back to how things had been, but it was hard.

Too hard.

He withdrew into an emotional safety zone, and then had to endure Lucie's puzzled looks for the rest of the day. He found a watch, the same as the one that he had smashed in his accident five weeks before, and the saleslady was able to adjust it so it hung loosely on his still tender and swollen wrist.

'It's taking a long time to get back to normal,' Lucie said as they left the shop.

'I've been giving it a hard time,' he said shortly. 'I've had no choice, unless I resigned myself to total dependence, and I didn't have anyone to depend on.'

'You could have depended on me,' she said softly, and he gave a brief snort.

'I could. I would rather not.'

'So you've pushed your wrist too hard and probably damaged it more.'

'It's my wrist,' he said flatly, cutting off that line of conversation, and Lucie fell silent. He felt a heel, but he was having enough trouble with his own emotions, without worrying about hers. Damn Fergus, he thought, and had to consciously relax his hands because they were clenched into fists so tight both arms were rebelling.

'Let's go home,' he said, without bothering to ask her if there was anything she wanted to do in town, and then had a pang of guilt. She'd driven him there, after all. 'Unless you want something?'

She shook her head. 'No. We can go back.'

The journey was accomplished in silence, and when they got back she said she was going to sort a few things out and disappeared into the cottage. He let himself into the house, patted Bruno absently and checked the answering machine automatically.

Nothing. No distractions, nothing to take his mind off last night and Lucie's beautiful, willing body under his.

He slammed his fist down on the worktop and gasped with pain. Damn. He really, *really* had to stop abusing this wrist. He massaged it gingerly with the other hand, and could have cried with frustration.

'You're better off than Amanda,' he told himself, and decided he'd swap places with her in an instant if it gave him a chance with Lucie.

There was nothing, of course, to stop him competing with Fergus—except pride.

Fergus had a car that cost more than he earned in a year, flash clothes that would never have seen the inside of Marks and Spencer, and he'd stake his life that Fergus didn't live in a tumbledown, half-restored excuse for a farmhouse in the middle of nowhere, miles from the nearest habitation and out of range of a mobile phone transmitter!

There was no way he could compete with Fergus for the heart of a city girl, and he didn't intend to try. He'd just take last night as a one-off, the night that shouldn't have happened, and cherish the memory for the rest of his life.

He struggled unaided into the long veterinary glove, had a bath and then lit the fire, opened the Scotch and settled down for a night's indifferent television. Nothing could hold his attention—not drama, not talk shows, certainly not puerile comedy.

He was about to go to bed when the phone rang, and he got up to answer it, to find that it was Fergus.

'Could I speak to Lucie, please?' he said in his carefully modulated voice, and Will grunted and dropped the phone on the worktop in the kitchen, going across to the cottage in bare feet and rapping on the door.

Lucie opened it, looking bleary-eyed and sleepy, and he wanted to take her in his arms and rock her back to sleep. Instead, he glared at her. 'Fergus on the phone,' he snapped, and, turning on his heel, he strode across the yard, ignoring the sharp stones that stabbed into his feet.

Lucie followed him in and picked up the phone. Will didn't want to hear her talk to him. A huge lump of something solid was wedged in his chest, and he shut the door into the sitting room with unnecessary force and turned up the television.

'Fergus?' Lucie said, looking at the firmly shut door with dismay. 'What is it?'

'I miss you.'

'I know. Fergus, we've had this conversation a hundred times now. I can't do anything about it. We aren't right for each other.'

'How's Will?'

Sexy. Amazing. The most incredible lover, better than I could have imagined in my wildest dreams.

'He's all right.' Actually, she didn't know how he was. Short-tempered, but that was no surprise, he was usually short-tempered.

Except just recently, and last night.

Last night…

'Sorry, Fergus, you were saying?'

'I was asking if there's any chance for you with Will, or if there's any point in me coming up to see you tomorrow. I want to see you, Lucie. I want to ask you something.'

Oh, no. But, then again, maybe a little competition might sharpen up Will's act.

'Come for lunch,' she said. 'I'll see you at twelve.'

'OK. I'll bring something, don't cook.'

'OK. See you tomorrow.'

She hung up, contemplated the firmly slammed door and shrugged. Will could find out for himself that she was off the phone. She went back to her cottage, shut the curtains and curled up on the chair and howled.

She'd really thought they were getting somewhere, but this morning he'd been so unapproachable, and then he'd said that they shouldn't have made love last night!

How could he believe that? It had been the most beautiful experience of her life, and she didn't think she'd been alone, but there was more going on here than she understood. There had been pain in Will's eyes, a real pain that hinted at some deep and terrible hurt.

A woman in his past? Had he been terribly hurt by her, and was that why he didn't do the morning-after thing very well? Was it that he couldn't bear to confront his feelings, or had he—please, God, no—pretended she'd been the other woman? Had *that* been why he hadn't been able to look at her in the morning?

Lucie scrubbed at the tears on her cheeks, and stood up. Whatever, she couldn't get any closer to understanding him by thrashing it round and round in her head any more, and she might as well go to bed.

Except that the sheets carried the lingering traces of his aftershave.

She sat up in the midst of the crumpled sheets and took her diary on her lap. 'We made love last night,' she wrote. 'At least, I thought we did. Perhaps it was just amazing sex.'

A tear splashed on the page, and she brushed it angrily away. 'Fergus coming for lunch tomorrow. He wants to ask me something. Hope it isn't what I think it is. Amanda and Henry came to grief on the track by the river. Very dramatic. Thought we were going to lose them both, but apparently not. Oh, Will, I love you, but you drive me crazy. Why can't you just open up with me? I thought we had something really special, but it must have been wishful thinking.'

She put the diary down, lay down in the middle of the crumpled bed and cried herself to sleep.

* * *

Fergus turned up at twelve. Will saw the car coming down the track from the end window in the house. He was struggling to strip the window, working with the wrong hand, and he paused and watched the car's slow progress. On second thoughts, maybe he wouldn't do anything about the track, and maybe Fergus would stop coming down.

He threw the stripping tool to the floor with a disgusted sigh, and shut the window, abandoning his hopeless task. He went down to the kitchen, arriving coincidentally as Fergus drew up, and he watched as Lucie came out to greet him with a kiss on the cheek.

Oh, well, at least it wasn't a full-flown no-holds-barred kiss of the sort he'd shared with her on Friday night. He should be thankful for small mercies—or perhaps Fergus was just too well bred to do it in public. He opened the boot of his car—a ridiculously small boot—and lifted out a wicker hamper.

If it hadn't hurt so much, Will would have laughed.

Game, set and match, he thought, and turned his back on them. He'd seen enough.

CHAPTER TEN

THE atmosphere between them remained strained over the next couple of days, but Lucie refused to let Will ruffle her, and by ignoring his moodiness it seemed to defuse it a little. At least, it brought a professional edge to their relationship, and for the first two days of the week it was all business.

Then, on Tuesday afternoon, he found her after her clinic and suggested visiting Dick and Pam. 'Dick's had his balloon angioplasty, and it's sort of on the way home. I thought it might be nice to pop in and see them.'

'And scrounge a couple of plants? You could take her back the pots from the others—they're lying dead by the back door, I noticed.'

'I know. I couldn't get them into the ground, and it's been dry,' he said shortly. 'You could have watered them.'

'I could have painted the outside of your house, but it's not in my job description,' she retorted, and put the cap back on her pen. 'Shall we go?'

'Only if you promise not to tell her they're dead.'

'As if I would.' She tossed the car keys in the air and looked at him expectantly. 'You coming, or walking?'

'Coming.' He stood up and headed for the door, holding it open for her so she had to brush past him. She felt him flinch and wanted to howl with frustration.

Why, when they'd been so close?

She drove to Dick's and Pam's in silence, pulling up outside the right white house this time, and she followed Will up the path and stood a little way behind him, admiring the front garden.

It had been five weeks since she'd first seen it, and now it was May, and everything was getting lush and starting to grow away. The bulbs were out, the daffodils finished but the tulips starting to nod their heads, growing up through the perennials that would soon rush up to swamp them.

So different from the boring, orderly town gardens she saw in London, which more often than not had a motorbike or car parked in them and a tattered fringe of forgotten vegetation round the edge.

She heard the door open, and then Will was hugging Pam, and she was smiling at Lucie and beckoning them in.

'Dick will be so delighted to see you—he's so much better. I'm amazed. He's back to work next week, and he certainly seems ready for it. The difference in him is incredible. He's in the garden, helping me with the daffodil leaves. Come and see him. I'll put the kettle on—can you stop?'

'Just for a short while,' Will agreed, arching a brow at Lucie, and she nodded.

'That's fine. A cup of tea would be lovely.'

They followed her through the house and found Dick bending over, tying off the tops of the daffodils, and as they went out he straightened up and beamed at them.

'Hello, there. Is this a social call?'

'It is, really. I just wanted to see how things were. I gather from Pam you're feeling much better.'

'I am, and it's all thanks to this young lady. My dear, I'm going to kiss you,' he announced, and, putting his hands on her shoulders, he planted a smacking kiss on her cheek. 'There. You're wonderful.'

Will shook his head and laughed. 'What did she say that I didn't?' he asked wryly, and Dick shrugged.

'Probably nothing, except you assumed I was afraid to die. Lucie here pointed out what a waste of my retirement it would be if I wasn't here to enjoy it, and I thought of the years I've paid into a pension just to let Pam sit back and squander it on a cruise, and I thought, Blow it, I'm going to do this! So there. That's all she said—just another angle on the same old theme, but it worked, and I can't tell you how grateful I am.'

Lucie laughed. 'Well, I'm delighted to have been of service. I must say, you do look well.'

'I am. Ah, look, here's Pam with the tea. Let's go and sit down in the conservatory.'

He led them up the garden, a riot of blue and yellow with the aubretia and alyssum foaming over the paths and tumbling down the walls, and they sat in the conservatory in the warm spring sunshine and talked about his operation, and how he'd felt, and they stayed far longer than they'd meant to.

Lucie didn't mind because as long as they were with Dick and Pam Will wasn't cold and remote.

Finally, though, he stood up to go, and on the way home he managed to keep the civilised veneer intact.

They got back as the phone was ringing, and he went in and came out again, calling her across the yard.

'Lucie? Phone—it's Fergus,' he said, and the coldness was back.

How odd. Surely it wasn't Fergus that was causing the problem, was it? Goodness knows. She went in, and as before he went through the door and closed it firmly in her face.

'Fergus?'

'Lucie, hi. How are things?'

She looked at the closed door. 'Just peachy, Fergus—just peachy,' she said heavily. 'How are you?'

Fergus again. Damn the man. Will looked morosely out of the window, staring at Henry's empty field. It seemed so odd without him. Apparently it was touch and go, but they were giving him time. Amanda, however, was making progress, and had recovered fully from her head injury. She would be in a neck brace for the next couple of weeks until her cervical fracture healed, and she had an external fixator on her pelvis to hold it, and her femur had been pinned and so had her lower legs, so that she didn't have heavy casts dragging her down once she started getting up and about.

Knowing how ruthless the physios were, Will thought it quite likely that she'd be up and about sooner than she thought or wanted, but he had it on good authority that she was a pretty tough cookie.

He wished he could drive. He wanted to go and see her, but he didn't want to ask Lucie. He was putting on her a lot, and he didn't want to—especially not now, when he was tortured by that night.

He could hear her voice speaking softly on the other side of the door, and, although he couldn't hear the words, every now and again she laughed, a soft, intimate little laugh that turned a knife in his gut.

He gulped and stared hard out of the window, down towards the river that would never be the same again since she'd been down there with him. Now he could see her there, outlined against the morning sky, her hair like a soft cloud around her head, and every time he went there he could feel her presence.

She hung up. He heard the clatter of the phone, and then her voice talking to Bruno, and then a tap on the door. 'Any news of Amanda?' she asked, coming through without waiting for the gruff invitation that was still locked in his throat.

'She's doing well. Everything's pinned and fixed and propped, and she's probably damned uncomfortable, but she's alive, and so is the horse, by a miracle.'

'That's good. I thought I might go and see her. I wondered if you wanted to come?'

Damn. She'd pre-empted him, and now he couldn't escape from her company, because he *did* want to see Amanda and it was more important than his personal feelings.

'I was thinking of going. I thought I'd get a taxi, to save you having to do all the running around.'

'I don't mind.'

So that was that. No way out, and anyway it would have been churlish. He snorted softly to himself. That didn't normally hold him back, he thought, and hated himself a little more.

They arrived at the hospital at seven, and Amanda, although obviously in pain still and very weary, was pleased to see them.

Lucie gave her some flowers to add to the many she already had, and Will showed her the card and hung it on a string over the bed with the others.

There was a cradle over her hips, keeping the bedclothes off her fixators, and she was lying flat, of course, because of the neck injury, but she said the worst thing was the boredom.

'And it's only been a couple of days!' she wailed laughingly. 'What will I be like in a month?'

'Longing to lie down,' Will advised her. 'You wait till the physios get hold of you!'

'Oh, don't. There's one girl who's already having a go—she's lovely really, but she makes me do all sorts of things and it hurts! Still, it's my own fault. I shouldn't have been galloping along there on the verge. You don't know what it was he fell over, do you?'

'An iron bar, part of a bit of old farm machinery,' Will said. 'I've had a word with the farmer and he's moving it. He said he's very sorry to hear you had such a bad fall, but he pointed out it isn't an official bridleway.'

'Oops,' Amanda said with a grin. 'Oh, dear. My father was muttering about compensation. I'll have to talk him out of it!'

'Might be wise. Anyway, it's gone. Any news of Henry?'

'He's had an operation—they've splinted it with a bit of bone from a rib, and wired it all together, so goodness knows how he's managing to stand up, but he seems to be all right. They don't know how well he'll heal, but he seems to have settled down there, at least, and he's taking an interest in his surroundings. Of course, that's easier if you haven't got your neck wrapped in a plastic tube!'

They chatted a little longer, but then it was obvious that she was tiring, so they stood up to leave, and she reached out and took Will's hand. 'Thank you so much for helping me. They told me you saved my life, both of you, and I don't know what to say.'

Her eyes filled with tears, and Will bent and brushed his lips against hers. 'You don't have to say anything. I'll put it on your livery bill,' he said with a twisted little smile, and Lucie knew he was touched by her words.

She was, too, but she hardly knew Amanda. Will knew her all too well, and had spent months avoiding her. Odd, how he had now been cast in the role of hero.

Amanda held out her hand to Lucie, and she bent and kissed the girl's cheek. 'You take care, OK? We'll see you soon.'

They left her there, surrounded by her flowers and cards, and passed her parents on the way in. It meant another brief delay and another round of thanks, but then they were out and heading for the car.

'Fancy going to the pub for a meal? Or an Indian?'

She met his eyes, and wondered at his motive. Was this an attempt to mend fences, or would it be a chance to find out what had happened between Friday night and Saturday morning? Or was it simply that he was hungry and wanted to eat tonight?

Whatever, she was starving.

'Sounds fine. We'll do whatever you want—I'm easy.'

They went to an Indian restaurant, and discovered a shared passion for chicken korma in a really thick creamy sauce, with lots of twiddly bits to go with it and heaps of plain boiled rice, not the fancy pilau rice with spices, but just the clean, fresh flavour of basmati.

And Lucie wondered why it was that they could be so close in so many ways and yet she couldn't ask him what had happened and why he didn't want to talk to her after she'd given him her soul.

They didn't fight, though, and they kept the conversation trivial and away from anything that might damage the fragile truce that seemed to have sprung up between them.

And when they arrived back at the house, Lucie looked across at him and took a leap of faith. 'Coffee?' she offered, but to her relief and disappointment he shook his head.

'I won't. Thanks. I've got a couple of letters I ought to write and it takes ages with this stupid cast on. Maybe another night.'

'OK.'

She locked the car, handed him the keys and let herself into the cottage. Minnie was there, curled up on the bed, and she stretched and wandered out to the kitchen, asking for food.

'I don't do catfood, you'll have to speak to Will,' she told Minnie, and opened the door for her. Half an hour later she was back through the bedroom window, licking her lips, and curled up on Lucie's bed again.

Lucie was in bed herself, with her diary on her lap, telling it about Will and their meal.

'It was a really nice evening, but we were both walking on eggshells. What's happened? I must ring

Fergus tomorrow and give him an answer about those concert tickets for Saturday. Bet I forget.'

She did. She forgot on Wednesday, and so on Thursday morning, she stuck herself a note on the front of the fridge.

GIVE FERGUS AN ANSWER! it said, in big red letters, but she still forgot to ring him.

The truce with Will was still holding, and it really seemed as if they were about to make some progress. They got back from the surgery shortly before seven on Thursday evening, and on impulse she turned to him in the car and invited him in.

'Goodness knows what I've got, but you're welcome to it. I can probably throw something edible together.'

'OK,' he said cautiously. 'I'll just feed the dog and cat, and I'll be back.'

It took him a few minutes because he took Bruno for a run, but by the time he returned she'd thrown together a scratch supper with eggs and pasta and bacon, with a grating of cheese over the top.

'Perfect timing,' she said, handing it to him with a smile. It was gorgeous, and he sat there in the comfy armchair opposite her and wondered if she really felt that much about Fergus, or if there might be a chance for him.

Then Lucie got up to make coffee and he followed her through to the kitchen with his plate. 'Here, you can make the coffee, I'll wash up,' she suggested, and put the dishes in the sink while he started pottering with the mugs.

She'd tied her hair back in a scrunchie and he could see the nape of her neck, and he bent, unable to stop himself, and nuzzled it gently. 'I've got a better idea,' he murmured, and drew her into his arms. His kiss was gentle, nothing too demanding, but his pulse rocketed and his knees felt weak and it was like coming home.

'I tell you what, let's forget the coffee and the washing-up, shall we?' she suggested softly, and he smiled.

'I'll put the milk back,' he said, and then he saw the note. GIVE FERGUS AN ANSWER! With great care he put the milk in the fridge and shut the door, and turned to her, slamming down the pain and refusing to let it take control of him. Fergus again, he thought. And what answer?

'On second thoughts, maybe I'll have an early night,' he said, his voice sounding as if it came from miles away.

'What?'

'I—I can't stay. I'm not feeling all that good—my arm. I need some painkillers.'

'Is it all right if I come over and use the phone in a minute?' she said.

'Sure,' he agreed, and with great reserve he managed not to bolt for the door, hanging onto his control by a thread. Once he was in his kitchen he leant back against the door and banged his head against it firmly.

'Idiot,' he growled. 'How could you be so stupid? You know damn well Fergus is still after her.'

The door pushed behind him, and he moved away from it to let her in.

'Sorry, I was leaning on it, doing up my shoes,' he lied, and kicked them off anyway in favour of his boots. 'I'm walking the dog. Help yourself to the phone.'

'OK.' She dialled while he struggled into his boots, his right arm still too weak to pull hard enough, and then she started to speak before he had time to escape.

'Fergus? Hi, it's Lucie. The answer's yes.'

Will slammed the door behind him, taking the steps in one and veering onto the track at the end of the yard, heading down to the river at a run, Bruno at his heels.

Hell. What answer? *That* answer? Please, no, he thought, and ran faster, his legs pumping, his heart slamming against his ribs. Please, no, please, no, please…

Lucie hung up the phone, looked out of the window at Will heading down the track like a greyhound and shook her head. What the hell had got into him tonight—unless it was her ringing Fergus? He didn't seem to like it but, anyway, it had been before then.

She went back, cleared up her kitchen, watched television and then just before it was pitch dark she saw Will coming back, walking heavily as if he was exhausted.

Idiot. His arm would be playing up if he was treating it like that. She shut her curtains, went into the bedroom and turfed the cat off the pillow then went to bed with her diary.

I GIVE UP! she wrote. 'I can't rescue him, he's unrescuable. I'm going to London for the weekend, I've had enough. I told Fergus yes, so must meet up with him on Friday night. At least he's reliable and won't change his mind every ten seconds about whether he likes me or not.'

And throwing the diary on the floor, she settled

back and glared at the ceiling while it went slowly out of focus and blurred. She blinked and it came back into focus, but only for a second.

Damn. Not again!

She sniffed, pushed the cat out of the way again and turned out the light. To hell with him. To hell with all men. They were more trouble than they were worth.

Except that this one, she knew, was worth ten of any other man, and she couldn't seem to get through to him.

Defeated, she let the tears fall, and in the morning she packed her case, put it in her car ready, turned the cat out and shut the windows. She'd come and pick the car up after work, when she brought Will back.

And then at least she'd have the weekend to cool off before trying again.

If she could bring herself to try any more. Just at the moment, she wasn't sure she could.

'Oh, Minnie, no! You are such a pain, cat. How did you get in there?'

The cat mewed at him through the closed window, and Will went into the house, fetched the spare keys of the cottage and went back to let her out. She must have darted in when Lucie left for London, he thought, and a great heavy lump settled in his chest.

He might as well get used to it, though. He went in through the cottage door, and Minnie ran into the bedroom and jumped on the bed, settling down to wash herself.

'You, little cat, are a nuisance,' he told her, and scooped her up.

A book caught his eye, fallen open on the floor, and he sat on the edge of the bed and bent to pick it up. Then he froze, suddenly realising what it was.

A diary, written in Lucie's neat hand. Three words stood out in bold—RESCUING DR RYAN! Rescuing him? From what—apart from her? Oh, lord.

Slowly he picked it up and scanned the entry, guilt nudging at him, but he ignored it. She was writing about him, and somehow that made it seem less wrong. He read, 'He kissed me. Don't think he meant to. Don't think he means to do it again—we'll have to see about that! I have a feeling he needs rescuing from himself. It can be my next challenge—RESCUING DR RYAN!'

Rescuing me from myself? Am I so tragic? Yes, his honest self replied. Tragic and lonely and an object of pity. Oh, hell.

Will went on, flicking through the pages, scanning the odd entry until he arrived at last Saturday, almost a week ago. 'We made love last night,' she'd written. 'At least, I thought we did. Perhaps it was just amazing sex.'

There was something so poignant about that that he felt tears fill his eyes. He blinked them away. There was a smudge on the page, as if it something wet had splashed on it and been brushed aside. One of Lucie's tears, to match his own? He swallowed hard and read on.

'Fergus coming for lunch tomorrow. He wants to ask me something. Hope it isn't what I think it is. Amanda and Henry came to grief on the track by the river. Very dramatic. Thought we were going to lose them both, but apparently not. Oh, Will, I love you, but you drive me crazy. Why can't you just open up with me? I thought we had something really special, but it must have been wishful thinking.'

I love you? *I love you?*

Oh, lord. He read on, but there was nothing very much. Comments on his temper, on their fragile truce, and then last night, after she'd phoned Fergus, she'd written, 'I GIVE UP! I can't rescue him, he's unrescuable.'

No, Lucie, Will's heart cried. Don't give up! I didn't know! Give me a chance. He read on, and horror filled him. 'I'm going to London for the weekend, I've had enough. I told Fergus yes, so must meet up with him on Friday night. At least he's reliable and won't change his mind every ten seconds about whether he likes me or not.'

Oh, lord. She'd given up on him, and gone to Fergus, and she'd told him yes. Yes to what? To sleeping with him? Living with him? Going back to London?

Marrying him?

'No,' he growled. Flinging the diary aside, he scooped up the startled cat and strode out of the cottage, locking it up and taking Bruno out to the kennel he used sometimes if Will was going to be out for long.

'Sorry, old boy,' he told him, giving him another bowl of food. 'I'll be back in the morning, whatever happens. On guard, eh, mate? Good lad.'

He shut the pen, and locked the house, throwing his light overnight bag in the car. He had to go via the surgery and pick up Lucie's address, but he'd already got Fergus's card which Lucie had pinned up on the board by the phone the other week and left there, so that would give him two places to start.

OK, he shouldn't be driving, but needs must, and he had to get to her before she did something irrevocable.

Like what? Sleep with him?

'We made love last night. At least I think we did. Perhaps it was just amazing sex.'

The very thought of Fergus touching her brought a surge of bile to his throat. 'She's mine,' he growled. 'She loves me, not you. Don't you lay a finger on her, you bastard!'

Will went up the track far faster than even the rugged Volvo was designed for, dodging the potholes whenever possible, and shot out onto the road with unwary haste. He picked her address up from her personnel file in the surgery, and then jumped back into the car and headed for the A12.

He needed a clear run and a following wind, and he got both, amazingly. He was in London in record time, probably picked up on scores of speed cameras, but he'd deal with that if and when it mattered. He cruised up and down, scanning the *A-Z* on his lap, and finally found her little street.

And there, right outside her address, was her car, squeezed into an impossibly tiny space. The nearest space he could find that he could fit the car in was three streets away in a residents' parking zone, but that was tough.

He slotted the car in, grabbed his bag and ran back to Lucie's, staring at the bells in puzzlement. This was her address—or it had been. Had she left it completely? He'd thought she'd handed it over to her flatmate, and still had a room here for emergencies. And maybe she was out with Fergus already—or up there with him.

His patience snapped, and he went for the right flat number, standing with his finger on the bell until he heard her voice on the intercom.

'Hello?' she said softly, and he felt suddenly sick with fear.

'Lucie, it's Will. Let me in.'

'Come on up. Third floor.'

The buzzer sounded, and he pushed the door open and ran up the stairs, his heart pounding, and there she was, standing in the doorway with a wary look on her face.

'Is everything all right?' she asked, and he pushed past her and swept through the flat, throwing the doors open, searching…

'Will?'

'Where is he?'

'Who?'

'Don't play games with me, Lucie. Fergus, of course. You said you were coming up here to see him. You said you'd see him on Friday.'

'No, I didn't.'

'Yes, you did, quite clearly—in your diary—'

'My *what*! You've been reading my *diary*?' She flew at him, her fists flailing, and he grabbed her wrists and held her still, wincing as she struggled.

'Yes, I've been reading your damn diary,' he growled. 'Only tonight, not before, but it was on the floor when I let the cat out, and I saw my name—'

'Where?'

'RESCUING DR RYAN. In capitals. And for your information, it wasn't just amazing sex,' he bellowed. 'We *did* make love.' His voice softened to a whisper. 'We did make love, Lucie—didn't we?'

Lucie looked up into his eyes, and her own filled with tears. 'I thought so.'

'You were right. It was just, with Fergus in the background, somehow it seemed wrong, making love to another man's woman—'

'Hey, hey, stop! I'm not Fergus's woman—'

'Don't go feminist on me, Lucie, you know what I mean.'

'Yes, I do,' she said, 'and I'm not. I'm not Fergus's woman! I've never slept with him—'

'Never?'

'No, never. I never will.'

He stared at her, stunned, unable to believe his ears. 'But…you said yes—didn't you?'

She frowned. 'Yes?'

'I don't know. You had to give him an answer.'

She started to laugh, and he let go of her hands and stalked across to the window, bracing his arm against the bar. His stomach was churning, and all she could do was laugh. 'It's not funny, Lucie,' he warned.

'Oh, Will, it is! He wanted to know if I wanted concert tickets for tonight. I said yes, but not for me, for my flatmate and her partner. That's where they are—they've gone to a rock concert in Hyde Park. He wanted me to go with him, but I wouldn't, so he offered me the tickets anyway. Said maybe I'd like to go with you.'

'He did?'

Will turned to face her, and she smiled and walked towards him. 'Uh-huh. He's on your side, Will. I can't imagine why, he's not into Neanderthal behaviour, but he's very magnanimous.'

'Witch,' Will muttered, and Lucie tutted and put her arms round him.

'Don't. No more fighting. I've had enough of it.'

'Me, too,' he said with feeling, and drew her closer. 'I love you, Lucie Compton,' he said softly. 'I'm sorry I didn't say so, but I really thought you were just toying with me, and Fergus was the love of your life, and I didn't want to make a fool of myself.'

'That stubborn pride of yours again,' she teased, and he groaned and dropped his head onto her shoulder.

'Very likely. Will you forgive me?'

She took his face in her hands and stared up at him, and her eyes were like luminous green pools. 'Oh, yes, Dr Ryan, I'll forgive you—just so long as you promise never to jump to conclusions again, and remember to tell me you love me at least three times a day, just so neither of us can forget.'

'You have to do the same.'

'Of course. I love you, I love you, I love you.' She smiled impishly. 'You're two behind.'

He kissed her, just the lightest brush of his lips. 'I love you,' he murmured, and kissed her again.

Then much later, after she'd agreed to marry him, he lifted his head and said again, 'I love you…'

* * * *

0106/03a V2

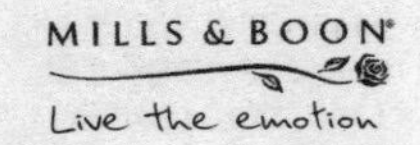

Medical romance™

NEEDED: FULL-TIME FATHER
by Carol Marinelli

The grand opening of Heatherton A&E doesn't quite go to plan, so nurse manager Madison Walsh must rely on, and trust, new consultant Guy Boyd to save the day. Trusting turns to loving, but Madison has her daughter's happiness to consider...

TELL ME YOU LOVE ME *by Gill Sanderson*

John Cameron is a loner, travelling the world as a professional diver. For reasons of his own he's wary of getting close to anyone – until he meets Dr Abbey Fraser. John instinctively knows he needs to be part of her life. Then they discover they share a secret...

THE SURGEON'S ENGAGEMENT WISH
by Alison Roberts

Nurse Beth Dawson has chosen small town life for some peace and quiet. The last person she expects to meet is Luke Savage, the high-flying surgeon she was once engaged to! Luke has changed, mellowed – realised what's important in life. But will he forgive Beth for leaving him?

A&E DRAMA: Pulses are racing in these fast-paced dramatic stories

On sale 3rd February 2006

Available at WHSmith, Tesco, ASDA, Borders, Eason, Sainsbury's and most bookshops

www.millsandboon.co.uk

0106/03b V2

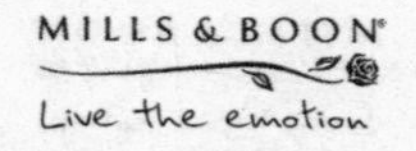

Medical romance™

SHEIKH SURGEON *by Meredith Webber*

Dr Nell Warren fell madly in love with Sheikh Khalil al Kalada – but he could never be hers. Now Nell must journey to the oasis city where Kal is a successful surgeon. He is the only man who can save her son's life. Not because of his skill – but because he is Patrick's father…

THE DOCTOR'S COURAGEOUS BRIDE
by Dianne Drake

Dr Solange Léandre has dedicated her life to the rural clinic in Kijé island. When specialist Paul Killian visits, he's mesmerised by her. But how can this city doctor show Solange that he has the dedication for life in the jungle – and the passion to care for a strong-willed woman?

24:7 Feel the heat – every hour…every minute… every heartbeat

THE EMERGENCY DOCTOR'S PROPOSAL
by Joanna Neil

Consultant Mark Ballard is challenging and demanding – yet somehow he awakens doctor Sarah Marshall's desires. As they work together, Sarah secretly hopes their professional respect will become personal. When she gets another job offer – from a former lover – it's time for Mark to take a stand!

On sale 3rd February 2006

Available at WHSmith, Tesco, ASDA, Borders, Eason, Sainsbury's and most bookshops

www.millsandboon.co.uk

0106/02 V2

FATHER BY CHOICE *by Rebecca Winters*

The majestic beauty of Yellowstone is the perfect place for Gilly King to find peace after a tough few years. Then she meets Alex – and in him finds the courage to love again. They have a second chance to change their lives – and the life of a troubled teenager who needs someone to take a chance on him…

PRINCESS OF CONVENIENCE *by Marion Lennox*

(Heart to Heart)

Raoul needs a bride – fast! – if he's to be Prince Regent of Alp'Azuri. His country's future is at stake – and so is his nephew's life. Beautiful and vulnerable Jessica agrees to marry him, but must return to Australia the next day. She could all too easily risk her heart in Alp'Azuri, married to a man like Raoul…

A HUSBAND TO BELONG TO *by Susan Fox*

Adopted at birth, Marla is overwhelmed to discover she has a long-lost sister – but a tragic event means she must keep her identity secret. One man stands in the way of her happiness – sexy rancher Jake Craddock. Jake can't figure out what Marla's hiding, but he does know that her vulnerability makes him want to cherish her…

HAVING THE BOSS'S BABIES *by Barbara Hannay (9 to 5)*

Like all the staff at Kanga Tours, Alice Madigan is nervous about meeting her new boss. When he walks through the door it's worse than she could ever have imagined! They once shared one very special night – and now they have to play it strictly business! But for how long can they pretend nothing happened…?

On sale 3rd February 2006

Available at WHSmith, Tesco, ASDA, Borders, Eason, Sainsbury's and most bookshops

www.millsandboon.co.uk

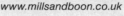